JONATHAN WILKINS

Writer, husband and father to two young men, Jonathan lives in a small village in Leicestershire, with his beautiful wife Annie. A former teacher and book shop worker, Jonathan started writing late in life when he stopped coaching basketball.

www.jonathanwilkins.co.uk

Copyright © 2017 by Jonathan Wilkins.

First published 2017.

Published by Words from my Keyboard.

Email: jonwilkins@btinternet.com

All rights reserved.

No part of this book may be reproduced in any form or by any electronic or mechanical means including information storage and retrieval systems, without permission in writing from the author. The only exception is by a reviewer, who may quote short excerpts in a review.

This book is a work of fiction. Names, characters, places, and incidents either are products of the author's imagination or are used fictitiously. Any resemblance to actual persons, living or dead, events, or locales is entirely coincidental.

Cover photograph courtesy of Liselotte Gijzemijter

Maps: Carto Studio Amsterdam

Utrecht Snow

Jonathan Wilkins

Visit my website at www.jonathanwilkins.co.uk

Printed in the UK

First Printing: May 2017

ISBN: 9781326200039

Utrecht Snow

Jonathan Wilkins

To Annie my darling wife.

My two wonderful sons David and Charlie.

To my Dadda, who I miss terribly

Acknowledgments:

With grateful thanks to Raymond Dörr, Rotterdam Private Detective and Kelly Goris. Hilde Bakke, Arthur van der Vlies, and Emile Vermeulen for an insight to the Dutch Police. Tony Jones of Cedars Judo Club Earl Shilton for advice on the technicalities of the sport. David Wilkins for Cross Fit nouse. Stephen Booth, Stuart Hill, Clare Hardy and Niki Valentine.

Behold, thou desirest truth in the inward parts: and in the hidden part thou shalt make me to know wisdom.
Purge me with hyssop, and I shall be clean: wash me, and I shall be whiter than snow."
Psalm 51

Vagevuur.

She closed her apartment door and shivered, but wasn't sure why. It was cold outside for sure, but here in the foyer it was reasonably mild. She nodded to her next-door neighbour Mevrouw Hanninga, who was walking towards her, then started to button up her coat. She could still taste last night's love on her lips and smell her lovers scent despite the hot shower she had just taken. She smiled to herself and looked forward to her return this evening remembering the picture of her lover in bed as she had slipped away for her day at Universiteit.

She skipped down the stairs happy with life and happy with herself. A cold blast of air struck her as she opened the outer door and she was faced with the greyness of the day; snow and mist seemed to swirl about in equal measure. Across the road, she saw her drably dressed neighbour shuffling along and she waved a greeting, but was ignored. She shrugged, best not attract her attention anyway. Along her pavement, she saw another neighbour, recognising him she thought, but just couldn't place his name. She had her studies to go to today and wasn't really looking forward to it especially after last night's pleasure.

She finished buttoning up her coat and wrapped her scarf around her chin, sinking into it before facing the swirling snow. Looking up into the grey sky she breathed in a gulp of freezing air before determining to get on. She turned and the man was there again, in her way, she made to step past him but for some reason he stepped the same way. He smiled and she thought, this is silly, then he hit her.

He punched her so hard in the face that she felt as if her nose had exploded and as she raised her hands to her face, speechless, he hit her again, this time in the stomach and she doubled over. Pain flashed through her body like an electric shock and she had no time to make a sound. He spun her round and she felt his hands on her neck. He's going to kill me flashed through her mind, he's going to kill…

Chapter 1

Donderdag, November 6, 2014.
Number 8 Bus, Utrecht. 08.54.

Cases Heda was normally about 185 centimetres tall; but today he was hunched up against the cold and felt like a goblin at half his normal size. He shivered yet again and breathed out the cold air imagining it freezing on his neatly trimmed beard and moustache.

Caes could just see the Dom outlined against the grey morning sky. It was towering above everything, it made him smile. Even as the snow feathered down it was still the centre of their universe. It watched over Utrecht from a height of what, over one hundred and ten metres and could more or less be seen in Utrecht from wherever anyone stood, whatever the weather. True, it was a bit faint today, covered as it was in snow. No melting due to no heat leaving the building the Dom was always cold, always frozen, it mirrored how he felt. Cold and alone he just wanted to be alone. All of a sudden, Caes just didn't fancy going to work. He just wanted some peace and quiet and to be left on his own, to wallow in his sudden misery.

Unfortunately, all his defence mechanisms didn't stop the woman from sitting next to him, well almost sitting on him in fact, as the bus picked up from Bleekstreet. She wedged Caes against the window and started talking to herself or was it to him? He opened his left eye and taking a closer look, saw what it was. Dirty faux fur coat and then the sickly smell of snowy dampness and then, yes it was urine. Caes had to start breathing through his mouth to try to avoid the smell. He couldn't get his arm away from her; he was stuck and she muttered on, words incomprehensible to him, Greek? Russian? He couldn't tell, maybe it wasn't a language at all; he was suddenly too tired to think. The half hour it took the bus to get to work was a torment, where had she arrived from? He'd never seen her before on this route, though to be honest he did spend most of his journeys to work with his eyes closed.

It was such a welcome relief when she stood and got off the bus. Her smell though, was hanging in the air, he hoped it wouldn't hang on his clothes. The pressure on him at last relented as she moved, typical it was also his stop. She shambled to the exit. Caes followed the smell.

He got off and found himself trailing the woman as she shuffled across the road and through the snow. Her muttering increased, talking to no one but everyone. People avoided her, even in the snow they could see her and they must have thought she was mad. She was going his way; in fact, she was going all the way. She entered the Bureau at Kroonstraat. Caes followed.

Caes Heda was Hoofdinspecteur in Utrecht. Thirty-nine and in charge of Crime at Kroonstraat Police Bureau, not committing it obviously, but tidying up after it had been committed. If he could catch them great, but he felt there was not much chance of stopping them all. It was a full-time job!

He did enjoy it though, it was a bit like a game, but he was never sure who was winning. They had success and then the criminals had a win. They locked some up, but more and more were getting community service and prisons were closing. He had always thought that saving money this way was a false economy as there seemed no deterrent anymore, but he was but a simple policeman.

Kroonstraat Police Bureau, 09.25.

Young Police Agent Frederik Meijer was at the desk alongside one of the civilian staff; but he had drawn the short straw. He gave Caes a disgusted '*why did you bring her in with you?*' look as his nose wrinkled at the odour that she had trailed in with her and now shared with him.

"My daughter…"

"*Mevrouw?*" Freddie asked.

"My daughter, she has disappeared…"

"When was this?"

"Don't know, I can't remember…"

He looked at Caes; he looked back, not knowing what to do or say. Caes shrugged his shoulders towards him, a madwoman?

"Let's start at the beginning…" Freddie said.

"She looks after me."

"She lives with you?"

"No, she comes by and looks after me."

"I see, when was the last time you saw her?" Freddie tried to get some clearer information.

"I can't remember."

"Then how…?"

Freddie Meijer was trying to be professional, but Caes sympathised with him as he started to get frustrated.

"I know she is missing, I feel it!"

"*Mevrouw…*" Freddie started again.

"I feel it… I know something is wrong."

"Her name?"

"Elise. Elise Cuijper, she is… I'm sorry, I do not know her age."

"Description?" Freddie asked helpfully.

Caes left them to it, heading towards his office and a fresh cup of coffee to warm himself up. He sniffed at his clothes, he thought he had got away with it, but how very odd this situation was.

At the morning briefing, Caes sat on the edge of his desk. He had a good team around him, they all worked well together. Freddie Meijer, he liked, he was young, so enthusiastic, he used his initiative and he was always asking questions, wanting to get better, wanting to improve. His fellow Police *Agent* was Maaike, his twin sister, she was lovely, and if possible had an even brighter future than Freddie.

Freddie was tall, blue eyed and blond with a chiselled face., a handsome young man, his sister Maaike was attractive as well, she had auburn hair with sparkling emerald green eyes. They were big and happy eyes.

"Oké, listen up everyone. We have had a resurgence of pickpocketing, especially around the Stadhuisbrug area, I want Freddie and Maaike to go plainclothes and just stroll around together for a couple of mornings, *oké*?" Caes said.

"Baas," agreed Maaike, "Should I hold his hand?"

"Baas, please no!"

Freddie complained. Everyone else laughed.

"*Moder* always made me hold his hand when we went shopping, she says Freddie can't be trusted on his own."

There was even more laughter as Freddie went redder by the moment.

"Anything you like, Maaike, but best hold onto your purse first." Caes smiled.

He couldn't understand why people had started delving into other peoples' pockets during this weather, he'd have thought their fingers would have been frozen solid before they could start. Wasn't everything tucked away, or did people not bother, thinking this would only happen during the summer. Oh well, such was life.

Madelon Verloet, one of the two *Hoofdagenten*, and most recent addition to the team spoke:

"As you know we had a nasty rape last week and as you know two sexual assaults last week. We know they are linked and we think we know who it is; we are waiting for DNA tests, but we'll see. I'll be looking after that and may need Maaike at some stage."

Madelon was newly divorced and had moved from Tilburg, another attractive woman about the same age as Caes. She was professional and capable with a sense of humour most of the team were getting used to.

"An unprovoked attack on a French visitor, not sure if it was robbery or race related, but we need to have our wits about us, at the moment, it's you, Danny and Adrie looking into it?" Caes asked.

"Yes, *baas*, we think it may be one of the Moroccan gangs going by early descriptions. The victim is concussed, but described them well, but still asking around... May or may not be linked to the pickpocketing so we'll keep in touch with the Meijer siblings. But I think they will both need to take care." Adrie said.

"That's very thoughtful of you, Adrie," Maaike smiled, "But knowing you are on the case as well, I feel so much safer already!"

"Oké dank for that, Maaike." Caes intervened, "Right, I know that Ernst is still looking into this stolen car business?"

Ernst was a monster. *Brigadier* Ernst Hoewegen. Nearly two metres of solid muscle, a mountain of a man. He had an amazing moustache, just like *Hoofdagent de Gier* in van der Weterings *Amsterdam Cops* series of crime novels; but without the Zen influences. Ernst thought he was Gods' gift to women, just like de Gier. He made Caes smile, but he was a hell of a police agent. He was unique at Kroonstraat. He could go back to his very first day at work and recall events that he had covered then or had read up in files. He was the 'go to' guy if you needed any information. He was like a magician. Ask him a question and he would always come up with the goods. They didn't need computers when he was about. Sometimes staff thought he took files home to learn them off by heart. It didn't do them any harm that's for sure!

"We think it is a local gang, but I've some help from Organised Crime."
He looked around the room.

"I have a few ideas of my own as to who it is, but need confirmation. Wait to be updated."
Caes smiled, this meant they were doomed.

"Madelon is also looking at some violence towards some working girls by their pimps." Caes said moving things along.

"Yes, we have seen quite a few girls with bruising recently and it seems that some pimps are becoming more violent. I cannot understand why. We know they don't have to be with a pimp, but think this is affecting the foreign girls more than our Dutch ladies, so there may be more to it. The girls, as usual, aren't too keen to talk, but again if Maaike and I can have some time to talk together and then interview the girls?"

"Yes, no problem. Do we interview the pimps?" Caes wondered aloud.

"We'll have to see what their girls want us to do, it is pointless talking to the scum if we cannot prosecute them. They will just laugh at us."

"It could make them think twice?" Caes ventured.

"That sort don't think!" snarled Maaike, "We need to find a way to make them…"
There were murmurs of approval from the group.
Caes could not understand why the girls seemed to feel they needed a pimp for protection; still…

"This is when we should have some type of vigilante group, to beat the crap out of a few of them," said Freddie with evident anger as red again flared up on his cheeks, but he was not embarrassed this time.

"I know it is difficult, Freddie, but we are the law and even though it might not seem to be working at times, we have to abide by it. I hope their time will come and I want to be there when it does, but in the meantime, we go with the flow." Caes said grimly.

Caes truly believed this and wanted all his team to have a bit of faith in the system. It didn't always work out, but more often than not it was successful.

"Leave this to Madelon, if anyone can persuade the girls to lodge a formal complaint I am sure it will be her."

Madelon nodded just as grimly,

"I'll try my best, *baas*, Freddie…"

"Do we need to talk to the *Rode Knop*?" Caes asked.

"The *Rode* what?" asked Danny.

"Prostitutes' collective, Danny!" said Maaike sharply.

"Oh, yes, sorry Maaike."

"I have an appointment fixed, we'll see what they think." Madelon said.

Looking at the group Caes moved on,

"Adrie, the increase in drunks, anything?"

"*Baas*, it's not me, but I am talking to bar staff at a few targeted pubs and clubs. There is no real pattern." Adrie laughed.

Hoofdagent Adrie Voelmans and *Surveillant* Danny Meeuwen were both good solid men. They were like two peas in a pod. Dark haired, both with beards. Danny was a little taller, but they were both very athletic and tough. They played rugby for our local team.

"Sorry, *baas*, one last thing, the friend you brought in this morning with you…" Freddie started.

"*Agent* Meijer…" Caes warned.

"Sorry, *baas*, anyway she reported her daughter missing, details on the sheet, one Elise Cuijper, no age known, but at *Universiteit* Utrecht, it's odd though, strange she doesn't seem to know too much about her."

"A fantasist perhaps? She was quite strange; I shared my seat on the bus with her this morning."

"Not sure, baas, but I recorded it all the same."

"*Oké*, to recap. Madelon you will be *teamleider* on the rape case and also on the prostitutes. I'd like Maaike to work as *informative coördinator* on both. Ernst remain *teamleider* for the cars, Danny *informative* and Adrie look after..."

Having allotted everyone a role, some with more than one, it was meeting over and they went their separate ways.

Caes loved Utrecht, it was the perfect place to him. Students overflowed in it while in term time, but, even though they were a city, it always seemed like a small village. They all knew each other. Walking across the Stadhuisbrug or along Vredenburg you would always see someone you knew. It did upset him that crime would always be there just like the poor, but they tried their best and kept taking them off the street. Sometimes though it didn't seem quickly enough.

He went to his office to catch up on paperwork. They had so much on their plate at the moment as he had outlined in the briefing. There were reports on the sexual assaults, on the attack on the Frenchman, Utrecht didn't want to get a reputation for being a no go area for tourists. Drunkenness could be controlled; it wasn't usually nasty. It was the violence Caes didn't like. The most worrying thing to him was the increased violence against prostitutes. More were appearing bruised or battered and they couldn't see a reason for it. The girls didn't need a pimp, they were free to act independently, but it seemed someone wanted to control them. He wondered if it was because of where they came from. Dutch girls knew the ropes and their hard-won rights. Foreign girls were another matter. They were soon going to face a crisis in this he was sure.

He badly needed to catch up on things he had put to one side. He didn't fancy going outside again, his feet had just started to thaw out and he still felt damp and needed to warm up and get dry.

Two hours later there was a knock on the office door.

"Come!"

He shouted, rather louder than he meant to.

"Come? Really, Pappy, you are so pompous sometimes!"

It was Truus, bearing gifts of coffee and cakes. She smiled her beaming smile, teeth bright against her tanned face. Her red hair seemed to explode as she pulled the damp beanie from her head and she ran her fingers through it to try and calm it. Her eyes were sparkling blue, the same as her pappy's and she laughed with her eyes as much as her mouth. She plonked two plastic cups onto the desk and retrieved a paper bag from under her arm.

"*Koffietijd* for you!"

"That's sweet of you *Schat*."

"Coffee with *gevuldekoek* or *peperkoek*, a choice or both?"

"What do you think?" Caes laughed.

"Pappy! Too greedy!"

She leaned over and kissed his cheek.

"What brings you here?"

"Oh, you know, I got into Universiteit early, did some work in the library then found my lecture was cancelled, sooo as I am now avoiding uni… avoiding work, avoiding people, I thought I would pop back into town and see my favourite pappy. You know how it is."

"What is it you want from me?" Caes was at once suspicious.

"Pappy, how could you, I want nothing save your love."

She smiled her mother's smile. But she did talk nonsense sometimes.

Caes snorted, "That's fine, but I have lots on."

"Oh sorry, Pappy, should I go?"

"No, no, I'll always have time for you, but you know police work…"

"I do, Pappy, I do indeed." She mocked him.

"At the moment, we've a missing girl, a rape, assaults on prostitutes, a car theft ring, pickpocketing, an assault on a tourist, all in my area, there is no time."

"There is actually too much time, Pappy, you just need to use it more wisely."

"Sagely said, Truus," He smiled, "but in reality, there is no time. Upstairs, as per usual as the cliché goes, want these cleared up by yesterday and then there will be more in as today goes by and then more tomorrow. We Dutch solve the problem of keeping the sea back, but we can't keep this tide back."

"Good one, Pappy." Truus laughed.

"Yes, just thought of that one. Anyway, we drip results back into the system, solve a crime when we least expect it, then another pops up, same crime, but a different offender. It's never ending. Now on this sheet…"

He waved a paper at her, "it seems as though we are ten per cent down on crime in the whole of Utrecht, but we at Kroonstraat are only down three."

"But still down, Pappy!" Truus admonished.

"I suppose…"

"I understand, Pappy."

"Though I'm not complaining, Truus."

He threw his hands up and smiled.

"I know, Pappy, but if you feel so negative why continue?" Truus suddenly sounded serious.

"Well I don't actually feel negative, most of the time. It's just it sometimes never seems to end, we have success, put them away and someone pops out from the sewer to do the same thing. It is a conveyor belt of crime."

"Tidal wave, conveyor belt. Too many metaphors, Pappy."

"I know!" Caes laughed.

"That's the world though Pappy. Fix something, only for someone to break it again. You are just doing remedial work all the time. If society was equal, we would have no need for crime. Fix our capitalist society and as Marx said there would be no crime. Simple. I leave you with that contribution."

"*Dank*, Truus, very radical. I'll explain that to the guys here at Kroonstraat."

"You should, they would be impressed."

"And the mayor!"

"An idiot, don't bother, he wouldn't understand."

"Well I must get back to work."

"*Oké*, Pappy…"

"Oh," Caes suddenly thought, "Do you know an Elise Cuijper?"

"Vaguely, she's in some classes with me, why?"

"Seems she's disappeared."

"Well I don't take much notice of stuff around me at Universiteit, I don't really know her," she paused thoughtfully, "sorry that sounds a bit selfish."

"No, it's fine, just listen out for anything, would you?"

"Of course, Pappy."

"This has been really nice, *dank* for the cake, the coffee and for you coming, the best part of my day so far." Caes said.

Truus again smiled her sparkling smile and pulled on her beanie.

"Oh Pappy, you are such a softy, don't let your boys hear you. I've got to escape, I've a lecture on something or other to prep for in the library as long as he turns up. A real treat for me indeed!"

"*Oké, lieverd*, you take care. Wrap up warm, more snow this afternoon."

"Will do, *hou van je*."

She blew a kiss.

"*Doeg!*"

"*Ik van je ta!*" He replied with a smile and a wave.

Universiteit Utrecht, 12.55.

Truus had returned to *Universiteit* and sat in her Sociology class, looking around. She wasn't too sure what was going on today. She hadn't bothered to prepare for the lecture after all. Her head was spinning and she felt a bit strange, a bit disconnected from what was going on. From nowhere Truus suddenly remembered watching her mammie play basketball in a game for Utrecht. It just came to her, clear as day. Her mammie was amazing. The image just appeared from nowhere, Truus didn't even know that she had stored this memory, it had come from nowhere...

Truus hadn't seen her mammies face in her mind's eye for a while and then there she was. Running so smoothly, ball looking as if it were attached to her hand or spinning through the hoop, arrowing it to a team mate. Smiling, laughing, and cajoling her team, leading her team. She was so beautiful, so elegant. Femke Heda, her mammie, the announcer had to keep repeating her name as she scored or gave an assist or made a steal. Truus had forgotten this, she had always loved to watch her mother play, but it now became as clear as day. Her beautiful mother, wearing an all red kit, a white band in her golden hair, caressing the ball around the court. Her beautiful, smiling, laughing, mother. People watching her play, seeing how good she was and Truus knowing she was her mammie. Truus wanted to tell her how proud of her she was, and wanted to be just like her, she wanted to tell her how her life was going, how everything was so, so... but no. Nothing, she could only speak to a memory and get nothing in return, no answers, no advice, no mammie daughter girlie chat, nothing... no hugs or kisses, no private confidences that only she and Truus could keep, the secrets that mothers and daughters kept from everyone, the shared secrets that would have meant so much to each of them... but then what would they, what could they say? She was not there, so why imagine what could have been? What should have been? What would never, ever be...

Truus had loved her, still loved her to bits, but could never, ever again tell her how she felt, never, ever feel her warm body, her hugs, her kisses when she was down, never again hearing her laugh, see her beautiful, beautiful smile, never have her wipe away her tears as Truus wished she was doing now, tears that were streaming down her face, never have her mend her breaking heart, Truus felt her heart shattering into tiny pieces... her beautiful, beautiful mother...

Truus could not concentrate and her gaze kept getting drawn to the window and the snow again, she felt cold, but there was also a thin sheen of perspiration on her brow. She was trying to focus on what the *docent* was saying. Her brain started to engage with the *Docent, meneen* Medel's, voice. She was finding this so difficult, but then it became a little clearer as she concentrated harder.

"Thinking about bullying at work offers real, though often uncomfortable, opportunities to confront what have been called by Bolton, the damp and dark corners of organisational life. We know this and the studies have shown the effect it has on people. Truus, your thoughts, please?"

She knew this, "I think too often in such organisational spaces, episodes of bullying and harassment are all too commonplace and seek to humiliate, degrade and subordinate certain people. It is always a question of absolute power for the bully. They seek to demean the victim to show that they have the power, that they are the power. It is a sick use of their energy."

"What effect does this then have?"

"Though often difficult to define, the bullying is often highly visible and in many cases' accepted or taken for granted. People often know victims of bullying, but will not try to defend them, many fearing they will take the place of the victim. People see the bully, but do not stand up against the bully. They fear repercussions; they fear if they speak out they will perhaps face other retaliation. Bullies thrive on this; they have the power over the victim and relish it. They will always deny what they do, but they know all along that it is this power they strive for."

"Excellent, Truus and what is the result of this, the outcomes?"

"Well the victims of bullying at work carry with them the hurt, the pain and the violation of their dignity. It goes beyond the workplace and into their life outside of work, it cannot help but do. Family life and relationships are critically affected. If they are a victim at work, they can start to replicate the behaviour at home. It becomes a vicious downward spiral for them. To allow this to continue is a denial of human dignity and leads to negative consequences for everyone involved, but especially the victim and their immediate family."

"So, the answer?"

"Shoot the bully!" Truus got up and left the classroom.

Korte Jansstraat, 13.05.

Maaike and Freddie were trying to keep warm as they sat outside a café. They kept scanning the paths for likely villains. The pickpockets seemed rather shy this afternoon. Freddie was bored and was teasing his sister. She would always bite, she never seemed to learn. Freddie knew this.

"You must like gammon." Maaike laughed.

"I don't like pig." Freddie was insisting.

"But bacon?"

"Is thin gammon." Freddie assured her.

"But you eat bacon."

"I don't eat pig." Freddie was firm

"What about sausages?" Maaike asked.

"Pig sausage?"

"No, pork sausages."

Maaike was exasperated. She looked across at her brother. His blonde hair damp, his nose going red. There was frost on his eyelashes. He looked frozen, Maaike knew that she too felt frozen, but she carried on regardless. He was smiling, she knew he was teasing her, but she had to respond.

"You like pork, don't you?" Maaike asked, frustrated.

"Yes."

"But pork is pig." Maaike was maddened by her brother.

"It's the pig I don't like."

"You don't make any sense, Freddie, they are the same."

"Pigs are horrible, dirty creatures, how can you eat them?"

"Freddie, are you being serious?"

Maaike found it hard to believe her brother.

"Do you like the idea of eating them?" Freddie asked.

"We eat them all the time."

"Unless you are a veggie." Freddie teased.

"But..." Maaike started.

"I don't like vegetables either."

"Freddie, you're just taking the piss."

"Who knows, Maaike, what do you like about vegetables?"

"Freddie..."

"Pig, cow, it's all the same." Freddie was firm.

"I'll turn you into a vegetable!"

"Maaike, that's not nice." Freddie moaned.

"*Aardappel hoofd*, that's what you are. Nothing is ever serious with you."

"Well what's the fun in a boring life? We need to change it up."

"For sure, Freddie, let's talk about pigs; that changes it up." She mocked him.

"No, getting you mad changes it up and that works every time."

Maaike hit him hard on the shoulder.

"Assaulting a police officer, Maaike, that's big trouble for you."

"No one would believe you."

"But we are in public."

"No one takes any notice, think about it. We are looking for the pickpockets, no one

18

Sees anything. No one feels anything." Maaike complained.

"It's too cold to feel anything."

"But even in the summer they see nothing." Maaike said.

"Own worlds to live in, Maaike."

"But it's our world. They don't pay attention to what's going on."

"Do you? When you're off duty, do you pay attention?" Freddie wondered.

"I think so. I haven't had to act, but I think I'd notice if a crime was being done."

"And do something about it?" Freddie asked.

"For sure, we all should."

"We all should, but we all don't. It's too risky for some."

"I know, anyway; let's move and see what we can see." Maaike said standing up.

"What about cow?"

"You mean beef?" Maaike snorted.

"No cow..."

"Remember I have a gun, Freddie!"

Flora's Hof, 14.45.

Truus wandered down Floridadreef towards the Dom then saw that her favourite quiet place in Utrecht was open. Flora's Hof, a tiny secret garden that in the summer smelled of honeysuckle and fruit blossom, but was now a sheet of white snow. She could see her favourite bench, sticking out like a ships prow and after clearing several days' worth of snow from it she sat, hunched, and bundled up against the cold, her hat pulled down low over her ears and her hands gloved.

'Shoot the bully' she thought sniggering to herself under her scarf. What a good idea, shoot all bullies. She had no idea why she had left the classroom. It was spontaneous, she just had to leave the room. Her mind was spinning, she had really thought deeply about the bully at work, she despised bullies. Was this disappearance of Elise an extension of bullying? A pretty extreme extension, but where was Elise? If someone had her they were executing an extreme sense of power over her. The ultimate bully.

Why was she thinking so hard about this? Because it was wrong? Because Elise had apparently disappeared. Truus only cared because fate had allowed her to know. If her pappy was not in the police, her ignorance would have been bliss, nothing for her to worry about. Blissful ignorance, the fate of the young. No worries about anything, except about themselves and how many took that too seriously? Blissfully ignorant. She had not been in blissful ignorance about anything since her mammie had died, she knew only too well the facts of life and how there were always consequences. Shoot the bully indeed.

Her seat was cold and damp, but she stayed put looking at the rows of trellis that would bloom in the summer. She imagined the scents and the sights that would burst into the air once the hot weather came and this made her shiver. She needed to go home to Jutfaseweg and to her bed, but decided reluctantly to go back to the Universiteit library to do some more work.

Universiteit Utrecht, 15.55.

Truus looked at her textbook in the library. She looked out of the window at the snow falling. She looked at her textbook. She looked at the clock at the far end of the room. Was that the ticking of the clock she could hear? She looked at her textbook. Her pen was drawing little arrows on her notebook. No words, just arrows pointing in a circle, an ever-decreasing circle, tiny little arrows with neat pointy points on them, floating on her page, between the lines, on the lines, pointing, prodding, painting a rain storm of arrows, flooding her page. She looked back at the textbook and saw nothing of the slightest interest to her. She looked back out of the window to the snow and thought, how nice it looked, great lumps of cotton fluff sinking to the ground against a backcloth of steely grey. She felt herself floating in the snow; it sent a shiver down her spine. White on grey, drifting, floating, almost hovering, ever so slowly down. Like goose down, feathery and oh so light making its way gradually to the ground. She looked at her textbook again, nothing, nothing of even the minimal interest. She couldn't bear it.

"Fuck this; I'm off to the gym,"
Then blushed as she realised she'd spoken aloud.

Vismarkt, 16.30.

Madelon sat down in the *Rode Knop* prostitutes' collective's office. Opposite her sat their secretary, Anastasia Groen. Madelon had become quite friendly with her over various liaison meetings and there was a mutual understanding. Trust would be a bit harder as there was history between the police and prostitutes, but at least Anastasia gave credit to Madelon for trying.

Anastasia said, "We know it is the foreign girls, the girls who aren't members."

"What are they afraid of?" Madelon asked.

"They don't understand our work. We try to find translators, but it is so difficult, so many nationalities."

"They must see it would help."

"That and their pimps, we see a lot of trafficking, they are afraid of being sent back. Their pimps of course, give them the kind of advice they find hard to turn down." Anastasia smiled grimly.

"We think there is a lot of coercion at the start." She continued.

"But aren't most of them here legally?" Madelon asked.

"More and more from Eastern Europe, a lot of Africans. We are truly a multi-cultural business here. Utrecht should be proud." Anastasia didn't try to hide the irony, she smiled, but there wasn't really any humour there.

"Under age?"

"Some, but we usually report those to Marlous Siegers, she then gets on to the Bureau Jeugdzorg to see what they can do."

Marlous was the liaison officer at Schaverijstraat police Bureau, the *Bureau Jeugdzorg* looked after children's welfare. Something that it seemed some parents could not.

"But they tend to disappear quite quickly once spotted." Anastasia said.

"Brothels?" Madelon wondered aloud.

"Not as many now, paying rates at business costs has driven them out and so sex now seems to involve cars, some hotels, and a couple of squats... I could give you a list," offered Anastasia.

Kroonstraat Police Bureau, 17.20.

Caes got back to his office and bumped into Ernst Hoewegen who had a pile of files in his arms.

"What gives, Ernst?"

"Just checking on something..." the big man replied.

"That bodes well?" Caes wondered aloud.

If he was on the job, it wouldn't be long.

"Not sure this time, baas, it's just a feeling rather than knowing for certain." Ernst didn't share his positivity.

"The cars?" Caes confirmed.

"Yes. Also, thought I'd give Freddie 'the talk' soon."

"Good idea, we need him to focus more. Stop being so hot-headed."

"He needs to be more like his sister." Ernst smiled.

"We are all different, Ernst. I like Freddie. I like his approach."

"He needs to be a bit more serious though..."

"Agreed and we need to unwind Maaike a bit, she is too intense." Caes said.

"She needs to be more relaxed, not take things to heart."

"Trouble is, that's what makes her so good. Need to find a way to do that without limiting her."

Caes did worry about Maaike, he would never want to blunt her enthusiasm, but he also wasn't too sure about her reactions at briefings where she would take things so to heart. They all cared, or at least Caes hoped they did, but they mustn't care too much and then lose focus.

"Perhaps give her more responsibility?" Ernst wondered.

"Possibly. Madelon can help there, I know she has some ideas. Anyway, car thefts?" Caes asked getting back on track.

"Local knowledge, stolen to order. That's obvious."

"It's where they are getting done up that's the key. It has to be somewhere pretty isolated if no one has seen anything." Caes pondered.

"But they don't want to be on the road too much if they need to hide it." Ernst replied.

"We need more CCTV that would help so much."

"But we know we Dutch don't like our privacy invaded." Ernst scoffed.

"Privacy! It's all well and good until it affects them, then they could have a camera on every street corner as far as they would be concerned."

Tamada Kick boksene, Johan Buziaulaan. 20.03.

Truus high kicked the bag. Pim, who was holding it grunted loudly. She then went high and there was another grunt. Next, she kicked hard and low, he moaned again.

"For goodness sake, Pim, stop being such a wimp!"

"You kick too hard!" Pim bleated.

"No, I just kick, man up!"

Two more high kicks, not giving him any time to moan.

She wiped her forehead with her forearm, sweat was pouring from her. She spun around and kicked high again.

"Nice, Truus!" said Tamada, "Go through the drill now."

She did, like a blur, Pim's moans melded into one long groan. Front kick using her heel, side kick with the side of her foot, semi-circular kick, roundhouse kick, Axe kick. Bang! Bang! Bang! Bang! Bang! Pim collapsed on to the floor gasping,

"Where'd that come from, Truus?" he asked.

"My mind, it's all Zen!" she laughed. "Do you want to spar?"

"No, you've bruised my ribs. Ask Robbie." Pim said.

"No, I will." It was Tamada the owner.

That made her shiver. Truus towelled herself down and looked at this amazing specimen in front of her, all Malay, all muscle. A rock-hard slab of a man, his very presence was intimidating.

"Remember what we said last week about defence, Truus."

I'll need to she thought! She didn't want to just cover up, it would hurt too much, but taking all his kicks on her arms would also take too much out of her physically, so she decided she would try just to slip, hoping that she would be able to anticipate the speed of Tamada and let every one of his incoming kicks and punches pass harmlessly by her head. Some hope, but she could but try. She smiled at Robbie who gave her the thumbs up. Pim helped her tighten her gloves. She pulled on her protective head guard and clumsily fitted her mouth guard in.

Tamada stood opposite, they bowed. Then he almost caught her full in the tummy, but pulled it at the last moment. He smiled, it was a wicked smile. He was still smiling when he hit the floor after she swept his legs from under him and her foot stopped millimetres from his head as she performed a perfect axe kick.

"Nice, Truus, very nice." Tamada was still grinning.

Then he finished it. He never stopped smiling.

Amaliastraat. 22.45.

Caes watched Femke score the winning basket and her stern game face suddenly changed into his beautiful wife's face. This image was repeating over and over again in his head. Her face wreathed in a smile, sweaty hair pinned back in a messy bun, but starting to flop over her face. Her eyes sparkling, running towards him; and then leaping into his arms to hug him, only for her body to instantly change into a skeleton and the bones crumble in his arms. Caes felt as though he had stifled a scream, but once again was sweaty and cold. He hated this. It made no sense. He had no idea where the image came from and why it came. Caes remembered when Femke had leapt into his arms. It was the last game she had played. Five weeks later she was dead. Taken before her time.

Utrecht had won the National Cup for the first time, Femke had led them to the win, scored the winning basket. Caes had coached the team. It had been his last game as well. Truus had run around, pigtails flying behind her, pompoms in each hand, leaping and squealing with joy along with all her basketball friends. She had never played since either. It had been the end in so many ways. But why should that joy be tainted by the revolting image of the skeleton? Caes turned over and closed his eyes, knowing that it would take some time before he would get to sleep again. He kept having this dream, repeating over and over again. Sometimes every night for weeks and then a break. But one thing for sure was that it would come again. There was no rhyme nor reason for it. Stress wasn't the reason. It was just an horrific memory that returned to his mind's eye at regular intervals. Repeated for five long years. Years he should have had with his darling Femke. Years that had broken his heart.

Vagevuur.

He smiled to himself as he watched her. This was all coming together, it was too easy, just too easy. He knew she wouldn't be missed. Who was looking for her, he didn't care. She was his. To do with as he wished, all his.

She sat on the floor, it was concrete and cold. Freezing cold. She had only slid off the thin mattress to try to go to the sink in the corner, but for some reason felt exhausted. Her face ached, she had put a hand to it and found it swollen and bloody. He must have hit her. The spinning in her head wouldn't stop. She felt dizzy and sick, but worse than that she felt terrified. She had no idea where she was and what had happened. She looked down at her bare feet. Where were her shoes? Why had she no shoes? She shivered and winced as pain shot up into her temple. She tried to think back. A man smiled, she knew him from somewhere, but couldn't think. He asked her for… what had he asked her? She had turned away, her face seemed to explode and then she had woken up here. Blood in her mouth, head aching, freezing cold with no shoes and frightened. She tried to get to her feet, but felt too unsteady, her legs like rubber, so had to crawl along the concrete floor, scratching her legs, towards the tap in the corner.

Who had done this to her? Why? What had she done? She felt tears start to burn her cheeks, she rubbed them away and finally reached and turned on the tap. She splashed water on her face and felt it sting as it hit the cut she must have below her eye. She shivered again. She was all alone. She didn't know where, she had no idea why. Who had she upset? Things had been going so well of late and now she was here. She saw her shoes by the door, where were her leggings, oh god has he taken her leggings, had he… no she remembered being sick when he tried. What was she doing there? Then she thought what if she had been brought here to die?

Chapter 2

Vrijdag, November 7, 2014.
Kroonstraat Police Bureau, 10.13.

"You took the report Freddie, what do you think?" Caes asked.

"I thought she wasn't all there baas, but that doesn't mean she didn't tell the truth." Replied Freddie.

"Where did she say she lived?"

"Vaaterstraat."

"Did you check with the Universiteit?" Caes asked.

"I did, they haven't seen her for almost a week."

"So, she is missing?"

"Seems like it. I have circulated the details top all our stations. Logged a missing person's report and now need to find where she lived."

"Not with the old woman?"

"She said not, but didn't know where she lived?"

"Odd..." Caes mused.

"Especially as she said she was her mother." Said Freddie.

"Universiteit dealing with that?"

"Yes, they'll email address and next of kin. Might be here now."

"Well you take on the role of *researcher* as first contact and see where it leads you. Oké?"

"Right baas."

Oudegracht, 11.50.

Maaike and Freddie were walking slowly. Freddie was moaning about his lot. Maaike was unsympathetic.

"I'd love to oversee a case Freddie, don't know why you're so unhappy..."

"It's that woman. She stank. It was awful..."

"So, because she smells, she shouldn't have an advocate?"

"Advocate?"

"Someone to support her when she has a problem."

"I think she's the problem. She's not too stable. I dread to think what her home is like..."

"Well you probably won't have to go around to it. Anyway, don't be such a *sufferd*!"

"Ouch Maaike, don't you be cruel to me!"

"You need to take these chances Freddie. If you want to impress you have to do menial tasks."

"This won't be menial Maaike, I can feel it in my bones. Something isn't right. I don't want to spend ages tied up with social services and psychological services. I want to be on the front line."

"Tell Caes then. Though I don't think he will understand your reasoning. We have to take on all roles and ways to find the truth."

"Even if the truth is this woman hallucinating about her daughter?"

"I think there is more to it than that. Have the Universiteit got back to yet?"

"Not yet, I'll have to pop around there as well. They keep moaning about data protection and that stuff..."

"Best safe than sorry Freddie. Be patient."

Utrecht Centraal, 17.30.

It had been a long day and Caes was tired. Nothing much had happened, except that the snow had continued and it seemed even colder. They had made no progress with any of the cases and more had started to pile up. Caes was of a mind to throw all the dockets up into the air and escape them, but he knew this was a fantasy that could not come true. He stepped over to Centraal Station and found his bus. It was almost empty. The driver gave him a cheery "*Hoi!*" and he replied in kind. The drivers were almost always jovial across the city, despite this current weather and consequent traffic hold ups.

There were still building works all around Centraal station. Utrecht 2030., the grand building scheme, couldn't come soon enough for Caes; not that he was wishing his life away, but when all works were completed it would be a fine thing. At the moment, all was static. Snowbound indeed. The deep foundation holes were filled with ice and snow. He smiled to himself as he imagined someone sinking neck deep in the drifts that had built up. There should be warning signs up outlining the danger. No wonder they were taking the Tour de France outside the centre. Utrecht wouldn't want the world to see all their holes! What a disaster if the peloton ended up in some sinkhole. Amusing, but also unthinkable.

He was pleased he had no responsibility for the great bike race. This was going to take over the city in July and Caes knew crime would not stop. Indeed, an extra million visitors to the city would surely add to the load. He would have to have his wits about him. He had already had Adrie and Danny delegated to some task force for the week of cycling events, he didn't need to lose anyone else. Problems piled upon problem. The bus passed near Vaartsestraat and he saw some police officers out canvassing. A lot of good it seemed to be doing them. Caes grimaced. They looked rather forlorn in their navy uniforms battling against the snow and boredom and unanswered questions. Caes closed his eyes and willed himself home.

Albert Heijn, Vondellaan. 17.55.

He called into the brightly lit *Albert Heijn*. His eyes screwed up as he entered and shuffled around the aisles. He threw the odd package of *boter* and *lamsvlees* into his basket, not really thinking about what he needed. *I must make a list* he said to himself as he finally got to the cash till; when he was suddenly grabbed by the red headed whirlwind that was his daughter and dragged back to the aisles.

"Oh Pappy, what have you got us, you know we need *brood* and *kaas*?"

"I don't, when did that all go?"

"What about *melk*, you finished the last this morning. Why do you never do a list? Wait till I get a trolley!" and pulling the basket from him she disappeared.

What would have taken Caes two minutes turned into half an hour and cost a fortune. He had no idea what they needed it seemed and as the groceries piled up he wondered what an earth he could have been thinking. This was constantly being reinforced by his red-haired daughter, who took time out every so often to push the trolley forward and career at speed down the aisle, using it like a bob sleigh, making him wince every time she came close to wiping out an entire family or an older shopper. She was so dangerous. he just wanted to escape the embarrassment.

Amaliastraat, 20.12

Truus and Caes were back at the table eating dinner, just chatting about their day. Caes looked over at Truus and thought how much she looked like Femke; she was such a pretty girl, if a bit of a tomboy. Granted unlike his late blonde haired wife, she had a shock of dyed red hair, but otherwise she was her mirror image and so beautiful. She did have rather a pale face and a bit of a black eye though, bloody kickboxing he thought.

For some reason Caes suddenly imagined a young Truus with her pigtails and ribbons, writing carefully in her school notebook, then saw her mother, her arm around her, encouraging her and carefully describing how to do things as Truus perfectly formed each letter and word onto her page. Caes had to blink himself back to reality. Where had that come from all of a sudden?

Truus snapped him back to the moment.

"Pappy, look at this!" she stood up and lifted her shirt and turned to the side.

"Put it away, Truus!" He said making a pained face.

"No look at these…"

The whole of the right side of her torso was a mixture of yellow, blue, and black bruises.

"Christ, Truus, run over by a bus, were you?" Caes spluttered.

"No, it was Tamada."

"Shall I get a warrant for his arrest?"

"Could be the only way to stop him, he's a monster."

She really was black and blue. Literally black and blue. It must have been one hell of a series of kicks.

"Why so much bruising, how many…"

"We were practising defence."

"So, you failed?" He laughed.

"*Vader…*" she warned him, "He just gets through, he is so quick. Look."

She pulled up her right sleeve, her forearm was also mottled with yellow and blue bruises.

"He even does this to me through the pads."

"Truus, if *Bureau Jeugdzorg* saw you, they'd think you were beaten up."

"I did put Tamada on the floor today, Pappy."

"That's good, but is that why he gave you the bruises?"

"No Pappy, he's not like that. He's too cold if anything, he never gets cross or raises his voice. He is the iceman!" she laughed.

"What can you do then?"

"Learn from him…"

"Is he sharing everything with you?"

"Yes, he's a really good teacher, so are Pim and Robbie, but…"

"What? Too good for you at the moment?"

"I'm afraid so, he is just so fast. I think I have everything covered then bam, he does me."

"Any way of beating him?

"Pappy, he is the veteran kick-boxing champion of Holland, not in my life time."

"You sure, there must always be a way?" Caes asked.

She smiled and shrugged her shoulders,

"Anyway, back to what you were saying…"

"Which was…" He had lost track.

"I was at school with Elise before Universiteit…" she said between mouthfuls.

"Mmm?" Caes couldn't speak, his mouth was full. *I at least had good eating habits* he thought.

"Elise Cuijper."

"That's her."

"So, she really has disappeared?"

"Mmm, her mother thinks so, weird though she doesn't know when... or anything really. She was a strange one..."

"Yes, she was."

"You knew her mother?"

"No, Elise, Elise Cuijper. But her mother? Her mother died I'm sure of it."

"No, she was at the station today..." Her smell came back to haunt him, god how could I have missed her he thought?

"Tall, slim with brown hair, like Elise?"

"No, no a really large dumpy woman and really, really smelly."

"No, unless she has really let herself..." Truus snorted, "No Pappy, she's dead, both her parents are dead, how could...?"

"Strange, then who is the woman?"

"Where is Elise Cuijper?" Truus asked the more important question.

Vagevuur.

She lay there. She was in shock, she felt stunned and frightened. She had no real idea of what had happened or even when it happened. She no longer had any notion of time. She smelt the vomit that had splattered down her front and wanted to be sick again. At least it had saved her from god knows what.

She had left her flat and had felt so happy. Things were going so well, then the man, the smile, the punches. That was it. She had woken up here. She looked about her. The room was empty save for a tap in the corner and the mattress she was lying on. She pulled her knees up to her chest and got another overpowering waft of the smell of her own vomit. She gagged, but swallowing hard she tried to block it out.

He had stood over her. She recognised his face, but could not place him. Letting her see his face scared her. He had no worries. He had stroked her face and she had slapped his hand away. He had yanked her hair towards him and she had lashed out with her foot and caught him on the shins. He slapped her again and pushed her to the mattress. Her face stung and she was crying. She could hear herself begging him to leave her alone. He had a horrible smile. He had pulled her leggings down; she had tried to fight him off. He had continued to slap her and swear at her. She had flailed with her hands and her feet, determined not to give in to him. But he was too strong. He had forced her hands down and had dropped down onto her, knocking all the wind out of her, but that was what had saved her. She was sick all over him. It didn't save her from being slapped again in disgust, but at least he had left her alone. Who was he, what did he want? Well, she had fought off one thing that he had wanted, but would he return?

She had lain there on the mattress. She had tried to clean up, but she didn't want to take off her clothes in case he could see her. She had washed her blouse as best she could. She had her coat, but that was now smelling as well, but she was so cold. She wanted to go to the toilet, but there was nothing in the room. Just the grate by the tap. She felt ill at the thought, but knew eventually she would have to give in. The trouble was the light had not gone out once and she felt so exposed, she didn't know where he was, what he wanted or when he would enter the room again. She had no idea how long she had been there, she was scared. She had never known a feeling like this before, her stomach was icy cold and felt numb. It wasn't just the temperature causing this feeling.

Her face still stung where he had slapped her and her head was sore from when he had tugged at her hair. She concentrated on the pain for a moment, feeling the throbbing beat through her head down to her heart and then echo around the room. As long as she had some feeling she knew she was all right. She closed her eyes and squeezed her legs together. She just wanted to sink into sleep to escape this, but she was so cold.

Chapter 3

> Zaterdag, November 8, 2014.
> Amaliastraat, 07.24.

Caes Heda showered then dressed slowly. White tee shirt, checked shirt. His good jeans, and wandered quietly downstairs. Silent ruminations were quickly and rudely interfered with by his daughter.

"Think, Pappy!" she insisted.

He had missed what she said as he'd entered the room.

Truus was sitting at the table, red hair all over the place wearing her favourite dungarees and DM boots. She had made coffee and was in irritatingly high spirits, way too talkative for this time in the morning. Caes just wanted to sip his coffee and wake up gradually, but she was always too alive in the morning, too bubbly, just too loud.

"Take de Welt…" she started again.

"Take him where?" she was maddening.

His head was starting to ache already.

"Take? No, not *take* him! Don't be dense, Pappy, de Welt. Take de Welt."

"De Welt?" He had no idea who she meant.

"A new car every week."

"A rich man?" Caes suggested.

"But a new car?"

"I don't know."

She was exasperating. Truus had this awful habit of thinking and then talking. Mind you, it was often not thinking and still talking which made it even more painful, but today she had a particular bee in her bonnet. She had never fully understood mornings. No matter how grumpy her father was; she would always construe it as interest.

"Exactly, Pappy, theft, it's obvious."

"You can't just accuse…"

She slopped more coffee into his cup.

"But why a new car? He's not honest." She was adamant.

"You can't…"

"It's obvious!"

"I don't know him." Caes tried again.

"So, he could be a thief."

"Because I don't know him?" Caes was losing patience.

"Exactly!"

Her logic was impeccable!

"Truus, you can't just accuse…"

She held out a toasted bagel to him, slathered in butter and *stroop*. Honestly, Caes thought, did he look like a ten-year-old?

"Nee, bedankt, Truus, you eat it."

"Well I'll find out; it'll be my first job." She said through a mouthful.

"Job?"

"And the Blekkiks?" she ignored him.

"Who?"

"Next door but one."

"I have no idea, what have they done?"

"You have to ask? Do you not see?"

It was as if Caes was a barely tolerated small child.

"I have no idea."

"What do you do for a living, Pappy?"

Now it was she who was exasperated.

"Well I don't spy on any of my neighbours, that's for sure."

He smiled at her, which only seemed to add to her frustration.

"But perhaps you should, have you never noticed…"

"Sorry, Truus, I'll be late for work, we can talk about this tonight."

"I'll be out."

"Doing?" Caes wondered.

"How old am I, Vader?" she was suddenly using her serious voice, Caes was being warned!

"What?"

He hadn't taken the hint.

"Vader, I'm nineteen, do you have to?"

Caes was not supposed to respond to that. It was clearly rhetorical, therefore he stayed silent.

"Truus, what did you mean job?" Caes suddenly thought about what she had said earlier.

"I've got to go, Pappy, see you tonight. Doeg!"

With a sticky *stroop* kiss on the cheek and a slam of the door, she was gone. Silence reigned. Caes finished his muesli and yoghurt, the coffee had gone cold.

Caes washed up, everything had been left as usual; well she had made the coffee he supposed. The silence without her was deafening, he glanced up at the photo of Truus with her mother and smiled grimly. Femke was looking radiant, wearing her Utrecht Dames basketball kit of vivid red, so athletic, and full of health. Truus was playing with a ball by her feet. Both were so happy. How long had it been since he had lost Femke, five years? Bastard! Caes dried his hands and got his scarf and coat.

Caes and his daughter lived just off Jutfaseweg a pleasant part of south eastern Utrecht which at the moment resembled a series of Christmas decorations as every house was covered with snow. Icicles hung from windows and guttering, threatening death to anyone who stayed too long underneath them. Windows were frosted, it wasn't sure if it was on the inside or out. It had been a seriously cold winter so far and there seemed no end to it.

They were well connected to Utrecht centre by public transport so Caes decided to take the bus into work again. He drove a car when he wanted to, which wasn't very often, but at the moment it was sitting under several centimetres of snow. Public transport was great in Utrecht, just as it is around most of Holland. He drew the line at cycling to work though, as he didn't want to get sweaty before the day had even begun. To him cycling was a thing to do for pleasure on days off and certainly in the sunshine not the sleet.

The snow may have put him off driving to work this morning, but he soon realised what a mistake he had made during his walk to the bus stop on Vondellaan. What should have taken Caes less than five minutes was more than doubled as the pavements, although continually being cleared, had been covered in deep snow once again. It was freezing with a body cutting wind. It knifed into his bones and Caes struggled against the downfall of snow as it was whipped into his eyes. It was gritty and painful. He thrust his hands deeper into his pockets.

At home, it was usually Truus diving in to take his chair or place at the table or into a bath he'd been running. Whatever he had chosen to do, Truus had this almost pathological knack of going just where he was about to. She amazed him sometimes with this ability to second guess him. It was perhaps the bath thing that got to him the most. Caes would run it, ready for a long soak; she would take it and innocently say she thought he'd done it for her and what a lovely pappy he was, so thoughtful and so caring. He was so good to her, even though she didn't deserve it. She did love her pappy. She had this mantra rehearsed and ready for every occasion. Caes found it impossible to get angry with her in spite of this. Truus completely cracked him up. Caes loved her so much. He didn't know what he would have done without her after Femke's death. She had kept him going, kept him strong.

Thinking like this wasn't good Caes though, he had to concentrate on the moment, not sink into the past. The sudden earlier thought of Femke had jolted him. He had been so depressed when Femke

34

passed away, as should be expected he knew and he didn't want to revisit the black moods he had suffered. He didn't want to forget, but he had hated the pain, he didn't want to revisit it all over again.

Caes swiped his card as he climbed onto the number Eight bus again. It was so cold, too cold. At least the bus was on time, or was it an early one arriving late or a late one arriving... Caes knew he needed to stop thinking as he slumped into a seat and folded his arms tightly and closed his eyes. He was as usual on the defensive, daring anyone to sit next to him. He liked his own space wherever he was, at home or on the bus. There she was again, the old fur clad woman, shuffling along, but at a different bus stop this time. She got on and luckily did not sit next to him. He could still smell her though. She had a seat to herself this time, it was as if there was a no go area around her. She was again muttering to herself, that and her odour putting anyone off from approaching her. She did not get off at his stop so Caes thought why not, I'll follow her and so he stayed on the bus with her. He allowed himself to think back to yesterday's briefings and the joys of what todays briefing would bring. The success rate from yesterday so far? Nil. Good police work from the Crime staff at Kroonstraat Police Bureau! He looked out of the bus window at the whipping snow, swirling and circling the town. It was going to be a long, cold, dark day.

Well, the old woman seemed content to sit and mutter to herself, safely wrapped up in her world and her smells. She remained alone for her whole journey. Caes was almost dozing off and the bus was pulling into Centraal Station when she got off, and started walking, this time across to another bus. *Where was she off to?* Caes wondered, as he continued to follow her. She got onto the number six bus and swiping his card again, he followed. She sat alone of course and he waited as they drove through the snow. The bus was almost at the Zamenhofdreef terminus when she stood up. Like a lap dog he followed and she made her shabby way to what turned out to be another Police Bureau, Kaap Hoorndreef, which she entered. Strange he thought and followed her into the building. It was déjà vu.

"My daughter is missing," she told the female officer at the front desk. Caes could see her nose almost visibly turn up at the smell.

"Your name Mevrouw?"
Professional to the last, Caes loved the police staff.

"Her name is Gisele, Gisele de Groet."

"Your name is?" The clerk persisted.

"I haven't seen her for a week; I don't know where she is..."

Now he knew that he should have stepped in then, but something held him back. This was too strange. Two different missing girls. Two missing daughters. One dead mother. One mother who was not their mother or was she? What an earth was going on? It made no sense.

Caes watched as the clerk looked down at her notes and suddenly the big woman just left, melting away outside into the snow. He was dumbfounded and was just about to follow her when Commissaris Aartsen called out to him.

"Caes, how the hell are you? What brings you to our neck of the woods?"

"I was just following… Shit! Bet I've lost her now."

Caes left him and rushed outside, but somehow, he had lost her, she had just disappeared into the snow. He went back inside from the cold, shivering and a bit puzzled.

He had known Frans Aartsen since they were in the Academie together. He had been a bit of a high flyer and had shot up the greasy pole of promotion quite quickly. He had gone off training the Surinam Police force a few years ago. All sun and sea and a lot quieter than even Utrecht.

"What was that?" asked Commissaris Aartsen.

"Oh, nothing, Frans, how are you, star turn in all the newspapers?"

"Steady Caes, just AD."

"Well it was a beautiful picture." Caes mocked,

"Though I can't remember what it was about."

Aartsen laughed.

"Fame is fleeting Caes." He smiled.

"How are things?" asked Caes.

"Good, good now I'm back in post."

"Not seen you for a few years, how was Surinam?"

"I learnt a lot. Training, leading men. Good experience."

"I'm glad it all worked out."

His face went a bit sour, but then he smiled,

"Yes, well these things can't be helped, got anything on?" said Aartsen.

"Not really, two missing girls' maybe, not too sure…"

"That woman?"

"No idea really, your clerk had some notes."

"Truus oké?" Aartsen asked.

"Yes, she's well, enjoying Uni… I think." Caes replied.

"You never ever know what's really going on, do you?"

"No, I don't suppose you ever do."

"Right, I have briefings now, want to pop in to listen?"

"No, I'll get back to Kroonstraat. You take care!"

"Don't know what you're missing, Caes!" he said cheerily.

"Oh, yes I do, Frans, see you later!"

"Cheers, Caes."

Madelon sat down in the Rode Knop prostitutes' collective's office. Opposite her sat their secretary, Anastasia Groen. Madelon had become quite friendly with her over various liaison meetings and there was a mutual understanding. Trust would be a bit harder as there was history between the police and prostitutes, but at least Anastasia gave credit to Madelon for trying.

Anastasia said, "We know it is the foreign girls, the girls who aren't members."

"What are they afraid of?" Madelon asked.

"They don't understand our work. We try to find translators, but it is so difficult, so many nationalities."

"They must see it would help."

"That and their pimps, we see a lot of trafficking, they are afraid of being sent back. Their pimps of course give them the kind of advice they find hard to turn down." Anastasia smiled grimly.

"We think there is a lot of coercion at the start." She continued.

"But aren't most of them here legally?" Madelon asked.

"More and more from Eastern Europe, a lot of Africans. We are truly a multi-cultural business here. Utrecht should be proud." Anastasia didn't try to hide the irony, she smiled, but there wasn't really any humour there.

"Under age?"

"Some, but we usually report those to Marlous Siegers, she then gets on to the Bureau Jeugdzorg to see what they can do."

Marlous was the liaison officer at Schaverijstraat police Bureau, the Bureau Jeugdzorg looked after children's welfare. Something that it seemed some parents could not.

"But they tend to disappear quite quickly once spotted." Anastasia said.

"Brothels?" Madelon wondered aloud.

"Not as many now, paying rates at business costs has driven them out and so sex now seems to involve cars, some hotels, and a couple of squats... I could give you a list," offered Anastasia.

"That's great Anastasia."

"Would you like to meet a couple of our clients?" Anastasia offered.

Binnenstad, 08.32.

Freddie shoved Maaike playfully in the back as they walked past O'Connells bar.

"Freddie," she admonished, "not now."

"Sorry I find it hard to concentrate sometimes." Moaned Freddie.

"Just because we don't have uniforms on doesn't stop us behaving."

"Sourpuss!"

"Freddie!" Maaike reprimanded.

"Oh Maaike, where's your sense of fun?"

Freddie smiled, without an obvious care in the world.

"It's not a game!"

Maaike was getting cross with her brother.

"Caes thinks it's a game."

"His game is not like your game," she laughed. "Your game is always a big joke."

"Maaike, you are so cruel."

"No I don't mean you're a joke, you just think everything's funny."

"Not everything."

"But this is serious, if people are robbed it is so horrible…"

"I know."

"Caes sees the game like Sherlock Holmes, trying to outwit the bad guys, you see the game as just having a laugh."

"I do my job," Freddie was hurt.

"I know, Freddie, but you have to be serious. Just put yourself in the place of the victim."

"I try to, but I don't want to get too involved. I want to catch the crook, bang him up and get the next one."

"That's only part of it, Freddie."

Then she calmed down,

"Let's get a coffee."

"I'll buy you a cake,"

Offered Freddie as an attempt at a truce.

"We may have to run after them."

Maaike protested half-heartedly.

"Look at you, Maaike, not a gram of fat on you. I don't know how you do it."

"I work at it, you know that."

They sat at the table and again looked out on the Vismarkt. Once again, they were cold and bored. There were a few tourists, but maybe they looked odd as everyone else was indoors shivering under duvets whilst they fought nature and sat looking out. The heaters above them worked well and Freddie had graciously placed one of the colourful blankets available over Maaike's legs. No crime was visible. Unless it was crimes against fashion! They watched the groups of students and didn't think it would be them, they were just having fun. Perhaps Freddie should go to Universiteit, Maaike thought. He would enjoy that. He had enjoyed Police Academie in Utrecht, they both had, but he didn't ever seem to want to graduate, he wanted to stay put and lead the life of riley. It wasn't that responsibility worried him, he just liked having fun without responsibilities. Maaike had loved it that after a period of classroom training they'd go out on the job and get real practical experience, then go back to training to learn something new. Freddie had enjoyed his time back at the Police Academie most. Maaike on the other hand was a little more serious about her work and couldn't wait to escape the Academie to get hands on experience.

The Dom towered behind them, the snow had stopped and there was slush everywhere. Cyclists still whistled by, not seeming to have a care in the world, chatting to their fellow travellers or just pedalling manically on their way to who knew where. Bundles of clothes on wheels, it made Maaike laugh. She wished she was on her bike, speeding out of the city in the sunshine, but that would not be for a few months yet. Freddie was chattering on about people in front of them, suggesting possible crooks and Maaike had to laugh at his suggestions as they all seemed to revolve around the aged or the infirm. She looked across at her brother and saw the silly grin on his face. How could she ever take him seriously if he never took himself seriously she wondered? Maaike finished her apple cake and coffee and suggested they get up and stroll about a little to keep warm, so Freddie put his arm through hers and they began their search again.

Amaliastraat, 08.35.

Truus had heard her father leave for work and rolled onto her side. For some reason, she had endured a restless night. Thoughts of all sorts had gone through her head repeatedly. Trouble was she couldn't remember what the thoughts were. She looked up at the window and saw the snow drifting down, she hadn't closed her blind, and maybe that was what kept her awake.

She closed her eyes and her mind started to wander again, half awake, half asleep. She was fourteen; she had just gone up to *Vortgezet Onderwijs*, trying to get established after being top dog at *Basisschool*. It was so exciting, new friends, new opportunities, a great adventure Truus had thought. Then it all came crashing down, collapsing, tumbling, shatteringly down. Mammie got cancer. It took just five weeks before she lost her. She died. So quickly, just like a nightmare only it was all too real. Pappy didn't cry. Truus couldn't cry, at least not then. They spent nights hugging each other. That's all she could remember, rushing about, going to school, spending time at the hospital, hugging Pappy. Mammie getting paler, thinner, weaker. Just five weeks, Mammie so beautiful, laughing, smiling then just gone. She was just gone. No more laughter, no more smiles. No more Mammie. The home suddenly became so empty. It took just five weeks, Truus had had no time to at all to prepare herself, to get ready for a life without her mammie, but then she thought, how do you prepare for that kind of loss, the loss of one that you love so much, the loss of one who is everything to you, who is your very heartbeat. How do you? You just don't. You just can't and honestly, why should you have to? It was so unfair, so wrong, and so very cruel. Slowly, but surely, over the years Truus had begun to miss her more. Time and distance did not make her feel better like experts said, time made it worse. She had her pappy and her pappy was Pappy, but there was no Mammie. No Mammie to talk to, to hold her, to smile and pick her up when things got bad. With Mammie, Truus thought that all would have been fine, without her it was just empty and dark and cloying. With Mammie, here there would of course have been none of this sadness, there would have been no need to be sad, no need to mourn, no need to cry.

Kroonstraat Police Bureau, 10.15.

Caes had decided very early as a policeman that he needed to lose many of the typical Dutch traits. When he entered the force, he had always seen crime as very black and white. You did wrong so you should be punished. There was no dispute. He saw the rule of law as the ultimate sanction. He had always thought it was right. But as time went on and he faced the different types of crime that people carried out that it was harder to keep that view. People committed crimes for different reasons. Greed or desperation were two extremes. Could we or even should we think that the man who steals a loaf of breads to feed a starving family be prosecuted to the full extent as a bank robber or burglar. Greed and desperation. Caes looked out of the window at the snowflakes drifting against the glass. Crime was almost as opaque as the window. Grey would be the best way to describe it. Caes pondered, should he ignore petty crime if the stakes were low or should there be a zero tolerance. He had changed. Even to be thinking like this showed he had changed, but he knew that the 'I am always right' mantra would never work, especially when he left the streets and started to lead a team. He had to be unDutch and look at a wide variety of views and opinions. There was never just one answer, one way of doing things, unless you are Dutch and were always right! Caes liked to think that he was right, but on the law of averages there would be times when he would be wrong, so if he was considering a murder or some serious crime he couldn't be dogmatic anymore. He had to question himself as well as question others. Caes tried to convey this to everyone. Don't be content with the first response, always make a second and third guess. Work towards the truth gradually. There had to be sense in that approach, it was one of very few things that he would impose, if that wasn't an oxymoron, we needed to give our questions every chance of being answered.

Madelon called Caes over.

"The DNA test is a match."

"He would have known that all the time the bastard." Caes said.

"I know, but maybe he doesn't understand science." Madelon was scathing.

"Will he still be there? He won't have done a runner?"

"I'll fetch him. Can Maaike come with me?"

"Why?" Caes wondered.

"I want two women to arrest him." Madelon was stone faced.

"I see, very appropriate. She's out with Freddie looking for the pickpockets."

"I'll radio her. We need to show him women are not weak."

"Don't hurt him, Madelon, give him no excuses…" Caes warned.

"All we'll hurt is his pride…unless he starts."

"Well, let us hope he is a fool and does start!" he smiled, "Just take care, Madelon."

"No worries, *Baas*. Oh yes, I've arranged to meet some of Rode Knopes clients."

"Excellent, see you soon…"

UMC, Utrecht. 14.19.

He was a fool; he did start and so Maaike broke his arm. Simple as that. It wasn't deliberate, she had just put too much pressure on his limb replicating one of the many judo holds she knew. There again she had thought briefly, it could have been on purpose. He was an absolute shit. She now sat by the shit at the hospital as he moped and whined and complained. She smiled grimly to herself as Madelon berated him and belittled him. He was nothing, he was not a man, he was pathetic, a parasite. He was all of this and more. Or less if you were Madelon. There was no question of Madelon being PC about this one, she seethed with anger at what he had done. They had him cuffed to a chair as they waited for him to be plastered up. Madelon called in two uniforms to finish the job. She thought she had made her point quite clearly. She and Maaike went to talk to his victims to tell them what had happened and what they had to do next. Madelon drove them towards the first address.

"Why, Madelon, why do we have this?" Maaike was upset.

"I don't know; some men just need to be in this position."

"What?"

"Of power, they need to control."

"It's all so wrong." Maaike almost sounded as if she was pleading.

"I know, it is the ultimate thing isn't it, rape as control."

"They must hate women."

"I think they hate themselves more."

"I'm not too sure about this then." Maaike said.

"What do you mean?" asked Madelon.

"I find it so hard where one part of society is actively oppressing another."

"It's not that bad, Maaike."

"You don't think so? One bastard of a man, one raped woman and two other victims. It's terrible."

"Don't be discouraged, Maaike. It is too easy to say this is all an unpleasant fact, but men have oppressed women as long as history. You will be a great asset to the Police, but don't let yourself get bogged down like this. It's right to feel angry, that can help, but we just have to keep fighting for what is right. Things will change, things must change."

"They change much too slowly for me."

"Yes well, come on let's try to give these girls some nice news at last."

"Will I face an enquiry over his arm?" a worried Maaike asked.

"No, not at all. Reasonable force. Anyway, can you see that little piece of shit making a fuss about a woman hurting him? I don't think so. I saw everything. I won't even have to lie!"

Madelon smiled,

"*Kom nou*, let's go!"

Vismarkt. 15.10.

Truus sat in Coffee Company. She was not even pretending to work today. She looked out of the window at the whiteness and couldn't understand why it looked so dark.

"Truus, you silly cow!"

She turned and saw two of her Sociology classmates. She smiled thinly.

"Shoot the bully, really, Truus!" Guusje laughed.

"Yea, what were you thinking?" Arnie asked.

"I hate bullies,"

Was all Truus could reply. Arnie and his girlfriend, Guusje, slid into the seats either side of her.

"But murder, Truus, really?"

Guusje was laughing.

"I know, I've no idea..."

"No one bullying you is there, Truus?"

Arnie was suddenly concerned.

"Do you think anyone would dare, Arnie?" Guusje said.

"What with her dad a cop?" Arnie laughed.

"No, her fighting skills!"

Guusje playfully punched Truus who laughed.

"Do we know any bullies?" Truus suddenly asked.

"Not since *Bassischool*." Guusje said.

"Do you think people grow out of it?"

"No," said Arnie, "They just meet a bigger bully."

"You think?"

Guusje looked quizzically at her boyfriend.

"Not ever thought about it..."

"No, it's weird, isn't it?" said Truus.

"We never do think about it, but maybe it goes on all the time, all around us." Arnie said.

"Were you ever bullied, Truus?" asked Guusje.

"Not physically, name called after Mammie died for some reason..."

"What?" Guusje was horrified.

"Can't even remember their names, just made me mad. I punched one, didn't do it again..."

"People are such arseholes." Arnie snarled.

Truus smiled, "God, hadn't thought of that in ages."

"Not a very nice thought..." Guusje said.

Bleekstraat, 16.00.

Caes had got off the bus stop which was close enough to where he lived to walk the last bit home, but thought he'd look around where the old lady said she'd lived. It was of course snowing again and he slipped over into a pile of darkened slush as he made his way towards Vaaterstraat. Caes stood in the road, brushing himself down. To his right was a small park. It was deserted save for two young lads who were shooting a basketball. Every time they hit the backboard the snow that had just settled fell off. They kept wiping the ball dry, they must be mad he thought and so cold. He slid along a frozen mud path through to Vaaterstraat. It was lit dimly. The snow was floating down like white rose petals, but every so often one would catch him in the eye and like a thorn, scratch him and make him blink. The sky was black and foreboding, though he wasn't sure what it was warning him about. The snow caught in the lamp light, sparkled then faded as it drifted down. This was just an ordinary street, in ordinary Utrecht. Nothing different here from a hundred others, so what was the confused old woman talking about? He stuck his hands deeper into his pockets and walked towards Cathrinjsingel and turned around. Flats on his right, town houses on the left. Snow everywhere, making everything look the same, cold, white. But dark. Caes decided to go home, he had a lot to do and though it was dark, the night was still young.

Amaliastraat, 18.45.

Caes got home to a quiet house and found Truus asleep on the settee. She looked so peaceful, just like the little girl she used to be, rightly or wrongly like she would always be to him, all curled up like a little mouse. Caes felt his heart jump. He must have woken her as she opened her eyes sleepily.

"Hi, Pappy, sorry, I must have dozed off..."

"No worries," Caes said, "Hard day?"

"Strange, been thinking a lot. You?"

"The usual, fighting crime. Keeping the streets of Utrecht safe for the likes of you. Fancy coming to lift some weights?"

"What from off my mind or at the *Zweet Fabriek*?"

"*Zweet!*" Caes laughed.

"Love to, now?"

"If you like, will it take you long?"

He suddenly had doubts, but was relieved when Truus said,

"No. I'm good, let's go!"

Caes changed out of his wet clothes and they went to the car. It took a moment to wipe the snow from the body and thanking the car spirits above, it started after only a couple of tries.

Det Zweet Fabriek, Herculesplein. 19.30.

Caes had got Truus to start weight training about six months ago. She had complained of not being powerful enough for kick-boxing. Tamada had said she needed to do work on her strength. She had taken to weight training like a pro. Caes had told her that this was where all the best weight trainers went, tongue firmly in cheek. He thought she half expected there to be sawdust on the floor as it was pretty seedy from the outside, but it was just what they needed. It was unpretentious, a place where people simply went to work out. There may have been a few poseurs, but none like you saw at some of the more corporate type gyms in Utrecht. The gym was aptly named *Det Zweet Fabriek*. In fact, it was just an old converted factory and it smelt of sweat, hence the name Caes supposed and it looked really serious. It was very basic, but there again, what did you need, just weights and bars, then more weights. No bikes or steppers or rowing machines here, just bars and literally tons of blue or silver weights.

"This is hard core,"
Caes had told her outside when they had first got there,
"Don't look anyone in the eye. They're all on steroids. Make no eye contact."
Truus had looked worried at first, but soon realised her father was trying to be funny; they were now used to it.

Caes couldn't believe that the two skinny Moroccan lads in baseball caps were on illegal drugs anyway as they struggled with the smallest of weights. They were just trying too hard. They were always offering their advice on how to do stuff that was completely bogus. They really had no idea and just made him laugh. If they went near to Truus though, she told them to push off, she would have none of it, wouldn't give them the time of day. She was too focused to waste her time when in a gym of any type.

A couple of huge Polish guys were on the bench next to them. They always greeted Caes with handshakes and laughs and were always quite chippy as they had got on well since he had first visited without Truus. They took it very seriously and had bodies like the proverbial. The two scrawny Moroccan lads were on their way out when one of the Poles roared something at them, Caes nearly jumped out of his skin and off the bench and hid, as the lads returned and started to put the weights they had been using back into the racks.

"Etiquette,"
Caes told Truus,
"Never ever forget to put the weights back."
"I know! And no eye contact." She repeated to him.
"Roid rage!" he muttered.
"Shush, Pappy, not even in jest!" she looked serious.

"Who's joking?" he said.

It was a really good, but challenging, work out. They were both concentrating on their arms and legs today, so he was bench pressing and then doing squats and other tortures. Truus stood behind him making sure his form was correct. She was a great help and had learnt a lot in a short time. Caes supposed her kick-boxing helped her when it came to fitness and exercise work outs. Then he did the same for her. She was very strong for such a slim girl. One of the Poles said something to Caes and he couldn't help but laugh.

"What?"

Truus snapped, she was cross, she knew he had said something about her.

"They say you lift like a man."

"That's good is it?"

she said abruptly, obviously thinking they were being rather rude.

"Well you do, I think they were being serious, it was a compliment, because you are being serious. They like that."

"Pappy, I lift like a girl!" She snarled.

You couldn't argue with the feminist Truus. Caes laughed out loud and told the Poles, and they laughed and high fived each other grinning broadly at Truus who tried to ignore them, though her blushing face showed she was embarrassed...

What was nice, and this was a rough old place, was that they just accepted her as a lifter and she had no need to feel like this. There were none of the sideways looks or comments you could expect in other gyms. They were here to work and they respected you if you were working too.

But God, this was hard. After a final set of six reps Caes would have to stop, his legs were turning to jelly. Truus shouted encouragement and he finished, then it was her turn and she worked herself to an even redder face and into the ground, but finished her set. So, determined to make sure she finished. She made Caes very proud; she would never let herself be beaten.

She mushed her sweaty hair up with her fingers.

"It's getting too long, Pappy, gets in my eyes when I lift."

"I thought your eyes were closed when you lifted."

"Pah! No I need a haircut."

She wiped her face with the towel.

"That was a good effort, Truus, feel better?"

"Carry me home, Pappy."

She muttered through clenched teeth as we went for a shower.

"I can't feel my arms... or my legs. Am I dead?"

"You'll be fine, just get showered…"

They decided to stop off at a restaurant to end the day. Truus was recovering from her fatigue, though Caes didn't think her mouth would ever get tired!

Vagevuur.

She was tired after a long day at Universiteit. The Number 12 bus was crowded and she was standing. Stop after stop went by and the bus gradually emptied and she found a seat. She yawned and tried to stifle it with her mittened hand. What a day. Psychology had dragged, Sociology had been boring. Tutorials and seemed endless and mindless. She didn't think she was going anywhere. She glanced up and noticed a man staring at her. She tried to ignore him. She knew she was quite pretty and was used to men looking at her, but they bored her. She had no time for anyone at the moment. Work was getting on top of her and her free time was limited. She closed her eyes and sighed. They passed by Vondellaan and she got to her feet moving towards the exit. She pressed the bell and was irritated as someone else rang it after her. Were they deaf or just stupid. Then the bell went again. If she had been the driver she would have shouted at them for being stupid. She looked out at the snow floating down as the bus pulled into Bleekstreet. She stepped carefully off and made her way towards her flat. It was downhill and treacherous. A few kids were playing basketball on the local court. They must be mad she thought. Someone passed her, jostling her as they did causing her to stumble. 'ignorant bastard' she hissed under her breath. A sudden gust of wind blew snow into her face and she wiped her eyes, blinking away the sting. She was about to turn into her flat when the man from the bus appeared. He made her jump and she tried to go past him, but he moved into her again. She felt a sudden blow in her stomach. He'd hit her for God's sake. Then he hit her again. She was just about to scream...

Chapter 4

Zondag November 9, 2014.
Amaliastraat, 09.45.

Sunday morning in a cold and wintery Utrecht. Caes had gone for a run through the snow trying to exorcise the demons of the last night. The streets were deserted, no hustle and bustle and as he ran towards the new railway station on Vondellaan he felt refreshed and at ease. He jogged under the bridge and looked up at the unfinished electric wiring wondering if it was a safety risk. Not unless you were four metres tall he supposed. He carried on and did a small circuit down Albatrosstraat and back onto Briljantlaan, parallel to his house, before he got back onto his road and started to sprint to show how fit he was. He lasted twenty metres before he settled back into a jog. He got back to find that Truus was up and had the coffee on.

Truus was wearing jeans and an old sweatshirt. Her red hair was controlled by a blue handkerchief. She had outlined her eyes with mascara and her lips matched her hair.

"Shall we go for lunch somewhere, Pappy?"

"You have nothing on?" He asked.

"No, nothing really."

"Oké, where would you like to go?" asked Caes.

"Pizza. Near the canal, what's that bar called?"

"I know it. We can watch the sad tourists on the canal getting cold and wet."

"Well, get a shower and we can get off, we can have a walk if you like?"

She bossed him.

"What's brought this on?"

"Just want to spend some time with you, Pappy." Truus smiled her smile.

She smiled and looked just like her mother. He again felt a lump in my throat. He truly believed that he would not have survived without her after the death of Femke. She was the reason to go on living. When Femke died, it wasn't a cliché to say it was like his heart had been ripped out of his chest. It was only the thought of Truus that had swayed him. He could not leave her on her own. He had never told her this. She was too important to him. A part of Femke lived on in her obviously, but added to last night's nightmare he suddenly missed his wife terribly. Caes shivered and almost physically shook off the feeling. He showered quickly, got dressed and was drying his hair as Truus grabbed his arm and dragged him to the door.

"Come on, Pappy, let's be going!"

After their pizza, they went on to O'Connells bar for a drink and saw the Meijer twins sitting in a corner. They joined them and Freddie disappeared to the bar.

Freddie returned shortly as it wasn't too busy and brought over a tray of lagers. He placed them in front of everyone. Maaike protested.

"Freddie, you know I don't drink beer!"

"Sorry, sis."

"Can I have a coka as well please, Freddie?" Truus asked.

"Sorry, bit thoughtless…"

Freddie said going red and disappearing back to the bar.

"He is an idioot!" Maaike snorted.

"Not to worry." Truus said.

O'Connells was starting to fill up. The big screen showed football from some part of the world, but it was only background colour to the conversations that went on in the pub. No one was paying any attention to the game.

"Had a good weekend, Maaike?" Caes asked.

"Quiet, I went to the judokan yesterday for a work out."

"What belt are you?" Caes wondered.

"Black at the moment working towards my next stage." Maaike said.

"Will that take long?" Truus wondered.

"I have a few grading competitions so not too long."

"Never argue with Maaike,"

Freddie smiled as he set two coka's on the table,

"It gets really painful. Her choke hold…" continued Freddie.

"I always thought judo looked a bit slow…" started Truus.

"Not at all Maaike, its very technical, but not slow…"

"All that grappling and looking for position though."

"That's the fun," said Maaike warming to her subject. "You are looking for an advantage. It starts with the grip…"

"I see that, but it can take forever…"

"I look into their eyes and know when I have them. I make the grip. Feel it."

She pushed her hand across towards Truus and took her hand and squeezed gently. Truus winced, it was like a grip of iron.

"Ouch!" she smiled.

"Well I am gripping her jacket, not her hand, then I assert myself."

50

"You are pretty strong..." laughed Truus.

"I keep low and have hold of the *Gi*, the jacket and then it begins."

"Like dancing?" suggested Truus.

Maaike laughed.

"A war dance, I try to get them off balance. Like you do in kick boxing I suppose, but a slower process."

"That's what I wouldn't like. I want it to be quick."

"But you must have long bouts?"

"Not really, it's all pretty quick. A kick or a sweep, they go down. I kick them in the head. Bingo!" she laughed.

"Maybe we are a little more scientific. We use levers and angles a bit more. But when we attack it is fast. They go down."

"Do you often go for submission holds?"

"Sometimes if they lay themselves wide open, but I prefer not to. I do like the action as well. I'd always prefer a good clean throw. That's the most satisfying..." Maaike smiled.

"I like the kick to the head most!" Truus laughed.

"You are a bit violent aren't you Truus?"

"I suppose I am at times. But not out of the ring. I'm a pussy cat."

She smiled and looked into Maaikes green eyes and felt her stomach turn somersaults and had no idea why.

Caes and Freddie were talking about the football game on the big screen. Both the young women hated football. Caes, a long-time supporter of FC Utrecht was trying to encourage Freddie to attend a game at Stadion Galgenwaard.

"I don't think so *baas*, I made too many enemies when on patrol there as a cadet..."

"Long time ago Freddie, they won't recognise you now." Caes laughed.

"Don't be too sure..." said Freddie.

"I remember in my teens running away from the Cops. We were a bit silly in those days."

"You a hooligan *baas*?" Freddie was shocked.

"Not as such, but if you were near them the police in those days didn't stand around and ask, it was batons out swinging and we had to be sharpish."

"Ever get hit pappy?" Truus asked.

"Never, I've always been quick." Caes laughed.

"Even now pappy?"

Vagevuur.

When her parents had died, she had felt afraid, but never as afraid as this. Her parents had left her provided for so she had no fear for the future though it would be a future on her own. That didn't scare her. She was scared now. She was alone and in the middle of her stomach she felt a heavy weight dragging her down into what she thought was a deep pit. She didn't think she could escape. Locked up, the light constantly on, she had no idea how long she had been there. She sniffed her clothes. She stank of sick and sweat and that made her feel worse. She looked over at the dirty sink, but felt too scared to move. She felt safe on the mattress, as if she was marooned on a boat and this room was an ocean. If she left the safety of her boat she would suffer. She still hadn't moved to get her shoes or look for her leggings, she was too frightened to move. It was irrational, but it was how she thought. Her body seemed weighed down by something inside her, something that was gnawing away at her, trying to escape. She knew if it escaped she would end up a screaming, sobbing mess and she didn't want that. She didn't want to lose control. It was all she had left. If she gave in she knew that it would be the end and whoever had taken her would have won. She couldn't let that happen, she couldn't let this man whoever he was win. Who was he? Where had she seen him? He was so familiar, so ordinary. The way he came into the room and threw over food and bottles of water without a word or seemingly a care in the world made her feel even more alone. He wouldn't speak, not since he had sworn at her when he had tried to rape her, he just looked at her with contempt. What had she done to him to make him act this way?

Chapter 5

Maandag, November 10, 2014.
Amaliastraat, 09.20.

Truus thought long and hard about what to wear. She usually just flung things on, things that were clean! She always seemed to be dressed well, but she wasn't one to over think things. Last time she had had to dress smartly was for her interview at Universiteit Utrecht, though she could have dressed in a sack and got in there she thought.

So, dress? No, a skirt, not too short, not too tight, with white tights, not leggings and some boots. Her new white blouse, her smart denim jacket, not Pappy's scruffy one, with her favourite silk scarf. Nice. A light brush of makeup and some ruby red lipstick, she was dressed to kill, though that probably wasn't appropriate. She ran her hands through her *Heet Chili Rood* hair, mushed it up a little and then decided to tie a ribbon in it. She felt she looked good, no, she knew she looked good. Let's get to this interview and yes, let's kill it!

The cold almost knocked her back into the house. How can it be this cold in November, she wondered? She tucked her hair into her hat and wrapped a scarf around her neck, feeling her eyelashes start to freeze. She blinked a few times and rubbed her eyes, before putting her head down and marching purposefully towatds the bus stop on Vondelplaan.

Staring out at the slush on the road didn't dampen her mood. The bus was noisy, she stood at the back hanging onto a strap; too many school children on it this morning all with a story to tell their friends. Truus was jostled and bumped by youths with back packs that they didn't seem to have any control over. It was a short journey into the centre and she was relieved when it ended and she could get off.

The biting wind attacked her as soon as she stepped onto the pavement. She waited as brave cyclists passed her before skipping Across the cycle lane and to safety. She was amazed that so many still travelled by bike. It was so cold and the cobbled were covered in thin layers of slush which were like land mines in her view. Hands deep in her pockets, she made her way to Blokstraat and the possibility of a brand new adventure in her life.

Gemoedsrust Psychotherapie, 11.30.

Caes looked across his therapist's desk. As usual it felt odd, although he wasn't being interrogated, it always felt like it. The long pauses were the worst, it always made him feel really uncomfortable and almost forced into saying something, but Caes always resisted. He really didn't want to share his feelings with any psycholoog. He didn't know why he attended, but his medical dokter kept urging him to, that he should talk it out, try to come to terms with it. It? The death of Femke, his wife and his world, nearly five years ago. Come to terms with it? How? Caes couldn't imagine how any amount of therapy could help him to come to terms with it. Nothing could help. He didn't want to live in the past, but felt himself rooted to the time that Femke died. Caes was trapped and could not move on, no matter how hard he tried to.

Dokter Jozefzoon smiled as he always did raising his hands prayer like in front of his face and pursed his lips between his fingers. He must have read somewhere that that was how he should look. He was very mannered in everything he did, always calm, perhaps too calm.

"Ever had thoughts about ending your life?" Jozefzoon asked.

"No…" Caes snorted, thinking how many times was he going to ask that same question, how many times would he give the same answer.

"Have you ever made plans to end your life?"

"No!" Caes almost shouted, this was absurd, always this mantra to open proceedings. Always the same responses, week in week out. Perhaps he should answer in the affirmative one week and see what the reaction was. Why would he want to kill himself, why did he keep asking? It made no sense to him, checklist or not.

"It's oké, you must know by now that I have to ask. How have you been since I saw you last week. Better? The same?"

"Not too good, I keep on wanting to cry. I just really can't help myself, it's for no reason; I just sit down and I just want to cry."

Caes explained his recurring nightmare to him yet again. He just nodded. Caes supposed there was no surprise that he should have that dream.

"So you feel there is nothing, not any reason, besides dreams, anything to make you start crying?" he wondered.

"No not really I just… I just start…"

Caes suddenly felt like he wanted to cry now, he felt ridiculous, weak and pathetic, not understanding why. Though really he knew only too well.

"How's work in general, away from the sadness?" Jozefzoon asked.

"It's oké, I get on with stuff, keep myself away from most people."

"Friends?"

"They are always there. I try not to let them in though; I don't want to make them get fed up with me moaning about how I feel."

"Do you think they would?"

"I don't know and don't really want to find out, it would not be fair. I just want to get on with it, but..."

"Yes?"

"Well, I feel I got into this and need to get myself out of it."

"I don't think that it's a question of you getting into depression."

"Well I can't see any other way to describe it...one day I was not depressed then the next... after I lost Femke, I suppose it just exploded on me..."

"It would not be a sign of weakness to ask for help."

"Well I see you don't I? I am trying."

This felt even more frustrating. Five years of so called therapy and not really getting anywhere closer to getting better. There again, Caes wasn't sure what 'better' meant anymore. This cloud of depression had hung over him for so long now. He remembered the wonderful days of his marriage and how happy he was and he still had Truus, she was all the goodness in his life, but he also had this unbelievable feeling of loss and emptiness that he don't think he would ever come to terms with. No matter how much therapy he was to receive. Truus filled his life, but there was a huge black void where Femke had been.

Jozefzoon asked. "How's it going outside work?"

"Good, I enjoy life. It's what I enjoy; I love life!"

"You should list three things then, things that make you happy..."

"And?"

"Every day you list three things that you have done that you've enjoyed and that made you happier."

"That does what?"

"Well we can then see that things are not as bad as you think, that there are positives, that you have good things in your life." Jozefzoon said.

"Well I know I have good things, it still doesn't…"

"Caes, be a little more positive please. Now your medication, you are still talking it?"

"Of course, I don't like to, but I am taking it."

"Any difference?" Jozefzoon wondered.

"Well it's been a few months since I increased it. I can't honestly say one way or the other. I never know how I should feel anymore. I've almost forgotten what it was like before I felt like this"

Caes never knew whether he felt okay because he was on this huge dose of antidepressants or whether he was getting better. Getting better would be a fine thing.

"It does take time to take effect; we increased it last month didn't we? So we can leave the dose the same I think. Come and see me in a week, oké?" He smiled, but Caes didn't really have anything to smile about.

"Oké." Caes shook his hand as he always did and bid farewell, feeling empty and that he'd wasted good time again.

After Femke had died, the police dokter and psycholoog thought seeing a therapist was a good idea. At the time Caes couldn't be bothered to argue and this had now gone on for too many years and with no positive result. He changed medication, changed therapists, changed the actual therapy and was getting nowhere. Caes sometimes shared his feelings with Truus, but never about his actual anxiety. Work and life went on as best it could. He didn't think his mental health impacted on work as he tried really hard to keep normality at the forefront of things, but sometimes he would descend into such a desperate low that he couldn't concentrate on anything and felt himself sinking deeper and deeper into a pit of despair. These times were awful and Caes just wanted to be on his own, to not involve anyone in his world, but this was almost impossible so he would battle on, knowing that at these times his performance at work was inhibited, that his concentration was not what it should be. He had a good team he would repeat to myself, not expecting them to carry him, but knowing that he could rely on them, but could they rely on him? Caes didn't want to go into anything half-cocked and not give them all the support they deserved. It was hard, but he just felt that he had to battle through it all. He knew that he needed to do something, but had no idea what. This was a battle, a five-year battle so far and there was no prospect of any type of victory as far as he could see; drugs kept his mood stable. This was a good thing. Caes had his ups when I would feel euphoric for no reason and then hit lows where I could sink into a real pit. The lows came and I had no idea why other than the feeling of complete loss. How long could I keep feeling like this, what was it doing to me? I shivered and pulled my collar up ready for the snow and the wind. It was freezing. It matched my mood.

Particulier Onderzoeks Bureau, Blokstraat. 12.45.

Truus Heda sat across from Thijs Orman; he looked her up and down almost dismissively, but also coldly and critically.

"There's not very much of you."

"What do you want, a gorilla?" Truus snorted dismissively.

"No, but you need…"

She interrupted him,

"I keep myself fit. I run, I work out, I kick-box, and I am very capable of looking after myself. Anyway, I prefer to talk my way out of things if I ever have a problem."

"You any good at that?"

"Well, I don't really get too many problems, but yes I am."

"You are very confident about yourself?"

Truus didn't feel it, but thought she needed to act this part out to the end.

"Yes…?" as if that was the most stupid of questions.

"What other skills do you bring to the table?"

"I understand computers, not that it seems to mean anything in the office here…"

Why was she being so rude to him, she almost kicked herself, but it seemed to wash over him for some reason. She desperately wanted this job. Toe the line or be yourself? If being yourself was to be rude, best stop. Now!

She looked around the musty office and saw a telephone and a typewriter, filing cabinets, sink, an old coffee machine and a fridge. That was it. Orman was a small man behind a big desk in a tiny slightly dirty office. Some job! But she wanted it, she wanted to be doing something away from her Sociology textbooks that were just boring her. Sending her to sleep. She wanted to be alive.

"Look, you knew my father when you were in the force. He is a good man. I am a good student. I learn quickly. I'll work hard for you. It's what I want to do. I offer you a lot."

"I have built this up from nothing. I had to wait for a long time before I could get my licence. I don't want to waste that effort by making the wrong choice."

"I'll work hard." Truus said defiantly.

"Why not the Police like your old man?"

"Too many rules and regulations. I don't want to be tied down by a book. I know right from wrong, but I don't need a book."

"Well…"

"Look, my father said that you are a good man."

She knew that was a lie. So too did Orman,

"Now we both know that's not true."

"Well he did say he liked you."

"Well I liked him, but how long has it been, eight years? Too long to trade on good will"

Truus suddenly felt guilty and shamefacedly started,

"Look, sorry, I should not have mentioned his name. That was crass. I'm sorry and I don't want to rely on any good will, real or imagined. I want to be chosen on merit. So anyway, just let me know, what's it to be? Yes, or No?"

He paused looking her in the eye,

"Oké we can give it a try."

"Thank you. You will not regret it. When do I start?"

"Tomorrow at nine. I'll have a job for you."

"See you, Meneer Orman."

"Call me Thijs."

"Oké, Thijs."

She made her way to the door, and closed it behind her, glancing at the dirty brass name plate. *'Thijs Orman. Particulier Onderzoeks Bureau'.*

Truus skipped down the steep stairs. She felt good about herself as if a load had been taken off her shoulders. She opened the door to the outside world and was blasted by the snow. Her face seemed to freeze immediately. She pulled up her collar and pulled down her hat so that only her eyes were exposed.

It was the final part of the briefing.

"Two girls missing…" said Caes

"Are they connected?" asked Adrie.

"Same woman reported them missing." Madelon said.

"Says they were her daughters. We know one wasn't according to Truus." Stated Caes.

"The Universiteit haven't got back to us about Elise yet." Said Freddie.

"Give them a kick up the arse Freddie." Madelon smiled.

"Baas." Replied Freddie.

"Also I think this is a bit bigger than I first thought so Madelon will take lead on this."

"Oké baas." Freddie was relieved.

"we need addresses and lists of friends. Parents if there are any, where they live. The usual. Oké Madelon?"

"Yes, no problem baas."

Amaliastraat, 16.00.

Truus lay on her bed at home hugging her rather worn childhood Nijntje. It was quiet and peaceful, her mind started to drift and she suddenly really wanted to hear her mammie's voice, where was she? She wanted to hear her tell her that she was doing the right thing, how she was making her so proud, whether she saw herself in Truus, how at… but nothing, there was nothing, no hugs or kisses, it all came flooding back to her, no private confidences that only she and her mama could have kept, the secrets that mothers and daughters kept from everyone, the shared secrets that would have meant so much to each of them… but then what would they to each other, what could they say? She was not there, so why should she imagine what could have been? What should have been? What would never ever be…Truus still loved her mammie, loved her memory, she loved her to bits, but could never ever again tell her how she felt, never ever feel her warm body close to her, her hugs, her kisses when she was down, never again hear her laugh, see her beautiful, beautiful smile, never have her wipe away her tears as she wished she was doing now, tears that were streaming down her face, never have her mend her breaking heart, her heart breaking into tiny pieces…her beautiful, beautiful mammie…Truus buried her face into the pillow and sobbed her heart out.

It was a strange crooked little man taking Mammies funeral, in a freezing cold kerk. He had a soft, rasping voice that faltered every so often. He looked just like a crow Truus remembered, with a hooked nose, small eyes, leaning forward, his cassock like wings on either shoulder. He was saying she had been loved by all and remembered by many. It's true. There were lots of people Truus didn't know at her funeral. Former pupils, friends, fellow teachers, relatives, all caring, but Truus felt she just did not care. Her mammie was gone, it was empty, and she was only fourteen.

Truus remembered her pappy standing at the front, squeezing her. Words like the 'sweetest, most beautiful girl' were spoken and floated into the air. That's all Truus could recall, then the freezing cold, the faces, nothing else and then the *pastoor* again, rasping, faltering and loved by all remembered by many.

And Mammies favourite hymn, so sad and haunting, the organist had played the tune so beautifully. *Calon Lan*, a Welsh hymn Pappy had explained later. They had it played and sung at their wedding and now it was being reprised at her funeral. Two such sad bookends on their married life. Truus for some reason clearly remembered just one part of one line,

"*The riches of a virtuous, pure heart will bear eternal profit.*"

How do you know at the age of fourteen whether your mammie has a pure heart? Truus did know that her mammie was full of goodness, her pappy sometimes says he sees her mammie in Truus. Well she was her mammie she always thought, she should be there in me! It's when Truus laughed that he says this most she remembered. Truus thought to herself bitterly, why should she keep seeing the image of her mammie in hospital? Wasting away, painfully thin, smiling through the pain or the picture of her smiling at them in her pink sweater, looking happy. Hear her laughing as they splashed in the sea in Wijk aan Zee, as she screamed at Space Mountain in Paris, as she scolded Truus for eating too quickly or for getting muddy after playing out, knowing she didn't really mean it. Pure in heart, pure in every way. Taken from them before her time, before she was ready, before any of them were ready, after just five weeks.

When are you ready for your mammie or your pappy to die? You never can be, but you don't expect them to go when you are still at school, thought Truus. Pappy had lost both his parents at nineteen, then lost his wife after only eleven years of marriage. At least they had spent all their thirty years together as neighbours, schoolmates, friends, then lovers. Truus thought she would never have been ready. She felt she couldn't see her mammies' face as often as she wanted to, and had to check the photo to make sure that she remembered her right. Truus heard her laugh and saw her smile, but her face was fading, she wanted to hold her hand, to feel her warm body. She wanted her to laugh, to smile. She wanted to hug her tight, to share her thoughts and feelings, she wanted to kiss her beautiful face to tell her how much she loved her and how much she missed her. This was so horrible. Truus just wanted her mammie. She pressed Nijntje to her chest. She couldn't hope to stop crying.

Caes put a plate in front of Truus. She as usual started to hoover it up. Finally taking a breath, Truus looked up at him,

"Gisele de Groet? I think she still lives in her vaders old house somewhere down in Binnenstad. Why?"

"No reason."

"Pappy?" she pressed him.

"Well it seems she has disappeared as well. Her mother, well she said she was her mother, but it was the same person who said she was Elise's mother the other day, who you say is dead. It's too fantastic! It's just too confusing. What do you know of Gisele's mother?"

"She went to live in America, she divorced many years ago. We never ever saw her at school."

"So she could be this big, smelly woman?"

"No, no she's in America with a new family, I'm sure of it."

"How very strange."

He said, how very strange indeed he thought.

"Her father?"

"Dead, again before we even knew her, her mother left as soon as she graduated from the VWO, left her to it after that, gone, what for at least two or three years?"

"Nice of her, poor girl." Said Caes.

"Yes she was only seventeen or so when she went, nasty really. It is all very strange, Pappy…" Truus got out her laptop and a textbook, dinner plates and pans ignored again.

"Do you want any help, Pappy?" she asked as an afterthought.

"No, it's alright *lieverd*; you get on with your work."

"About that…" she started.

"Yes?"

"Yesterday, I sat in the library…" said Truus.

"Yes?"

"I was just so bored; I just sat and watched the snow fall…"

"Well, is it a boring module?" asked Caes.

"I honestly don't know, Pappy, I can't get into it." She shrugged.

"Well, I suppose you may have to start to look long term, is this what you really want to do with your future?"

"I don't know anymore, at first it was really interesting finding out new things, but now…"

"Too technical?" wondered Caes.

"Yes, too dry. I need something to bring me alive."

"Why not swap subjects?"

"I had thought I might."

"To Literature or writing?" Caes emphasised, "I could never understand why you went for Sociology."

"I thought I ought to, now I don't know why as well," She laughed.

"Well, arrange a meeting at your *Universiteit*, see if you can swap. If not this year, you should be able to take a break and restart next semester. It's fine, you have to do what you enjoy, there really isn't any point in doing anything else and…"

Caes flourished some papers in front of his daughter.

"More, Pappy?" her face brightened.

"I have a gift for you."

"Christmas so soon?" she smiled.

"No, two tickets for Depeche Mode, take a friend..."

"Oh, Pappy!"

She jumped up and hugged him.

"I wanted to go but had no money, how did you..."

"Took me hours and hours, but here they are."

"Thank you so much, Pappy."

She kissed his cheek, took the tea towel and started drying up. With a final flourish, she folded it up when finished.

"*Dank wel*, Pappy. I've got to go, dinner was nice, see you later. *Doeg!*"

Det Zweet Fabriek, Herculesplein. 19.30.

Caes had to stay in trim so it was a return to *Det Zweet Fabriek* with Truus and some late night hard core lifting. He didn't like going to the police gym it was too clean, too sophisticated. Also, it was too distracting as there were always people there saying 'Hi' or wanting to catch up or look at cases they were running. Here it was private, sweaty and dirty! The two Polish lads, Bogdi and Ofim were also doing some heavy lifting in a corner. It was late, darkness had quietly covered the snow outside. Inside there was the normal gaggle of noisy Moroccans who as usual spent more time arguing than lifting, but as all they really wanted to do was strut around as peacocks they didn't care whether they lifted or not. They weren't doing any harm, so good luck to them! Bogdi and Ofim both had amazing senses of humour so were laughing between lifting. At the Moroccans, more often than not and definitely not at Truus and him, Caes hastened to add in his head! There were also their two beautiful Polish girlfriends, who had come to work out as well. One, Nadzia came over to Caes just as Truus was in mid lift and going puce in the face and said admiringly,

"Bogdi say you amaze him as girl who work out, he talk all of time about you. We get jealous so come and do it ourself to check you out and show him we too women of strength!"

"He not say you pretty and strong, that you just strong," said Zuzana.

Truus had to take that as a compliment and Caes smiled to himself, thinking how she had resented their 'lift like a man remark'. But they really did just see the athlete, not the woman which was kind of refreshing, though he was sure she would wish to be described as pretty sometimes rather than just strong! No, he thought, she can't have it both ways! But he was her vader and he thought she was pretty!

Nadzia and Zuzana went back to their lifting, while Truus and Caes did more work on their arms. Caes spotted as Truus pressed, getting faster as she built up her power and stamina. They didn't want the pretty Truus to look like a man, but Caes felt that he now wanted her to be able to punch like one! She just looked exhausted after her three lots of ten reps,

"Can't feel my arms, Pappy, are they still there, it's all going black."

Caes finished his sets with Bogdi spotting him. Bogdi and Ofim were going to enter an Utrecht 'strongman' contest and asked if Caes would like to join them. He thought best not! Sounds too much like hard work and if these two monsters were typical of the entrants, there would be very little point!

Kroonstraat Police Bureau, 18.50.

Maaike and Madelon sat on the settee in the 'Sex Crimes Suite'. It was way after midnight and they were both tired. Not as tired as the girl with them though. The girl opposite, Jeltje, looked about thirteen, her face swollen, her left eye closed.

"He beat you for what?" Madelon said.

"It was my fault."

"How can it be your fault that he beat you?"

"Yes, it was, he told me he didn't want to, but I had to work harder."

"You have sex for money, Jeltje, you don't keep your money."

"No, but he takes care of me…"

"By beating you?" Maaike said.

"He loves me, I love him. He keeps me safe, I have a home."

"How old are you?"

"Nineteen."

"Really, Jeltje?" asked Madelon.

"Truly."

"Is this what you want from your life?"

"It's for him… "

"Jeltje, it's not about him, my love, can't you see…" Maaike despaired.

"He's using you to make money for him, then does this…" Madelon tried.

"You don't need him, you're able to work without him, you do realise that don't you?"

"I need him. It was my fault. Look have you finished?"

"You don't want to press charges?" Maaike asked.

"Why'd I do that?"

"So he doesn't do it again."

"He won't, he loves me." Jeltje smiled.

The bastard smirked at them as he kissed Jeltje as she went through into the foyer and then held her close, like two lovers out for a stroll.

"I want to be sick, Madelon, how can we stop this?"

"You're too old fashioned, Maaike, it'll always go on. But the violence, I don't like this…"

Klasina was just the same, but with a different pimp, though her affection for him was a little worn. She was older, harder.

"Nothing to do with you, I can handle this." She said.

"But why should you?" Madelon asked.

"We can help…" Maaike felt she was almost pleading.

Klasina laughed,

"Because it's the way it is."

"It doesn't have to be, Klasina. You can work alone; you don't need him." Madelon said.

"Who'd look after me if he didn't?"

"There are others…"

"Yes, with his friends? His connections?"

"You don't deserve this…" Maaike tried.

"It's my own fault, I wasn't working hard enough."

"Look, Klasina, why not find someone else to take care of you, if you've your card why him, why someone so violent?"

"And then what? Do you think he would let me go? Why should he anyway?"

"You are your own person; he doesn't own you!" Maaike was angry.

"He takes care of me, in his own way. I know the score; I know what's what."

"Klasina, please help us to help you…"

"Leave it will you, I need to get back to my work."

"With your face like that?" Madelon said.

"Yes, with my face like this. No work I get the same." She snapped.

"And you are happy with that?"

"It's my choice, it's my life. Look I've got to go."

"Klasina…" Madelon started.

"Dank for thinking of me, but there is no point. I'll see myself out shall I?"

And there he was waiting, a great smile on his face as if she were returning from holiday. Arm in arm they left the station.

Maaike was almost distraught when she spoke to Madelon.

"But people like that, the bastard pimps we saw, why are they allowed?"

"As long as we allow prostitution they will be around, it's the organised crime involvement that is the problem, the underage girls. I can't believe that Jeltje is nineteen, we'll have to check."

"But if gangs are involved, why can't we stop it?"

"I'm sorry, Maaike, we have to deal with it as we see it, trust me you'll see worse as you go further in your career."

"I might not want to go further then," she muttered to herself.

They had one more girl to talk to. Alida sat opposite them, she had a bit too much make up on, she looked tired, her hands were in old lady's mitts, her nails chewed and the polish was starting to flake off. She just looked a bit scruffy. But you could see she had a beauty, though it was fading. Maaike wondered how old she was, though the cliché, old before their time, did seem to ring true with her.

"...don't you want to stop all this?" Madelon had asked.

"No, I'm happy..."

"Really?" Maaike couldn't hide her surprise, "How can you be? Sorry, but how?"

"It's my choice, what's your name?"

"Maaike..."

"Maaike, what if I don't want to stop?"

"But you have a choice, there is always a choice, you can stop."

"What if I don't want to?"

"Don't you?"

Alida paused, her dull eyes were looking darker and sadder.

"You don't understand."

"Try me," Maaike demanded.

"What's the point?"

"I want to understand; I find it so hard to understand. Some of the girls I think get pushed into it and are then controlled, but you? I don't want to sound patronising, but you sound too bright, so clever, why?"

"I did my degree at Groningen Uni, couldn't get a job, went out with lots of blokes, had sex, then I thought why not? Joined an Escort Agency, they took too big a cut, so went freelance, needed a bit of help, my fella found me, the rest is history."

"But why not get a job, use your degree?"

"I'd like to stop working this way, but don't know what else to do, how would I make a regular income?"

"I suppose you're right at the moment, jobs being short as they are." Maaike felt that seemed such a trite thing to say and hoped Alida didn't think she was trying to be sarcastic.

"Yes, it's a vicious economic climate, but men'll always pay for sex!" Alida smiled grimly.

"Would you ever be able to have a, I don't know what to call it, a 'normal' relationship with a man?" Maaike asked.

"Even if I found a man who I could tell what I'd done in the past, at the back of his mind he'd never trust me and who could blame him? It puts you in a no-man's land. I know I could never trust a man again."

"But that's so sad!"

"In fact, I'm almost glad that I have done this because I know what men get up to. Their wives don't know. The likelihood of him cheating on you is probably quite high."

"I don't really believe that!"

She looked at Maaike me as though she was stupid.

"I don't know why I'm telling you all this."

"Because I asked?"

Alida smiled,

"Maybe, probably. When I first started, I thought I was getting my own back. Men were meeting me and expecting sex for nothing so I thought, why not make them pay? It does sometimes bother me especially when they get a bit rough, but that's why my fella is about. I don't know what else to do. I try to make clients think. Don't know if I get too far. Like, when a man asks me to do a three way, to be with another girl I say, 'Well, would you go with another man?' I try to make them stop and think. I don't think it works though. We're not dealing with too many Einstein's in Utrecht!"

"What about your man, does he hit you like others seem to be getting hit?"

"Not really, he sees us as too valuable, so just looks after us on the street. Sometimes he gets a bit pissed when we don't have enough money, but well it's water off a ducks back to me."

"But how does it make you feel? You can't like it can you?"

"It's not about liking it, it's a job. I tend to ignore them," she laughed. That made Maaike and Madelon smile as well.

"The trouble is, girls, are being made to value themselves by what they look like and by men's definition of how we should be valued. You see music videos celebrating pimps and hoes, lads' mags, everything. Women are being told that their bodies should be accessible to men. It's like there is a conspiracy to turn women into semen receptacles."

Maaike shuddered at her language, but it seemed so true.

"Men are twisting life to make women think it's all level and it's equal and liberating. No, it suits men, it's convenient for men. That's what's so nasty; it's a fucking rotten state of affairs."

Alida was almost getting angry, but more resigned than anything else.

Maaike felt really cold, but it was from the inside, it was horrible. She looked despairingly at Madelon.

"Maaike, look, I have a choice, at the moment I choose my life to go in this direction. I don't do drugs, I may look a little scruffy, but I have been out since nine tonight, what time is it now, nearly three? I brush up well when I need to."

"But men dominating you, paying you…"

"No, I charge them, I win in every sense. My fella takes a cut, but I have money. Not thousands, but I survive."

"You could do so much more though." Maaike was almost pleading.

"I will, when I choose to, that's the choice I've made. Look love, you're young, still have your ideals and you must keep them, but this is the real world. I chose my life. We all have to make choices when we finish at Universiteit. If you went maybe you would see the world differently?"

"I doubt it."

"I am oké, well, Maaike… Madelon," she nodded to them both, "it's been nice, take care getting home the pair of you." And she left.

Maaike looked at Madelon who sipped her coffee, it was cold, she thought about what she had said.

"What an awful view of men, is that what this work did to her?"

"Well, you couldn't blame her, but she seems determined to carry on, she's bright, she knows she has choices and has chosen this. What can we do?" Madelon asked.

"At least she is not getting hurt like the others."

"Well, not physically, but she hasn't got a very nice view of men."

"Can you blame her? What a world we live in."

"Go home and go to sleep with a smile on your face. That's all you can do, Maaike. Try to leave it all here."

"I will try. *Tot ziens!*"

Amaliastraat, 21.00.

Once back at home, Caes sat on the settee. He could hear the beat of some band or other coming through Truus's earphones. She looked up at him and smiled. She was stretched out on the floor. She looked happy as she returned her gaze to her book. Her feet bounced up and down on her bottom as she responded to her music. Every so often she would sing a short phrase or verse. Caes had no need for his own music, she was entertaining him with hers. She pulled her ear plugs out.

"What ya thinking, Pappy?"

"How your ears are going to explode." He smiled.

"Sorry! Was it too loud?"

"No, not really. Not loud enough to know who it was." He lied.

"You must know the band!" she was horrified.

"Depeche, who else."

"Good, Pappy, on the cultural ball as usual."

"The zeitgeist, Truus, the cultural zeitgeist."

"Whatever."

She dismissed him with an affected wave of her hand.

"My culture, my music. You weren't even born when they started."

"Anyhoo, what you thinking?"

"The missing students…"

"Remember you always tell your guys to leave it at work."

"I tell them that, Truus, but don't actually believe it."

"Pappy!"

"I don't want the youngsters worrying off duty. The older they get, fine they can, but I want to let them live."

"Wait till I tell, Maaike!"

He kicked out gently at her bottom, but she was too quick and rolled away.

"Don't you dare! I need my management secrets. Anyway, we are just going nowhere. We've spent hundreds of hours going nowhere."

"Well at least you've ruled things out which must help?"

"I know, but I'd rather it was the other way around."

"But you know who hasn't got them which is a start."

Caes smiled at her logic, but it was a thin smile.

"I want to know why Thijs. Why Sterre? What has Thijs done or is it Sterre?"

"I can't see it. He seems quite nice really. A bit gruff at the start, miserable now of course."

"He's on edge, not the normal Thijs, whatever that is now."

"I wonder how he's been these past few years growing his business."

"Professional I think." Caes said.

"I'd have thought really business like from how he operates in his office. It seems basic, but he is very organised with an amazing filing system. He is distracted now, but still sounds so competent on the phone, he does seem very professional."

"That's how I remember him before the drugs took hold, really capable and professional." Caes agreed.

Totale Judo dojo, Balearen. 21.50.

Maaike grabbed the *judogi* of her opponent. There had been the usual slapping and feinting of movements as each tried to get the upper hand. They seemed to grip each other simultaneously and he pulled Maaike towards him trying to catch her off balance, but she was nice and low, her feet wide. She felt his superior strength almost course through his hands. She looked into his eyes and then saw him smirk. This didn't happen often. Judo was all about respect. That was the thing she liked the most about fighting here, it was all left on the mat. Her opponent today was disrespecting her and she felt her teeth bite hard into her gum shield. She released him and stepped away.

Sensei Korbert called *hajime* and Maaike went straight for the *Ashi-Guruma*. I may be small but I am quick thought Maaike. I am strong she said to herself as he slammed onto the mat, so unexpectedly that the quizzical look on his face only appeared after he stood up breathing deeply. She bowed and smiled inwardly and walked away from the mat, grabbing her weights towel as she did. She pulled off her *judogi* and wearing just her sports bra and scarlet shorts she went into the weights room.

Instinctively she felt her right bicep. It was firm and muscled. She moved towards the bench and put weights onto the bar. There was no one to spot for her but she knew she would cope. She started to pump her arms up and down, locking her elbows with each lift. Ten quick reps later she was on her feet and jogged across to work on her shoulders, pulling a heavy blue weight down from above her head, feeling the lactic acid build. Then it was over to the leg press and she felt her thighs trembling as she pushed against the board, the weights moving slowly with the agony of it. It was then up onto her feet to skip on the spot twirling the rope like a professional boxer. It made her smile the tricks she could now do with the rope. Except for double turns they were mostly for show and she didn't do this if anyone else was in the gym. Despite the amusement this all gave her she felt her body crying out to stop, it was complaining and large beads of sweat were seeping into her eyes making them blink as it stung her. She wiped her face, then back to the bar to start on her power press; onwards and upwards, she could not stop. She found the twenty-five-kilo weight and moved over to the wall. She slowly slid down the wall into a sitting position and lifted the weight out in front of her. *Mind over matter*, she thought as she held her arms locked in front of her. She spat away sweat as it dribbled into her mouth and closed her eyes to stop the stinging. Her legs began to shake as she continued the torture. She felt her arms start to quiver and breathed deeply through her nose. She looked over at the clock willing the second hand to move but it seemed to be stuck. She could almost hear her arms screaming and her legs were crying. She jumped to her feet and started to press the large weight above her head. She had to do twenty or she was a failure. At fifteen she felt she could do no more, but started to berate herself inwardly. Her arms shook, her body was telling her no, but up the weight went, slower and slower, until she had reached her goal. She almost threw the disc to the floor and sank to her knees, shaking her arms as she did. They felt like lead. But she had to go on, rolling over to pick up her skipping rope she went back into the dojo and waited her turn to fight again.

Vagevuur.

How long had she been here? She had no idea. It was painful to exist hgere with the light always on and seconds turning into hours without her knowing her. As for the days... she kicked at the bags of brioche he had thrown into her. Six bags, some with mouldy bread, some empty, but had it been six days? She was so hungry, she pulled up her blouse and looked at her stomach, she was getting thinner. She almost laughed as she thought what a good diet the brioche one must be. Brioche and water. She actually did laugh then her insides turned to ice as she heard the key in the lock and the door open. He stood there looking at her.

"What do you want?" she snapped.

She had to take control. She'd read that somewhere. Probably in her psychology lectures, but he wouldn't let her. He stood and stared as if she was an exhibit. She shivered.

He threw her a bottle of water and a polythene bag. She ignored them as they landed on the mattress.

"Who are you?"

Nothing.

"What do you want?"

Silence.

"You bastard..."

He left the room and she heard the key turn. She pulled her knees up to her chest and started to cry. What was to become of her? She still had stomach ache from where he had punched her. She remembered the punches and then waking up in this room. At first she had thought she was dreaming that she was in the middle of a nightmare. She remembered how tired she had been after her day of lectures, then it had dawned on her that this was no dream. The pains were real. The isolation was real. She shivered. And reached for the bottle. She drank it greedily and then tore open the bag. Stale bagels, but she couldn't remember when she had eaten last. Everything was merging into a long nightmare that was a living horror. The bagel cloyed at the back of her throat. She became only too aware that she was wide awake. She rubbed tears from her eyes and drank the last of the water. She needed more and got unsteadily to her feet and stumbled as she felt dizziness overcome her. She put a hand on the damp, cold wall and tried to focus. She moved slowly to the sink and splashed water onto her face, trying to liven herself up. Liven up for what though she wondered. She refilled the bottle, drank some more and topped it up again, before stumbling back to the mattress. She slowly sat down, her head spinning, her mind all over the place and closed her eyes.

He stood outside the door. He felt good. This was proceeding as he had wished. Clues were being laid by people who had no contact with him, he couldn't have wanted better.

Chapter 6

Dinsdag, November 11, 2014.
Particulier Onderzoeks Bureau, Blokstraat. 09.37.

Next morning, at his office, Thijs Orman was straight to the point.

"Photo, home address, Sterre Vossen just find her."

"Sterre Vossen? She is in one of my classes at *Universiteit.*"

"You know her?" He suddenly seemed very interested.

"Not really... she's pretty, very quiet... keeps herself to herself. Who wants to find her?"

"It's none of your business. Just look for her, find her if possible and be discreet. Oké?"

"*Oké,* Thijs."

He was such a miserable bastard she thought.

"Now this is off the books. You need to be discreet."

"Is there an issue?"

"You don't hold a private investigators licence yet. You will have to go to college to get it. Will you have time?"

"I think so..."

"In the meantime just be prudent. *Oké?*"

"For sure, Thijs."

"Be careful how you act. I am a *beroepsvoyeur*, 'a professional voyeur', you might not like that, but that is what you must become."

"*Oké,* Thijs. See you later."

Truus got onto the bus, it wasn't crowded. She looked out of her window at the snow. It was still very cold, more snow had fallen, there was lots of white, but some dirty black slush scarring it. She did like the snow though, it struck her as being so very pure, so very clean, almost as if it were cleaning up all the ills of the earth beneath it. If only that were true she thought, we'd be in a much better place.
Now why would Thijs want this girl? She wondered was she a missing heiress, an escaped prisoner, a fiancée to check up on, who could she be? Best be practical, Truus thought. Not too exotic, just ask where is she, have you seen her, do you know her, those kinds of things. She could start by asking herself, but though she knew that Sterre was at Universiteit Utrecht, she couldn't think of anything of note. Sterre was pretty, a quiet girl who kept herself to herself. She didn't seem to mix with any of the circles that Truus knew; she didn't seem to have any friends that Truus could think of, no one she seemed to knock about with, what subjects did she take? God, she was awful at this. If she couldn't think of things

that made someone she knew, however vaguely, stand out, what chance would she have with a stranger? Right! Start again. Treat this as if she is a complete stranger. Sterre Vossen. Good, my stop, Bleekstreet. She checked that she had the right address. Excellent, let my new job commence!

Vaartsestraat, 10.20.

Bleekstreet by name, dour by nature. She walked down a steep path towards Vaartsestraat and got her bearings. To her right were ten oldish looking houses. The owners must have been pleased when they decided to build the thirty odd flats on the opposite side of the road, though she had no idea what they were replacing, so they might have seemed a good idea at the time. Now they just looked plain and utilitarian. Ahead at the end of the street was a main road and beyond that a canal. *What else would there be?* she laughed to herself,

Truus climbed the steep stairs to the second floor of the third lot of flats, and knocked on the door of Flat 11, no reply. She looked through the curtained window pane on the door, but all was obstructed. She knelt down and looked through the letter box, nothing, only some garish flyers for night clubs strewn about the floor. She knocked on the next door.

"Hey, have you seen Sterre? We were supposed…"

"Who…?" A suspicious old woman asked.

"Next door, Sterre Vossen?"

"Sterre? Is that her name? No," she closed the door.

Nice.

Truus tried across the corridor on the other side. The door was dirty, but she had to find out so knocked loudly. The door opened and Truus nearly stepped back because of the smell from the flat. A scruffy looking young man regarded her up and down, she could smell his breath from where she stood, she had to take another step backwards, he creeped her out.

"No, why…?"

"We were supposed to meet, she didn't show, I just wondered."

"Not seen her for a few days, why not come in?"

"No, I have to go, but thank you."

Truus moved on. This wasn't very pleasant.

"Sterre? No not for a few weeks, but I've been away."

And on.

"Who? Sterre? No idea."

Next door.

"No."

This was disheartening. She left the building to enter the first set of flats. She knew it would be a really long shot to find someone who knew Sterre if even those next door to her had no idea. Four flats per house, nine lots of houses, she breathed deeply and crossed a corridor again, zigzagging between flats.

"Bugger off!"

She started up the stairs to the top floor. Of course, the lift didn't work.

"Don't know her."

And finally, at flat number thirty-six.

"Get lost!"

Her feet ached, she had tried every one of the thirty-six flats and then the ten houses. From nine there had been no replies and none of those had had a name plate. She would have to revisit them another time. Most had no idea who she was or just could not be bothered to think. But how could a pretty young girl like Sterre Vossen just disappear? Truus wondered again who had put Orman onto this job? Who wanted to find Sterre?

Universiteit Utrecht, 11.15.

Back in the library, Truus warmed up her laptop, she seemed to be going nowhere with her search for Sterre Vossen, though it was early days, now, where else could she look? She suddenly thought of and found Sterre's Facebook page, nothing on that, two hundred and ninety-seven friends. No messages for a while. She couldn't remember when she had 'Friended' Sterre, probably at the start of the term when everyone was going to be friends for ever. She looked for Elise and it was the same, though she had just twenty-two friends. Should she ask all of them? Indeed, what should she do? She decided to put in a vague, 'Hi not heard from you for a while, give me a call' type message, for both of them, just in case. Gisele de Groet, she didn't have as a 'Friend', but found her and asked to be her 'Friend'. How sad was this?

She looked at their photographs, nothing out of the ordinary at all. Two normal girls and Gisele she assumed must be the same. Yes, she found her page and she was normal, she too had the same silly photographs, with nobody twirling a villainous black moustache in the background to be seen anywhere. What could the connection be between the three of them? Did there have to be a connection?

She went back to her own page. A happy looking Nijntje looked out at her. She had precisely nine hundred and sixty-four friends, god she was such a failure, why not a thousand? Yeh, and who were these nine hundred and sixty-four 'friends'? She spent an hour scrolling down, reading and thinking and deleting name after name after name, a good old Facebook cull, who were her true friends? Nine hundred and sixty-four? That's just plain stupid, who needs that many friends, if indeed any were really true friends. She went back and started to cull again.

Kroonstraat Police Bureau, 12.12.

"The pickpocket?"

Caes asked from behind the front desk at Kroonstraat, watching as Adrie booked a young lad in. This search had taken quite a while to be successful. He wasn't sure about the manpower they had diverted onto this for just one man, well boy really, but at least it had worked.

"Well, one of them, baas, I don't think he's alone, but…" Freddie started.

"Adrie saw him in the act; Freddie of course didn't even know his fingers were in his bag!" Maaike scoffed.

"You neither Maaike!" Freddie said petulantly.

"Wasn't my pocket Freddie!" laughed Maaike.

"He was so gentle, baas." Freddie moaned, looking embarrassed.

"Like a mother's kiss." Maaike snorted.

"Well, not that gentle, Maaike."

"But you have them." Caes was pleased.

"One of them anyways."

"Not Moroccan though?"

"No a local boy, but he must have been trained."

"See if he will give you anything. Is there a Fagin about?" Caes said.

"Fagin?" Freddie looked nonplussed.

"Oliver Twist you *Hansworst*, Charles Dickens… English writer…" Maaike snorted. Freddie looked blank.

"Someone who controls the gang! See what I have to live with, baas?"

Maaike pretended exasperation. Caes laughed.

"Good work, have a go again, day after tomorrow and then we'll leave it."

"Baas," said Freddie.

"It's such fun, *baas*," said Maaike, "Oké if I take my break now?"

"Sure, I have something for Freddie."

"*Dank.*" She wandered off to the cafeteria.

"Is it those girls?" Freddie asked when Caes spoke to him.

"Yea, can you have a stroll about the Universiteit? We are still looking for those couple of girls who have disappeared. Don't change in to uniform, you'll only scare them."
Caes finished the morning briefing with
"So, Mevrouw Haan needs to be brought in. She will be easy to trace."
"Yes, just follow the stink!" Freddie Meijer laughed.
There were more stifled laughs, but Caes pitied the old woman.
"Freddie, that's not appropriate!"
"Sorry, *baas*..."
"She is distinctive though, just be kind; she is a sad old lady. Very lonely."

Maaike smiled as she looked up from her computer. Madelon raised an eyebrow.
"Nothing on Facebook I'm afraid. She hasn't had any threats or nonsense."
"What about Instagram?"
"Can't find any links."
"Not between them?"
"No they aren't friends."
"What about other social media?"
"Nothing. Quite solitary. If we had their mobiles…"
"Well you could go through the friends and see. I can check at the Universiteit, but you know how often you kids change them!" Madelon smiled.
"It's sad that we see our social success as the number of people we have on Facebook."
"That might not mean anything anyway. Do you have Facebook?"
"Used to then I joined the police and thought best to come off it. Don't want to compromise myself…"
"Oh yes Maaike, tell me more."
Madelon looked at her, eyebrows raised. Maaike felt herself going red.
"No, stop it Maddie. I just don't want one of my friends to say or show something stupid that puts me in a bad light."
"Friends shouldn't…"
"I know, but you know what happens to people's judgement sometimes. There's nothing like that on Gisele or Elises pages though."
"Is that good or bad though? Two very sensible young women it seems."
"Their few friends say so…"
"Perhaps we need to interview them again. Ask different questions…"

"But what? We can't second guess them. They seem to be normal sensible types. Would they go somewhere dangerous? See someone dangerous?"

"Did they put themselves in a dangerous situation. They didn't meet any one on Facebook as far as I can see. Maybe we can get something from Elise's computer, but…" Madelon hesitated and Maaike finished her sentence.

"Maybe they don't want to be found or maybe they are dead."

"It's a possibility. We need to get a time line to see how long it is since they vanished. I'll get Danny onto that."

It hadn't taken long to find Mevrouw Haan and bring her to the station. She was again dirty and dishevelled.

"My *kinderen*." She almost pleaded.

"*Kinderen*?"

"Elise. Gisele." She spluttered.

"Where are they?" Caes asked.

"I… missing, they left me." Mevrouw Haan said

"When?"

"I don't know…" Mevrouw Haan said.

"How?"

She was exasperating, she had no idea how frustrated she was making Caes feel.

"I can't be sure, they were there, and then they were gone."

"Did someone take them?" Madelon asked.

She just looked lost.

"Did you see?"

"Nothing…" Mevrouw Haan said.

"Who took them?" Caes tried.

"I don't know, just that they are gone." Mevrouw Haan said.

"They are your daughters?" Madelon said.

"Yes, my friends. My friends, they are my friends."

"How long have you known them?"

"It seems forever, they come to my flat." Mevrouw Haan said

"And you are sure of their names?" asked Caes.

"Elise, yes.".

"And Gisele?" Madelon said

"That's right. Such pretty girls."

"Where did you see them last?" Caes said.

"At my flat, my kinderen."

"And this was when?" asked Madelon.

"I cannot be sure, they were there, in my flat." Mevrouw Haan said

"Together?"

"Yes they are always together." She looked pained.

"When? When did you last see them?" Madelon pressed.

"I don't know, just gone, I don't see them anymore just…" Mevrouw Haan said

Madelon looked at Caes and said quietly.

"I'm not sure that this is going to get us anywhere."

"I will have to get home in case they come back…" Mevrouw Haan said.

"We can have a police officer wait for you?" Caes suggested.

"No, I want to be there, to welcome them. It has been so long."

"But how long, Mevrouw Haan?" Madelon asked again.

"So long, so long ago…" she was starting to get tired, her language faltering. The odour intensifying.

"No, excuse us for a moment please, Mevrouw Haan." I said quietly.

We left the room, the smell followed us, it was dreadful.

"She thinks she has two daughters."

"Perhaps she did once and is transferring…" Madelon said.

"But why these two. They *are* missing, that's for sure."

"How does she know them, where has she seen them and who with?" Madelon said.

"It's a mystery to me, look I think we'll have to let her go."

"She isn't unfit to go home." Madelon said.

"She isn't right though."

Caes was worried for her, but she was one of so many on the streets of Utrecht or any city really.

"I know, but we cannot take her into care, there are no real grounds. I need to see her own dokter, if she has one though." Madelon said.

"Do you think she may lead us to the girls?" Caes was thinking out aloud.

"No, she has no idea. Probably about anything in our reality at all, she seems to be living in her own little world."

They took her home. The car hummed with her odour. She got out and shuffled away. Caes got out at the far end of Vaartsestraat and wandered back. Her house was a ramshackle building that mirrored her own appearance. She was just closing the door. He looked around. There were houses on either side. Number Two, freshly painted and bright, the other, Number Four, rather dowdy, but with some of the windows brightly painted or full of flowers. The dowdy one had just seemed like Mevrouw Haan's. Madelon crossed to the other side of the road towards the long row of flats. Caes approached the nice house on his side and of course there was no one in and there was no name plate, no matter, he would return later, or send someone round.

The flats were another matter. Three floors, four flats in each section, so at least forty tenants I would have thought. Names on some of the bells, but not on others. This would take some time. Caes decided to get some help first. He wandered to the end of the street. A canal was flowing across from the Cathrinjsingel road, running alongside it with a steep grass bank, now covered in snow, separating it from the street. It meant that Vaartsestraat was almost a cul de sac with a main road at one end and a children's park at the other. Opposite Mevrouw Haan's house an old chap was walking his dog. What the heck he thought?

"Excuse me, *Meneer*, do you know a Gisele de Groet?" Caes asked.

He looked blank and shook his head doubtfully.

"An Elise Cuijper?" Caes offered.

"Ah yes... Elise, a lovely girl, but I have not seen her for a while."

"Where does she live, Meneer?"

"Across the way, second floor, number seven I think."

Universiteit Utrecht, 12.45.

Truus felt a little uncomfortable asking her friends about Sterre Vossen. It brought it home to her that someone was just on the periphery of her life and though she had no reason to, she was starting to feel guilty that she had not involved her more, not got to know her better, but as usual your own life got in the way and you were wrapped up in your own affairs, doing your own thing. You just didn't worry unduly about other people, or even think that they might be lonely or just plain alone. Of course, this was irrational, you couldn't look after every single lonely person in the world, but when she is the very person who stands next to you in a queue or sits behind or beside you in a class, shouldn't you do something?

But being rational, how was she to know. What could she have done about it? Made herself available she supposed. Been there for her, if she had wanted her to be, but had she even wanted friends? She must have, we all need friends, we might not want a boyfriend or a girlfriend, to be in a relationship, but we all need friends. Someone to talk to, someone to share things with. Truus knew that her pappy was her best friend, the one she could always, always talk to, the one she could say anything to. She also knew friends who never spoke to their parents, who could never confide in them. This saddened her, but then she wondered was she so close to her pappy because her mammie had died. She would have certainly shared everything with her mammie, she had done up to the age of fourteen, they had shared everything, then nothing. She missed her mammie so much. She just stood there for a moment shaking her head, thinking of her mammie. She had to concentrate back on the present, back to today. Asking the same questions and getting the same answers was soul destroying. The police must get so bored.

"Sterre? No, two weeks ago? I honestly can't remember…"

"Not seen her for ages…"

"She just stopped coming to lectures…"

"She did the right thing; they are just so boring…"

Over and over again no one had seen her, no one knew where she was, they all knew of her which seemed to make it even worse. Here was a pretty young girl who everybody seemed to know of, but nobody seemed to know.

She decided to ask her father. He would know what to do.

Then Truus spotted Freddie Meijer in the bar, he was out of uniform and looking a bit lost.

"Hi, Meijer, how's it going?"

"Fine, Heda, what's new?"

"Nothing really, just on a job."

At the moment, she didn't think she could tell him about Sterre being missing, that's why she had to talk to her pappy.

"You here about Elise and Gisele?"

"You know about them?" Freddie asked.

"Yea, I know them vaguely."

"They've moved from addresses they gave to Universiteit and no one has a clue as to where they live." said Freddie.

"That's ridiculous. They can't just drop off the face of the earth." Truus said.

"Well they appear to have done just that."

"So did they disappear before they moved or after?" wondered Truus.

"Don't complicate matters Truus. Their attendance is sketchy. No one's seen them for ages, but they can't be sure. People sign each other in even if they don't know them." Sighed Freddie.

"I've seen that. So, they could have been missing for weeks or…"

"Stop right there young lady. I need to take something positive to the baas." Freddie smiled.

"Life is so complicated Freddie!" smiled Truus.

"I've just finished with their professors and a few friends. I really do mean a few. Gisele was at De Machine, on her own, as usual apparently and that's about it, do you know anything? We could form a team. Anything new?"

"No, I know they were both loners. Elise has a bit of a temper sometimes or did when I knew her better at school and Gisele is just a really nice girl who no one has a bad word to say about. But nobody really knows them."

"Just two ordinary girls?"

She laughed. "Just like me! Want a drink?"

"Just a coka please..."

Meijer watched as she just ploughed her way to the bar, not a mean feat for such a slight looking girl, but they all moved away for this little pixie as she greeted each with a word or a laugh or a kiss on the cheek.

She returned with the drinks and slumped into the couch.

They talked till about seven, joined now and then by other friends or acquaintances of Truus Heda. Meijer didn't need to take part; he just listened and tried to remember names and faces. Truus kept bringing him into the conversation so that he didn't feel out of it. He noticed how Truus's hands moved as fast as her mouth, she was so confident, so exuberant, but in a totally natural unforced way. She kissed everyone who came to the table, hands on, very touchy, very real, and very nice. Everyone seemed to love her. She kissed Meijer goodnight on the cheek, told him to give her love to Maaike, pulled her hat over her ears, then was on her way into the snow.

Kroonstraat Police Bureau, 13.50.

Ernst, of course, had traced the mother of Gisele de Groet in America with the help of detective colleagues over there. She had lived in Syracuse for a couple of years. She was not happy to hear from Utrecht. Some mother Caes thought.

"Your daughter has disappeared." He told her.

"She's old enough to look after herself."

"You are not concerned?" asked Caes.

"We don't speak."

Caes couldn't help it,

"Well you did leave her."

"I have my own life."

"And hers?" Caes wondered.

"She can do as she wishes. I have no idea where she is."

"Or if someone may wish to harm her?"

"What do you mean?"

"She has disappeared..."

Caes tried to re-emphasise the fact, but to no avail.

"Probably with friends, she is of an age."

She had no concerns.

"You don't seem worried by her disappearance?"

"Why should I? We live separate lives."

She was cold, detached.

"Not through Gisele's choice though."

Caes almost snapped.

"She has managed. We do not speak, now if..."

"Your daughter could be dead."

Caes almost shouted, but managed to keep calm. There was a long pause, then,

"I have my own life, a new husband. I have no time to worry about the past."

"If we find your daughter I'll be sure to tell her."

Caes replaced the receiver. What a bitch.

Tamada Kick boksene, Johan Buziaulaan. 13.55.

Truus slid her way through the snow. She was very cold and felt lethargic. She needed an adrenalin rush. She saw Robbie and Pim sparring. She threw her bag at Pim who brushed it away.

"Great parry, Pim. Getting warmed up for me?"

"No, Robbie will spar with you today, I still have bruised ribs!" Pim moaned.

"Oh, Pim, you are such a disappointment.

Pim kissed his partner Robbie and went to get some drinks.

"How goes it, Robbie?"

"Good, good. You?"

"Just a bit fed up, I feel like I need to explode! Full of pent up energy!"

"Pim, you fight her! No, it's fine, just joking." Robbie laughed. "Anything you need to work on?"

"Not sure, there are lots of things that need work." Truus said.

"What especially?" Robbie wondered.

"Maybe defence, I need to be able to counter Tamada and his Flying-punch, his 'Superman', he

83

just gets me every time."

"Yea, it's a tough one to stop, but not impossible." Robbie winked.

Robbie proceeded to show Truus some footwork and body movement that would help. He was a good instructor. Pim just watched throwing in the odd word of advice. He wasn't really hurt; he just loved to play the goat, to be the victim so that Robbie would dote on him which he did anyway so the point was lost on Truus. He made her smile though. They both did.

"It is just a flashy move, Truus, but it's the follow up that always seems to get you."

"Well he hits so hard with the superman punch; I get caught off balance." Truus said.

"Yes that's why we work on the feet and the stance. Always remember your guard. Look for his fake to punch again and look for his foot. That's how he put you down last time. Punch to the chest, kick high to the head."

"Yes, my black eye shows that!" laughed Truus.

Sweat pouring off her once again Truus went through the moves Robbie showed her. She learnt quickly. Maybe not quickly enough or well enough to counter Tamada, but he was rather unique. He stood at the side watching like a hawk.

"Truus, why don't you fight competitively?" he finally spoke.

"This is just fun for me," she said, kicking Robbie in the head.

"If I had to win every time,"

She leg swept Robbie and he crashed to the floor,

"I don't think I'd have so much fun!"

The axe kick finished him, hovering above his eyes like a thunder clap ready to break.

"Thank god you don't take it too seriously!" shouted Pim.

Kroonstraat Police Bureau, 14.50.

Hoofdcommissaris Coeman sat opposite Caes. He didn't look happy, but then he rarely did. He wouldn't force things, he usually let them get on with their cases, but he did want an update.

"Unusual three girls, have we a madman on the prowl?"

"No idea, *baas*, it's just so strange. Only one girl really missed and that's Orman's daughter."

"What do we read into that?"

"Again not sure… "

"With the other two it could be random or targeted?"

"No idea, I know this sounds a bit pathetic." Caes was at a loss.

"Dead?"

84

"Again we are in the dark. We have to see if there are more similarities. All the same age, all pretty, all at *Universiteit*, each one alone..."

"It is strange, Caes. Do you need more staff?"

"Not for now, if we have to re-canvas areas maybe..."

"News conference?" Coeman smiled, knowing what Caes's response would be.

"Not yet..."

"What about the cars?" Coeman changed tack.

"Nothing yet, but de Grier is on to it." Said Caes.

Coeman smiled at the use of Ernst's nick name.

"Just as long as you don't see me as the wizened old Commissaris." Coeman said.

"Never, *baas*!" Caes laughed.

"Though we do have a mystical Zen approach."

"Take more than a bit of Zen to sort this out."

"Well if you need anything let me know and I'll see what we can do."

"Thanks, *baas.*"

Well that was easier than it could have been, Caes thought. *Hoofdcommissaris* Coeman was good at deflecting the pressure, but that was going to come in spades if they didn't have a breakthrough soon. They all knew the time line for these things, so many hours and this scenario takes place, another few hours and that may be the outcome. Caes didn't buy in to all that, each case was so different, but here we had three girls gone. Where were they?

Caes sat at his desk, looking out of the window trying to concentrate. His mind couldn't stay on one problem, it kept drifting back to Femke. He needed to focus, but when he saw a picture of one of the missing students his thoughts turned almost automatically to his late wife. His *late wife*, he shivered and thought back to her last few days as she just seemed to drift away from him. She died holding his hand. Her breath had become so shallow that it was only the gentle release of his fingers that told him she was gone. It had been expected, but it was still a shock. One moment there, the next nothing only memories. Telling Truus was the hardest thing. She insisted on seeing her mammie and he remembered standing by the bedside holding his daughter's cold little hand as she stared at her mother. Her grip was firm as if she would never let him go. Fourteen years old, her mother gone. She had leant forward and kissed Femke on the lips, then told Caes,

"Vader, it's time for bed, let's go home..."

So, they had gone home and tried to move on. Eight years on and he was still trying.

Vismarkt, 16.05.

Truus saw a crowd outside the Coffee Company and decided against being a voyeur. She stepped into the cycle lane to pass them, but glanced over and her eyes met those of Maaike who was kneeling over an old man who was lying in the snow. Her face lit up when she saw Truus and she smiled a dazzling smile. Truus felt an odd tingling in her stomach, but smiled back. Maaike's eyes dropped back to the old man on the floor and Truus could see her saying soothing words to the old fella. She heard the siren of the paramedicus and waited as they came to deal with the patient and Maaike came over.

"Slipped in the ice bless him."

"Is he *oké*?" Truus asked.

"Broken wrist I think."

"Ouch!"

"I know, poor old chap. I've got to go around to his flat and tell his wife. That'll be nice."

"Well at least he's alright." Truus said.

"I hope so." Said Maaike.

She smiled again.

"Anyway I'd best get going. He lives quite close. See you Truus."

Amaliastraat, 18.17.

Caes was still working when Truus slammed into the house. Like a whirlwind as usual.

"Truus, what if I'd been asleep?" He tried to complain.

"Well, you'd be awake now, so all is well, Pappy."

"Truus..."

but how could he ever be cross with her?

"How has your day been, Pappy?"

"Good, good and yours?"

"Working hard as ever, you know me, Pappy." Truus smiled.

"Only too well..."

"I saw Meijer tonight at Universiteit. He hasn't come up with much, but I suppose he will tell you all tomorrow."

"You talked about the cases?" asked Caes.

"Not really, I told him what I remembered about the two girls from school, but like I said, there wasn't much. That was *oké* wasn't it?"

"Yes, no problem at all."

"Vader, what ever happened to Thijs Orman?" Truus ventured.

"God, that's a name from the past. Thijs Orman, why do you ask?"

"I just wondered, I thought I saw him today."

"He left the force, what, six or seven years ago? I think Americans would say he was let go."

"What do you mean?" Truus asked.

"He beat up a child molester. He did what many of us would have done."

"But you never…"

"No, because no matter what, the law is the law, I often felt like him, but I can so far always draw the line."

"Why wasn't it covered up?" Truus asked.

"Well perhaps it would have been, but there were so many more complaints."

"About?"

"He roughed up junkies and pushers as well."

"Again it's what many would do." Said Truus.

"But the last time it was a serious assault and he stole their drugs for himself, he'd developed quite a habit. He had a bad drug problem of his own."

"I see…"

"But last I heard was that he had got over it and had set up…"

"I know, it's my new job." Said Truus.

"What is?"

"I'm working for Thijs."

"No…really? What as?"

His heart sank. Was this what he wanted for her?

"Office help and… and I am looking for someone for him." Said Truus.

"Yes?"

"Sterre…"

"His daughter?" asked Truus.

"What? He never said that, he called her Sterre Vossen."

"His wife."

"Who is?" asked Truus

"Laure Vossen. Divorced, she lives up in Haarlem now I think. Nasty business I seem to remember. What about you and your Creative Writing then?"

"I have a meeting with them soon, I can do both, I can fit both in. I've only just started with Thijs anyway."

"Oké."

"Oké? I thought you would be cross." said Truus

"How? Why, if it's what you want to do, just make sure you are careful, don't do anything rash, if that's possible."

Caes knew that if he railed against her it would go badly. He couldn't win, he had to support her, but he wasn't happy, he didn't really think that it would be the safest thing, working for Thijs, but she was nineteen years old and of an age when he couldn't start telling her what to do. Christ, she wouldn't even do the washing up if he told her to! She had to think it was her idea! Her confusion over Universiteit became clear as well, this was a difficult time for her and he supposed what she needed was time.

"Just be careful."

"I will, Vader, I know my limits!"

"I hope so, anyway, now three missing girls." Caes intoned seriously.

"Yes, I know them all which is odd. One missed just by her pappy and two by a strange smelly woman."

"Yes, if we hadn't had that and then checked the attendance at *Universiteit*, they would still be missing." Caes said.

"If you hadn't followed her to Taap Koorndreef no one would have known anything."

"If she didn't smell so much!"

It was still with Caes. Not on his clothes but in his memory. He didn't like the feeling.

"Link?"

"All the same age."

"Very few friends."

"Or relatives and they all lived alone." Caes said.

"No one has reported they are missing, not even Thijs yet."

"Except for the old woman…"

"Who nobody would have believed, if you hadn't seen her go to both stations."

"Well, we don't know that, but probably." Caes said.

"And why didn't Thijs tell the truth?" Truus was puzzled.

"Yes, that's interesting; does he know more than he is letting on?"

"Where do they live?"

"Well it's interesting, Elise has a flat in Vaartsestraat." Caes said.

"Really? So, does Sterre! I spent ages looking for her there."

"I think I need to visit again, at last a link." Caes decided.

"There was a creepy bloke on the third floor in Flat 9, he may know more, and he just felt a little bit sleazy." Truus recalled.

"Is that your de Welt radar working?"

"No it's my Girldar, we know a scumbag when we meet one! Sterre lives across the floor in Flat Eleven."

"*Dank*, I'll check." Caes said.

"Happy to help my local police agent!"

"*Oké*, let's eat; I have some other work to do."

Caes went into the kitchen,

"Do you make notes on all your enquiries?" He asked her.

"I hadn't thought to…"

"Well I think you should start. Always have a system. List everything you have done in order. Gives you something to hang on to when you feel you are going nowhere and you will have many days when you feel like that I can tell you." Caes said.

"*Dank*, Pappy. One last thing though. It seems only Thijs has an interest in a missing girl. The other two are nobody's really; they have no one, is that important. Is the link between all three that there is no link?"

Had his darling girl hit upon what this could be? How insightful, how grown up. Caes hadn't thought of it in that way. She then surprised him even more.

"You go and sit down, Pappy, I'll make our dinner. Is *andijviestamppot oké*?"

Caes was too stunned to say more than "Lovely, dank."

"With *rijstebrij* to follow, lay the table and then put your feet up."

They had a really pleasant evening. Truus surprised him with her cooking, she never usually made the effort. It always seemed that cooking was his job, along with everything else!

"What are you writing at the moment, Truus?" asked Caes.

"I am writing some poems, but I find that quite tricky. I'm never sure if I should rhyme or be a prose poetess."

"Prose poetess, that sounds interesting."

"Well it's not really, I just have to cut long sentences or paragraphs shorter to make sure they have patterns and scan…"

"Do they scan?" Caes asked.

"Usually, but I have to edit then re edit and keep them on the straight and narrow."

"Your novel?"

"A young girls coming of age… it's brilliant!" Truus smiled.

"Brilliant, Truus?"

"I think so; I am writing about this young girl who cannot find what she wants from life and has adventures that lead her on the path to what's right."

"And what is right, Truus?"

"Not sure yet, but that's the joy of it all."

"Autobiographical?" Caes smiled.

"Perhaps…" Truus gave her most dazzling smile.

They had a really pleasant night, just talking about things other than police work. About what was going on in the world, about holidays, about music which they both loved and was highlighted when Truus put some Metallica on the CD player. They sat in front of the fire and spoke long into the night. Finally, it was time for sleep and Truus kissed Caes goodnight and went to her room. He was left sitting staring at the fire thinking that he was a lucky man in many respects. He may have lost his wife, there was nothing good about that, but he had Truus. She breathed life into him and made everything worthwhile. She was everything to him, everything in the world.

Amaliastraat, 22.20.

The front door crashed open, peace shattered once again; I heard her laughing then smelt….

"That you, Truus?"

"Yea!"

"You been smoking dope?"

Someone reeked of it.

"No, it was Meijer!"

"What… no, baas, we've just been to a Kaffe."

"You stink of it; hope you're not leading my daughter astray." Caes teased him.

"No, baas, we just bumped into each other again." He was flustered.

"Yea, he threw away his spliff when he saw me!"

Of course, Truus wasn't going to help.

"Truus!" Freddie moaned with exasperation.

"Anything to report?"

"Pappy, he's off duty! We met after my kick boxing."

"Never off duty, perils of coming to the baas's house!" Caes laughed.

"No wonder I never bring anyone home."

"Truus!" Caes complained.

"Nothing, baas, saw their professors again, went to the Uni bar again... met your Truus, again"

"There will be a lot of repetition, someone might remember something."

"No, it's as if they don't exist, none of them are memorable. They all remember Truus though!"

"Freddie!" Truus warned.

"Truus?" Caes wondered.

"She is just memorable though, *baas*! Got to go, Mama is waiting at home with my dinner!"

"*Oké*, Freddie, see you tomorrow."

"*Doeg!* Freddie. *Dank wel* for the ride."

Truus kissed his cheek and went to the door with him.

"Give Maaike a kiss from me!" Truus said.

"Nice lad Freddie, pity he's taken!"

"Pappy! We are just friends!"

"For sure, I wasn't fishing, had a good day?"

She then proceeded to tell him all about it.

Vagevuur.

He looked through the small peephole in the door at the girl who was sitting in the corner. Hugging her knees to her chest, she was silently sobbing and rocking. She was petrified, lost in her terror. He sniggered to himself and went to the next room. Another girl was asleep on a mattress, looking dirty and dishevelled. She kept shuddering in her dreams. No one to miss these two yet, it had been a good practice. He went back to the first door and put his eyes to the peephole and leapt back as the occupant hammered on the door screaming soundlessly at the barrier. There was hatred and anger in her tear-filled eyes. He felt his heart hammering at the initial shock, but then looked back satisfied to see her slide to the floor, sobbing. Her hands wrapped around the back of her neck. Sterre Vossen, her father must be missing her by now. He put the light out in the corridor, locked the door at the end of the passageway and went up the stairs. He locked the trapdoor to the cellar, covered it with the mat, slid the table over that and only when he was satisfied that all was well, he took his coat from the hanger, brushed himself down and left the building, locking yet another door behind him and stepping into the snow.

"Hi, Mevrouw Haan, ben je oké?" he said cheerily.

The old woman shuffled past him in her own lonely world, not recognising him, not recognising anything. Just lost in her own world.

Chapter 7

Woensdag, November 12, 2014.
Amaliastraat, 08.35.

"Truus, get up!" Caes called through her closed door. He was a man on a mission.

"Pappy... No!"

She moaned at him,

"What time is it?"

"We're going out." Caes said.

"Where, no!"

"Get up, a bright sunny day, we are off to the seaside."

"It's snowing." Truus was pleading.

"No, it's stopped, the roads are clear." Caes said

"Pappy!" Truus exclaimed.

"I have your breakfast; I have your bucket and your little spade."

"Vader, are you insane? What's the time?" groaned Truus.

"Ten, you've had enough of a lie in!" Caes said

They needed a break, Truus needed a break, Caes didn't really want to drive, but what the hell. They would go to Wijk aan Zee beach.

"Only if I can drive..."

"You try to negotiate? Just get your coffee, eat your bagel and make sure you wrap up warm!"

She slumped at the table.

"Where is the *stroop*?" Truus sighed.

"I'll get it, what on earth did you do last night, Truus?" Caes said

"You know; I was in early! Boxing, I'm so knackered..."

"Sleep in the car, I'll drive, you can take over later. It will be milder at the coast."

"For sure, more coffee first, please." Truus moaned.

"It might be good to surf today?"

She perked up

"Would you like to? We haven't done that for ages." Truus was excited.

"I know; I don't think I can remember how to!"

"You big liar, Pappy! Yes, lets surf that will be good."

93

Wijk aan Zee, 12.00.

Truus was wide awake throughout the journey down all the A's A2; A4 and A20. She had suddenly become really animated, chatting, laughing and gesticulating wildly as she told Caes what had been going on with her at Universiteit Utrecht and at kick-boxing. It took them a little under an hour to get to Wijk aan Zee, but time and Amsterdam, Amstelveen and Haarlem flashed by. As usual it was really windy. Perfect. The sea was high, white splashes on top of the crowning waves. The wind was catching sand and snow and sweeping it down the empty beach, it looked a bit like a wintry desert. Truus shouted something into the wind, but it was carried away from me, she looked in such a good mood.

Caes loved to see Truus as happy as this. She then made him happy. He took her hand, she squeezed it and smiled.

"This is nice, Pappy."

"Yes it is. What did you shout to the wind?"

"Just *hoi* to Wijk aan Zee, come on let's get down to the front." Truus grinned.

She raced off leaving him standing; again, there was the flash of her with her pigtails and ribbons flying. Caes tried to blink the vision away as she turned and waved, but no, there she was a twelve-year-old at the seaside again.

They stood together on the North Pier, looking over at the Tata Steel factory. The sky above it was a cloudless grey blue, but what with the white fumes that were coming from the dark industrial complex it provided a surrealist backdrop to the beautiful white sandy beach and the white snowy dunes. It all seemed so out of place, which of course it was! How did they get permission to build it there of all places Caes wondered?

They found the *Surfenkit* store and rented the gear. Caes squeezed into his suit as Truus waited impatiently for him. How was she so quick he wondered? They headed down the beach, to Velsen Noord.

No matter how much arm work you do in the gym, it's still hard work paddling on a board out to the surf. It was also freezing cold. Caes eventually found his balance lying flat on the board, though it had been a while since he had last been there. The summer sun had beat down that weekend and the beach was packed. It was still as windy today as it was then, but the sun had taken the edge off the cold. Not like today! It was also an empty beach; no one else had been as foolhardy as they had been. He couldn't blame them; it was making his teeth chatter! Had this been such a good idea after all?

He checked the leash on his ankle and looked for Truus. She was miles ahead, just starting to stand. She seemed to be walking on top of the water, her board hidden from sight by the swell.

Her balance was amazing, that's why she was so good at kick-boxing he supposed, she was out there, positioning to catch the wave, with immaculate timing, and balance. She was off, he could hear her squealing with delight, just as the pigtailed Truus had done with her mother all those years ago when she had first started. Her mastery of the techniques to break through oncoming waves was almost otherworldly. Caes found this really difficult, often getting caught off balance as board and wave crossed, but not Truus. Caes finally got up to above the waves and waited, he saw Truus returning from the shore. He knew his take-off positioning needed to allow him to predict where the wave would set and then where they would break. This came naturally to Truus, he really had to study the waves hard to make sure of the right time and here it came. Up he got and down he crashed back into the sea, his board tugging at his ankle as it tried to head for the shore on its own, just as he should have headed for the shore, but on the board, looking good. They hadn't been surfing for months, yet here she was catching the waves as if born to it. She amazed Caes at times. This didn't come easily to him, but to Truus...

He heard Truus squealing with laughter again. She was closer, giggling at him. She was paddling wildly towards me, then stopped and criss-crossed her arms waving at me.

"Surfed before, *Meneer*? Do you want some help?" She gasped, laughing.

"Sod off, Truus!"

Caes knew he had to pop up quickly as soon as the wave started pushing the board forward. He judged it better this time and made about twenty metres before he was wiped out. He could see Truus once again riding to the shore in all her glory.

It got better, it had to get better. He forgot the cold and the battering his body was taking as he finally got the hang of it again and started to make complete journeys into shore. It was just like riding a bike, you never forget! Truus was flying, she looked happier than he had seen her for a while, she was laughing just like her mother had used to.

"One more, Pappy?"

"Yes, it's getting darker..."

"And colder, my toes are going Arctic blue." She smiled.

He looked at her happy face.

"So are your lips, come on I'll race you in."

Caes was exhausted. It was no contest. If Truus had been on the road she would have been spewing pebbles in his face as she charged to her destination.

She was flat on her back gasping for breath as he finally hit the shore and he flopped beside her.

"Too cold, Pappy, can't move, get the car!"

"Just get up, you wimp. I see *olienbollen!*" Caes pointed.

She was up in a flash, running towards the kiosk.

They stuffed their faces with them and drank hot coffee from a stand next to the pier.

"Getting too old for this…"

Caes said as he limped to the car, aching all over.

"Never, Pappy, you'll never be too old."

"You drive." Caes said.

"Really?"

"Yes, aim for Haarlem, we'll eat there."

"I'm still so famished that's good."

"After three massive *olienbollen*? You're truly a dreadfully greedy girl."

"A girl has to keep her strength up, Pappy."

"Wake me up when we get there." Caes yawned; he felt exhausted.

"It's only ten minutes."

"That's long enough. I'll take a power nap. God I'm so old…"

Caes had to complain,

"Bones bruised and battered, I'm getting past it."

Was he getting too old for this, at thirty-nine? My god! What a thought.

"Pappy! For goodness sake, be a man!" Truus was laughing at him.

She drove carefully into Haarlem and they stopped at an Indonesian restaurant and enjoyed a lovely meal. This had been a nice day. Truus was still sparkly eyed even though it was late. This had done her a lot of good. They again chatted about lots of stuff, then just before they left the restaurant;

"Do you ever think of dating again, Pappy?" asked Truus.

"Can't say I have given it too much thought, lieverd."

"Do you think you ever will?"

"No, but what about you?" Caes decided.

"Don't change the subject!"

"I really don't…"

He hadn't given it a thought for a long time.

"That's sad isn't it, Pappy. Don't you want to?"

"No, I don't think I do actually. I know I should not think like this, but no one could replace your mother. So why bother?"

"But it's not about replacing her…" Truus tried.

"But there is also you to…"

"Or worrying about me, it's what you want, not what I want."

"I think it is what I want, there's plenty of time if I change my mind. I'm still young!"

"Yes, Pappy!" she snorted.

"What about you, lieverd, anyone?"

"No, boys don't interest me, they smell!" Truus said.

Caes laughed,

"No really, that's twelve-year-old Truus talking, what about nineteen-year-old you?"

"No, Pappy, I have no interest at the moment in anyone." She said seriously.

"No one at Universiteit?"

"Nope, sad, isn't it?" she smiled.

"Well, plenty of time for you!"

"We should be getting back, Pappy, I never thought I'd say this to you, but I have to get ready to go to Uni in the morning!"

Kroonstraat Police Bureau, 19.05.

The day at Kroonstraat had almost ended when Maaike was handed a message from the front desk. Apparently, a Marie van Hoorn had left a message to say that a Tyson Groot had threatened Gisele during the summer. He was on his way to the station to be interviewed. Adrie would join her when he arrived. She sighed and shoved the note into her desk and waited for the call. Freddie popped his head in to say he was off home.

"Lucky old you," Maaike replied.

"Tell mammie I'll be late."

"Will do old thing, see you later perhaps."

Maaike shrugged and smiled and went with her brother to see him off and get some coffee. As she returned to her office, Adrie called her and she went to the interview room and sat down. Coffee steaming and pencil and pad next to it. She looked up as Adrie and a surly looking Tyson Groot entered the room. Adrie seated Tyson and came around and sat next to Maaike.

He switched on the tape and followed the niceties of protocol. Adrie looked across the desk and smiled at Tyson Groot.

"You understand why you are here?" he asked.

"Not really..." Groot sneered.

"Gisele de..." Adrie started.

"That tart!" responded Groot.

Maaike smiled and rotated her pencil between the middle three fingers of her right hand. Groot looked her in the eye and quickly switched his gaze to the slowly spinning pencil. Maaike stopped playing with the pencil and jotted a few things down on her pad. Groot seemed fascinated.

"What you writing. We've got the tape, haven't we?" he sneered once again. His face was a real picture of contempt and anger.

"Nuances Tyson, all the nuances the tape misses."

"What d'you mean?"

"Well it's hard to see how angry you are on tape…"

"I'm not! Just don't see why I'm here…"

"Nuances Tyson. Trying to see if you are telling the truth…"

"But I've done nothing…"

"Then there is the constant sneer on your face as if we've actually done something wrong. All we want is some help…"

She jotted something else down and looked him in the eye. She and Adrie waited. Groot crumples first.

"What is it you want?"

"Gisele has disappeared…" Adrie started.

That brought Groot to life.

"Well its nothing to do with me I've not seen her for months…"

"Would that be in the summer?" asked Adrie quietly.

"When you told her she'd be sorry if she kept ignoring you?"

"How… What's that got to do with anything?"

"You threaten her and a few weeks later she disappears." Maaike said, still looking him straight in the eye. Groot looked at her then at Adrie, then at his knees.

"She was full of it, I didn't mean…"

"Tell us what you meant." Adrie interrupted.

Groot seemed to collapse.

"When we were at school…"

"Which school?"

"Basisschool…then VMBO."

His face reddened. His sneer left his face.

"It's a long time ago. We met and she used to joke we were brother and sister. Our surnames…" He shrugged.

"We were friends then, but drifted apart. I saw her in the summer in Willhelmspark and she seemed really happy. I went over and she cut me dead."

"That upset you?" Adrie asked.

"Sure it did. We had been pals then her parents died and she was sad. I didn't know what to do. We went our separate ways... you know how it is?"

"This summer. Was it an argument?" asked Maaike.

"Not really. She was happy. I suggested a drink. She said no."

"As was her right." Said Maaike.

"I know, I know, but ... you see I had really liked her and I thought... you know we could be... then she cut me..."

"So you got pay back?" Adrie said.

"No!" Groot shouted.

"No, I was angry, yes. No one like to be... you know cut, rejected... I got angry and said things perhaps I shouldn't..."

"Perhaps?" asked Maaike, "Shouldn't?"

"I know, I know, but I'd never hurt her. She was so happy, so content. It was like coming out of her. I just thought..."

"You thought wrong." Said Maaike.

"I did. I'm sorry, but I'd never hurt her..."

"When did you last see Gisele?"

"It was in the summer. I can't really recall, but not since I..."

"Was really unpleasant to her?" Maaike said.

His head dropped and he shrugged. Adrie glanced at Maaike she was jotting things down again. She circled the word 'truth' and Adrie stood up.

"Well thank you Tyson. That's been very helpful."

"You will find her, won't you?"

"We hope so Tyson, but we can't promise anything."

Adrie showed him out and Maaike doodled till his return. As he sat down she took a sip of coffee and grimaced.

"Pah, it's stone cold!" she laughed.

"Not him then?"

"Don't think so. You and your nuances. Trying to bamboozle him?"

"Well he can't fool me I could read him like a book. Just a silly boy with a crush."

"I agree, back to square one. Where the hell is she. Are they all together?"

Maaike was just about to take another sip of the cold coffee, then put the cup down

"We have no idea, do we? This is senseless. It could drive you mad if you let it."

"Well make sure you don't Maaike. Anyway, your shift is over, get along. I'll write up a report. Nuances and all!" he laughed.

"Nuances are key *Hoofdagent.*" Maaike laughed.

"Don't *Hoofdagent* me young lady! Get off home. We''ll talk tomorrow."

Vagevuur.

When you are truly alone with no one to talk to that's when your fears bubble to the surface. Sterre felt alone and she felt afraid. The man didn't care if she saw him and that scared her. She was alone and that scared her too. She had no idea why she had been taken and that scared her most of all. She sat on the mattress, hugging herself feeling as if she was the last person alive, it was so quiet and she could hear nothing save for a water pipe or something tapping away. She tried to put it out of her mind. She knew it had been snowing outside and could imagine that no one was out in the street wherever that was. She had no idea if she was still in Utrecht or out in the countryside. All she knew was that she was alone, alone and afraid. Loneliness had been something she had got used to over the past few months. She hadn't seen her father for ages and her mother had disowned her. She had been so fed up of the arguments and rows between her parents. From the outside, her side, she thought her mother was being unfair. She knew her father wasn't well, but had still been shocked when she discovered he was addicted to dope. It explained so much, but she couldn't understand why her mother hadn't been more supportive. Sure, he was an idioot, but he was ill and had to have support. She recalled the court case and how that revolting little man had accused her vader of hitting him. What was his name, Spraat, Stinger, something like that? And the big thug with the broken nose, who was he. God, she couldn't put a name to a face or a face to a name to save her life at the moment. Then prison. Had he felt like she was feeling now? All alone in a cell. He would have been segregated for sure, all alone. How had that affected him, she had never asked, never had the chance to ask. When he had come out of prison to no job, her mother had lost it. The constant bitching wasn't helping him. Because he lost his job she wanted a divorce and that seemed so wrong. The marriage over she had to fend for herself, her father had taken time to sort himself out and she was left alone. Alone to go to Universiteit, eventually alone to find a place to live. Alone in classes. She was fed up with her peers and fed up with everything, but how she wished she was amongst those silly, irritating students and boring staid lecturers now. She didn't want to be alone any more. She wanted to speak to someone, anyone, she just wanted company...

Chapter 8

Donderdag, November 13, 2014.
Amaliastraat, 07.45.

Caes liked his Doc Martens shoes, he remembered being kicked by a few DM boots in his FC Utrecht supporting days when hooligans seemed to rule the roost at the old Galgenwaard stadion. He sometimes felt he still had the bruises of his rookie cop days when anyone he seemed to try to arrest would lash out with their high cut DM's looking to inflict as much pain as possible. But back to his shoes, cherry-red today and shining. Truus had been at her helpful best and had been the family shoe shine girl last night, so Caes felt he had to wear them out in the snow. He'd pressed all his clothes neatly and feeling fit for purpose he made his way out into the cold and of course, snow. It was bitter. Grey and nasty. Blowing not quite at blizzard speed, but at a fair rate of knots. He closed the door quietly not wanting to wake his slumbering daughter. He had walked a few metres down Amaliastraat before he heard a great slam of the door behind him and then the sound of a banshee as said banshee jumped onto his back.

"Truus, not you again..." he sighed.

"Pappy," she jumped off and kissed his cheek.

"You must stop this, I'm a finely tuned master of martial arts and you put your life at risk."

She snorted and playfully punched his shoulder,

"Too slow for me old chap, I'd have you down and begging for submission before you knew it was me."

"I only let you live because I know it's you." Caes laughed.

She grabbed his hand.

"Anyhoo pappy, thought I'd share the walk as far as Vondellaan. Then I'm off to Universiteit."

Oudekirkstrasse, 08.30.

Freddie had been stupid enough to challenge his sister. She now had him in an armlock and he was moaning with pain.

"I didn't mean it Maaike." He pleaded.

"Shouldn't have said it then!" she grunted through gritted teeth and twisted his arm.

"Maaike!" Freddie squealed.

"Take it back then..."

"Allright, allright!"

Freddie squealed again as she tightened her grip.

Maaike let go of his arm and got up from the floor. She pulled her brother up and he scowled at her as he rubbed his arm.

"You are such a bully Maaike…" he moaned.

"For goodness sake Freddie, man up! You can't call me names and expect no retribution…" she giggled.

"I can't complain to anyone. No one believes me when I say you terrorise me!"

"Terrorise? Oh Freddie…"

"Well show me how you do that move."

"No way. If I show you how, youll be able to get out of it. I'm not risking that!"

Freddie had to laugh and returned to sit at the breakfast table and sipped at his coffee.

"Why don't you take up judo anyway Freddie?"

"No time, you know that…"

"Maybe not, but it would help."

"I have my running and the gym. I need my reboot time."

"Reboot, you are an idioot."

"You know what I mean."

Universiteit Utrecht, 11.35.

A Social Psychology module! That was all that Truus needed at the moment, but psychology had to be faced. The blank hour in the Library was only a preface to a blank two hours in the classroom. She was going through an anti-Psychology phase as well. Truus was trying hard to remember why she had opted for it. She looked around at the group and didn't really know anyone there, not like in Sociology where there were always some of the girls to have a giggle with; here they were all a bit, well, geeky, so fitting in here was a bit more difficult. They all got on oké, but were not close as a group. Nobody was really pally with anyone in particular. Truus thought that they could have started a psychological study on the whys and wherefores of that. Maybe it was because they had all put this down as a final option, not knowing what else to do? Maybe, Truus seemed to recall that she had had the faint interest in it, thinking that she may be able to get inside her own head and see why she felt like she did, but that hadn't worked out too well. Anyhoo, what was the teacher saying?

"… are looking at Motivation and educational performance."

Truus thought that it might even be interesting.

"What types and theories of motivation do we know?"

Had she been reading the wrong text?

"Linset?" the *docent* asked.

"Well there are extrinsic and intrinsic types." Linset replied.

"Good yes, what theories? Paul?"

"Behaviourist." said Paul.

"Study by?"

"Brophy is it?" Paul suggested without a lot of confidence.

"Good that's right, anymore, Linset?"

"Humanistic with Maslow and Cognitive, but I'm not sure on who wrote that study."

"McClelland," Truus said, where did that come from she wondered?

"Good, Truus, now we have the types and theories of Motivation, but what do we do with them?"

"We use them to start improving motivation. In Behavioural it would be by using effective praise and in cognitive we would need to see achievement and need to avoid failure."

"Excellent, Truus, you've done a lot of research on this."

"I think it's my sporty background, *Meneer* Sands, I actually listen to my Coaches!"

"Not to me then?" he smiled

"No, sorry, yes of course, but it's very hands on, my coach of course uses motivation techniques a lot, he's very positive in his outlook, uses praise a great deal, everyone is different, everyone needs a different approach, it's quite interesting actually to see how he speaks to different people in different ways, what type of reinforcement, that kind of thing…"

Truus had also seen her father at work and seen how he spoke to each of his team, how all were different and needed to be treated as such. She could not see him talking to Hoewegen in the same way that he spoke to Freddie. It just wouldn't work. The same as with Adrie and Danny either, all so very different. She carried on,

"…particularly in weight training where you really need to be motivated at times. It can be very solitary. you against the bar, so a second voice is vital. My *vader* is my second voice at weight training."

"Yes, the second voice, we'll discuss that next week, but perhaps we should get *Hoofdinspecteur* Heda in for a masterclass?"

Vaartsestraat, 12.10.

Madelon and Caes entered the flat. Spotless. Nothing out of place, clothes all folded neatly in drawers, not too expensive, a young woman's wardrobe, just like Truus. Books on Sociology and Economics neatly stacked in the bookcase. Lecture notes neatly piled on the desk, unlike Truus. What he assumed was her laptop was open, but switched off.

"Take this Madelon and see what's on it just in case."

"It all seems so normal, baas."

"Yes, nothing, though I wish Truus was as tidy as this!"

"Kinderen!" Madelon sighed.

Caes stood in the middle of the room and looked about. Freshly polished floor. Kitchen spotless, all dishes put away, drainer clear. Bedroom on a mezzanine at the top of some steep stairs. The bathroom was sparkling clean as well. He envisaged his daughter living in a flat like this. Hopeless she'd be, running home to him after a few days unable to cope with washing up and cleaning. He smiled to himself. He was sure she would have to try soon, but he hoped not for a while. He had to shake the thoughts away.

"But nothing, it's just so normal... thoughts?" Caes asked.

"None really, it does seem normal, like she just popped out and, well disappeared... Scary really."

"Oké, let's wrap it up and get back into the snow."

Vismarkt. 13.00.

Truus and Caes sat in the Coffee Company, it was not as busy as usual with mostly students and their steaming mugs of *munt thee* flavouring the air. It was a strange mixture of damp and mint that filled his nostrils. He sipped his cappuccino and could not take his eyes off his daughter. Truus was vacuuming up an apple cinnamon cake. How on earth did she stay so trim? She looked up at him and he noticed her eyes were full of tears. Caes reached across and put his hand on hers.

"What is it lieverd?"

"Pappy, I really miss mammie..."

"Where has that come from, lieverd?"

"I don't know, these past few days I have been thinking about her a lot, I'm not sure why."

"What's brought that on?"

"Not sure, maybe seeing how Thijs and Sterre were..."

"Were?"

"Well how they've no relationship, then the other two girls. Alone, with no one."

"That's awful I know, but you're not alone."

"Yes, I know, but it's horrible. I know I've you…"

"Is that so horrible?" Caes smiled.

"No, silly man, it's lovely, but I do miss Mammie, she was, well you know better than me…"

"Yes she was, she still is so beautiful to me. But without you, well what would I have?"

"Pappy…"

"I see her in you every single day. You are so beautiful. She really does live on through you."

"Oh, Vader," she started to cry again.

"Truus, no, that's a good thing. Don't cry because you make me happy, you make me so proud, every time I see you."

"*Vader*, that's so sweet of you."

"No, it's the truth, wipe your nose," He gave her his handkerchief, but she used her sleeve,

"Except when you do things like that!"

"Sorry, Pappy! I'm *oké* now. I have to get off to Thijs. Duty calls."

"You'll be oké though? No more tears?"

"No, I'll be alright, *hou van je* Pappy."

"*Hou van je te lieverd.*"

She kissed his cheek and was gone.

Caes looked out through the window into the snow as she ran skidding across the icy path and for some reason he saw Truus as a child again. She was careering across her school playground, dodging parents and pupils and teachers, her pigtails and ribbons flying behind her, one side of her denim dungarees undone, her backpack a lethal weapon as she trailed it swinging behind her. She had leapt into his arms and hugged him, almost knocking him over. He remembered just squeezing all his love into her. How she was growing up. It scared him, she was never going to be his little girl again, but she was becoming her own woman.

What Truus had said the other day about there being no real link at all, that these were two separate incidents struck Caes. Why Thijs's daughter, they were kind of estranged, but did have minimal contact? The other two didn't, one was an orphan, and the other ones only relative lived in the United States. So, was there a target? If there was, it had to be Sterre. Caes decided to see Thijs again. Or was this all random and Universiteit the only link?

Meanwhile, he had to stir up everything he had set in motion. They were checking houses and flats. They had traced and spoken to Gisele's mother in America, there was no father de Groet. Gisele was alone, no other relatives in Holland. Caes remembered Laure Vossen vaguely from the past and called her up in Haarlem. She blamed Thijs for everything; it was as if even todays snow was his fault.

Caes knew she must have had her reasons, but didn't know the ins and outs of their marriage, just that she seemed to hate him and this was yet another stick to beat him with. Poor Thijs, he was trying so hard to sort himself out after messing up his life and this is what he got for trying. Well Laure Vossen at least agreed to stay in Haarlem and not come beating at Koonstraats door or beating up Thijs. Elise had no one, both parents were dead and there were no relatives. A lonely girl, even lonelier now.

Oudegracht, 14.30.

Truus was making her way back to the Orman office when she glimpsed a sight of a slim figure in a navy and yellow police uniform. Maaike. She felt her heart jump and she felt herself blushing. Maaike caught sight of her and waved. Truus waved back and didn't understand the feeling she had in her stomach.

"Hi, Truus, you alright?" Maaike asked as she approached.

"Yea, just on my way to work, you busy?"

"Nothing happening at the moment. Freddie wandered off somewhere."

"Avoiding work?"

"No probably the opposite, looking for someone to arrest. He makes me scream."

"Are you enjoying your work?"

"Today's much better. It's when you get the harsh realities of life overpowering you that it becomes hard." She smiled.

"I can understand, I have only just started looking for this girl and am feeling a bit lost and hopeless. You are looking for three girls on top of this prostitute problem and everything else, I can hardly imagine…"

"I think your pappy is right. You need to compartmentalise, but it's not easy."

"But it's also about not taking too much home. Pappy rarely talks to me about his work. It must be hard if you and Freddie are always talking about stuff."

"We don't that often, but I do get a bit fed up at times. I know Freddie cares, but he seems to let it wash over him. He does take it seriously, but… I don't know."

"Don't over think, Maaike. Look forward to something. I've got to get to work, but let's meet up and dance somewhere."

"Alright. There's Freddie. I'll give you a call."

Particulier Onderzoeks Bureau, Blokstraat. 15.00.

Truus went off to work.

Truus asked, "So Thijs, missing your daughter, are you?"

"How?" He shrugged, "Your father?"

"Yes, but why not tell me who she was, what difference would it have made?"

"I'm not sure. I think there is something going on, but I'm not sure."

"My father is looking into the disappearance of two other girls."

"Oh yes?" He was suddenly interested.

"She may have disappeared, or she may just have gone away for a break. That's why I asked you... but this, if other girls are missing, well...," he continued.

He shivered and seemed to shrink into an even smaller person, "This is a bit scary. What does your father think?"

"Nothing solid yet. Both the same age, same kind of girls as Sterre, now all three are lonely, they don't seem to have any friends..." Truus said.

"Don't say that, she must have..."

"No, she was at Uni, but no one seems to have really known her."

"Someone..."

"She was in one of my classes, I didn't really..." said Truus guiltily.

"But no one?"

He looked crestfallen. "Maybe they have gone off together somewhere, were they friends?"

"I'll ask again; I'll also go round to her flat again. You don't have a key, do you?"

"Yes, I'll give it to you later. No. I'll come along with you."

"Might see my father..."

"Well, for old times' sake..."

"Oké, I have to go to Universiteit now, I have a class in an hour, but then I'll meet you at back here at six pm. Oké?"

"Thijs, how are you?" Caes smiled his greeting as he entered Ormans office.

"Coffee, Thijs? Hoofdinspecteur Heda?" his daughter, the assistant, asked.

"Please..." Caes said.

"Yes please," said Thijs, he wasn't smiling.

"Thijs, we've been thinking through things and can you think of why you might be the target?"

"Me? No, why do you ask?"

108

"It was something Truus said, you have had some contact still with Sterre, but there is no one else in contact with the other two girls."

"Not as much contact as I should. I haven't seen her for weeks and can't remember when we last spoke."

"Perhaps you are the target, so has anyone been in contact?"

"No, I just thought she had been taken, a random snatch after I heard about the other two girls."

"Well..."

"I just assumed all three were random, but..."

"Well, have a think if there is anything, think back..." Caes said.

"I did a lot of bad stuff, but that was a long, long time ago."

"I know, but we also know some people have very long memories, it may be a surprise."

"But to be honest though, no one I upset was really that bright, they were all pretty low life, not particularly motivated, they wouldn't have the nerve, would they?"

"I really have no idea, Thijs."

"It's not a period in my life that I'm particularly proud of, Caes. I ruined everything with the drugs and then my behaviour. I've taken a long time to get anywhere close to where I was. I lost my wife, though I think she had long been looking for a way out."

"I'm sorry, Thijs."

"But it's Sterre, I've messed everything up for her. She supported me and I took that for granted and just wasn't there for her. Now when she needs me most..."

"As I said, just have a think."

"I will. Dank, Truus."

They drank the coffee she had made, not talking, and then Truus suggested,

"What about your wife, Thijs? Could she be involved in some way?"

"Taken Sterre?"

"No, could she be a target, are they trying to get to her through Sterre?"

"No idea. It couldn't be could it, Caes?"

"Perhaps, it's a thought. I have spoken to her, but just to let her know what was happening, I'll send Madelon over to see her tomorrow. Dank for the coffee, Truus, but I have to go. See you tonight? See you, Thijs."

Vaartsestraat, 16.50.

Freddie Meijer called Caes over grinning,

"Hi, *baas*, what brings you to our mean streets?"

"Just looking, anything going on?" Caes asked.

"We are just on our way to a call; some woman says there's something strange in the canal." Maaike answered showing her radiant smile.

"When is there not?" Caes snorted, "Whereabouts?"

"End of Vaartsestraat, across Cathrijnesingel." Freddie said.

"Oh yes, where else? Everything seems to be leading us to Vaartsestraat this week. I'll come with you.

There was indeed something strange in the canal, it was a body. Not that this was so strange in cities with canals these days to be honest, but this was ridiculous Caes thought, why everything here in Vaartsestraat? Why had it suddenly become a crime destination?

It was a man, pale, skinny, still recognisable, though Caes didn't know him. He was of course dead but had not been for long, his body wasn't bloated or anything, just a bit damp and well, just a bit dead.

"Any idea who he is, Freddie, Maaike?"

"No, never seen him before." Freddie said.

Maaike shook her head.

"His papers?"

"None…"

"Call the boys in, I'll ask about while we wait. Fish that bag out as well would you Freddie and then tape it all off, inner and outer zone."

Freddie Meijer reached into the canal for the black bin bag that was floating just off the body.

"Just clothes, baas… old clothes and some shoes… Maaike!" Freddie called.

His sister had started off to the other side of the road.

"You oké?"

"For sure, Freddie, don't fuss. Anything for me, *baas*?" she asked.

"Yes, go and canvas that side of the street, Freddie will stay here. I'll get to the other side."

So, the soul destroying routine of knocking and asking the same questions started. But as usual, no one had seen anything. It was no surprise, though, it was a funny little street. The canal was hidden almost by the corner of the end building. The two rows of houses were all looking forwards. The canal was sideways of them. If he had entered the water where they had found him, then he would have been shielded from their sight. Looking on the negative side, if anyone had helped him in, they too would have been hidden. As Caes came out of the first block of houses Freddie called him over.

"A lot of blood on the clothes, baas."

"A wound?"

"Can't see anything without pulling his clothes off, but it looks like it."

"So may be an assault that went wrong, a robbery perhaps. We'll wait for the techs. You take over canvassing. I'll stay here."

Caes wrote a few notes down whilst waiting for the medical examiner. It didn't take long for the flashing lights to highlight the street and it was soon all very business-like.

Kroonstraat Police Bureau, 17.45.

Of course, it was Ernst who told them all about the dead man. Once he had the name he didn't need to do anything else, he just knew,

"Jouke Spliker just released from Wolvenplein, thirty-seven, paedophile, so no real loss, served four years and three months. Obviously rehabilitated and back in society, but for one day only."

"Just one day? Adrie, get on to Wolvenplein, see if he was met by anyone. Who was his cell mate? Was he seeing anybody? Out of prison contacts, visitors, well you know the drill…"

Caes thought was there anything else? Yes.

"Danny Meeuwen, house to house, flat to flat at Vaartsestraat …"

"Again? They are going to be so pissed off, baas."

"Not as much as Spliker was, just do it!"

"Yes, baas."

Freddie Meijer said,

"I just love the name Wolvenplein, pity it's going to close soon…" to no one in particular.

Madelon joined Caes over coffee to discuss Thijs's former wife.

"His wife hates him; she simply hates him."

"Hates him enough to hurt their daughter though?"

"She's had no contact with Sterre for nearly three years."

"Oh?"

"She took her father's side in the settlement, testified for him at a hearing. She cannot forgive her."

"Really? God, divorces are a bitch."

"You don't have to tell me, Caes."

He felt himself going red,

"Sorry, Madelon I didn't mean..."

"It's nothing, baas, anyway it's weird then that he doesn't seem to have had very much to do with her since the divorce."

"I know, it's strange, but he has been starting a brand-new business."

"But if he loved her..."

"Yes, he would have found a way, you are right."

"Does he love her? Is this all a gigantic double bluff?"

"He is mad with worry and grief, it's not him."

"Then who? His wife had no ideas about anyone who could have done this, she just has this poisonous hate for poor Thijs."

"Poor Thijs indeed, but if he really loved Sterre?"

"People love in their own way." Madelon said.

"Or not at all. He doesn't really know much about her at all."

"Sad, but so true of so many families."

"You think? Mind you I have no idea why Truus chose to study Sociology at Uni."

"There you go then, Caes!"

"Yes, it is the family that is the greatest mystery!"

Amaliastraat, 22.00.

Truus was flicking through magazines on her bed, listening to music on her iPhone. She turned over and looked at the ceiling. She suddenly thought that she could not remember ever kissing a boy. Did she ever kiss one at basisschool for a joke or a bet? She had no recollection. Truus had never felt anything for boys. It was weird from an early age she just did not fancy them. Girls? It was only now, when she met Maaike, that she felt a real attraction. For nineteen years, there had been nothing really. This is when she really missed her mammie, someone to talk these feelings over with. She knew that her pappy would understand, but for a deep discussion on her feelings she needed her mammie. If she thought back she had always felt more attracted to girls, but never made a move, not because she thought it was wrong or anything, she had just never felt she had the time or the inclination. Odd, Truus knew. She felt the odd tingle when she saw a beautiful woman, but men, Nee, bedankt!. Then Maaike, she met her but had not realised her feelings, then she thought that her green eyes were so beautiful and from then the tingles in her tummy had started, the warm feeling between her legs had started. It was the eyes, it was just that they sparkled and shone and just burned into her, telling her something she had never been told before.

Maaike lay on her bed, she still had her uniform on. She flicked through her notes. How many houses had she called on today? Her feet were sore and she rolled onto her bottom so that she could untie her boots. She squeezed her toes as she freed them from her socks. She breathed out deeply and then tugged her trousers off, but was too tired to do anything else at that moment so slumped back into her pillow and breathed out deeply again. She looked out of her bedroom window. The sky was navy blue, but the snow stood out like feathers against it. Floating slowly and gently but surely towards the ground. It seemed like the world was acting in slow motion outside her window, just as results to her questions this morning had come in slow motion or rather negative motion. No one knew anything, no one had seen anything. It was if the whole of Utrecht was snow blind, all they could see were the noses in front of their faces and very little else.

What a hell of a day. Maaike sat up on her bottom and pulled off her blouse, balling it up and throwing it into a corner where her wash basket was. She brought her knees up to her chest and hugged them towards her. This had been a wasted day. A day that had gone nowhere. She had to have days where something happened, where she could make a difference or at least feel she was making a difference. All this routine was just that, routine, she wanted something exciting.

She thought of Truus and a smile came to her lips. She had come to a decision. It was quite late when Maaike rang Truus at home.

"Can I come around tonight?"

"Pappy's out at the gym tonight."

"To see you, Truus, I need to talk to you."

"*Oké*, what time?"

"I'm quite close now, a few minutes…"

"*Oké* see you…"

Maaike looked flushed at the door as she pulled off her coat and brushed snow from her hair.

"It's so cold outside."

"Coffee, Chocolate?"

"Chocolate would be lovely please, Truus."

"*Olienbollen?*"

"That would be a treat!"

Truus set the mugs down on a tray in front of the fire. Maaike put her feet under her bottom and gazed at the flames.

"Your pappy gave me a good idea."

"About looking into violence against women?"

"Yes, it will do some good."

"I am sure. Do you know who to get in touch with?" Truus asked.

"Yes, a lot of groups, but I need to talk to the girls more to find out why."

"They see nothing else for them?"

"Some, but those forced into it are just victims."

"So many foreign nationals are here now, more than Dutch girls."

"It's those girls from the East or from Africa who think they are coming to a new life as a dancer or a nanny who then get forced into it," Maaike said.

"But surely they don't believe this, they can't be so naïve."

"But if a woman comes to you and says 'here you are, love, I've got the chance of a lifetime for you…'"

"But can't they see it's too good to be true?"

"I don't know, it's what they want to believe, they want to get out of poverty and they see that as a way out, but they don't know what they are really getting in to."

"So perhaps we need to go to Eastern Europe and explain to them there what is really for them over here?" Truus wondered.

"The trouble seems that the brothels are closing now the business rates are so high in the city, the girls are forced out and into the hands of people who abuse them."

There was silence. Maaike was staring into the fire, avoiding eye contact, but then reached for Truus's hand.

"This is tricky, Truus."

"What?"

Truus was suddenly confused by her touch. She realised she was not breathing and could feel her heart pumping against her chest. She looked up at Maaike who was still gazing into the fire. Then she turned towards her.

"I feel I am quite attracted to you."

Truus smiled, all of a sudden relieved, she found she was breathing again, but in short deep breaths.

"And me to you." She gasped.

"Really?" Maaike seemed surprised.

"I've had funny feelings in my tummy whenever I've seen you lately."

"I really wanted to kiss you the other night…"

"I think I really wanted you to…"

"You are not horrified?" Maaike looked scared.

114

"Horrified? No, I feel quite happy to be honest."

Truus squeezed her hand. She felt a little embarrassed, as was Maaike. Maaike looked into her eyes.

"I have never been with a woman..."

"Me neither, Maaike, but then again I have never wanted to be with a man."

Maaike lent forward and her lips brushed gently against Truus as if by accident. Only for a second, but the electric shock it sent down her spine was incredible, jolting Truus alive. In that instant, she could feel that Maaikes' lips were soft and cool, her scent musky and heady. Her body close and warm. Her arm wrapped around her body. Truus heard herself whisper,

"Again."

The lips found hers, softly, more deliberately, tenderly moving against them. They kissed. Truus had her eyes closed, she felt as if she was floating. Her heart was racing. Blood was pumping loudly through her head into her ears. Maaike kissed her eyelids, brushed her cheeks with her so soft lips, gentle, little movements that caused chills to jump down through her body. Her breathing seemed to have stopped again and she gasped.

"Maaike..." Truus started.

"Shush," Maaike stopped her, "it's *oké.*"

Truus leaned forward and caressed her lips against Maaike's. Maaike pulled her close and responded to the kiss passionately. She then pushed her away, her turn to be breathless.

"But will it be alright? Your pappy?"

"He loves me, Maaike." She kissed her again, "Pappy will want what I want."

"And you want me?"

"I think I do..."

"Only think?" Maaike whispered

When Maaike first kissed her it was an explosion of delight waiting to happen. Truus wished she had done it sooner. Her softness was amazing; her tongue eased between her lips and entered her mouth, Truus felt herself dissolving and shuddered. This was blissful, it was what she had wanted for so long she suddenly realised. It had never before crossed her mind that this was what she desired, what she wanted. Truus felt Maaike's hand on her breast. This was meant to be. She could not take her lips from Maaike's, it felt intoxicating, but Truus had to push her away to gasp for breath. Maaike had looked worried then, it was one of her looks,

"You don't mind?"

"No. I've waited for you forever,"

Truus sighed, realising as she spoke what a cliché it was, but she felt like that.

Their love making had progressed as the night went on and they discovered more and more about each other's bodies. They lay naked on Truus's bed and traced their fingers on each other, this was such a beautiful game and they were not embarrassed in the slightest. Truus had imagined fumbling and blushing and giggles. They did have the giggles when something didn't work, but neither of them were ashamed of what they did.

Words cannot describe the feelings that showered through Truus's body that first time. The world seemed to stand still and then explode in Technicolor. It was a beautiful moment that she would never forget, but the moments went on and on.

It was late when Maaike left and at once Truus felt like there was a great part of her life missing. Why had she allowed her to go when she wanted to lie next to her in bed and just wallow in love. She wouldn't let her go home again. She would have to spend night after night with her. She needed her and hadn't realised this, now she did, she never wanted to lose her. She had to tell her pappy, but wasn't sure how. That could wait. She just wanted Maaike, instead she pulled her Nijntje close and kissed her fur. She closed her eyes and fell asleep seeing her beautiful girl, her Maaike.

Vagevuur.

He hadn't felt so satisfied since he didn't know when and almost rubbed his hands in glee. He felt excited and so damn pleased with himself. This was all working so well. He looked through the peep hole again and saw the whimpering shape of the girl. This is what your father deserves he said to himself. After all this time, he is getting pay back. Did he really think he could have got away with it? The man was a fool and now he had his daughter. One would go; one would live. He hadn't decided which yet and smiled again. He felt a surge of power through his body. Who was the boss now? It was like the old days. He was in charge. No one knew about him and he was in charge. He flicked the light off.

Suddenly the light went out. Sterre could not remember ever being in such total blackness. She couldn't see anything. She forgot where she was and started to moan softly to herself. Her eyes were blind. She put a hand up to her face and couldn't see it. Why was this happening? Was he trying to torment her or was it a power cut? She tried to remember where the door was, but couldn't see any light anywhere. She became very afraid. What if there were rats? Would they find her? Would they come out into the darkness looking for food? She shivered and told her self not to be silly. But then she thought of the horror movies she had seen where victims became surrounded by tiny bright red eyes and sharp teeth. She shuddered and held herself tighter. She listened to the whimpering sound and tried to ignore it before she realised it was her. She felt bile rise at the back of her throat, making herself sick with fear that was a new one. 'Pull yourself together woman' she ordered. 'Be strong' Platitudes and clichés flashed through her head, a head that was spinning and whirling, trying to understand. 'I can't bear this' she thought, 'I'm going to go mad' She felt a scream rising in her head and the lights went back on.

Sterre wondered what was going on. She had no idea how she had got here. She was worried, she was hungry and she was very cold. She wanted to use the toilet, but didn't fancy the bowl covered with a cloth in the corner. She assumed that was what it was meant for. She almost smiled at the thought of seeing a sign with W.C. written on it and an arrow pointing to the pot. Well, a girl had to have her pride. She had to keep hold of something, trapped as she was. She didn't know how long she had been there; her watch had disappeared. The light was on all the time and there were no windows, just four blank walls, a mattress and a pot. Nice. She had no idea what was happening. It would be too easy to say this was a nightmare as she knew she was wide awake and it was actually happening. Thoughts flooded through her head. Who was the man? Why was she here? Where was she? She felt numb, an icy cold feeling weighed her stomach down, it was fear, she recognised that. It was a feeling she had never had before. She recognised despair, she had felt that when her parents split up, but this feeling of abject terror was something new and she hated it. She was alone and that scared her more than anything. No one would know she was here, she had no real friends who would miss her. She shivered and started to cry. Warm salty tears streaked her face. She hadn't realised just how alone she was since her parents separated. She had no one and nothing. Her stomach tightened and her sobs filled the empty room.

Chapter 9

Vrijdag, November 14, 2014.
Amaliastraat 07.35.

Caes started to button his shirt and think about a tie, but it was only a thought. He knew he would be ridiculed if he wore a tie to work. Ernst tried it last week and it was strange to see this giant of a man curl up with embarrassment after the ribbing he took. 'Save it for when you are Commissaris' was the mildest of remarks. Maaike had been the worst, she had a right mouth on her sometimes. He straightened his button-down collar and brushed his hands through his hair. There was no need for a comb; he thought his beard could use a trim, but he hadn't really got time. He also didn't want to make a mistake then have to shave it all off before work. He tucked his shirt in. Well, all was shipshape, neat and tidy, it was time for breakfast.

Surprisingly Truus was up. This was rare and Caes was foolish enough to say so. The answer was rather a cold stare and a noise like a snuffling beast. He smiled and she had to smile back. She pushed across a coffee and Caes took a sip.

"Why are you up so early then?" asked Caes.

"Pappy I have work; did you see the paper?"

She shoved it across.

"Meisjes nog steeds vermist!"

"Of course the girls are still missing, we only told the press yesterday!" he snorted.

"They want results pappy." Truus said as she pushed toasted bagel into her mouth, almost camouflaging what she said.

"Miracles more likely..."

"Well you are the magician pappy."

It was Caes' turn to sound like a snuffling creature.

"What are your plans liefje?"

"Universiteit first, then off to Thijs and then the gym, you still want to go?"

"And let the world miss the sight of this body?" Caes laughed.

There was a snuffling sound from Truus again, followed by,

"That's a yes then, seven o'clock?"

"I'll be there, start without me if I'm late you…"

"Yes I know, no eye contact, etiquette, no steroids…" Truus parroted.

She kissed his cheek leaving a residue of *stroop* and *boter* and slammed out of the house, my sweetest daughter Caes thought.

Willelm Bilderdijkhove, 11.10.

Maaike had the rather unpleasant job of going through her allocated part of the sex offenders list, though she couldn't be sure whether a sexual offence had taken place. She hadn't thought that there would be so many as she cross-referenced by offences against teenage girls, then against aged women. Her long trawl resulted in the names she has had in front of her. Now she had to find them; three were in jail in Wolverplein, which left her just two. One regularly attended meetings at the sex crimes centre and one seemed to have dropped out of circulation and was in violation of his parole.

Alfred De Freitas and a Serb national called Marko Adamović would have to be interviewed. She wondered why the latter was still in Holland's and not been deported. He had now gone to ground so would probably be hard to find, but they would ask Ernst. He would find him. Having been made *rechercheurs* for this part of the case, Maaike and Danny called on De Freitas both dressed in the attractive navy and yellow uniform which didn't stop the woman who answered demanding to know who they were and to see their identification. She was a small unfortunate looking woman, her greasy tied back, her face weathered and lined, an obvious smoker with a cough to match her nicotine stained fingers. She was slovenly dressed obviously not caring about how she looked. Reluctantly she showed them to the kitchen, it was filthy, table greasy and littered with bits of food and dirty plates. The dirty sink was festering with what could have been a week's worth of crockery.

"Wait here I'll get him." she muttered.

De Freitas followed her into the kitchen. He was a small weaselly man dirty I did not shake the proffered hand. He shrugged, he must be used to rejection Maaike thought. He sat down, Danny led the way.

"De Freitas…"

"That's me." he answered sullenly.

"Just a few questions."

"It always is, what's happening now?"

"Not seen the news Heren De Freitas?"

"No..."

"No TV?" Maaike asked.

"Don't you read?" Maaike asked.

"No money."

"You have no job?"

"I get by; my record doesn't help."

Whose fault is that thought Maaike.

"We are looking for two girls."

"Aren't we all?"

De Freitas smirked. It wasn't a good look.

Maaike slammed her hand on the filthy table top and immediately regretted it.

"It's no laughing matter!" Maaike snapped.

"Who's laughing?"

"Two women are missing do you know anything?" Danny asked.

"Why should I know anything?"

"It's what you do isn't it?" asked Danny.

"Not for a long time, I am reformed." He whined.

"Reformed?" Maaike asked, "or just watched too carefully?"

"If you're watching me then you know the answer."

"Every dog has its day!" Danny said.

"No need to be rude." He whined again.

"What do you know Heren De Freitas?" asked Danny.

"Nothing I don't do that sort of thing..."

"What sort of thing?"

"Attack women!" snapped Maaike.

"They have disappeared..." started Danny again.

"Well search the place, ask my wife, she'd have my balls if I started again..." interrupted De Freitas.

"No urges De Freitas?" Danny asked.

"Piss off why can't I be left alone?"

"The women you attacked, can they forget?" Maaike asked

"Done nothing wrong..."

121

His whining voice was starting to grate on Danny and Maaike. His wife was at the door.

"What is he supposed to have done now?"

"We are just making enquiries Mevrouw De Freitas."

"He knows better than to get mixed up with any funny business," she sneered.

"Last time was the last time wasn't it Alfie?"

"Yes."

He seemed to shrink to an even smaller size.

"Done nothing, I just want to be left alone…" he whined again.

"Like your victims did?" Maaike said.

She looked at Danny he shrugged.

"You mind if we take a look around?" Maaike asked.

"Be my guest, nothing to hide." said the woman.

Maaike went upstairs trying not to touch anything; she had put some blue gloves on but was sure that she would not be protected from the germs and squalor. The house was filthy; how did people live in places like this one Maaike wondered, but there again she had seen worse. There was nothing up the steep stairs except dirt and rubbish, she met Danny on the landing.

"What do you think?"

"Squalor, pathetic little man, wife or partner keeps him under the thumb…"

"Pity she didn't do that earlier." Maaike said bitterly.

"Nothing, best get out of here, my skin is crawling."

"They went into the snow realising how claustrophobic the house had been. Snow was starting to fall again. Maaike pulled her gloves off road then rubbed them in the snow to clean the grease off."

Danny smiled

"Teach you to be dramatic Maaike."

She laughed,

"We need to find this Adamović now where should we start?"

"I'll ask Ernst he'll know he knows everything." Declared Danny.

Maaike laughed if only he knew where the women were, even he was not perfect.

Maaike looked up into the sky and allowed the snow to settle on her face, she felt her eyelashes become heavier as the snow dropped faster. She couldn't see it ever stopping. She looked to the West and saw the Dom Toren rising into the morning sky. The drifting flakes making it look like the centre of a giant snowball, lights seeming to highlight every flake that fell. Christmas was a while ago, but it still felt festive even though things were not very pleasant. At the moment, they made their way back to Kroonstraat after another dead end.

Korte Minrebroederstraat, 11.19.

Ernst Hoewegen and Freddie Meijer were strolling through the city.

"And what do you want, young Meijer?" asked Hoewegen

"To be just like you, sir!" Freddie smiled.

"*Idioot*!" smiled Hoewegen.

"I want promotion. I want to be a detective. I like it when the baas gives us more responsibility."

"You think you can handle extra responsibility."

"Don't you think I can?" asked Freddie.

"You oké working on your own?"

"I enjoy it, makes me concentrate more."

"I have noticed…"

"I do find it hard concentrating on menial run of the mill things."

"But that's so much of our work, Freddie, this weeks extra are just that. Maybe extra isn't the right word, but you know what I mean…" Ernst said.

"I do. Maaike now, she's one hundred per cent focused all the time, on everything she does."

"Maybe too much?"

"I'm not sure…"

Freddie didn't really want to talk about his sister.

"Caes feels she needs to unwind a little, be less intense."

"She told me. I'm very different. I do care, but I don't take it home."

"So, the cases we have at the moment, what do you think?"

"I know each is important"

"Any more so?" wondered Ernst.

"The missing girls. We can't be sure how long they've been gone. They may be dead, they may just have gone away together. They may not know each other. It's really strange."

"It is a puzzle, what do you think?"

"They've been taken, but we don't know why. I think they are still alive, we've found no bodies after all, but it is all so weird." Freddie was puzzled, but so was everyone.

"The cars?"

"Probably as you said, one gang. Stolen to order. We need to find out where they are being fixed up and who is sending them."

"If we knew that…"

"I know, I meant from where. It must be obvious to someone. You can't keep driving posh cars somewhere and have no one notice..." Freddie said.

"A garage?"

"Probably, with a high turnover so it doesn't look odd."

"But we have checked every known garage in the city and a few that aren't known and nothing..."

"Industrial estates to the west?" wondered Freddie.

"Maybe, we can ask our friends over at Schaverijstraat to have a look. "

Ernst Hoewegen then brought it back to the girls,

"What about the two students though..."

"Both disappeared and no one cares. No one has missed them save for the old woman who isn't really anything to do with them." Freddie answered.

"So they may have been targeted because no one knows them?"

"What, that no one will miss them? So not kidnapped for money, for something worse?"

"I hope to Christ not. We can do without a pervert or sex traffickers in Utrecht..."

And so, the discussion went on. Ernst Hoewegen trying to mentor young Freddie as asked to by his baas, just as he had with Danny and Adrie in the past. It was an ongoing task of personal development and one that Ernst relished. He liked to think of himself as an important figure in his young charges development, not in a pompous way, but he knew he had a lot to offer. Ahead for Ernst was promotion as well and he looked forward to the next step in his own journey.

Vaartsestraat, 15.07.

Caes got to the scene just after three o'clock. He saw Thijs and Truus standing by the canal. The trees by the canal were snow covered, of course, indeed it was almost polar like. The pathway between houses and canal was again about twenty centimetres deep in snow, all hard pressed, but not thawing or slushy. From that, white washed walls of the flats formed a dirty frontage. It looked bleak. Maybe it looked different in the summer. He couldn't remember. There had been too much snow to think of a time when there had been no snow, but for the moment the flats still looked cold and bleak. It was all white and mixed with the grey sky it made him feel even colder. Caes saw some sunshine as Truus looked over and waved.

"Truus."

"Vader." Truus grinned.

"Thijs."

Caes greeted him with his hand outstretched. He took it and gripped it firmly and shook,

"Caes. You well?"

"Yes, you? How's it going?" Caes said.

"Good, good."

"Any news?"

"No, nothing."

"Any thoughts?" Caes said.

"Not really..."

"So you think it's random?"

"I really don't know, now that I know there are two others..." He paused, broken.

"Random? Have you been upsetting anyone?" Caes said

"No, Caes, that's long gone, I couldn't keep my licence if I wasn't legit. I was foolish then..."

"What about your daughter then? Has she got any enemies that you know of?"

"No, that's stupid!"

"You don't really know her Thijs..." Caes said

"What! Who says?" He paused. "No you're right. Truus said she had no friends, I didn't realise..."

"Drugs?" Caes had to ask.

"I hope to God not, God..." He broke down in tears.

"I don't know her, my own daughter, who she is, what she does, I don't even know her..."

He was sobbing, Caes had no idea what to do, he put his arm around his shoulder, he grabbed hold of Caes and hugged him, his chest heaving. Truus looked at me over his shoulder, smiling thinly. She pointed up and mouthed 'I'll go look upstairs' and disappeared.

It seemed pointless talking to Thijs in this state, Caes followed Truus into the flats. He heard a bit of a racket and as he got to the second floor landing he could see that Truus was arguing with a weasel faced young man, he raised his hand. Caes made to step forward to stop him, but Truus interrupted me,

"Pa...Piet! I can handle it!"

Who is Piet Caes wondered?

She whipped his legs from under him, but held onto his arm as he fell. He squealed in pain.

"Don't ever think to touch me or any woman uninvited you little bastard or you'll lose more than the use of your arm."

"Oké...oké ..."

She twisted it and he squealed again as she threw him to the side like a piece of rubbish. God, she is good, Caes thought.

"Now, Piet Keizer here..."

Piet Keizer? Former Ajax football star? What is he doing here Caes wondered?

"Piet and me are looking for Sterre. You seem the type who might be able to help as you seem to be a bit sleazy and would know where girls go?"

"I don't. I haven't seen her for ages, like I told you…"

"Do we believe him, Piet?" Truus asked.

Piet? Oh, yes, that was me.

"No, you seem the type who just watches girls, likes to watch girls, so what did you see?"

"I've not see her for over a week, I can't remember the last time."

"So you watch her?" Truus said.

"No…Yes…I do see her, but I'm not stalking her."

"No?" Caes asked.

"No, I have a life!" he almost shouted.

"Not much of one it seems to me…" Truus snarled.

"Look, I've done nothing wrong."

"You tried to assault me." Truus said.

"That was a mistake. I'm sorry…"

"Do we believe him now, Piet?"

"I believe he needs to reassess his approach to life. Tell you what, I may just get the police to call around." Caes replied.

"I have not seen her I swear!"

He was starting to panic and Caes don't think they had anything to worry about. He was a voyeur not a danger. Hopefully ending up on the floor with a bruised arm and ego would be a warning. He hurried back into his foul-smelling room.

"Why Piet Keizer?" Caes had to ask Truus.

"Well I know you loved him when he played."

"But…" Caes started.

"I started to call you Pappy, but that felt so wet when we were out on a job together."

"On a job together, Truus? How proud you make me…"

"Don't be daft!" Truus laughed.

"But in case you had forgotten I am actually a real policeman and have no need for subterfuge, though I have now, it seems, impersonated a former Ajax footballer."

"I had to think fast."

Truus explained, going slightly red.

"Yes… I'll give you that, but best not to lie. 'Daughter of fake footballer assaults weasel man' is not what I want to see on the front page of De Telegraaf."

"Sorry…"

Her embarrassment was now complete and she smiled guiltily.

"No, it's *oké*. Right what do we know so far?" Caes said.

"Thijs doesn't know Sterre. Do you know me, *Vader*?"

"I think I do… not everything." Caes smiled.

"A girl must have her secrets…"

"But the important things, I hope I know." Caes really did.

Truus squeezed his hand,

"You're my best pal, Pappy. Anyhoo. Sterre is lost."

"Thijs is ashamed."

"Is Thijs involved?" Truus asked.

"We don't know."

"Do we think so?"

"We have no real idea, but probably not." Caes said.

"About anything!"

"Well we do know she is missing!"

Truus replied seriously,

"Yes, we do know that, all too well!"

They went downstairs into Sterre's flat. Thijs was sitting on the bed; he looked as if he had been crying again.

"Anything, Thijs?" Caes asked.

"Nothing, but I wouldn't know really would I?"

"Well, I wouldn't either if I was in Truus…" Caes started.

"No, Caes, I have no idea, nothing. Her clothes, what she wears, what her favourite things are, do you, Truus?"

"No, I'm sorry…"

"How'd I know if anything's missing?" Thijs asked.

"You don't, it's just if anything unusual hits you."

"What would be unusual? I've no idea."

"Her Uni work? Letters, phone messages, we'll need to take her laptop and check through it…" Caes interjected.

"There's a photo of you here, Thijs." Truus pointed to the bedside table.

"Something I suppose…" Thijs smiled thinly.

"Well better than nothing, Thijs, come on get yourself together man, you're no use nor ornament if you are just going to mope!" Caes snapped.

He couldn't be having him sink into a pit of despondency, he needed to have his wits about him.

"*Oké*, alright, I'm sorry. Shall I leave you both to it?" Thijs said.

"If you like, leave the key with Truus. I'll have a proper look."

But there was nothing, just like in Gisele's flat, everything in order, tidy, clean. Caes smiled to himself at the thought of Truus and of her organised chaos.

"What you thinking, Pappy?"

"Of you, come on let's go, there's nothing here."

"Flyers for two clubs. De Machine and Roze Fluweel?" Truus wondered.

"They new are they?" Caes should have known this.

"I've heard of De Machine before, a bit grim, there was something to do with De Machine and Gisele as well I think, Freddie said, probably just an advertising splurge?"

"*Oké* ..."

"Look at all her shoes and boots, Pappy, all lined up so neatly."

"Yes, why are yours never like that?"

"I'd never know where to look for them Pappy, come on..."

Universiteit Utrecht, 15.45.

Truus sat in the so called quiet room in the library. She had people talking all around her. So much for rules she thought. She plugged in her laptop and her mobile phone. She didn't want the charge to run out. She pushed her iPhone earplugs in and started to listen to The Cure. She looked around to check if people could hear her music, then turned it up a notch. She pulled out the plugs and was pleased that she couldn't hear anything so punched it up another level and put them back into her ears. Beautiful Robert Smith was singing 'Charlotte Sometimes' and Truus closed her eyes and drifted off into another world for a moment where she was dancing in a flowing dress of purple damask, whirling around between the trees of a forest that had suddenly appeared. She was scattering flowers around from a basket she was carrying under an arm, then was spinning between library shelves, in and out of stacks of books and desks. She woke up and felt herself going red. No one was watching her. No one cared; they were all in their own worlds. Some working hard, others, the majority, just talking. She looked down at her laptop and swallowed hard. She had to get this work done. Four thousand words finished, another thousand to go and she was stuck. She looked at her notes and looked into the air. The ceiling seemed a long way off, she looked at her notes again. The ceiling was suddenly just above her head. Everything seemed to be closing in. Her notes made no sense, she closed her eyes and the snow began to fall again. Her notes were covered in a fine white frozen dust, getting thicker by the second. She looked at the floor. Her feet had disappeared under a layer of ice and the snow was settling and reaching up to her knees. She shivered and tried to move her feet to escape its clutch, but couldn't move. Her waist was suddenly covered by snow and she could not see her laptop or the desk. All around her ghoulish figures of Nijntje, dressed all in white were standing and crowding around her, all pointing into the distance where she could vaguely see a face. The snow was now at her chin, she could not move, but the face was becoming clearer and closer, then it moved away before surging back towards her.

Sterre, it was Sterre and she was crying great snowflake tears and then the snow obliterated everything and she was frozen and alone. Truus jerked awake again. This had to stop. She unplugged everything and tucked them into her backpack. She pulled on her coat and left the library. She needed fresh air, but needed most to wake up. The freezing air slapped her face as soon as she left the building. All around was white. It had once again covered the road that had been clear when she had entered the library. Trees heavy boughed and grey, pricked the white backcloth. The flakes were so big, they drifted down and froze, flake on flake, layer on layer, getting deeper as she stood there. Pulling her hat down over her ears and pushing her hands into her pockets she set off for Orman's office. She had to do something.

Kroonstraat Police Bureau, 18.00.

Maaike and Madelon sat on the settee in the 'Sex Crimes Suite'. It was way after midnight and they were both tired. Not as tired as the girl with them though. The girl opposite, they had met earlier in the week. Tonight Jeltje's, face was swollen, her left eye closed.

"He beat you for what?" Madelon said.

"It was my fault."

"How can it be your fault that he beat you?"

"Yes, it was, he told me he didn't want to, but I had to work harder."

"You have sex for money, Jeltje, you don't keep your money."

"No, but he takes care of me…"

"By beating you?" Maaike said.

"He loves me, I love him. He keeps me safe…"

"How old are you?"

"Nineteen."

"Really, Jeltje?" asked Madelon.

"Truly."

"Is this what you want from your life?"

"It's for him… "

"Jeltje, it's not about him, my love, can't you see…" Maaike despaired.

"He's using you to make money for him, then does this…" Madelon tried.

"You don't need him, you're able to work without him, you do realise that, don't you?"

"I need him. It was my fault. Look have you finished?"

"You don't want to press charges?" Maaike asked.

"Why'd I do that?"

"So he doesn't do it again."

"He won't, he loves me." Jeltje smiled.

The bastard smirked at them as he kissed Jeltje as she went through into the foyer and then held her close, like two lovers out for a stroll.

"I want to be sick, Madelon, how can we stop this?"

"You're too old fashioned, Maaike, it'll always go on. But the violence, I don't like this…"

"But…"

"Her papers seemed oké, she didn't want to press charges. We'd have to have her name the attacker…"

"The odds are all stacked against us…" Maaike said softly.

"If it turns out she is younger than she says and I think that is likely, we can do something…"

"But if her papers say…"

"And the address she has given. It's a mine field." Said Madelon.

"What do we do?"

"Keep an eye out for her. I'll get in touch with Anastasia at Rode Knop and the Bureau."

"Schools?"

"If it's her real name, we can check it out."

"We can't just take her into care?"

"Not really. I know she looks very young, but we have to be sure…"

"And in the meantime…"

"I know Maaike. It's not perfect, it really isn't, but we are hamstrung by the law."

"The bloody law," hissed Maaike. "I thought it was designed to help people. This seems to actively protect the bad people."

"I'll make the checks Maaike. Try not to worry."

"I can't help it Madelon. It breaks my heart."

"Listen Maaike!" Madelon said firmly.

"You cannot take this to heart. If you do every nasty incident will break your heart and you will be overpowered by them. Each one will add to your load and soon it will be too heavy and you will break. You must put it to one side…"

"But is caring wrong?" Maaike almost pleaded.

"Caring is fine, but you cannot be the conscience of the world. This is your job, but it's not your life. You must leave it at work in the office. You cannot carry it around with you. It will break you, not your heart."

"I don't…"

"But I do Maaike. I used to feel like you. I think caring too much messed up my marriage. I took it home. I didn't have time for a life, it all overwhelmed me. I couldn't carry it all and expected my husband to take some of the load. He refused and we drifted apart. I felt if he didn't care about my work, then how could he care about me."

"So he left?"

"With another woman." Madelon laughed.

"He wasn't that picky in the end and I gave him a good excuse."

"But if you love…" started Maaike.

"I don't think he truly loved me, but I didn't help. I gave him the excuse. I wanted him to share everything. I thought that's what couples did, but really they don't always want to know the truth. You'll have to be careful when you find a partner not to overload them with your hopes and fears at work."

"I think I see…" started Maaike.

"What is it that Caes says? Compartmentalise. Try to put things in boxes and close the box when you leave work at the end of your shift. It will still be there when you go the next day. Sometimes time is of the essence, but most times we can be methodical and sort it all out. A few hours here or there isn't usually vital."

"I hope you're right Madelon."

"I am usually!" Madelon laughed.

"I'll try." Smiled Maaike.

"Well try really hard or you'll be in my bad books and you won't want that young lady!"

"No, I don't think I would. Thanks, Madelon…"

Vagevuur.

He felt a stirring between his legs. He had been so close, but when she puked on him that had changed everything. He had fancied her and would have taken her, but not now, not when she smelt like she did and looked like she did. There had been an attraction, he had seen it in her eyes, but then she had been sick and that desire had quickly ended. Why bother anyway, he could have any woman he wanted and didn't need the snivelling little bitch in the corner, not if she begged him. He wouldn't dirty himself.

Elise shivered, she sat on the mattress with her knees hunched up under her chin, and she was so very cold. She was very scared as well. The man terrified her. His dead eyes were horrible. She had completely lost track of time and didn't know if it was day or night or how long she had been there. Or why she was there. What had she done to deserve this, just as things were starting to look up for her? What the hell had happened to her?

She smiled to herself at the thought of Gisele. Now that had also happened so very fast, but she thought she knew what had happened there. She almost laughed, but shivered instead.

Gisele and her, they had passed by each other for almost a year at Universiteit Utrecht after leaving school. They saw each other in the corridor, in the restaurant, in the bar and never spoke, it was weird. They had known each other at school, but just drifted apart even though they were often so close together. Then by chance Gisele had sat beside her in the library and they had gone for a coffee and then two days later Gisele and she were sharing her bed at Vaartsestraat. They had held each other close, as close as two people could be, as close as lovers needed to be. It had been so beautiful, it was what she had been waiting for, she had realised. Someone who loved her for who she was and someone she could love as well. It had been so perfect, but all too brief. She had to get out of this and back to Gisele, she loved her so much and needed to be with her so much. How had she not known that Gisele was the one? They had passed each other so many times and not known it, then eventually found their bliss. From that bliss, to this, the final irony, Elise thought. I find happiness and then this monster takes me. Well at least we had some fun together, and this time she did laugh, but it soon turned into sobs as she hugged herself against the cold and cried herself to sleep again.

Chapter 10

> Zaterdag, November 15, 2014.
> Kroonstraat Police Bureau, 09.00.

Briefing was over and Caes and Madelon were sharing a coffee in his office. Madelon had been quiet. Caes looked across at her, she smiled.

"What you thinking about?" he asked.

"Promotion Caes, a post in Maastricht."

His heart sank.

"Really?"

"I'm not sure, is it the right time?"

"Is it ever Maddie, you've been here what eighteen months?"

"About that, is it too soon?"

He wanted to say yes, way too soon.

"No, but if it's the right fit for you…"

"Is there anything coming up here?" asked Madelon.

"Not with all the cutbacks, if it's what you want go for it."

"I'm not sure Caes, I'm happy here."

"What do you want, to climb the greasy pole?"

"I thought so, Commissaris Coeman gave me the details."

"Did he now?"

That was a surprise, especially with the current problems, but there again, if she went euros would be saved. There always seemed time to cut budgets, it didn't matter if crime was up or down.

"What did he say?" asked Caes.

"Oh, that this is an exciting post…" Madelon was noncommittal.

"Is it?"

"I think he's over egged it, but it would be a challenge."

"Maastricht is very nice."

"Caes, what do you really think?"

"The selfish part would like you to stay."

He felt himself going red.

"But professionally, it could be the right time."

"You ever think of promotion?" asked Madelon.

"Not for a long time."

"Why not?"

"I suppose it's because I'm content."

"Is that good?"

"I love Utrecht, it's my city. I was born here; anything else would have to be in a bigger city, miles away. I also have Truus."

"But she is growing up…"

"I know but…"

"She may want to move away soon."

"I don't think she'll leave Utrecht either. I know she may look for somewhere new to live and if she does I may have to move as well, but not from the city."

"Has nothing ever attracted you?"

"To be honest, no. I'm happy here and you lot are a good team."

"We are that, but anyone could move on…"

"I realise that. I'm not staying here out of loyalty and you mustn't either. If you want to go for it that's fine, I'd never stand in your way."

"Do you think I'm ready?"

"More than Maddie…" Caes smiled.

"It's such a lot to think about, after my divorce Tilburg seemed to close in on me and I was glad to move away even if it was a sideways move. I've learnt a lot from you."

"Thanks Maddie, the feeling is mutual."

"But to uproot again and to Maastricht it's like the end of the world." Madelon grimaced.

"It's not that bad, it does seem isolated, but your friends could meet up."

"That's the other thing, I just started with a new circle of friends, do I really want start all over again at my age?"

"You sound like an old woman Maddie," laughed Caes.

"Sometimes I feel like one."

"Don't be silly."

He looked at her, she was so attractive, all blonde and blue-eyed. How could she feel old Caes wondered?

"Why not visit, take a few days to have a look."

"I can't right now."

"We'll still be here when you get back; we can give Maaike a little more responsibility if you have any meetings…"

"I do with the Rhode…"

"There you go then, let Maaike handle that and you visit Maastricht."

"If you're sure?"

"Course I am."

He reached across the desk and squeezed her hand.

"Take your time it's a big decision…"

"Tell me about it," she smiled, "thanks Caes."

"My pleasure."

Caes smiled, but he didn't mean it. Did he care that she wanted to leave or had been pushed towards leaving? Yes, he did was it selfish for wanting her to stay? Again, yes it was, but was it just for work reasons? When he had squeezed her hand a tingle had gone through his body. A feeling he hadn't had for a long time. He rejected any thoughts of romance, but the seeds were there, but so was his love for Femke.

Vismarkt, 10.11.

Maaike had somehow lost Freddie and was walking down the cobbled street on her own. She felt content. Admittedly the crimes they were investigating weren't being solved, but she did like patrolling the street in her smart navy uniform trying to be nice to people who didn't always deserve her politeness back. She liked to help people, be it showing them the way somewhere or helping them through the piles of snow. She liked the interaction with the shop owners and bar keepers along her patrol route. Best of all, she liked that they knew her name and would actually wave or smile if they saw her. She wanted so much to be part of the community and not have them be fearful of the police. She knew that some had had poor experiences with her colleagues and that made her even more determined to do and say the right thing. She didn't want to give anyone an excuse for disrespecting the police or more importantly disrespecting the community they lived in. She also knew that she was being given more to do than a normal police agent would be given, she loved the responsibility. She loved to be able to go out and act upon her own initiative. It made her want to be a detective even more, she knew she had to work hard at this, to gain experience, but being trusted to do things meant so much to her.

What would mean even more to her would be if she could get a breakthrough on th kidnappings or the way the prostitites were being treated. She felt sick to mher stomach when she thought about what they had to endure. Sure, some had chosen the life, butn what other options did they have. Her worst fears were for those who had no options, who had been lure dto Holland with promises of a better life only to have their papers taken away and then been brutalised into a life they had never dreamt about. A living horror with the constant threat of violence and disease and drugs laid out at their door. They had no way to get home, indeed if they wanted to what would greet them as there was the threat of violence towards their families. It wasn't the cold that made Maaike shiver, it was the absolute disgust she felt for the men who took such obscene advantage of these girls. The law didn't seem able to help. The refuges did a little, but it was so hard. So hard for the women who were trapped and those who helped. She thanked god for her position in life, but it didn't make her feel much better.

Kroonstraat Police Bureau, 12.00.

Caes had a visitor.

"Thijs? Don't see you in how many years and now it's every day, what's up?"

"Spliker." Thijs replied.

"Who, the body from the canal?"

"Yes, you'll find out soon enough."

"What?"

"He was the child abuser, the one I beat up all those years ago." Thijs said bluntly.

"Yes I know, it's here in front of me. So, you finished the job?"

"Don't be stupid, why…"

"Well, I'll have to speak to you…"

"You'll want an alibi?" Thijs asked.

"If you have one, I would appreciate it." Caes smiled.

"I was probably with your daughter."

He was with Truus. One down, how many to go? Caes had put Madelon on to trawling through the list of Spilker's victims and Ernst on to any of his contacts from Wolvenplein. If anyone could find anything it would be Ernst. Caes didn't really want to, but thought he'd better talk to some of the slimier characters on the list.

Michel de Wuurt was the first; he had been a cell mate until recently and had been released on parole. Why did all paedophiles look the same? Why did they act the same? Why could they not control their sickening urges? De Wuurt was just so typical, a smarmy self-righteous bastard.

"No, Hoofdinspecteur, he did not say he was meeting anyone outside."

"You sure?" Ernst asked.

"We had arranged to hook up when he got out, to discuss certain private matters, but he did not show."

"Any visitors for Spliker at Wolvenplein who was different or might have been out of the ordinary?" Caes asked.

"No, Hoofdinspecteur, no one."

Caes didn't believe him.

"Hoofdinspecteur Heda, how many more questions must I answer? I have made certain plans for tonight."

"Forget them you little bastard and just answer the questions!" Ernst snarled from behind de Wuurts chair.

"Is he allowed to speak to me like that, Hoofdinspecteur?"

"Not really, I must apologise for Brigadier Hoewegen, it's just that when he sees a pile of shit like you, all his manners go out of the window."

Ernst slapped de Wuurt hard across the back of the head.

"Which is where you will be going as well, if you don't answer us." Hoewegen snarled.

Caes looked at Ernst, he looked back shrugging and smirked. He put both hands down heavily on to de Wuurts shoulders. De Wuurt jumped as if an electric shock had gone through his body. He was so pathetic.

"Oké, oké, he said he had had contact with a new man, a man who would tell him about a new club where we could see boys. He told me it would be fantastic and he would share everything with me."

"Name?" Ernst asked.

"No, no names, but he was excited."

"The club?" Caes said.

He looked flustered. Ernst Hoewegen made him jump again as he slammed his hands back onto his shoulders.

"Twilight Club."

Caes looked at Ernst; he shook his head and mouthed 'no idea.'

"Where's this club, Utrecht?"

"No it's not like that..."

"Where then?" Ernst shouted.

"Twilight, its online I have a password."

Later that afternoon they interviewed another low life. They really were quite disgusting human beings. What had society done so wrong that they had to put up with them? That society had even generated them? It may be a cliché, but the room did smell of fear, but the man at the desk tried to cover his trepidation with bravado, just as de Wuurt had. Caes knew it would not last. These people are devious and unpleasant, but they always cave, they always tell you what you want to know, but it was always at their pace.

"Well, Hoofdinspecteur?"

"Who did Spliker talk to about the Twilight Club?"

"No idea, he kept that to himself, trust issues, wanted to enjoy it all on his lonesome I'm sure."

He smirked.

"We know that's a lie, you all love to share. He shared with de Wuurt, who else?"

"We heard it was you, Bulle." Ernst Hoewegen put in.

"Well de Wuurt was his special friend."

He sickened them both.

"Do you want to get transferred to Demersluis Bulle?" Caes asked.

Demersluis was where the hard men went to, no special unit for the weak there.

"You couldn't!" a suddenly ashen faced Bulle almost begged, bravado gone.

"I could and you know I would."

"We need a name!" Caes slammed his hand on the desk.

Bulle was sweating and looking flustered.

"So give me something or mistakes will be made in transfers," Ernst threatened.

"You will go mainstream; wouldn't that be fun for you?"

"No, no, he did meet..."

"A visitor?" Ernst asked.

"Yes, I don't know who, moustache, no a beard, I was a distance from him. Beard, long hair, look in the records, I have no name honest to god."

"God, you ask for god? Do you really think you may ask him for help?" Ernst asked.

"We thank you for your help though, Meneer."

Caes said and breathed clean air as he left the room.

Ernst again checked through Wolvenplein visitor's register, then the visitor's details, and then after cross checking their own data base found he had never existed. He had used a false ID. There was no clear CCTV picture, nothing, a phantom. What the hell was going on?

Oude Hortus, 14.25.

Truus strolled along the snowbound paths at the botanical garden of the Universiteit. Summer time saw a blaze of colour, today it was all white. Her hands were cold, but she pulled out her notebook and started to jot down some thoughts and ideas. The cold, the silence echoing in the air, the grey sky melding into the white covered ground. She imagined all the plants resting below the surface waiting to bloom and thought how amazing it would be if they thrust through into the snow above. She imagined the noise of the summer compared to the restless quiet this winter. She saw tracks of visitors and of dogs and imagined what their story had been, why they were, where they were going and why. She suddenly couldn't stop thinking and writing down ideas and thoughts. It really was a wonderland that was tempting her mind to travel far and wide. This was why she loved to write, to escape, to feel she was on this amazing journey into the unknown; that she was the only one who could find her way, as she was the only one who knew where she was going. A snowball suddenly thudded into the ground by her feet and she whirled around to see Freddie Meijer there, looking all innocence, complete in his police uniform. She wondered if it would be assault if she threw one back, but then thought why not and quickly formed a small ice ball and hit him right between the shoulders as he turned to try and avoid it.

"Young lady!" he boomed across the frosty air.

"I saw her officer!" another voice called and she saw Maaike and a thrill shot through her body. Then it was chased away as a snowball hit her in the head.

Truus could not believe it, she was being attacked by two police officers in broad daylight. She hurled a snowball at Freddie and it hit him flush in the chest. She half expected him to take his baton out, but he just picked up more snow and sent a missile fizzing towards her. She ducked and it missed by miles, only for Maaike to hit her again. This time on her back. She howled, not in pain, but in mock anger and started to run at Maaike, who turned tail and ran away.

Freddie could be heard laughing and Maaike suddenly turned and let fly another snowball, but this time at her brother. He got it flush in the mouth and stood stunned. The laugh wiped off his face. Maaike rushed over to apologise and he sagged to his knees.

The two women were suddenly concerned and ran closer. Their big mistake, as he emptied a huge handful of snow on their heads. Truus just stood there shivering and groaned. Maaike, suddenly put her sensible hat on and said,

"Best stop now whilst we haven't spilt any blood."

"Killjoy!" said Freddie, but he knew she was right.

"You wait till I tell my pappy..." Truus threatened.

"I have my pistol, Truus!" warned Freddie.

"What, you'd shoot me to stop me reporting a snowball attack?"

"I'd do what was necessary, *mejuffrouw* Heda, whatever it takes to keep the peace."

"Pig!" said Maaike.

"Maaike!" reproved Truus. "Will I see you later?"

"I'll come around at eight...*doeg!*"

Amaliastraat, 19.45.

Maaike was at the door. Truus took her coat and scarf. She stood there rubbing her hands together. She wore a crisp white blouse and white tights and a very short lacy burgundy skirt.

"No wonder you are cold!" Truus smiled.

Maaike knelt and untied her black Doc Martens and then looked up at Truus.

"Not cold, so much as frozen!" she laughed.

Standing, she straightened the white ribbon in her hair. Her green eyes were sparkling, her lips blood red. Truus took her hand and led her into the dining room before kissing her gently on the cheek. Maaike in return pulled her close and kissed her lips fiercely.

"I've missed you today, Truus..."

"Not with the snowballs, you bully!"

"Truus!"

"Well we are here now... let's sit by the fire, we can keep each other warm."

"All I wanted to hear, Truus."

"Though I do have a bit of work to finish..."

"You pig... can I help you though?"

"Not really, the English lecturer said to keep a journal. I keep putting it off, but suddenly got inspiration this afternoon, but was rudely interrupted by you two at Oude Hortus."

"I must be your muse!"

"Maaike!" Truus reprimanded, then mellowed, "when I return from a day of artistic excess you will await me naked in my boudoir. You will be on my bed and when I return you will feed me grapes and bathe me in Asses milk."

"Asses milk?"

"Indeed I will be a veritable Cleopatra. You will dry me with butterfly wings..."

"Truus you go too far!" giggled Maaike.

"You will feed me nougat and fine wines and we shall make love till midnight."

"You are sending shivers down my spine Truus. Stop it." Moaned Maaike.

"But I adore milk and wine and love."

"But not now Truus, please stop..."

"I wait then with bated breath." Smiled Truus.

"Yes with bated breath we wait." Laughed Maaike.

"I cannot wait." Truus protested.

"And I need a cold bath now." Maaike leant forward and kissed Truus on the forehead and whispered, "You have to wait."

Then kissed her on the mouth.

"I really do need a muse, I've been stuck for a while, too many things to think about. Put some music on and I'll get a drink." Said Truus extricating herself from Maaikes arms.

"No, I'll make the drinks. You finish what you are doing." Smiled Maaike.

Truus smiled and sat on the settee, curling her feet underneath her. Maaike returned with coffees and then went across to the CD pile.

"These all your pappy's?"

"No," Truus snorted. "We have the same taste, you know that. What is it you really like?"

"Dance music, trance, anything dreamy…"

"Not so much of that, Depeche Mode I suppose, but put something different in…that old Peter Green CD."

Maaike slotted in *I've Got a Mind to Give Up Living* and as soon as the honey flavoured blues guitar started she was in rhythm, moving as one with the ambient sounds. Truus was too distracted to work as her movements seemed to be erotically charged as she tried in vain to concentrate on her words, but Maaike kept sweeping into view and was so off putting. It was hopeless, her body was so lithe and smooth and almost seemed to be floating across the floor, Truus grabbed her and pulled her to the settee.

"You win…"

"What?" Maaike said in mock puzzlement.

"I'll stop."

"What do you mean?" Maaike laughed, "I was just dancing…"

"That's not dancing, that's teasing…"

"Tease?" she kissed her lips. "I just dance…"

She climbed onto Truus's lap and facing her, looked into her eyes. Truus wrapped her arms around her slim waist and pulled her close.

"I feel so good with you…"

"I know; I feel it too. So comfortable, as if we have been together for ever."

"I never imagined this," Maaike whispered and moved forward and kissed Truus on the nose.

"Me neither, I hadn't looked for it."

"But you found it."

"Maybe that's the secret, it's so beautiful."

Truus wrapped her arms tighter around Maaike and pulled her closer still.

"All my life something has been missing and I never had any idea what it was. I honestly never thought of girls. But had no interest in boys. I preferred the company of girls, but never in any sexual way. Boys just made me shiver, except for Freddie of course! I hated their moves and their words. I was never comfortable in their company. Then I kept seeing you and every time I did I got these surges down below and didn't understand them…"

"Me too, my tummy seemed to dissolve every time I saw your face, holding you this close I can feel it melting again…"

"When did you know?" Maaike asked, her face next to her ear.

"When I saw you, ages ago. I knew something, but had no idea what it was."

Maaike laughed.

"My magic spell, it took eighteen years to work but work it does…"

"It's worked on me, let's go upstairs…"

Maaike again kissed her fiercely on the lips before Truus led her upstairs.

Vagevuur.

A packet of brioche had been thrown into the cell. Elise fumbled for the empty bottle and shuffled over to the sink. She felt like an old bag lady. She rinsed water over her face and used her shirt to dry herself. The smell of stale vomit was still there. She felt disgusting. She slowly made her way back to the mattress and pulled open the bag. She bit into a stale brioche. What was the matter with the man, even buying cut price food to give her? She wanted to spit it out, but was so hungry. She rubbed her stomach where he had punched her and pulled up her shirt to see the bruise. It was certainly there, he was horrible. Thoughts raced through her head. She wanted to be home, to be with Gisele. Where was Gisele.? Did he have her as well? If not, was she trying to find her? What had they been talking about when she last saw her? They had made love, she had showered, she had left the flat feeling so happy and now this. The smell, the squalor. This made no sense, no one hated her this much. No one would pay a ransom for her if that was his plan. No one really knew her. Save for Gisele, she was all alone. She started to cry and batted tears away with the back of the hand. Don't show you are weak she demanded to herself. Don't give him any more satisfaction the bastard. She closed her eyes and chewed on the stale sickly sweet brioche. What was she doing here? What could she do?

Chapter 11

> Zondag, November 16, 2014.
> Kroonstraat Police Bureau, 10.12.

Ernst of course knew where Adamović was. *Rechercheurs* Maaike and Danny faced him across the desk and waited. He had a neat crew cut and looked like a businessman; he probably was a businessman, but not in the conventional sense. He had been convicted of rape; two eighteen-year-old women in the early nineties. He had spent time in Wolverpleine and had then been paroled. Apparently, he had not met his parole officer for sixteen months; why we had not been told of that Maaike had no idea. Anyway, he sat across the desk from them looking smug. He didn't have hair out of place; it could have been a normal business meeting, but he was far from normal. His cold eyes stared across at Danny and Maaike.

"Missed your parole appointments." said Danny.

"One or two…" he smirked.

"Sixteen to be precise."

"As many as that?" Adamović sneered.

"You know it is; any reason?"

"I've been busy."

"Doing?" asked Maaike.

"Making a go of my life in Holland."

"Breaking the law more like." said Danny.

"You caught me for anything?"

"We have now," Maaike said.

"Slap on the wrist." he smiled.

"I don't think so, how come you weren't deported?" Maaike asked.

"Just lucky I suppose," the smile stayed.

"Do you think your luck will hold?" asked Danny.

"Who knows?" the smile remained.

"We have two missing women." Maaike tried.

"I read the news."

"Any ideas?"

"Probably dead by now, it's been too long. You know the statistics. What are you police doing about it?"

"We are searching your home as we speak. What will we find?" asked Maaike.

"No women unless my Petra is at home." Adamović replied.

"Petra?" asked Maaike.

"My girlfriend she is in and out."

"Anything else?"

"Well a real surprise; you will see what you see…I've been busy since Wolverpleine."

"Doing what?" asked Danny.

"You'll see…"

"Why stay in Holland Adamović?" asked Danny.

"I love Holland. In Utrecht, there are so many opportunities."

"What about home in Zagreb?" asked Maaike.

"Zagreb? Utrecht is my home." Adamović was adamant.

"How long do you think for?" asked Maaike.

"We shall see…" Adamović replied smugly.

His attitude was getting on their nerves. He seemed to be very confident. He looked up and smiled as there was a knock on the door. Ernst beckoned Danny over. They stood outside.

"OCU say there's a bloody armoury Danny, so far twenty Glock guns and at least fifty percussion grenades. We've no idea what he's planning."

"Or just selling?" Danny wondered. "Thanks Ernst who's got it?"

"Organised Crime they love us; we give them so much." he laughed.

Danny went back into the room Adamović looked up and smiled. Danny whispered to Maaike what Ernst had just told him.

"Buying or selling Adamović?" asked Maaike.

"Do you want to buy?" he asked.

"You're probably right about not going back to Zagreb, not for a few years anyway." Danny said.

"Look policeman I can help you. I do not have the women as your men have seen."

He was so smooth, so smug, thought Maaike. How had he been able to get away with this for so long? Police intelligence wasn't very good if this was the case; he had dropped off the radar completely to make his fortune. Someone must've known something about him.

Danny and Maaike left him and reported to Caes. He was just as surprised as they had been. As they left the room they were passed by Commissaris Coeman. He didn't look happy. It was followed by Rijsbergen. Caes knew he worked the AVD, Dutch secret services, but why were they in the building Caes wondered.

"Boss can I help?" asked Caes.

"Rijsbergen has a request..."

"Well not really a request, good to see you Caes." Rijsbergen said.

"Tell me what you want first." Caes said knowing this would not be good.

"Adamović is one of our..." Rijsbergen started.

"A rapist!" Caes exploded.

"Needs must Caes."

"A bloody rapist! This had better be good Rijsbergen."

"He's worked for us for nearly a year, a middleman in various deals, various lots of Intel we're working on with the Americans..." Rijsbergen explained.

"So that's fine then..." Caes snapped.

"Caes..." Coleman warned.

"So I'll take Adamović home now that the OCU have left his flat I'm glad they were so discreet." Rijsbergen smiled.

"You're welcome; close the door after you." Said the Commissaris. He sat down.

"Baas..." started Caes.

"I know Caes my hands are tied."

"He raped two women."

"He served his time."

"What kind of a punishment is it to be taken up by the AVD?"

"They are bastards, but they are on our side."

"You think?" Caes asked.

"Caes I have to think that; otherwise... Anyway, he is under surveillance by the AVD. It doesn't appear he's our man."

There was a banging on the door; Ernst burst in

"*Baas* they... Oh sorry, Commissaris..."

"Sit down Ernst. Caes could you call in Danny and Maaike I'll try to explain." Coeman said quietly.

Explain he did, but it didn't convince any of them. Coeman wasn't happy. None of them were, but at least he had been ruled out of the enquiry. This was when they had to think of the greater good in this case for some stupid silly plot that they would probably never hear about. Well, time alone would tell.

The Twilight club was not an actual club in the real sense, no premises, it was a virtual club. Using the password, Caes was able to access it from the so called Dark Net. From what little he understood about this, most of the Web's information is buried far down on sites, and standard search engines do not find it. Traditional search engines cannot see or retrieve content in the Dark Net, he remembered hearing at a briefing that the Dark Net was several orders of magnitude larger than the surface Web, it was all quite frightening to think there was this level of hidden information just floating about and that anyone could use it for what wasn't always very nice things. Maybe the Child Protection Unit had already seen this one, but Caes would pass this over to them before the end of the day. It made him retch, jpegs of suffering and contact details, all encrypted he supposed, so no immediate leads. It was like looking for a needle in a filthy rotten haystack. Caes rang the CPU and they followed his instructions, they had the manpower to access this information and the expertise to access the encryptions, so maybe some good would come out of it. They would let him know who they found as soon as they could. Caes thanked them and shivered, he did not envy them their task.

    What puzzled Caes was why he had got access to this club from a stranger. What was the point? Spliker could and probably would have found this site at any time he wanted to, why had someone given it to him? Why also was the person who gave it to him so enigmatic that they didn't actually exist? What Truus had said the other day about there being no real link at all, that these were two separate incidents struck him. Why Thijs's daughter? They were kind of estranged, but did have minimal contact. The other two didn't, one was an orphan, and the other ones only relative lived in the United States. So, was there a target? If there was, it had to be Sterre. Caes decided to see Thijs again.

Zoutmarket, 11.35.

Maaike and Freddie were patrolling down Zoutmarket. The ridiculous statue of the old farmer's wife and her chickens wore an extra coat of snow, but still looked out of place. Like so many statues in Utrecht it had its story, but it looked so weird.

    "I am so cold, Freddie." Maaike moaned.

    "Pity we can't just stop and go for a coffee."

    "I need more than that, I need a log fire."

    "A bed." Suggested Freddie.

    "Yes a four poster, I need a four-poster bed." Maaike smiled.

    "Double duvet."

    "Double duck down duvet!" Maaike was making herself laugh.

    "Very impressive alliteration, Maaike!"

    "I'm not just a pretty face!" Maaike grinned.

    "No sister, you are so much more than."

Freddie grinned back at her.

"On duty remember!"

"A hot drink!"

"Shall I get a coffee?" Maaike asked.

"No, I'll..." Freddie started.

Maaike spotted someone she knew.

"Shove off, Freddie..."

"Why?"

"I just need to talk to this girl... alone."

It was Jeltje, her nose had been bleeding and she had been crying. Maaike took her frozen arm and led her towards Coffee Company. She pulled away at first but then gave in. She was dressed for a summer's day in the freezing snows of Utrecht. Maaike sat her down, demanded that she stay put, pointed to Freddie as a warning and got two coffees.

"What's happened?" Maaike asked though it was rhetorical, she could plainly see.

"I did it again."

"So he hit you again?"

"It's all my fault, he only does it because he loves me." Jeltje said childlike.

"Jeltje, he doesn't love you, he is a bastard."

"No..."

"See that big lump of a police agent over there?"

She pointed to Freddie who gave a silly wave.

"Now he loves me. He takes care of me. Do you see any bruises on my face, is my nose bleeding?"

"No, but..." Jeltje started.

"If he touched me I would chop his balls off. He knows that, but he loves me so much that he would never, ever touch me."

"But..."

"He would never, ever touch me, he would never, ever hit a woman..."

Truus emphasised each word.

"If you did wrong?"

"What could I do that is so wrong to deserve a beating? What did you do that was so wrong? Jeltje, it makes no sense?"

"I... I'm not sure, I didn't have enough money again last night, I don't..."

Jeltje dissolved into tears. Nineteen? Dressed like a thirteen-year-old and probably not too much older. This was awful, it was breaking her heart. Maaike made a decision.

"I can help, Jeltje, I want to help, but you need to want to be helped."

"I don't know, I'm scared. Look at my face, look what he did to me, and it hurts so much, look at my arms."

She showed Maaike the bruises.

"Look at my tummy."

She pulled up her skimpy blouse to reveal black and blue bruises all over her tiny frame.

"Look at me, he kicked me. It made me be sick it hurt so much. He said he didn't want to do it, but…"

"I can see." Maaike grimaced inwardly.

"He still said he loved me, that he didn't want to hurt me."

"But he did hurt you and he will again, come on, Jeltje." Maaike said.

"I just don't know what to do. I'm just so frightened of him."

"I can help you. I promise I can keep you safe from him, at my own place if you want. You can't carry on like this, you don't deserve this. He cannot do this to you again."

"No, I don't deserve this at all, he said he loved me, he said it was forever, but he hurts me, he hurts me all the time…" Jeltje started to cry.

"That's not love, Jeltje, love is being safe, feeling trust for your lover. Look at him out there, how could he want to harm a fly? He loves me, I love him. We take care of each other. We keep each other safe. Do you ever feel safe?"

"No, never, not for a long time, I just feel so scared. I hate what I do; he tells me if I love him it is alright. It's not is it?"

"No, Jeltje, it's not alright. It never was. We'll go to Kroonstraat and sort this out. Is that oké?" Maaike started to take off her outer coat to wrap it around Jeltje's slim shoulders, just as Freddie came in with his coat off all ready for her.

"Too cold for you, Maaike, let her have mine, keep yours."

Jeltje just stood and sobbed into her cupped hands. Maaike put her arm around her and they went out into the freezing cold. She hoped to god this would work out, did Jeltje have the will to see it through? She hoped so.

Particulier Onderzoeks Bureau, 14.30.

At first it was a horrible, low moaning, then her begging, then her terrified whimpering followed by a scream so loud that it split the air. A cry so full of pain, Caes just didn't want to imagine what had caused it. He switched the player off.

"No message, Thijs?"

"My God, my Sterre," Thijs said, sobbing.

Truus was white faced. Caes squeezed her hand.

"No, no message, just that..." Thijs stammered.

"Bastard," Caes said, "Thijs, at least we know she is..."

"Alive? Alive to suffer like that, alive?"

"I'll get coffee..." Truus said, just trying to ease the atmosphere.

"Not for me, lieverd," Caes said,

"Thijs, at least we now know she's alive, hang on to that, man."

"Yes," Thijs slurred, "Hang on to that..."

So finally, we had part of it. Thijs was a target, or the target. There was nothing from the other two girls. Perhaps they were not linked, but if not, who would take them off the street and why? Was Thijs the End Game? Or would we hear from Elise and Gisele's kidnapper soon? But why had they targeted Thijs? Who had he upset? No one for quite a while if he was to be believed and I honestly could not see any of the low life junkies or pushers that he had slapped around in the distant past having the balls to do anything like this. Who had he stepped on in his police days or in his slide into drugs, or was it something he had done recently in his new business.

"Thijs, I'll need to look at all of your cases over the last five years and lists of clients who you've upset if any, what the outcome was of each case. Do you keep that kind of information?"

"I do, lists of names, contacts, results of inquiries, but not if I've stepped on anyone's toes, I've never had a section for that."

"How many cases you had?"

"Over the years? Maybe two hundred and fifty, sixty..."

"Oké, do you want this official?"

"I'm not..."

"I can check this for you, Thijs, I can see if anything jumps out. It can help me get to know your business as well," Truus said.

Horst Vos was not a nice man and had never ever been a nice man, but he had done very well for himself no matter how hard the police had tried. Even when Thijs had broken his jaw he had still been a success. For Thijs that was the last straw after Spilker, the attack on Horst saw Thijs thrown out, that and the stash of drugs that Thijs had taken from him, though for some reason Horst had never pushed for their return.

Anyway, despite everything the Utrecht police did, Horst did even better and was well thought of in certain low life areas of Utrecht.

"Well, Horst, how's business?" Madelon Verloet asked.

"Why am I here?"

"Just wanted a bit of a chat, to catch up." Madelon replied.

"About?"

"Business?"

"Going well, *dankjewel*, but you could have asked me on the phone, not dragged me in here."

"Any upsets lately, any problems?" Caes said.

"From the police?"

"Anywhere, the Turks? The Moroccans?" Madelon asked.

"Why should you care?"

"If you are happy, Horst, we are happy," Caes said.

"That's shit!"

"Well less blood on the streets if you are happy," Madelon said.

"Thijs Orman?" Caes asked.

"What about him?"

"Busted you up badly." Madelon interjected.

"A long time ago, Hoofdinspecteur, a long time, I've forgiven him. It's forgotten."

He smiled a rather sickening smile.

"Really?" Madelon asked, genuinely surprised.

"Yes, why hold a grudge?"

"I'm told you don't hold them for long." Caes said.

"Not sure what you mean."

"Anyone crosses you…" Madelon implied.

"Rumours, slander, I'm legit, and you know that."

"I know something, Horst." Caes said coldly.

"What's that?"

Vos answered in kind, confident in his position.

"Thijs Orman, you spoken to him?" Madelon asked.

"Had contact with him?" Caes tried.

"About what?"

"Anything. You do remember him?"

"Yea, but why should I bother…"

"His daughter…" Madelon started.

"Hold on now!" for the first time Vos was concerned.

"His daughter has disappeared."

"Hey, don't try to pin..."

He was suddenly angry.

"What?" Caes asked.

"It's nothing to do with me!"

"But your jaw," Madelon said, "Weren't you just a little bit miffed?"

"What would the point be now? If I had been bothered and it's a big if, Thijs Orman would have got his, a long time ago." Vos snarled.

"Really?"

"Yea, now though? There's no point now. He's nothing, no threat to me, so what would be the point."

And of course, he had a point, Caes looked at Madelon, she shrugged.

"Look," Vos said, "You think you know what I do. What would be the point in upsetting an old friend of the police? Why would I make things worse by getting involved with an ex-cop? You would still consider him your own. I know when to turn the other cheek." He smiled grimly, but he didn't understand the irony of his statement.

Caes believed him, not that he wanted to, but they let him go. Caes knew he had other faults and knew they would get him eventually, but not for this. Not this time.

Madelon shrugged,

"Well not him then?"

"Not for this I don't think."

"Maaike!" Madelon saw her at the end of the corridor,

"Maaike, that was a win with Jeltje?"

"I hope so," Maaike smiled thinly. "I had to pretend my own twin brother was my boyfriend for effect."

"Well it worked. Did you hear what she did, Caes?" Madelon asked.

"Yes, that was good work, Maaike."

"I felt so sorry for her." Maaike said.

"But you must try not to get too emotionally involved, Maaike," said Madelon.

"If I hadn't she wouldn't have come in, I had to get emotional. It's no life for a young girl like that."

She was right, if she hadn't showed she had cared, Caes didn't think that the girl would have changed her mind.

"Bureau Jeugdzorg involved?" Caes asked.

"Yes, they will be meeting with her and her parents." Maaike replied.

"Well Maaike, take on the role of *familierecherheur* in this case, liaise with family and the Bureau.

What about her family?" asked Caes

"Parents? They love her, can't understand how she got into this mess..." Maaike replied.

"Did they never see the bruises?" asked Caes.

"Obviously not, girls can be very clever..." said Maaike.

"Deceitful more like." Madelon said.

"It's this weird sense of secrecy that seems to be pervading everything at the moment. Thijs Orman has no idea about his daughters' life, the missing girl's no one knows about them. I don't understand where its leading to..." Caes was frustrated.

"The worst thing is she is just fifteen, *baas*. They had no idea she was doing this. She still lives at home. Madness..."

"Jesus, are we charging him?" Madelon asked angrily.

"Still not sure, baas, she is not sure." Maaike shrugged.

"Christ, how do people not know? Parents? Her school? How?" Caes asked.

"People can keep secrets, Caes," said Madelon, "We all have them, you'd be surprised."

"I hope not, is she too scared to testify?"

"I'm not too sure, maybe..." Maaike said.

"We cannot blame her if she doesn't, well keep me posted. That was excellent, Maaike, well done." Caes said.

Oudegracht, 19.10.

It was the mindless answers to questions that Freddie hated most. It seemed utterly pointless, the questions went out, and the answers came in. You'd think that was a good thing, but the answers bewildered him sometimes.

"Just like my sister..."

"Seen her in McDonald's just now..."

"She works in my office..."

Everything had to be followed up, all would prove fruitless. It was the looking without seeing that sent him into despair. All they could do was suggest answers that bore no relation to the question. In fact, they could be answering a totally different question at times and Freddie wondered what exactly he had asked them. She wasn't his sister. She did not work at the local McDonald's, there was no one like her at the office. He knew this but would still have to check. Where did they get this from? Who did they think they were helping? Were they just saying this to please him or to get rid of him? He was at a loss. He smiled grimly at the thought of how Truus had got on. She had received only negative replies. They all seemed to be going nowhere and of course it began to snow again. The cobbled path so assiduously swept some hours ago was starting to dust over again like icing sugar on a sponge cake. Freddie sniffed in despair. He looked ahead and smiled as he recognised his sister at once although her head was covered in a thick striped scarf, he knew the tiny tutu like skirt she was wearing over similarly coloured striped tights and the big black Doc Martens. He couldn't fathom her, he was so cold, but she must be freezing. Her hands were stuffed inside her hoody and her head was down. When he called, she looked up startled, before breaking out in her usual beautiful smile.

"Freddie, you lump! You scared me." Said Maaike.

"Could have been a mugger, Maaike, stay alert!" he laughed.

She snorted loudly,

"Let them try. How you doing?"

"Not very well, just finishing for the night. You clubbing?"

"Judo." Maaike smiled.

Freddie saw the ruck sack between her shoulder blades.

"On your own?"

"Nosey!"

"Could be with the Pope for all I care." Freddie scoffed.

"No, he's busy. I'm on my own."

"Shall I walk you there?"

"No, you get back to Kroonstraat and home. I'll be fine." Maaike said.

"Never doubted it, sis!" he grinned again.

Already he felt a bit better. Maaike seemed to have that about her.

"I'll see you at breakfast, Freddie. Bright and early."

She reached up and kissed his cheek, then melted into the snow.

Freddie shivered. He brushed the thickening snow from his greatcoat and headed back to the station. He stepped between shoppers and cyclists and kept his eyes open. He wasn't sure what for, as all he could see were figures shrouded by drifting snow as if in some monochrome cartoon. Heads down over shopping bags or handle bars, not looking up. No wonder the girls weren't recognised by anyone; he was surprised that they even recognised their own feet.

He turned into Steenwerg, when he saw two struggling figures, then he heard a scream and a yelp of pain. He got to the couple and grabbed the man's arm as he was about to bring it down on the girl. There was blood on the girl's face, he twisted the arm up behind the man's back.

"Calm down!" Freddie ordered.

"Bitch bit me!"

The girl took her chance and threw herself at him and booted him in the groin.

"Bitch kicked you!" she screamed.

Freddie couldn't help but laugh but regained control, "Steady now, Meneeren."

The man dropped to the ground groaning. Freddie had to let him go or break his arm. There was no more need to restrain him as he rolled into a foetal position and put his hands between his legs moaning softly.

The girl muttered,

"He jumped me, I bit him, he…"

Suddenly all the fight left her and she started to cry. Freddie put his arm around her and reached for his radio. Soon Steenwerg was heavy with medics and police.

Steenwerg, 20.15.

Caes wandered over to the shivering attacker, prone on the snowy pavement. His hands handcuffed, he was groaning. An ambulance had pulled up, blocking us from the onlookers.

"Bitch kicked me, I'll sue…"

Caes looked around then kicked him. He knew he shouldn't but this man was pathetic. A bully and a liar. He looked up at Caes.

"We can all have a go. You can sue us all. But you'll be in Wolverplein, so shut the fuck up." Caes snapped.

"You have no…"

"Don't give me any shit!"

Caes had suddenly felt really angry. It was like a dam had broken. He wasn't sure if this was a breakthrough or not, but a lot of tension had been building up over the past few days and it seemed to be escaping due to this.

Caes looked up and called Danny over,

"Put him in a car and take him to Kroonstraat." Caes said.

"I need a hospital…" the man whined.

"Count 'em and get up!" Danny snarled. He jerked the man to his feet. He immediately doubled up and was sick in the snow.

Caes was exasperated,

"Get the *paramedicus* to give him a check over. We'll do what they say."

"Brutality that's…"

Danny wrenched his manacled arm up his back,

"Don't start again, let's move!"

Madelon was talking to the girl. Freddie was standing nearby.

"Good work, Freddie." Caes said.

"No, baas, she did it all, very brave…"

He nodded towards the girl who looked up and smiled at him, sending his cheeks crimson.

"Who's the man?"

Flustered, Freddie handed Caes the man's ID.

"Jeroeme Verharon, lives around the corner. Married with two children."

"Charming! Do you know him, *Mevrouw*?" Caes asked the girl.

"Lotte de Vries, no I've never seen him before."

"Where do you live, *Mevrouw* de Vries?" Asked Madelon.

"The other side of town in Venuslaan."

Was he stalking her Caes wondered? He spoke to Freddie,

"Can you take a statement back at Kroonstraat, act as *familierecherheur* and then take *Mevrouw* de Vries home?"

"Pleasure, sir,"

Freddie said and then went red again. Caes rang the DA and told her what had happened.

"A breakthrough?"

There was excitement in her voice.

"We shall see, not sure. Do you want to attend the interview?"

Luckily she left them to it.

Kroonstraat Police Bureau, 21.47.

Caes switched on the tape,

"It's twenty-one forty-seven, present Hoofdinspecteur…"

All the information the state required before they could get down to the real business.

"You declined an *advocaat*?" Madelon asked.

"Yes," he mumbled.

"Please speak up for the tape." Madelon instructed.

"You knew…" Caes said.

"Who?" Verharon sounded puzzled.

"The woman you attacked?"

"I don't…" Verharon started.

"Don't know her?" Caes said.

"No, didn't attack her!"

"You were seen, *meneer* Verharon." Madelon said.

"It was a misunderstanding." Whined Verharon.

"Seen by one of my officers." Caes said.

They waited, minutes passed.

"I wanted to ask her the way home. I was lost." Verharon tried.

"You live two hundred metres away."

"You had the girl in a headlock. Where is the misunderstanding?" Madelon said.

"She wanted sex." Verharon snapped.

"*Heren* Verharon, that is so unlikely to be laughable." Madelon said.

"What do you mean?" Verharon was upset.

"Look at yourself. Why would an attractive woman...?" Madelon said smiling.

"How dare you!"

Verharon was outraged. Madelon made me laugh inside.

"I dare because it is nonsense, just tell us the truth so we can move on."

"She bit me," Verharon whined again.

Caes was getting sick of his self-pity. Madelon even more so,

"What was she to do? Let you rape her?" Madelon said.

"I never intended…"

"*Heren* Verharon, you were seen. Arm around her throat. You were attacking her, metres from your home."

He suddenly looked crestfallen.

"I didn't mean…" Verharon started.

They waited again.

"I don't know what happened." Verharon finally added.

"You had decided though, you wanted sex." Madelon said bluntly.

"No... yes... no, I have no idea what I was doing."

"Have you been drinking?" asked Madelon.

"Not a drop." Verharon was adamant.

"So you decided whilst sober to have sex with this woman who you had never seen before?" Madelon said.

He looked at us like a goldfish, his eyes glazing over.

"I am so sorry; I don't know what... a brainstorm... I've never..."

Which was true, he had never done anything like this before. Caes opened a file and placed the three missing women's photographs on the desk in front of him.

"Do you recognise these women?" Caes asked.

He stared at the three smiling women. A flicker of recognition lit in his eyes.,

"No... wait..."

Caes felt his heart leap. Was this the man? Would he admit to taking them?

"They've been all over the news and the papers."

"You don't know them?"

"Wait a minute...I know nothing about..." Verharon was suddenly terrified.

"You attack a woman in the street. Unprovoked, but know nothing about these three." Madelon asked.

"That's right." Verharon almost shouted.

"Why should we believe you?" Caes said.

"On my children's lives..." whined Verharon.

"Don't!" Madelon warned.

"I have no idea." Verharon said.

"We will speak to your wife." Caes said.

"No..." he groaned, "Can't we?"

"What, cover this up?" Madelon asked.

"Make it all go away?" Caes followed up.

"Pretend it didn't happen?" Madelon sneered.

"I don't know what happened to me. I'm sorry."

At last an apology, but to the wrong person.

"We need a DNA swab."

"But why?"

"You committed a sex crime. Do you not understand?"

"I... yes..." Verharon muttered, then started to cry.

Madelon had no sympathy,

"You were man enough when you had her at your mercy."

Caes showed him another photograph and asked,

"Do you know Thijs Orman?"

"Orman? No."

"He was a police officer." Caes said.

"Never had a problem with the police."

Verharon started to cry again.

"He has a daughter, Sterre."

Caes pointed to her photograph.

"Never seen her except on the news."

"Sure?" Caes said.

"Why would I lie?" Verharon said.

"Well you have already."

"I... I was wrong. I did attack the girl. I have no idea why. But she bit me..."

Caes sighed, Verharon really was pathetic, but he felt nothing for him.

"Don't start again..."

He had nothing more to say. Caes pressed a buzzer and the Duty Officer came in.

"DNA swab, then holding cell for *Heren* Verharon."

"Sir, Heren Verharon, this way please."

They left the room.

"Pathetic!" Madelon snarled.

"Yes, but is he our man?"

"Hard to tell, but I doubt it. He's not got the balls for all this. Fine when he's got one on her own. All power until he has no power..." Madelon said.

"So not our man?" Caes sighed.

"Don't reckon so. I'll go to his wife. What a pleasant meeting that will be."

"If it is him, where would they be?" Caes pondered aloud.

"Well I can ask his wife." Madelon smiled.

"You do that. If it isn't him though they may be dead already. Even Sterre, we have no idea."

Caes was trying hard to be positive, but listening to himself he knew he was starting to fail.

There was a knock on the door. The *Oficier van Justitie*, put her head around the door. She wanted to know what they had got so far. She wasn't at all like the DA's you see in American crime films, but did roughly the same job. Marie Hartmann was a high-flier, she was in her early thirties and a very attractive, athletic woman. Apparently, she played hockey for Utrecht, you could see by the shape of her legs that she could run. She smiled, but Caes was not fooled. She was a bit like a barracuda.

"Caes, Madelon..." she nodded, "What news?"

"Not our man." Madelon said firmly,

"He's too pathetic, back to square one." Caes added.

"What now then?" Marie Hartmann asked.

"I'm off to see his wife." Said Madelon.

"I'm going home." Caes said.

"Madelon, do you want company?" Marie Hartmann offered.

"Yes, if you're not too busy, don't fancy dealing with a hysterical wife on my own,"

Madelon smiled, relieved. She hadn't been looking forward to this.

Totale Judo dojo, Balearen, 22.20.

"It is the routine that makes us better."
How many times had she heard her sensei say this Maaike wondered as she used O-Soto-Gari to turn her opponent onto his back?

"Repeat skill, repeat skill, you get better..." Sensei said quietly.

She was slammed onto the mat by her opponent, but bounced back up onto her toes to repeat the move. They alternated the throw, it was a real killer. Fatigue hit and it became harder, but there was no chance to relax. It was throw, be thrown, bounce up from the mat, and repeat your part. She smiled across at her partner, Jordi. He grinned back. She liked working with him, there was no patronising. He had only respect for her. So, he should, she was a black belt after all. She wiped her face with her sleeve, her eyes stung from the sweat that seemed to be flooding from her body every time she hit the mat. Her hair was wet and getting in her eyes. She pulled her suit tighter and rewrapped her obi, she was so proud of it. Jordi looked as tired as she felt. Her internal organs must be mush by now constantly reverberating against her insides, but it was her turn to hit the mat. Regaining her feet, she bounced on her toes. Bowed and stepped forward engaging his arms and down he went again. She felt she wanted more aggression from her partner, she wanted a fight. All the drills made sense, but she loved the rough and tumble of a proper fight. Trying to outwit her opponent, rather than just swap roles. She finally had her chance as they lined up to face opponents.

At last, thought Maaike and she counted along the line opposite to see who she would be fighting. Others chatted, she watched and thought. She tucked her jacket into her belt again and breathed deeply. It was Dirk, bigger and so much stronger than her, she knew from battles of old.

Her turn came, they bowed. It took him over four minutes to finally best her. She loved it. Trying to outwit him. To be quicker, more agile she had all that. Her judo brain was an extra muscle, but he was too big and wore her down. They bowed and made their way to the back of the line. She replayed the bout in her mind, moving her head as she went through what she had done. How could she beat him? She often thought this and smiled to herself. She pictured what she could do and what his counters would be, then imagined herself countering his moves. He was slow and methodical, she could try to tire him out with her speed as he must have used a lot of energy against her, but that was a risky tactic as had just been proved.

Then she pictured another way and thought it just might work. She bounced up and down on her toes as she waited in line. When the time came, she was on the mat bowing low. Dirk bowed and was at her, too quickly, he was off balance from the start. This time she didn't allow him to engage her arms, she was underneath them and bang! He was down on the mat with an explosion of noise as the air left his body. She bowed even lower than before and then skipped off to the shower.

Vagevuur.

Elise sniffed her clothes again. The smell wasn't getting any better. She felt disgusting. She stank and that made her feel awful. She almost laughed. Here she was kidnapped from her flat and more worried about how she smelt. She suppressed a snigger and then felt tears spark in her eyes. She was a mess. A train wreck. What would people think when she got out of here she wondered. Would she get out of here? She must stay positive, she knew she was in the shit, but she couldn't give in. why was she here., who was the man that she dimly recalled from somewhere. She screwed her eyes together and trued to concentrate. Where had she seen him.? Who was he? Then all she could see was his leering face when he had tried to… she shook off the image and opened her eyes. She rolled over on the mattress and saw the water pipe and thought it had to lead somewhere. She could rip the pipe off the wall and drown herself or, she decided to try and attract attention with the pipe. She pulled off her shoe and started to tap the pipe. She didn't know Morse code. She knew there was the SOS signal, but had no idea how to do it. How stupid she was. What a ridiculous thing not to know it. She began to cry in frustration, but kept knocking her shoe against the pipe, slowly, rhythmically. Would anyone hear her?

Chapter 12

> Maandag, November 17, 2014.
> Gemoedsrust Psychotherapie, 10.05.

We had skipped over the self-harm and suicidal thoughts questions this time. I supposed I would never be a lost cause as long as I kept wanting to stay alive and not cut or harm myself. That was reassuring. Death or depression, perhaps not such a difficult choice for some of us! I could see what Jozefzoon was up to, just being hyper positive about stuff.

"Have you spoken to anyone yet about all of this?"

"No, not yet."

"Why is that do you think?"

I paused, thinking before I answered,

"Shame I think mostly... and I don't want anyone to worry about me... I do feel rather pathetic about this. Weak if I have to be honest. I don't see why my whole world should collapse at any minute..."

"But, Caes, it did collapse when Femke died, we understand that feeling..."

"But that doesn't mean I have to involve anyone else. I want to work this out myself, but I just want to know how..."

Dr Jozefzoon smiled, "But that's my job, I worry about my children all the time! We have said it's an illness not a fad, you didn't decide to become depressed."

"I know, but I don't want to tell anyone, though it is sometimes so hard pretending all is well in the world."

"And that is a problem in itself, Caes, you use so much energy hiding things, you will have to open up eventually. Does talking to me help?"

"Sometimes, though sometimes I feel worse." I smiled. "I just worry..."

"I understand, it's not a simple thing at all is it?"

"Not at all."

"You need to do more things."

"Bit difficult to fit them in though." I complained.

"No, I perhaps mean different things, if you are not careful you will soon only find pleasure in a few things. What if you were to start hating things you did or you hurt an arm and couldn't go to the gym? What would you do? Would you be unhappy? You need other targets. So what about finding..."

Afdeling Pathologie, UMC. 11.00.

Caes hated autopsies; he didn't suppose any one really enjoyed them, except perhaps the *lijkschouwer* who was performing them. It was a cliché, you see it on the TV all the time, stoical copper, fresh faced rookie, all in varying shades of green. Caes smiled tightly. It wasn't fun at all. To be honest though, Grete de Zueew always seemed to enjoy her work, ruddy faced and a real blusterer she was always so full of fun, it was weird or maybe just a defence mechanism for her, she saw a lot of horrible things every day.

"Caes, good to see you, now don't puke, again will you?"

"Once! Just once! My very first! How long ago was that?"

Caes had to protest every time he came here.

"Well it was memorable!"

"How many autopsies have I been to since then?" Caes asked.

Indeed, how many times had he since been to an autopsy? He had lost count and didn't want to remember. They were awful. The bodies, the smell, the crude blanket stitches holding everything in place, the smell. Yes, it was the smell that was the worst thing. Everyone would know you'd been to an autopsy. No one would say anything, but there was an almost universal wrinkling of noses and looks of disgust. Caes was sure he did that himself when he smelt it on others. Caes used to go home after an autopsy and shower for ages, he never wanted Femke to smell it, sometimes he would finish his shower, get dressed and sit down, only to smell that odour again and return to the shower to clean himself all over again. He didn't do that anymore, but still. He shivered.

"Cold, Caes?" Grete smirked.

"Not really, think someone just walked over my grave..." Caes tried to smile.

"Well, you have been a good lad recently, but you never know!" She was loud.

"Madelon, how are you?"

"Fine, Grete, dank." Madelon replied holding back a snigger.

"Well, just one stab wound, in the heart."

"From which angle?" Madelon asked.

"Front, he or she was facing him I think, bruising on the neck, probably where he or she brought him onto the knife."

"Nothing else?"

"A single upward motion, with no hesitation. They were strong. You can see the pattern of the knife on the screen, double bladed, and not unusual."

"Shit!" Caes spluttered.

"Yes, shit indeed, you can buy them anywhere, so nothing I'm afraid."

"Dank, Grete." Caes said.

Caes had to get out to breathe some fresh air.

"One small thing, Caes."

Caes had to turn back.

"I think the killer was wearing surgical gloves or something similar. There is some dust like substance in the wound."

"So not an off the cuff murder, definitely pre-meditated?" Caes asked stupidly.

"Unless they were in the habit of wearing gloves like that, no, Caes!"

Grete was almost patronising, but not quite.

Caes smiled,

"Dankjewel, Grete, as ever you have been invaluable."

"I am here to serve. See you later."

And she was back to the corpse as Madelon and Caes left to find some clean air.

"How can she survive in that atmosphere?"

Madelon asked as we stood in the corridor.

"I think she has disinfectant in her veins." Caes grinned.

Madelon laughed,

"She must be a hard soul the awful things she must see."

"She is the sweetest person you could ever meet, Madelon, she really is. You'll get to see that in time. Though I do wish she'd forget about me being sick!"

That still grated with him, he just hadn't been ready for it and he kicked himself even now as he should have been prepared, he'd seen enough corpses and autopsies before Grete had joined them but had obviously made a big impression on her first day.

Oh well, he thought, glad that was over, Caes made his way to the office of Orman Detectives, plural now that Truus was working there.

Particulier Onderzoeks Bureau, 12.00.

Thijs's record keeping had been surprisingly good. Caes looked over Truus's shoulder as she placed file after file into separate piles. She was taking a bit of a load off the police by doing this, but he supposed it was her case as well so that was fine. Divorce, infidelity, theft at work, neighbour's quarrels, background check ups, surveillance...two hundred and thirty-nine cases over five years. Thijs was quite a successful businessman it seemed. There was nothing much Caes felt he could do so as he went to the door, he called:

"See you later, Truus."

But she was so engrossed in her work that she didn't answer him.

Truus read of how he had watched a Victor Stevens for six weeks. In that time Victor Stevens, hereafter known as the subject, had slept with seven different women, spending an average of seventy-five euros per meal with each of them as he wined and dined them all a total of seventeen times. The subject had hired a car for each date, at an average cost of ninety-two euros a time. Hotel accommodation had totalled over nine hundred euros. Thijs had not recorded the wronged wife's reaction, suffice to say that she was not happy and that divorce proceedings had started. He did not say what the settlement was either, but Truus could imagine. It went on like this, meticulous recordings of dates and times and meals and costs and venues. Truus thought she wouldn't want Thijs on her case.

Then it struck her that if he had been so meticulous in his dealings with these people, why couldn't he have used some of this energy in engaging with his daughter. Sterre was the one who had sided with him through the divorce, the young woman who really needed him. How very sad all of this was for Thijs, for Sterre and for his own wife as well who had just given up on him and gone, when he probably needed her the most too.

Truus looked at the next pink file. Mattias de Boer, the subject, had stolen over six thousand seven hundred euros' worth of electrical equipment from his employer. The subject had just parked his car near a shop fire exit and loaded it up on various nights of the week when he was responsible for locking up the shop. Thijs had photographs of twelve occasions when the subject did this, over a period of five weeks. He had receipts for the equipment that he had purchased back from pawn shops throughout Utrecht and Amstelveen, along with photographs of the subject entering said shops and two street markets where the subject had been selling some of the stolen goods when Thijs could only buy some of the stock back. He had photographs of the other purchasers though. A neat and tidy effort by Thijs. Truus gave him ten out of ten.

Truus phoned Caes with the news she had discovered.

"Well I think this is the lot, seven cases of divorce where the man did really badly out of it so might be miffed, just two women in the same boat. There are four cases where someone got the boot because of Thijs's work. It seems one suicide because of some undercover work Thijs was involved in, may or may not be connected, so what's that, fourteen cases?" Truus had been very thorough.

"What do you think?"

"Well, some are very petty, most are really quite insignificant people."

"That's the thing, they all look it…"

"Yes, I know, we don't know what lies underneath."

"No, well, can you email me a list? I'll send Danny and Adrie to interview them."

"*Oké*, Pappy, right away"

This took them all day and most of the afternoon, but it got them nowhere, they were all insignificant and didn't have the wit to do anything about their anger with Thijs according to both Danny and Adrie. It was another dead end.

Nordse Park, Utrecht, 14.45.

Magda Haan lay dead in the snow. Caes got to the RV point on the outer ring and covered his shoes with blue disposables. He pulled on his gloves as he kept to the track towards the crime scene. Police tape surrounded the it. Danny lifted the tape and Caes made his way into the inner ring. An island of industry, surrounding the small sack like figure that was the victim. She had been stabbed, that much was clear as her dirty, stinky faux fur was soaked in blood, a dark liquid staining the white snow that was starting to cover her, her eyes just staring out at the sky. There was no red as you would have thought, no red on white like in the films, just a dark, dirty patch beneath her dark, dirty coat. A final extinction of her sad life, with her blood oozing out into the snow.

    Caes thought there was a look of surprise on her face. Well it would be a surprise to get stabbed, why would she expect that? What a horrible way to end her sad, lonely life he thought. But why was she there, so far from Vaartsestraat? Meeting someone he supposed by arrangement or did she have the wit to remember where to go? Was she lost or was it planned? Why would anyone kill her, she seemed harmless enough? Technicians scurried about, a tent was being erected over the body, photographs were being taken, measurements written down, casts being made and a nose to the snow search for any clues was being made by a half dozen officers. There had been more snow, so only one trail of footprints, all accounted for and roped off. She had died on a remote island of snow, all alone, as had been her fate all along. Caes gave the boys the usual instructions, and then looked back to Danny who had moved further away to the Rendezvous Point, checking people in as they entered the outer ring of the crime scene. Caes motioned him over and he gave his clipboard to another cop who was in uniform and strode towards him.

    "Danny, we need to get to her house on Vaartsestraat."

He nodded agreement and they made towards the car. I knew that this was not going to be pleasant.

Vaaterstraat, 16.00.

Marie Hartmann, was already there. She looked stern and business like, but her welcoming smile was warm. Caes held the door open and the stale smell of neglect eased its way into the street almost making me want to take a deep breath before entering. It was dark and uninviting. He looked for the lights and switched them on. There were no shades around the bulbs, it was so depressing.

Her house smelt as badly as she had smelt. Caes expected there to be cats, dozens of them for some reason, but no, it was her smell. The place was filthy; she had old food on all the surfaces, dirty plates and dishes everywhere, no bulbs in many of the sockets, dead candles everywhere. Windows with old sun stained Utrecht's newspapers covering them, instead of normal curtains. What had she done, who had she threatened, what the hell? How an earth could she have ever been a threat to anyone about anything?

Danny had gone upstairs and found it was the same, nothing, but the higher you went up into the house, the less furniture there was. Four storeys, all for one woman, and she had nothing to show for the whole of her singular life, just grime and rotten food and the stink. Christ, what an existence. The top floor was completely empty and surprisingly clean, save for the dust. It was also very quiet, nothing to disturb anyone except a faint steady tapping from the ancient heating system. Though in here it was freezing cold, so it must be next doors.

Caes shivered and wandered back into the main part of the house. Hardly any mail, a few bank books with very little invested. Her pension, little else. A few bills, nothing outstanding. Nothing outstanding at all, nothing for all those years, what a sad lonely house for a sad lonely woman. The house was quiet save for the incessant knocking of the water pipes. As they left Marie Hartmann sighed.

"Not a lot to look forward to, Caes?"

He smiled thinly.

"It all depends on what you leave behind I suppose…"

"She had no one obviously."

"That is sad, but we can't live other's lives for them."

"But should we be doing more for people like her, people who have slipped through the net?" Danny asked.

"In what way? She lived her life. We have no idea if she was happy or sad. She was I know confused, but what can society do for her?" Hartmann said.

"Make an effort I suppose, look out for people like her, give her friendship…" Danny said.

"It's not so easy is it? Would she want assistance? Would she even realise she needed it and really, who are we to say she does?"

Vos Holdings, 16.45.

Horst Vos was obviously more relaxed in his office. Madelon had Maaike with her and they sat opposite Vos sipping coffee. Vos was at ease on home turf, relaxed on his throne. He looked down on the two women. He didn't realise that there was no way they would be intimidated by him.

Madelon spoke.

"Since we last met, anything come to you?"

"Nothing *Hoofdagent* Verloet. Like I told you…"

"After Orman took your drugs…"

"I never said he took anything…"

"Strange that Orman said he had then." Madelon said.

"Trying to make his assault sound better."

"Perhaps, but then why would he use them?"

"He was a junkie; still could be for all we know. Have you considered his alibis?" Vos snapped.

"Alibis? Why more than one?" asked Maaike.

"Two women, two murders…"

"Are they all connected?" Maaike followed up.

"What do you think?"

"What do you hear *Heren* Vos?" asked Maaike.

"Nothing really."

He squirmed in his chair. There was a pause. The silence seemed to lengthen in the room. The two women were daring Vos to break it. He finally gave in.

"No one knows anything. Rumours about drug dealing…" Vos offered.

"Yours?" asked Maaike.

"A new man trying to enter the field… don't know if it's true." Said Vos.

"From where?"

"Not sure, lone wolf perhaps…" Vos said.

"And you are going to allow that?"

"I'm not sure that I understand. If I know of drug dealing I will be sure to let you know." He smiled.

Maaike smiled back pleasantly, but her smile seemed to disconcert Vos.

"That's very generous *Heren* Vos. You didn't always act with such public spirit."

"Young lady. I am a business man. I have laid all my cards on the table. You think you know about me, but your facts are wrong. My business is legit."

"So we keep being told Heren Vos, but your name keeps cropping up." Madelon smiled sweetly.

"Has anything stuck?" he smiled again.

"It will one day, you can't be lucky all the time." Maaike said sharply.

"My business was never about luck ladies. Look, as I said before. If and it's a big if, if I had wanted to sort Orman out I would have done it years ago. His daughter? That's not my style. If I was involved in any funny business, I would never hurt a woman. I love women." He showed his teeth with his smile.

Maaike finished her coffee and placed it on the table next to her. She looked at Vos. His smile started to fade. She didn't take her eyes off him. He was still looking a little disconcerted. He almost jumped as Madelon asked.

"What's your next project Heren Vos?"

"Importing goods, that's where the money is." Vos replied.

"Anything in particular?"

"Not women that's for sure. No, we do a lot of work with the new markets, Poland, Slovakia, old iron curtain states. There's a lot of profit there."

"You know Vaartsestraat?" Maaike asked.

"Not really, I'm more of a Western Utrecht type as you can see."

He waved his hand around his office.

"You live this side of the city?" asked Madelon.

"Close by, as you know. I don't stray far from here."

"For safety reasons?"

"Ladies, really. No one can intimidate me or my family. I just prefer it here. What's the point of having money if you hide away?"

"Indeed. So, you don't hide, you show your face everywhere?" asked Madelon.

"Charity dos, you know the sort of thing. Surely you've seen my face in the papers.?"

"Donating cheques to charities..." Maaike smiled.

"Yes, that sort of thing. I like to give. I like to be in the paper. I don't care if people see my face. I have nothing to hide."

"It appears not." Said Madelon getting to her feet. She proffered her hand and he shook it. He moved his hand towards Maaike, but she had turned her back on him.

"We'll see ourselves out Heren Vos." Madelon smiled.

They sat together in the car.

"He's not our man, is he?" stated Maaike.

"Don't think so. He's highly confident. There again he is a psychopath and knows nothing better." Madelon smiled.

"What about the suggested drug dealing?"

"Covering his back perhaps?" pondered Madelon.

"Or maybe someone is trying to move onto his turf and he's letting us know."

"But why, how would that help him?"

"Takes our noses off the scent…" Maaike said.

"Well he stinks to high heaven!"

"I know, all that money, most through crime. Why can't we nail him?"

"Too clever by half. That'll be his undoing. He will make a mistake." Madelon said.

"Like Al Capone and his taxes." Maaike started to giggle.

"Yes!" laughed Madelon,

"Something really mundane. Unpaid parking tickets or dog fouling the path." Maaike laughed with her.

"Can you get ten years for dog fouling?" Maaike wondered aloud.

Home of Laure Vossen, Haarlem, 17.35.

Caes took his car to visit Laure Vossen in person. Haarlem was sixty odd kilometres away and the main drag was quite snow free. She was a poisonous faced woman and was not welcoming. They had known each other when Thijs was in the force, but only fleetingly. She was not the kind of person you wanted to know. He'd always thought Thijs was well out of it and she didn't disappoint him.

"Caes?" She was a bit brusque.

"I have to do this, Laure…"

"Well there's nothing more to add."

"No one who would wish to do you harm?"

"Me?"

"Through Sterre?"

"I've had very little to do with her over the past few years."

"Still…"

"She decided to side with him… she lost me then."

"A bit harsh Laure, she was very young."

"But since then she could have made her peace."

"She's your daughter, Laure."

"She left me when I left Thijs."

"So no one you can think of who would want to hurt you or Sterre?"

"No one."

"Thijs?"

"A lot of the people he upset when he was in the force."

"But it's over five years…"

"I know, but he did upset many."

"No names?" Caes asked.

"He had stopped talking about work. He was taking drugs, was depressed, he was not the man I knew. Sorry, Caes, I have nothing for you."

"Please think Laura…"

"His boss didn't take too kindly to it, I remember that."

"Shall I say anything to Sterre when we find her?"

"You are confident." Laure said.

"I have to be…"

Laure Vossen suddenly started crying.

"I love her, but I don't know her. I'm sorry, Caes…"

Tamada Kick boksene, Johan Buziaulaan Utrecht, 19.00.

Tamada winced; Truus had never seen this happen before. It made her wince, not from pain, but slight panic. She had to admit that it had been a really great kick, but what on earth had she done? Why had she used it on Tamada of all people? Then he smiled. *Oh God*, she thought, *not the smile!*

She bobbed her head to the side as he attempted a high kick, then she weaved under the punch that came her way. She bounced on her toes, looking for a chance to kick again, she fell to the floor in an effort to leg sweep him, missed and leapt up before he could pounce. She bounced again, remembering Robbie's words to her. Tamada faked a roundhouse and came at her again with a spin and a high kick. It glanced off her head as she bobbed to the side again, but didn't do enough to stop her. Bob and weave she thought, stay on your toes, bob and weave. She looked through her sweat filled eyes at Tamada. His eyes were flinty black. Hyper concentration above his smiling mouth, though she knew it wasn't really a smile. This time she actually anticipated the super man and stepped back just in time, just as Robbie had shown her, the follow up trademark punch whizzed past her head by a fraction. She was still bouncing on her toes when he caught her full on the temple and sent her crashing to the floor. She hadn't even seen it start, let alone see it finish and hit her. But she certainly did feel it.

Robbie and Pim stood solicitously over her; Tamada had just bowed and was approaching her prone body.

"Nice, Tamada," she muttered.

"Not bad, Truus, you get better. You make me work today."

"You make my head ache today."

Tamada wandered off, Robbie was ecstatic, Pim worried.

"Fabulous, Truus, you actually hurt him today." Robbie helped undo her head guard as Pim took her gloves off for her.

"I know, that's why he hurt me."

"He's not like that, Truus," smiled Robbie.

"I know." Truus said.

"Spoils of war," said Pim, "he won't forget that."

"No he won't, but in a good way, Truus, you may make a fighter yet." Robbie laughed and helped her to her feet.

"Did it knock you out or just stun you?" Pim asked.

"Well it went all black, but that might have been the shadow of his foot or was it his fist? I have no idea."

"Foot, it was a kick," said Pim, "Hell of a kick."

"It had to be, anyway, Truus love, dokters or are you oké?"

"I'm fine, not even dizzy; I think I'll be fine."

"Do you want a lift home?"

"That would be very kind, *dankjewel*, Pim."

Vaartestraat, 20.30.

Maaike and Ernst had revisited Vaartsestraat. It was endless trudging around in the cold meeting blank faces, faces that showed contempt for the police, faces that couldn't care a less, old faces that were lonely and wanted a chat but had nothing to offer. The photographs meant nothing to most people. There were vague looks of recognition, but there was no follow up, no one had seen anyone with the girls. No one had seen Spilker either or anyone unusual. Maaike noted down all the flats and houses she had visited and compared notes with Ernst.

"Still some people who are not in."

"I know; we need to catch them up. I'll find them and phone them."

"Maybe away in the sun to escape the snow?" Maaike suggested.

"Maybe, though there doesn't seem to be a lot of money around here."

"I'd like to be in the sun," Maaike sighed.

"Wouldn't we all young lady, but as we're not, best foot forward."

"Should we widen the canvas?"

"I don't think so for the girls, it all centres around here and there aren't that many shops or houses anywhere near. Over the canal is quite a long way away, but they may have seen Spilker. Do you fancy going over there?"

"Not at all Brigadier Hoewegen …" she smiled at him. "I have nothing better to do."

"Don't be so cheeky Agent Meijer, remember how long it took me to gain my position of power and how far away from it you are…" he grinned back at her.

Minrebroederstraat, 21.05.

"Crime isn't everywhere Danny!" scoffed Maaike as she pushed open the door to The Delft Bar. They had decided to give O'Connells a miss, to try somewhere different, so had decamped just around the corner. Maaike was indignant as Danny seemed to see only the worst. Maaike hoped she was more open in her attitudes.

"Seems to be though, Maaike."

"But only to us as we face it every day it's our job to try to stop it so we must see it."

"So no one else does?" asked Danny.

"Only when it affects them…" shrugged Maaike.

"So that's why they don't help us. No one seems to help anyone today, Maaike."

"But for many if it doesn't affect them, they see no need to get involved. I don't suppose you can blame people for that."

"But it's so shallow." Said Danny.

"I don't think so; people are often scared and don't want to be involved. If they aren't hurt, then they just hope it goes away. Maybe we should ask them?" Maaike smiled as they sat down with Adrie.

"On a normal day, Danny, for normal people…"

"So we aren't normal?" Danny laughed.

"Hardly! You go to work, nothing happens. Still snowing. Do your job. Get home, wife has your evening meal ready. Watch telly, go to sleep. How has any crime affected you?" Maaike said.

"But people complain…"

"What do they complain about? Only when it comes to them. Drugs on the street corner, muggings outside their home or on the way to work. Vandalism. You know how it is. That pickpocketing we had. Me and Freddie were on the lookout…"

"Freddie not so well…" Danny laughed.

"But no one was bothered, they may complain, but they don't do anything. No vigilante groups… but when it effects their home, sending prices down that means something."

"Or if they'd had their wallet stolen."

"Yes…"

"We Dutch are selfish…" Adrie said.

"I'm not, do you know how much this cost me?" asked Freddie as he put a tray of drinks down on the table.

"Not that kind of selfish you *horstwood*!" laughed Maaike.

"Just saying that no one wants to help the police." said Danny

"Tell me about it!" Freddie was annoyed. "The girls who have gone missing, may as well have vanished into thin air. No one knows anything about them. People who live next door to them or who sit next to them at , they know nothing. I don't even think that they try to remember anything. It's out of sight out of mind."

"It's so sad," said Maaike, "It's oké to be quiet and withdrawn, but to be totally ignored as if they'd never existed. It's like they have no value at all."

"Except if this is a kidnapping." Adrie said.

"But there's been no demands. We have no idea how long they've been gone."

"They may even be dead."

"But what is their value and to who?" asked Maaike.

"If we knew that…" Adrie started, then felt better of it, "Anyway its night time at the Delft, let's try to forget work for a bit."

"Just let me get some food!" Freddie said, then, "Maaike, don't take work home. Danny, stop moaning, Adrie, come to the bar with me…"

They disappeared to order and Danny excused himself to go to the toilet.

Maaike sipped her *coka* and looked around. *Yea*, she thought, *everyone has their own lives to worry about why concern yourself with anyone else*. She scanned the room. Music blared over loudspeakers and the big screen was showing a Monday night soccer game. She couldn't make out the teams, but people didn't seem too interested in the match. She thought she recognised an English name, so lost any interest there may have been. Everything was swirling around her, conversation, soccer crowd noise, music. In the corner a man was arguing with a girl. He towered over her and she was obviously crying. Why couldn't people just be nice to each other thought Maaike? She realised the girl was trying to get away from the man as she was pushing at his forearm that was blocking her into the corner. He wouldn't let her move. Maaike looked around, everyone was ignoring them, even those closest to them. She hated this bullying, it was the worst.

She got to her feet and as she got closer she could hear the girl above the noise. She was telling him she wasn't interested and to let her go. The man wasn't listening, he seemed drunk. He leant forward to try to kiss her. Still it was being ignored as the girl turned her face away from him. How could they just sit around? This just reinforced all she had been thinking earlier. If it didn't affect me why should I bother? She knew the answer, because it is wrong and in an instant, she had his wrist up his back in the perfect arm lock and he was squealing in pain.

"Respect her wishes…" hissed Maaike.

"You're breaking…"

"I will break it, now get out!" she manoeuvred him towards the door and shoved him into the snow. The doorman came over aggressively.

"What's going on?" the doorman asked.

"Doing your job mate!" it was Adrie.

"Threatening that girl…" said Maaike, "You need to pay more attention."

"Thought it was a bit of fun…"

"Don't you dare…" snapped Maaike, flashing her ID.

He suddenly looked sheepish under her glare of admonition.

"No, you're right, sorry…"

He went over to the girl who brushed his apology off and then she mouthed '*danke*' to Maaike who grimaced in return.

Maaike watched her go back to a group of friends who had been oblivious to everything. This was the problem thought Maaike, no one notices. The three missing girls, the girl in the bar. She was surrounded by dozens of people and no one saw a thing or if they did they had ignored it. Was someone in the know about the missing girls? Were they ignoring something that had happened? Was Danny right? She sighed, even those paid to keep an eye open like the doorman misread signs, either intentionally as they didn't want a fuss or unintentionally as they didn't understand what was happening. Maaike asked herself are they not being taught the signs? What is the right way to behave, why did men feel they had the right to act like this? What was happening in their world?

Freddie sat down, "Maaike, you have to be careful…"

"Don't Freddie, no one was helping her."

"I know, but…"

"Don't... you know I had to help. Is it fair for someone to behave like that?"

"Of course not, Maaike, but..."

"Even if I wasn't in the police I would have helped out. We were brought up that way."

"I know. You're right as always." He smiled.

"Don't patronise me, Freddie, but I am." She laughed.

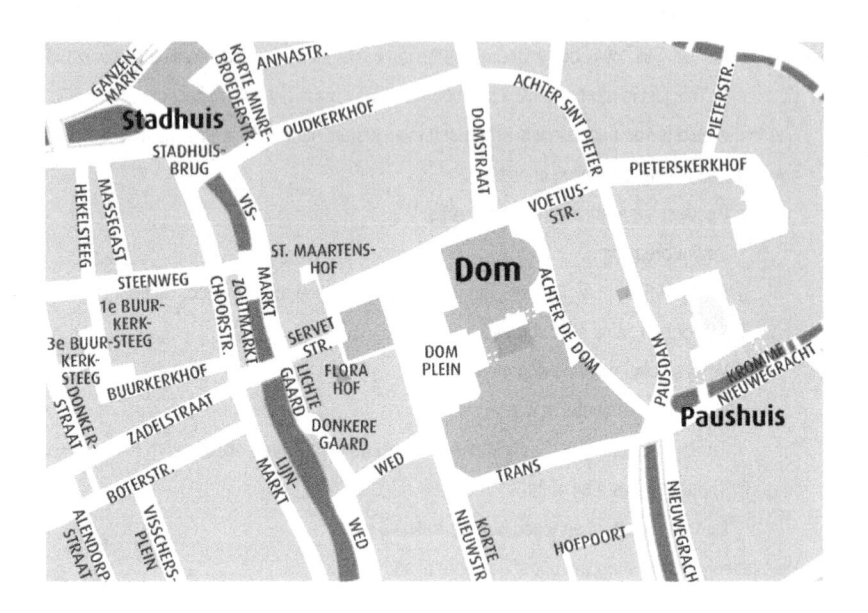

Domplein 22.15

Looking up at the Dom tonight made Caes feel as if he was inside a snow globe. He felt a little dizzy as it was so high, but with the light refracting through the heavy lumps of snow he wondered if he was going to get tipped up on his head for the snow to clear. The snow slowly drifted down onto the ground and would soon freeze underfoot unless the brave municipal workmen came out to clear it again. It was like the famous boy with his finger in the dyke, they would never stop it all. It was madness to try. Tyres were compressing the snow on the road between the Dom Toren and the Domkerk it would soon be impossible to drive down the ice fields as they became death traps. Caes shivered and brushed fresh snow from his coat, wishing he had his gloves on as the cold bit into his fingertips like tiny frozen daggers. He pulled his collar high. He hadn't realised how cold it was and stamped his feet to shock some warmth back into his body.

Caes turned from the Dom and even though it was so close he could hardly see the Domkerk across the road through the storm. The wind was whipping up snow from the ground and beginning to howl, unless that was his own moans. The number two bus sprayed him with slush on its way to the museum quarter and Caes decided to move to warmer climes. Maybe Spain, he laughed to himself. He had hardly taken two steps when someone suddenly leapt on his back. Mugger or what he had to decide instantly, friend or foe, but somehow instinctively knowing it would be Truus he thought it best not to throw her onto Domplein and pull out his gun and shoot her. She hugged him round the neck and shouted into his ear,

"Take me away, Pappy, to somewhere hot!"

"You're an idioot!" Caes said, "I could have shot you."

"You'd miss!"

She jumped off his back and kissed his cheek.

"How's your day been?"

"Slow, what are you up to?"

"Just finished Cross Fit and thought I'd come into town. Saw a funny old man in the street and thought he needed cheering up, so here I am."

"I'm not old, but I am funny!" Caes protested.

"You can say that again, Pappy, but don't. Anyway, shall we get a pizza?"

Vismarkt, 23.00.

So, arm in arm, they made their way back to the canal and to their favourite pizzeria. They took their lives in their hands as they stepped down towards the dark water on the so steep stairs. No matter what the weather though or the time of year, it was always busy. Students, tourists, locals, everyone.
Caes reported on his meeting with the therapist as they sat down.

"The Worry Tree! The bloody Worry Tree!" Caes snarled as Truus came into the kitchen.

"What?" she looked at him in surprise.

"I mentioned I get worried sometimes to the *psycholoog* and that causes me to get a bit low."

"And?"

"He introduced the Worry Tree."

"Does it bear fruit?" Truus giggled.

"Only nuts!" Caes scowled, which only made Truus giggle more.

"Listen if you notice a worry then you have two questions to answer. What am I worrying about and can I do something about it?"

"Sounds oké so far" she smiled.

"Yes, but then if you can do something about it you develop an action plan."

"Again, sounds reasonable."

"But if you can't do anything about it, you let the worry go."

"Where?"

"You just let it go and change your focus of attention."

"Focus of attention?"

"Yes, you let it go, what bollocks."

"You told him this?" Truus asked.

"No, I just could not believe it, you let the worry go! Christ if I could let it go I wouldn't be worrying."

"True, but the action plan?"

"Oh yes, once you have an action plan you implement it and then... drum roll please... you let the worry go."

"But how, Pappy?"

"Exactly, how? God this makes me sick..."

"Don't get down, Vader, it'll sort itself out."

"When though, it's gone on too long..."

"I know. I still miss Mammie as well. It must be normal to feel like this."

"I know, my darling." Caes smiled.

"I try to think good things about her."

"You only had good times with her!" he smiled.

"I was lucky, you knew her longer, you have more to miss. It can't be easy. It shouldn't be easy, she was special..."

"No, it shouldn't be...anyway, lieverd, pizza. What would you like?"

"You choose, I just need to go to the loo."

Caes watched as she wove a path between tables and another image came into his head. That of his wife Femke. The two women were so alike. Peas in a pod he thought. He reached out for Truus hand as she returned and squeezed it gently. He looked at his daughter with pride.

"Mammies basketball team always ate here." Caes remembered from somewhere as they sat down.

"Wonder where they go now?"

"Who knows?"

"Do you miss it?"

"Not really, I don't think. It used to be important, but more important things came along..."

"Like me?"

"Yes, *lieverd*, you did. Then work took over, taking more responsibility. There wouldn't have been any time."

"But it was something you liked…"

"I like being your pappy more."

"Even now I'm grown up?"

"Grown up, Truus? You'll never grow up."

"Pappy!" she was indignant.

"You'll always be my little girl."

Truus snorted.

"Though I do realise you are now a young woman and have grown…"

"Pack it in, Pappy." She smiled.

"But to attack me in the street and risk certain death…"

"Well you know nobody would dare attack you, *Hoofdinspecteur*. It had to be me, you must have known that?"

And he had. He knew it was her. He laughed and she sniggered.

"Anyway maybe when you leave home…"

"You want me to go?"

"If you should ever leave home I should say, maybe then I'll get involved again."

"You'll need a new hobby when you get rid of me."

"Well, we'll see, Truus…"

Somehow she had demolished her pizza whilst talking and Caes still had half of his own left. He offered her some. She didn't refuse. Finally, she finished eating and Caes noticed a change in the expression on her face.

"What is it?" He asked.

"I have news, Pappy."

"Yes?"

"I have found a partner…"

"That's nice, my darling." He was happy. He wanted her to be happy.

"It's…" she seemed to choke a little, "its Maaike."

Caes didn't care about her gender, though he had wondered why Maaike had been round to their house so often recently. Some detective he thought!

"That's good, she is a good person." Caes knew this was true. He had no issue with this. Part of him was a little upset that Truus had found it hard to tell him.

"You don't mind?"

"Don't you know your own Pappy? If you are happy, I am happy."

"That she works for you?"

"No problem at all, darling."

"That I am gay?"

"Why should that be a problem? I love you."

Caes meant this. It didn't matter to him in the slightest. The only thing would be, that police work could be dangerous for Maaike and he didn't want his Truus to be under any illusion as to the dangers. But Caes knew that she understood that full well already. Bottom line, he loved her and was happy for her.

UMC, 23.35.

Maaike sat by Jeltje's hospital bed. She was stroking her forehead. She was so pale, her face almost transparent, a deathly white. Both her wrists were bandaged, she had tried to kill herself. She had been found just in time, in the bath by her mother. Her first night home after leaving the care of the *Bureau Jeugdzorg* and she did this. Her mother, Aneke de Bruin, was sobbing outside in the waiting room with her husband. He sat there hugging his wife, not knowing what to do. Freddie Meijer sat opposite them, feeling very uncomfortable, he too not knowing what to do or what to say.

"I saw him; he was standing outside my home." Jeltje whispered.

"Jeltje, no..." Maaike said.

"He was watching me, looking through my window."

"He was with us..."

"No! He came into my room. Standing there smiling."

"Jeltje, we have him at Kroonstraat."

"He scares me so much, his smile, it scares me."

"Jeltje, you're safe here. No one can hurt you. Don't, you mustn't hurt yourself my love."

"It was him, he made me do it. He said he loved me and smiled and that I should just finish it, all for him."

"Jeltje, he was with us, you've been having nightmares."

"Stay with me, Maaike, can you just stay?"

"Yes as long as you like."

"I just need you here, with me."

"Do you want your mother as well?"

"No, I have let her down so badly, she must hate me."

"No, Jeltje, she loves you. She's breaking her heart. She loves you so much. She doesn't know what to do, your father as well. They are both here, they are so worried about you. They love you so very much."

"I'm worthless, what is the point of me living, he's right."

"No, Jeltje."

"I have been so dirty, so horrible."

"No, that's not true, don't think like that."

"I hate myself so much."

"No, Jeltje, do not say that. You must not hate yourself," Maaike insisted.

"I hate him then. I want to kill him."

"He can't hurt you anymore. You just have to be brave. I'll see this through with you. Just be brave. Look here's your mammie."

Mevrouw de Bruin came in, eyes streaming,

"My darling, Jeltje, are you alright?"

"Mammie. I'm so sorry…"

Maaike excused herself and passed Jeltje's father in the doorway. She moved zombie like towards Freddie and just fell into his arms and sobbed.

"What can I do, Freddie, what can I do?"

"You do your best, Maaike, that's all you can do, you can never do more."

"It's just so wrong, she nearly died. The power of one man, it's all so wrong, so horrible."

"But it's not your fault. If anything you have saved her, she would be lost without you, what kind of a life was it for her?"

"Her parents, how unhappy they must be?" Maaike spoke with tears in her eyes.

"I know..."

"But Jeltje, how sad that she is so scared."

"She needs a lot of special help, you can't do it all...you are not qualified, my love." Freddie advised.

"I know, Freddie, I want to be there, but you are right, I don't know what to do or what to say to her."

"Well we can but hope he gets sent down for a long time."

"He must go down; it would be impossible for Jeltje."

"Let's hope she can be brave enough and then maybe some of the other girls will be as well. Bureau Jeugdzorg has got involved and are checking out his girls. They will find any more underage ones. It will be rape, kidnapping, assault, sexual assault. He will be destroyed. No community Service for him."

"I hope not."

"I promise you I'll fix him if the courts don't, you've my word Maaike."

"Freddie!" Maaike was shocked at her twins' vehemence.

"No, Maaike, I will. Try not to worry, you care too much."

"I love you, Freddie."

"I know. Get back inside, I'll wait here."

"No, go home, tell Mammie I'll be late."

"No, I'll wait for you sis. Take all the time you need."

De Machine, 23.55.

After they got home, Truus thought about what she could do about Sterre. She needed to do something. She didn't feel tired. In fact, she felt alive and on edge. The nightclub flyers had linked Gisele and Sterre, so why not? She knew that De Machine was a late night, early morning hard core type of thrash metal club so decided to dress down a bit. She had no idea about Roze Fluweel, but could guess. So, her black Doc Martens and a short black leather skirt seemed very De Machine appropriate. She put a little more colour in her bright red hair with a yellow kerchief, but the rest was black, a blouse and her short black leather jacket. *Very Goth*, she thought. She printed off a couple of Facebook photos each of the three girls, shoved them in her backpack and set off. It was still very cold and the snow was not thawing, she was a bit under dressed for this weather so needed to get inside.

She could feel, rather than hear the beat as she turned the corner of the street towards De Machine, it was bloody loud, she half recognised Pestilence or was it Sinister? The street seemed to be throbbing, the snow flecked air almost pulsating with the thrash metal noise.

There were lots of leather clad men milling about the door, not too many girls, hopefully they were inside. She showed her student ID at the door and slid in to the sweating, heaving, decibel breaking mess that was De Machine.

She got a coka zero, not believing how much it cost, she wished she was back at the student's bar in *Universiteit*. *God Dethroned* now blasted out of the speakers. Truus wondered if her ears would soon start bleeding. The barman had not seen the girls or rather he could not be bothered to look or to try to remember. Truus was unsure how to play this. The place was damp and smelt of sweat. Not pleasant. Though people no longer smoked indoors, there was the stale smell sticking to everyone she passed.

The music was so loud; she couldn't hear herself think. She was starting to get a headache from the lump that Tamada had kicked earlier in the day. Brain damage she thought to herself. She scanned the room, no student types in here tonight, very few girls. The girls that were here were with men, none on their own. She realised she had made a huge mistake. What on earth was Gisele doing here on her own or to be honest with friends? She shivered and decided she would leave. She would ask one more person if they had seen any of them. She wandered over to a waitress and showed her the photographs, but she too had no real idea. Truus asked who might know. The girl pointed at a group of men,

"They are in every night, always looking for girls, but be careful, they are not very nice."

They didn't look too nice, but she felt nothing could happen here. There were five of them, Romanians by the look of them, she thought.

The nastily named *Prostitute Disfigurement* were the latest piece of so called music on the decks. Loud, spiteful insinuating music, but the De Machine clubbers were loving it as it throbbed through the air.

She put her backpack on her shoulder, swallowed her coka and went over to them. Taking a deep breath, she asked,

"Excuse me I know this sounds stupid. I am looking for my friends; they seem to have disappeared."

"Let me see in light,"

one of them said and before she knew it, she had been shoved through a fire exit and was outside.

The Romanian pushed her back against a wall. *That hurt*, she thought and then looked into his leering face, she was in the shit. He went to slap her across the face, but she blocked it and leg swept him to the floor. She followed through with her axe kick into his head and he grunted. Finished. She felt herself go automatically into her defensive stance, practised over and over again at the gym. She had her feet balanced and looked at her attackers through narrowed eyes. Another man came towards her and she round house kicked him in the chest, Doc Martens and all, but he didn't go down, oh shit she thought. He then produced a knife.

"So girly, you want this?"

She lashed out again at the hand, caught it fully and the man dropped the knife squealing in pain. He automatically bent to retrieve the blade and Truus kicked out again and there was the sound of two dull thuds as boot hit head, then head hit floor.

She knew from practise that she would be quicker than any one of these men, but there were too many of them. She stood there, eyeing the remaining three. On her toes, waiting

A hand grabbed at her from the side and twisted her arm, pushing her round and up against the wall. That really hurt her face as she collided with the brickwork. *Fuck, this is it,* she thought, but she managed to twist away as a fist flew towards her face and ducked, then slid over the Icey ground to the side, but she couldn't stop both when two men attacked. She feinted under another swinging arm, but cried out as she got a punch in the kidneys and felt her knees sagging. She struggled against a hand that had now got hold of her arm, trying to kick out, but it was too icy and she was off balance and couldn't get at him. Another hand grabbed her and spun her round and a Romanian was right in her face.

"So, what is your business here girl?"

"I am just looking for my friends…" Truus gasped.

"Do I look stupid?" He asked.

"Yes, you fucking do!"

Truus snarled, lunging upwards and forwards with her head catching him on the underside of his nose, his blood splattered everywhere, his nose broken.

"Good girl!" a voice cried out, she recognised it.

"That is real good move. We here now, Truus."

It was Bogdi of all people!

"You may leave her now, man, she is our friend." Ofim added.

"Fuck off, Bogdi, look at my face…"

"Look at mine, Izzie, let her go or I'll finish you."

"Bogdi…"

"Izzie, call off your dogs and fuck off or we'll start."

It was Ofim, his voice cold and clear.

Tears of pain had come into Truus's eyes, she wasn't crying, but she could hardly see. But there were Bogdi and Ofim and just to the side the lovely Zuzana and Nadzia, dressed up to the nines, beautiful, but looking a little concerned.

She felt the grip on her arm slacken and fall away, she kicked out in that direction and her heavy DMs again hit flesh. There was an accompanying moan and she prepared to lash out again, but Nadzia pulled her to the side,

"Come into club, Truus, we get drink, tidy you up, fix your make up, leave boys to play."

The boys didn't need to 'play' as the two unharmed Romanians lifted up their two injured mates, whilst 'broken nose' the man called Izzie, held a handkerchief to his face, glaring at everyone, but doing nothing.

"What you doing on own here, Truus?" asked Bogdi as they sat at a table.

"Just looking for someone."

"This not nice club, bit rough to be on own. Our girls come to protect us two." Ofim smiled.

"You see that for self?" Bogdi said.

"Yes I do now." Truus grimaced.

"Ask any question they think you spy for other gang or worse Police."

"You end in canal, Truus…"

"Where is father?" Ofim asked.

"At his work, this is my work."

"Not good work for pretty girl," said Zuzana.

"Exciting no?" said Nadzia.

"Too exciting, I didn't really like that at all. Dank Bogdi, dank Ofim, you saved my life I think." Truus said quietly.

"They not kill, but maybe do worse," said Zuzana.

"You want lift home?"

"Nee, bedankt!, I have to finish my work I was going to go to Roze Fluweel." Truus said.

"Tis gay club?" Nadzia squealed.

"We all go; it will be fun." Zuzana suggested.

"Will they let boys in?" Nadzia asked.

"Yes, they look gay!" the two girls screamed with laughter.

Bogdi and Ofim looked hurt, then roared with laughter.

So Roze Fluweel was a Gay club and Truus felt she again fitted right in with her black leather look. Not that she was quite sure before she entered. The Polish contingent drank heavily and danced and laughed. Truus showed the three photos around, but there was nothing. Truus decided she needed to dance as well. Zuzana and Nadzia were only too happy to oblige.

Truus had to take a break. She was exhausted, but then felt scared. She had left herself wide open tonight, it could have gone so wrong. She looked at the couples dancing and somehow felt more relaxed. Everyone seemed to be having a good time. The atmosphere was calm, not like at De Machine which had been so aggressive in every sense. A young woman came over to her and asked her to dance. *Why not*, thought Truus and she made her way to the dance floor and escaped into the music.

Amaliastraat, 23.56.

Caes watched Femke score the winning basket and her stern game face suddenly changed into his beautiful wife's face. This image was repeating over and over again in his head. Her face wreathed in a smile, sweaty hair pinned back, but starting to flop over her face. Her eyes sparkling, running towards him; and then leaping into his arms to hug him, only for her body to instantly change into a skeleton and the bones crumble in his arms. Caes felt as though he had stifled a scream, but once again was sweaty and cold. He hated this. It made no sense. Caes remembered when Femke had leapt into his arms. It was the last game she had played. Five weeks later she was dead. Taken before her time. Caes turned over and closed his eyes, knowing that it would take some time before he would get to sleep again.

It was no good, he went downstairs and put on the kettle. He thought a cup of tea would help. As he poured in some milk a sleepy eyed Truus appeared at the door.

"Good morning pappy," she smiled.

"Not really my love. Whats the time, midnight?"

"No idea, make me a cup..."

She jumped over the settee arm and sat down with a thump.

"Did I wake you?" Caes asked.

"No, I went to the loo. Thought you were a burglar!" she laughed. "Why are you up?"

"Thinking about things…"

Caes looked at the book Truus had picked up.

"Whats that?"

"A bit of Nordic noir pappy."

"What happened to your tartan noir you foisted off on me?"

"I've moved on pappy. This is all cinnamon rolls and coffee filled thermos flasks. Then the most vile murders…"

"Not like the whisky and football you set me up with."

"Well, just like you pappy all they want to do is to catch the bad guys."

"And it's always so straightforward to them. I can't imagine how they would cope with what we have on, missing girls, murders, all linked together…"

"A bit of Dutch noir pappy."

Caes laughed.

"Perhaps I shouls approach it as a novel. What would be my first step?"

"Motive pappy, it's always about motive. So, what is the motive behind all this?"

She looked at Caes wide eyed and innocent, with a half smile on her face. Caes shrugged. If he knew that he would have the killer. It was so simple.

Vagevuur.

Sterre woke with a jerk, she had been dreaming of being alone, locked in a brightly lit cell. Her eyes became accustomed to the light and she cried out loud. He looked down at Sterre with such hatred that she almost felt his eyes burning into her. She was stunned.

"What is wrong with you?" she demanded.

"Your father..."

"What? What has he done..."

He towered over her, trembling and clenching then unclenching his fists. She felt he was about to hit her, which scared her even more.

"What has he done to you. Why am I here?"

"So he knows pain. Your pain..."

"But I've..."

"He destroyed me, everything I had..."

"But I don't even live with him. He doesn't care where I am..."

"We'll see..."

He pushed his face into hers and then yanked her hair back. She tried to remove his hand but it was vice like. Then he moved his hand to her face, squeezing her cheeks together, forcing tears into her eyes.

"He will be made to miss you. He will see what the cost of his interference was. Your father..."

He pushed her away and her hands went to her face.

"Your father is going to know what it is like to lose everything..."

Once again, her stomach turned to ice and matched the tone of his voice. She could now see no escape and was truly terrified.

Chapter 13

Dinsdag, November 18, 2014.
Amaliastraat, 02.00.

Caes had nodded off over some paperwork, appraisals of Danny and Adrie and wondered what time it was. It was in fact gone three in the morning when the door suddenly smashed open and Truus careered in. It crossed his mind that if she entered like this sober, what on earth would it ever be like if she drank and came home drunk. It didn't bear thinking about! Why is she so loud and thoughtless? He supposed that as he had fallen asleep on the settee it didn't really matter. It never usually did.

"Lieverd, a good night?" then he saw her face, scratched and swollen.

"What's happened to you?"

She just started crying and fell into his arms, sobbing her heart out.

"Oh, Pappy, I have been so stupid, I was really scared..."

She outlined the nights' events sending a chill down his spine. Oh, for God's sake Truus Caes thought, what on earth were you playing at, but all he could say was:

"But you are safe now..."

"Bogdi and Ofim, if not for them."

"You would have got out of it, I'm sure, but no next times."

"No."

"Tell me when are you next going to play the hero."

"I didn't expect it to be like that, what must Gisele be like if she goes there regularly?"

"It does seem to be slightly out of character, but what do we really know of anyone? Anyway, dry your eyes, Truus, let's get you to bed..."

"I'm sorry, Pappy, I really am..."

"Learn from it, lieverd, you will need a backup if ever you do that kind of thing again. I always have someone nearby. You can't do it all on your own. You have learnt a lesson tonight. This man, his gang, any names?"

"Izzie, says Bogdi. They know him."

"Well I'd best get to know him as well."

"Pappy, is it worth it?"

"He can't hurt my little girl and get a free pass."

"I know, but haven't you a lot more important things on?"

"More important than you?"

"I think I've lost one of my nine lives tonight."

Truus tried to change the subject. Caes thought best to let her. He didn't want to argue.

"Well like I say, learn from it. I can't be doing with losing you."

That was a stupid thing to say as it started her crying again. Caes sat and stroked her hair.

He woke up an hour later, carried her to her bed, threw a duvet over her, tucking Nijntje next to her face and crashed into his own without washing. He suddenly felt drained. Truus was driving him mad! What was he to do? Should he put his foot down and say he didn't want her to do this? Should he encourage her to join the Police? It might not be any safer for her, but she would at least have some support. She would never forgive him if he went to Thijs and told him to let her go, but it crossed his mind that he should. There was a PD James book called *An Unsuitable Job for a Woman* and ironically, this was just what she was writing about, a female private detective. This didn't seem suitable at all for Truus, or was he just being old fashioned or sexist or just a worried father? Maybe they should team up. He could leave the force, maybes jumped on top of maybes and Caes fell asleep.

"Coffee, *Vader*?"

"Please, Truus. How are you feeling?"

"Better, I'll try to improve,"

She smiled at him and kissed his cheek.

"Thank you for listening last night and for not judging."

"That's oké."

"It means a lot that you trust me."

Caes actually did trust her, despite everything, he smiled to himself.

"Well, my love, only so far. Just be careful and stay safe."

"You want some cheese with your *brood*?"

"Please, what on earth are you eating?"

"*Gestampte muisjes*, Pappy, don't you remember them, when I was little?"

He remembered, coloured aniseed on a rusk spread thickly over butter, a customary breakfast food for their beautiful Dutch children. It was so sickly he remembered. This was madness from Truus!

"You aren't regressing, are you?"

"Nooo, just thought I would see if I still liked it."

"And?"

"Yes, Pappy, indeed I do!" she giggled and whirled out of the room.

"Got to go, Pappy, I've work to do. I'll see you later. Love you, *doeg*!"

and with a slam of the front door she was gone. He started to clean the bomb site that had once been his kitchen. Normality had returned.

Universiteit Utrecht, 10.24.

Truus was tired after her lack of sleep, but trailed into *Universiteit*, partly to show her pappy that she could work for Thijs as well as do her studies, but also because she needed to keep her brain active. Despite the fact that she was going to try a new course next year, she had quite enjoyed the motivation module they had worked on last week and though she had not followed up with any reading she thought it may be interesting today.

Meneer Sands smiled a greeting,

"How are you, Truus?"

He was obviously concerned by the scratches on her face.

"Well, *Meneer*, you?"

"Well indeed, Truus, been fighting?"

Truus laughed, "You know us students!"

The class filed in, Sands began.

"We'll be following up last week where we spoke about different types of motivation. Motivation is the force that initiates, guides and maintains goal-oriented behaviours. It is what causes us to take action, whether to grab a snack to reduce hunger or register in *Universiteit* to earn a degree. The forces that lie beneath motivation can be biological, social, emotional or cognitive in nature. But what about criminal motivation? Where does that come from?"

Nobody spoke, Sands continued,

"Believe it or not, you already know what the criminal is and what motivates him, you see it all the time in minor forms. What to most people is a minor character flaw, is to criminals, a major defining element of their personalities."

Truus thought about what was going on in her life at the moment and said,

"I think we need to look at extremes in behaviour. The criminal goes to extremes, but few people recognise them for what they really are. Extremes are everyday behaviour, thoughts and ideas taken and magnified out of all proportion. What happens with the criminal is that the normal checks and balances that keep them under control are missing, turned off or abandoned."

"Indeed, Truus. Each day we encounter attitudes, behaviour and ways of thinking that are annoying and selfish. Usually, there are forms of checks and balances that keep them in line with normal society. We assume these checks and balances are in place. This is the 'social contract' that allows people to function and get along together in their day-to-day activities. We don't realise how ingrained and unconscious these rules of behaviour and ways of thinking are. They temper our selfishness and prevent it from running amok."

"So in our daily lives, we rely on people to have moderating influences, but the criminal is unmitigatedly selfish, doing everything for themselves at the exclusion of all others. They don't recognise that they have a duty to conform to society. They make their own society with their own rules." Truus interjected.

"Yes, what I think Truus is saying is that these checks and balances are missing from the criminal or violent person. Nature abhors a vacuum. With this absence of counterbalancing influences, certain behaviour flourishes and grows, taking up that empty space."

"Yes, *Heren* Sands, behaviour that is apparent in a so called normal person ends up being enormous in the mind of a so-called criminal. The extremes to which a criminal is willing to go are unbelievable to most people. It is both shocking and unnerving when we see someone who doesn't follow these rules about controlling one's selfishness." Truus said.

"Thank you, Truus, it is indeed a sad fact that some people cannot see the connections of day-to-day behaviour to the extremes. They simply don't believe that the small, annoying conduct they encounter every day could grow to become such extreme evil. While others, until they see the extremes of behaviour, cannot recognise those same patterns in daily activities."

After her lecture, Truus had wandered aimlessly through the Universiteit for a while. She wanted to sit down somewhere warm, but everywhere was crowded and felt wrong. She found herself outside the weights room and like her father dismissed the notion of working in a spic and span shiny studio. She liked the rough and tumble of the Zweet Fabriek. She saw the door to the Sports Hall and was suddenly drawn to it. Inside were the sounds of the bouncing basketballs and the squeak of trainers on the floor. She hadn't heard that noise for years. She put her head around the door and the familiar smell of boys sweat reached her nostrils. Why couldn't it smell of girls she wondered? The boys were shooting at the nearest basket, trying to dunk and generally showing off. She remembered that as well. At the other end a group of girls were chatting and tossing balls between them in a very desultory manner. Truus made her way to the bleachers and sat down. She turned her music up louder and rummaged through her backpack for her notebook. Her search was interrupted when a ball bounced next to her. Automatically she grabbed it, feeling its strange rough pimples under her fingers for the first time in so many years. A boy gestured for her to return it. She stood up and drilled it back to him, so hard that it went straight through his hands and slapped against his head. Her proffered apology was drowned out by the hoots of derision from the group of girls and the mocking of his own mates. Truus felt awful and waved a further apology as a girl ran up to her,

"It's Truus isn't it?"

She recognised her from a long time ago,

"Matilde, God how long has it been? You playing here?"

"Yea. It's been years. How are you?"

Matilde hugged her tightly and kissed her cheek.

"I'm really well."

"God, Truus, how have you been?" asked Matilde.

"Fine thanks…"

"Sorry we didn't keep…"

"Don't it's the way things…" said Truus.

"I know but…"

It had been a long time. They had played basketball together till they were fourteen, that was the link. When her mammie died, she had stopped playing then they had gone to different schools. For a long time, grief was the only world Truus had known. She had lost contact with a lot of people over the years, but had made new friends so… but it was almost five years ago, five years since mammie had gone. A lifetime ago. Truus felt a lump in her throat. Matilde pulled her back from her memories,

"I didn't even know you were at this uni."

"Yea doing Sociology."

"Wow!" exclaimed Matilde.

"But changing to English next semester."

"That makes more sense!" Matilde smiled, "I'm doing science. No wonder we never meet!"

Truus remembered Matilde's love for all things scientific.

"We have a game tonight."

"Here?"

"Yea. Groningen Uni are coming over." Said Matilde.

"Will you win?"

Matilde laughed,

"Did you even know we had a team?"

"Vaguely."

"If you did you'd know we never win!"

Matilde laughed again.

"Really?" Truus asked.

"Really."

"But you were so good. We were good. You must be even better now…"

"One swallow, Truus…" Matilde said.

"Suppose so, what times tip off?"

"Hour and a bit away."

"Yea I can stay for a while." Truus agreed.

"Come and shoot." Demanded Matilde.

"I have some reading…"

"Truus! You know you want to." Laughed Matilde.

Truus smiled at her and replaced her notebook and followed her. At least she had her Converse on so was not totally inappropriately dressed for the sport.

"Who coaches you?" asked Truus.

"We do it ourselves. No money to pay a coach. Sometimes one of the boys will try to help, but as usual they are too full of themselves." Matilde replied.

Truus watched as the ball swished through the net. The sound made her tingle all over. She had always loved that swoosh as the net ripples as the ball passed through. She waited for the backspin to return the ball to her and handed it to Matilde.

She made introductions. A couple of the girls Truus remembered from way back as they were local, others were incomers from places all over Holland and further afield.

"Never goes away, Truus!" Matilde smiled as Truus scored again.

"What?"

"Skill, you have so much" Matilde said.

"I don't think…" Truus was embarrassed.

"It was such a shame you…"

Truus stopped her,

"I had to, Matilde. It was all too much, reminded me…"

"But now?" Matilde wondered.

"Don't know, I really don't know. I'm so busy with stuff."

"Stuff? Well you know where we are…" Matilde bounced the ball to Truus.

Again, there was the familiar swish as the ball hit nothing but net. Truus smiled to herself. It was as if she had never been away.

Truus sat in the bleachers, elbows on her knees. Head in her hands staring at the court but all she could see was her mammie. Her mammie smiled and kissed her nose, Truus felt awful. Had she betrayed her mother by playing basketball again? Would her mammie understand? Eight years was a long time. She had always loved to play, but reckoned it was only because of her mammie. After all she had driven her everywhere, watched her play, helped her pappy to coach her, it was she her passion had been shared with. True her pappy had coached her mammie and they had had such success together, winning cups and leagues until that awful day. Since then pappy nor she had been near a court until... A whistle split into her thoughts and she looked up. The game had started, a Utrecht player had double dribbled. Matilde was right. They were never going to win.

Truus felt a bit down as she got onto the packed Number twelve bus back into Utrecht city centre. The lights at Galgenwaard stadion were shining into the snow filled sky, there must be a game on, no wonder it was so busy. Traffic was slow and people kept bumping into her. She hadn't been able to find a seat, she needed to sort out her timing to make sure she did in future. No one cared though. Backpacks kept hitting students, students scowled at each other. No one was particularly civil. Truus couldn't wait until the snow melted and she could get back onto her bike. With relief, she saw they were turning into Vondellaan and her stop.

Kroonstraat Police Bureau, 11.35.

"*Baas*, the stolen cars. I have something!"
Ernst was almost jumping on the spot.

"What gives?"

"You know the pickpocket they brought in, well he was trying it on, mouthing off how he knew people, who knew people, you know what they are like..."

"And?"

"I didn't think he would have anything to offer, so I told him to piss off and sent him to the cooler."

"Come on, Ernst, I've got a lot on, what gives?" Caes said.

"Sorry, baas, he stewed for a bit and asked to see me again. Wanted to know if there was anything we could do. I said tell me what you've got and we'll see..."

"Ernst!" Caes warned.

"Izmir Rudescau is the player! He mentioned his name in passing really and I remembered I had come across it before."

"You would, Ernst!" Caes smiled.

"He takes BMWs, strips them down, refashions them, exports to Romania. Classic!"

The name Izmir also struck a chord with Caes. Could it be this Izzie Truus mentioned? He wondered. Caes had been meaning to set Ernst on looking for him anyway, this might kill two birds with one stone. He explained what had happened to Truus. His eyes darkened.

"How does the boy know him?" Caes asked him.

"Friends with one of the other Romanians in the gang."

"We'll have to move quickly then; he may suspect he's for the drop if the lad talks."

"Yes I spoke to organised crime an hour ago. We go tonight."

"Good man." Caes smiled.

"Want to come?" Ernst offered.

Dick Bruna Huis, 12.00.

Truus was at the Museum kwartier. She knew she was way too old, but this reminded her of when she was small and visits with her mammie. The home of Nijntje. When she was little she had so many of the toys and books by Dick Bruna and so returning to the Dick Bruna Huis made her feel so happy and yet so sad. She remembered holding her mammies hand tightly as they queued up and then how she would race away to the interactive games with her mammie laughing behind her. How she would sit on her mammies' lap looking at books or screens that you touched and brought to life. She remembered her mammie hugging her tight and laughing. Her laugh. She had to keep that sound in her head. Her smile. She had to keep that vision in her mind's eye.

    The collection consisted of hundreds of works, including children's books, book covers and poster designs and so every visit was the start of a new adventure, even if she had to beat away small children to look at things! She just felt peaceful amongst the noise and the commotion, felt a link with her past, a link to her mammie. *Nijntje, really,* she thought to herself, *at your age.* Then smiled as she knew whatever age she was Nijntje was part of her and her life. Indeed, Nijntje still sat on her bed at night and often shared the duvet with her. She felt tears prick at her eyes and wiped them away. A small girl looked up at her from a Nijntje jigsaw.

    "Are you sad?"

    "No, I'm happy." Truus said trying to smile.

    "Why are you crying?"

    "Because I am so happy, *lieverd.*"

    That seemed to appease the concerned child who returned to her game and allowed Truus to return to her memories.

Kroonstraat Police Bureau, 13.45.

The ringing phone brought Caes back to the moment.

    "Hi, Caes."

    "Grete, how are you?"

"Fine, I've got Madelon here with me at the autopsy, but thought I'd let you know..."

"Yes?"

"Same knife, one blow, same killer as Spliker I would have thought. Same talc residue from the gloves. I'll need to write it up for you, but that's what I'll be saying."

"Dank, Grete, anything else?"

"No, sorry, just the same upward motion. I'm checking the talc though."

Same killer. The same killer, everything was as one, three girls, one linked to Thijs. Two people dead, one linked to Thijs. One linked to two of the girls, in as much as she had 'lost' them. Linked by the killer. Are they linked to Thijs? The missing girls are both linked to Sterre. Were they over-thinking, were all the cases individual? No, too many links. God this was such a distraction. Caes just felt he did not know where to go with it, where to start. Everything seemed too jumbled up, too mixed up and intertwined. Where to start? But he had other things to concentrate on now, the Romanians at Mende Strasse, for a change, far away from Vaartsestraat.

Mende Strasse, 20.35.

That night, the lads from Caes' team met up with a unit from Organised Crime in Oudwijk, eastern Utrecht. Maaike had excused herself, she didn't want to play second fiddle to anyone and she had made Caes laugh with her serious tone. She was a tough young lady at times. This was a really nice neighbourhood though, with a lot of European and mixed race families. The Romanians would not have looked out of place here. The police converged on a small road with a series of lock up garages. It was away from the main routes, but surely people would have noticed a series of high-powered cars coming down here at all hours. Or maybe they were cleverer than that, Caes didn't know. But it was reinforcing his view that people didn't see anything, didn't know anything and certainly were less inclined to do anything about anything that was out of the ordinary. Ernst led the way.

He was always an impressive looking man. Tonight, he was wearing black overalls and a broad grin. His moustache bristled as he welcomed the OCU chief. They were in deep discussion for a while then he came over to Caes.

The OCU deferred to him, well he was two metres of solid muscle and moustache and he *had* found out about this place. They had arranged a unit around the back. There were no other exits, just the front one on Minervaplein. Caes didn't expect too much trouble, but felt they were prepared for all eventualities. Still, they had their stab vests on and there were two armed units with them.

Ernst explained his plan to him, then briefed Danny and Adrie. They moved quickly to either side of the door. Ernst grinned at Caes, made a thumbs up sign to both of the armed units who were in reserve behind the vans. He had told Caes they wouldn't be needed. He made Caes smile. Ernst went to the door, knocked and disappeared. Five minutes later, one by one, seven Romanian guys wandered out and lay down face first on the tarmac. One had a plaster over his nose, and had obviously been in a fight recently. Ernst strode over beaming from ear to ear.

"You should see the place, baas, four BMW's in various states…"

"What did you say to them, Ernst, for them to just walk out?" Caes was astounded.

"Nothing really, the usual that we've got the place surrounded… blah blah… sharp shooters blah blah… tear gas blah blah and that I would rip their balls off if they didn't get outside now. They believed me!" He roared with laughter.

"If only your women believed you, Ernst," Caes said.

He slapped Caes on the back and he almost toppled into the gutter.

"I think I'll just thank the OCU for their hard work." Caes said, his back stinging.

"Yes, baas."

"Well done, Ernst, we've done well. It's a good day!"

Inter group courtesies over, Caes strolled back over to the guy with the plaster. He had his foot by the man's head. He turned his head from the tarmac to look at him.

"Izzie?" Caes asked.

"Fuck off!" he snarled.

Caes laughed.

"Not your week is it, looks like you met my daughter the other day. Not done too well for such a big player…"

Oudekirkstrasse, 21.30.

Maaike kicked off her police regulation boots and pulled off her thick socks. She felt that one day she was going to get trench foot, though so far the wet was being kept at bay. Her trousers however were damp and splattered with slush; she stepped out of them as she tugged off her top and T-shirt. Standing in bra and knickers she looked at her body sideways to the mirror, it was hard and firm. Just as it should be, she thought, considering all the work she did on her abs. Her legs ached, but she had walked many kilometres today so it was no surprise. Racing after the shoplifter hadn't helped and she smiled at the memory. She pulled off her bra and cupped her breasts, firm but soft if that made any sense. She liked her breasts, they looked good and she knew they felt good, especially when Truus touched them. Stepping out of her knickers, she walked to the bathroom and climbed into the bath water. She tousled her hair then splashed it with hot, soapy, sweet smelling, water. She took a breath and sank beneath the surface; she was in a cocoon and she felt all the efforts of the day seeping out of her into the water and into the air and away from her body. She must have relaxed too much, too soon, as she gasped awake with a mouthful of water and surged to the surface feeling foolish that she had nodded off. Thank goodness she was on her own. No forget that, she wanted to be with Truus, but she was so tired and had to make a conscious effort to stay awake; the warmth of the bath was so intoxicating. She knew if she spent any longer in there she would fall asleep again. She didn't want to do that, she wanted to be wide awake for her visit to Truus.

Amaliastraat, 23.00.

Truus and Maaike were settled in for the evening in Truus's bedroom. Maaike had decided against being an observer at the car bust. What would be the fun in that, she'd thought? Leaving everything to the bully boys of OCU. Rather spend time with her new love Truus. Truus was sitting reading on the sofa, neatly wedged between the legs of Maaike. Maaike was fiddling with her hair; Truus liked this. It was the only time she wished her hair was longer as she enjoyed the closeness. Truus felt she would love to have her hair braided or plaited. There was such a sensual feel to having someone's fingers running through your hair. Maaike suddenly hugged her tight, almost crushing all the wind out of her.

"Really love you," she whispered.

"I know, Maaike. I know you do."

"No I really, really love you," she leant down and kissed her neck sending shivers from the spot down her spine into her tummy.

"I love to hold you close, feeling your warmth. I love everything about this..."

"It is nice..."

"Nice?" she protested, "is that all it is to you, nice?"

"Nice covers a thousand feelings." Truus said, "that's the beauty of the word."

"Doesn't seem enough to describe how I feel."

Truus could feel Maaike grimacing.

"One of my creative writer tutors I had, once said never to use the word nice in writing, but I think that's wrong. It does have so many meanings..."

"Happy!" Maaike interjected.

"Warm..."

"Pretty..."

"Beautiful..." Truus laughed.

"Safe..."

"Millions, stop. I need to read this."

"Why?" asked Maaike.

"Just wanted a different perspective..."

"On what?"

"Something I wrote; I need to see where it's going." Truus explained.

"Does it have to go anywhere?"

"It needs to make sense."

"Shall I read it?" Maaike asked.

"When it's finished, I want it to be just right."

"When do you know it's right?" Maaike wondered.

"You just do. You write then edit then rewrite. Lose words, add words, mix it all around. Eventually it all fits into place." Truus replied.

"Are you never happy with the first thing you write?"

"Usually I am, but you keep being told to trim it down, to edit and edit. Sometimes you seem to lose the meaning of what you first wrote. It's madness sometimes." Truus replied.

"But you do like it, don't you?"

"I love it. I love to write; it makes everything right in the world. I can escape and be someone I never knew, go to places I have never visited. It can be magical."

"I can see that."

"I find myself in a world where I am always happy. I can make the world my own. It doesn't have to be a bad place or a sad place, it can be perfect. A lot of the time when I write I just think nowhere could be a better place. Everything is as it should be..."

"But?"

"But I know that can't be true and that I have to reflect the real world.""

"Are you trying to escape then?"

"Sometimes I am. I can lose myself and no one can find me. It's perfect, the best of both worlds, but now..."

"Now?"

"I have you."

"Will you take me with you?" Maaike asked smiling.

"In my heart always." Truus smiled in return.

Caes returned home after the arrest and settled down in front of the fire with a crime novel. Busman's holiday indeed! Truus had told him that Tartan noir was the next big thing. He wondered what clothes had to do with anything until she explained. The plot was good though, there were even some believable elements to it, but he did think that if anyone on the Utrecht force had a similar drink problem they would soon be getting moved on, at least into some kind of therapy. Or maybe not considering what had happened to Thijs. They were pretty proactive here. Caes supposed his life bore witness to that with his now weekly visits to a therapist. People who drank as much as the hero here would not be tolerated. Why did writers have to give their heroes a flaw? Was it so necessary to make them different? Caes couldn't work out how he was supposed to react to the drunk. Should he admire him for getting the job done, despite his illness alienating all he worked with or should he despise him for his weakness and just take him to one side and explain the damage he was doing to everyone around him. Caes knew it would be the latter, no one is more important than the job. They were there to serve after all. Maybe a bit too goody two shoes!

Caes supposed you could say that they are all human beings first, but in this job one almost had to take on supernatural abilities. Yes, you had to understand your fellow man, but you also had to try to understand why they did what they did. If you thought their behaviour was the norm, what did that say about you? If you broke the law to keep the law, how did that help? Was this the flaw that critics wanted to see in their fictional detective? He wouldn't last two minutes in the real world. What was his flaw Caes wondered? He was depressed, did that affect his job? Sometimes he wanted to be on his own and wallow a bit, just wanting to be... well depressed. But at other times he could just push it to one side – almost.

Caes had constant reminders of Femke, especially as Truus was growing up to be so like her, and maybe that was a bad thing, always having her remind him of his wife. But there again he didn't want to ever forget her. Caes had loved her so much. Even now he still loved her. He missed her terribly, five years on there was still this huge gap in his life. She had gone too soon, but at least he had Truus. Maybe that was the problem, Truus was always there. Did she need to move on as much for her sake as his? Caes had no idea if he was holding her back or affecting her. Perhaps he should ask. But what would he say? You need to leave home, lieverd, as you remind me of Femke too much? That was ludicrous. But maybe not.

Did he need to find someone else, but how could he? It was almost as if taking up with someone would negate his time with Femke, well that's how he looked at it. Caes knew that Truus had said there would never be a replacement for her mammie, but as soon as someone else came into his house, his bed, how would that affect things. It was easier not to bother, to keep the memories, to hold onto the love he had, a love as far as he was concerned that could never be bettered.

Vagevuur.

The bastard had broken her little finger. He had almost teased her that he would; she saw the recorder and wondered what it was for. He was so cold, so flinty cold. He didn't care that he was hurting her; he wanted her to feel pain. It was as if he enjoyed it and that was what really scared her. She knew him from somewhere, but could just not recall him. It was his eyes, they were so empty, so heartless, so uncaring that was what really scared her. What on earth had she done to him to make him hurt her so much? She had screamed, she hadn't wanted to show any emotion to him, not to give him any satisfaction, but she could not help herself. She had begged him not to, but he just went ahead. She had heard it crack, that was worse than the pain.

She must have blacked out. He had left the room. It had hurt so very much and was sending stabs of pain throbbing through her body, it had already turned a nasty black and blue and it was agony. He came back in and had thrown her some tape and told her to fix it.

"Fix it, you bastard, how?" she snarled at him as he left the room.

What a complete and utter cold-hearted bastard. Then the door opened again, a girl stumbled in.

"Who the fuck are you?"

Sterre seethed, hardly able to get the words out through her gritted teeth. She was in so much pain, her fingers throbbing and on fire.

"Who... he sent me in... he said to help, I heard you scream, what happened? Are you oké?"

"Who are you?" she demanded again.

"Sorry, I'm Elise, Elise Cuijper. He took me some days ago, I think,"

She looked embarrassed,

"I'm sorry I stink, I'm sorry..."

"Elise Cuijper? Weren't we at school?" Sterre asked.

"Why, why are you here?" Elise said.

"I don't fucking know. Christ, what's going on?" Sterre seethed.

"God, your hand, is that what he did? What's he going to do to us...?"

Sterre had no answer to that.

"Sterre... just let me try to help, give me your hand..." Elise said gently.

"Why..." but there were no more words as she screamed again at Elise's touch and fainted.

Elise sat with Sterre's head in her lap. She had taped two of her fingers together, had tried to straighten the broken one whilst she was unconscious, but it had scared her so much, she didn't really want to touch it. She had done her best. She sat there, gently stroking her head, trying to soothe her.

Sterre was sobbing soundlessly. Her hand hurt so much, there was no relief. The throbbing was just bashing against the inside of her head, making every part of her ache and pulsate with every heartbeat. She was in such pain, her hand didn't feel as if it belonged to her, but no longer part of her, being stabbed repeatedly by the sharpest of knives, over and over again, now by the bluntest of weapons. Sterre wanted to be sick. She was terrified. He was so cold; he didn't care how he hurt her. She had no idea why he had, what had she ever done to him? She had never hurt anyone, she kept to herself, she worked hard, never harmed anyone. What had her vader done to him? What had she done to him? Who was he? What did he want from her? She knew him from somewhere, but it just would not come back to her, but whoever he was why was he hurting her? Sterre then realised it was not going to be a good ending. He was happy to let her see his face. Oh god, if he didn't care that he could be seen, what would this mean for them both? She was suddenly even more frightened, frightened for her life.

Chapter 14

Woensdag, November 19, 2014.
Willheminapark, 09.35.

It was early and Maaike was with Jeltje. She was finding life difficult. She was waiting to go home to her parents, but was scared. Bureau Jeugdzorg had suggested meeting up with someone she trusted, she had said she trusted Maaike. Maaike had asked Truus to come to Willheminapark with them, she felt it may be more appropriate with another adult there. Truus did not need to be asked twice, she would have an hour before the gym. She pulled on her hat and her warmest coat and was ready.

It was scary, flying around the ice and snow, avoiding little kids. They had taken a plastic sledge, more in hope than expectation as it wasn't that hilly. Truus and Maaike spent most of their time pushing or pulling the sledge until it got up speed before collapsing in a heap and watching it ploughing forward, falling, careering with no control or cares about safety. Jeltje was, all of a sudden, the fifteen-year-old girl she should have been all along.

Snow started falling again, they could not see the top of the small hill as the wind whipped it into their faces, it was getting colder, but they did not notice as they went running again, sliding down manically, falling, rolling in the snow, throwing snowballs, getting whacked in the face by ice and bits of stone. Jeltje looked so happy, it was wonderful, it was like she had learnt to smile again. Maaike knew this was not going to be simple. Her lifestyle had become like a drug habit and they had to get her off it. Bureau Jeugdzorg would help, a psychiatrist even more, but it was going to be her family that were vital. Why had she got into this in the first place, was she happy at home? Probably not, work was going to have to be done. Would they be able to prosecute the bastard who had got her into this? Time would tell, but it was going to be a long slow frightening process. Maaike was determined she would see it through with her.

The three young women were going mad with excitement and enjoyment, with their noses running, and howling with laughter, they were having amazing fun and all nightmares and worries were forgotten, if only for a brief moment.

Truus loved it when it snowed, it was always so clean and, well, white. It was also really quiet and she loved to walk or to run across Willheminapark or Park Lepelenburg in the snow, especially when no one else had been there first. Virgin snow, untouched! Today at the park it was noisy with screaming kids everywhere, including the three of them, but the silence of the snow, that was always nice. She had to leave to get to work, Thijs was out somewhere and she had to run the office. It was hard to break away from the fun, if only we never had to grow up and become responsible, Truus thought. Maaike kissed

Truus on the cheek and now she knew there was more in the kiss than a casual peck, she felt exhilarated. She hugged and kissed Jeltje and made off for the gym.

Tamada Kick boksene, Johan Buziaulaan, 12.30.

Truus was working out with Robbie, when Tamada called her over. As usual she felt a little intimidated by him, was it his eyes, the cold smile? His sheer size? She couldn't tell, she knew she had to listen to him though. No, she had it. It was his very essence, his very being. He was just pure intimidation! How Pappy could have done with him patrolling the streets she thought.

"This is all about totally fine-tuning your reflexes," said Tamada. "You have to train yourself to react instead of using a thought process. You can't think of what you're going to do, you do not have the time, it's got to just happen. Now give me one hundred sit ups, quickly!"

Truus would never argue with Tamada, she hit the floor and started counting.

"Let us go through your kick drill. Again, quality is the key!"

Front kick using her heel, side kick with the side of her foot, semi-circular kick, roundhouse kick, axe kick. Bang! Bang! Bang! Bang! Bang! There was no whining from Tamada as there had been from Pim, just,

"Again!"

Front kick, side kick, semi-circular kick, roundhouse kick, axe kick. Bang! Bang! Bang! Bang!

"One hundred sit ups!"

"Kick drill!"

"One hundred sit ups!"

"Kick drill!"

She stood hunched over, dragging in breaths, her chest was on fire, her legs burnt, her arms felt like lead, her tummy agony, lactic acid swimming everywhere through her body, weighing her muscles down. She was watching the pools of sweat forming on the floor in front of her. Truus had worked her heart out. This was so horrible, but it felt so good. Was she insane?

Tamada spoke quietly, "In kickboxing, it is better to have quality then quantity. So, it is vital you choose only a select few techniques to perfect rather than trying to perfect hundreds of techniques. You, Truus, have your axe kick, perfection, you have your defensive techniques that work. We have your high chest kick. We need a few more."

Truus nodded, still gasping for breath.

"Now, Truus, again, one hundred sit ups."

Her tummy was burning, but she bit her lip and dug deep.

"We'll look at the crescent kick another time, you have not tried this before, but look at how it works…"

Tamada demonstrated on Truus.

"This is a kick that can be used to break a guard down. To do an inward crescent kick move the left foot out, like this…"

He was in perfect slow motion.

"Then bring your leg up high and direct the ball of the foot to the target. The outward crescent kick is the reverse. Move the left foot to the right then sweep the high foot to the left. Pim, come here, you have pads?"

Pim came over, Tamada smashed him to the floor with the inward and smashed him down again with the outward.

"Thank you, Pim." Tamada said to a stunned and shaky Pim who staggered off looking for a hug from Robbie.

"Enough, Truus, one hundred more sit ups then shower. Good work!"

Work, thought Truus, I haven't even started work and I'm knackered already!

Amaliastraat, 22.08.

Caes called in at *Albert Heijn*. They were short of so many things. Caes recognised a couple of his neighbours and smiled a greeting to them. He was tired and didn't want to engage in conversation with anyone. He finally got home to find his daughter curled up on the settee.

"How's your day been?" asked Caes.

"I am exhausted, Pappy, that Tamada he is a monster. Then I had work at the office…"

"Oh poor Truus…" Caes smiled.

"I am so tired, *Vader*, can we eat on the settee?"

"Shall I feed you?"

"Would you?" she smiled thinly.

"Of course, let's just cook together."

"Maaike is good, isn't she?" Truus asked.

"A good cop, but an even better young person."

"Yes, she is lovely, I am lucky to have her." Truus smiled warmly.

"She cares too much sometimes; she's very involved with this girl Jeltje."

"Better to be like that, than to be cold though, Pappy."

"I hope so, she is young and wants to put the world to rights."

"We all do in our own way, there is nothing wrong with having a dream." Truus said.

"But she looks as if she would get very discouraged, very easily if things don't go just right. I'll have to talk with her." Caes said.

"Oh Pappy, my tummy, I must have done a thousand sit ups, I'm in agony." Truus suddenly moaned.

"I'll run you a bath later, it's like you are still my little girl; all I ever do is run around looking after you." Caes mock complained.

"But that's your job, Pappy, you know you love it…"

Caes supposed he did and smiled.

"I bumped into Flip today."

"Flip?"

"De Zeeuw." Caes said.

"Oh the old basketball coach." Truus remembered.

"Yea, it was nice to see him, not been in touch for ages."

"You never go to any games anymore."

"Well, since your mammie…"

"Pappy you are silly, you really loved basketball." Said Truus.

"But you never play anymore."

"Both as bad as each other really."

"I don't know whether I loved it because your mammie did…"

"Well, Pappy that might not be true. Though I stopped playing because…"

Caes knew she had stopped playing because of her mother. Her mammie took her to all her clubs. When Femke died Truus just closed off for a while, didn't go anywhere, didn't want to see anyone, do anything, just wanted to be with him. He knew the feeling. Caes just wanted to be with her. He was so frightened that he'd lose her as well, irrational as that was, he didn't want her out of his sight. He stayed off work, she stayed off school. Caes would often wake up holding the empty space where Femke had lain and would find his daughter wrapped in his wife's dressing gown curled up at the foot of their bed. They could have gone one of two ways, luckily the fourteen-year-old Truus sorted him out. She stopped sleeping on his bed. She insisted he get back to work. She became very much the independent young woman she was today, but she stopped playing the sport her mammie loved. There again, Caes had stopped coaching. It just didn't seem the same. He hadn't coached just because of Femke, but he couldn't go on without Femke. It was their thing, the time they spent together that was so important, the joy of seeing her succeed was so important. He just didn't see the point anymore. When she diedt, so did the coaching. It just didn't seem right.

"But I met Matilde the other day." Truus told him.

"Matilde Termeer?"

Caes remembered her.

"She's at Uni, she plays for the team."

"Really?"

"They always lose though…" Truus laughed.

"Interested?"

"Don't think so, but don't know. Got so much on…"

"Well you can think about it. Your mammie wouldn't mind, would she?"

"Don't know, Pappy, just don't know…"

Vagevuur.

He looked through the peephole at the two young women. He sneered as he saw their dirty faces and wondered why why couldn't have kept clean. They were a mess. They don't deserve to live. He had decided to kill them. He had no qualms about it. He just needed to work out how. Stabbing was simple and he did enjoy looking into their eyes as they died. He had shot people many years before on his way to the top, but the two recent killings had made him feel good. Not so much the old woman, he supposed. He had looked into her eyes as she died and there was nothing. Her eyes were listless and vacant. She showed no surprise when the knife entered her body, made no noise. Just slumped to the floor. Spilker though, he knew what was goiung to happen and his eyes had reflected that, first surprise, then terror and finally pain. He had felt a thrill going through his own body as life left Spilkers. It had made him shiver, but in a good way. It had actually excited him. When he killed these women would he be as thrilled as that? He hoped so. It was just how, strangle, knife? He had a lot to think about and closed the peep hole.

"Gisele was staying with me; we have just started a relationship, she is so sweet, I hadn't really spoken to her since school or at Uni until recently. We wasted so much time…"
Elise just needed to talk.
"I never even knew you lived in my block." Said Sterre.
"I know, it's hard, we all have our own worlds we live in. I had my own world which was not too nice, my parents were dead, Universiteit was getting hard and I didn't have anyone really, but Gisele and me had just met up after a couple of years…Then we were together, it was lovely. It was what I had been missing, I was so happy for once in my life. I couldn't remember the last time I had felt so good about myself. I actually started looking forward to each day. I had no idea what it would bring on, but I knew it would be something good. It's ridiculous and then the bastard just dragged me in, punched me in the face and I ended up locked in here."
"Where are we?" Sterre wondered.
"Don't know, somewhere close I think, unless he took us somewhere when I was knocked out."
"Who is he?"
"I have no idea; I don't really know anyone around here." Elise said.
"I am sure I know him from somewhere, but I just cannot place him. What about Gisele?"
"No idea where she is. Can she be looking for me?" Elise asked.
"I hope so. God, I feel so dirty, I know I am really dirty, but this is horrible."
"Yes, clean knickers wouldn't go amiss!" Elise said trying to smile.
"What has my father done to him?"

"He didn't say?"

"No, just implied stuff. He scares me. "

"He's evil. How he could hurt your hand without a thought…"

"Oh, he was thinking alright, thinking how much he could hurt me."

Sterre laughed despite herself. She put her good arm around Elises shoulder and rested her head there. She wanted to feel wanted. She breathed deeply.

"Since my parents' divorce I've been on my own, kind of caught between two worlds where neither wanted me." Sterre whispered.

"Like me though my parents died…"

"At least you knew there was no one there to rescue you."

"I suppose, didn't make it easier though."

"Course not, but knowing my parents are there but didn't want to know me…"

"A bit like Gisele's mother, she upped and went to America, left her to fend for herself…"

"Again at least she knew where she was. I still have no idea. Does my vader love me? Does my moeder still hate me? Will they even mourn me?"

"No need to mourn Sterre, not just yet. We'll get out of this, you'll see."

Chapter 15

Donderdag, November 20, 2014.
Kroonstraat Police Bureau, 11.35.

They had to do it, two murders, three missing girls; they had to officially involve the press. Caes hated the press. Generalisation or not, they just never went in the same direction. They always wanted more, more than he ever wanted to give to them. Could they help here? The baas, Hoofdcommissaris Coeman, thought so. The investigating officers sat together at a table, Madelon looking cool beside Caes, Marie Hartmann cooler still next to her. Caes just felt hot under the lights. Truus always said he looked guilty on TV. Caes decided to promote positivity, get his body language right. They had a fan blasting at them from the side to keep them all cool, so that was a start, no sweaty guilty looking copper for the masses to moan about.

"I am Hoofdcommissaris Luuk Coeman; to my left Hoofdinspecteur Caes Heda and to his left Hoofdagent Madelon Verloet, then Marie Hartmann from the Justice Department and finally Principal Ida de Vries from Universiteit Utrecht. Caes?"

"We have three missing female students, names and brief details are on the handout. There are no real connections between the young women. The dates we think they went missing are also on the sheet, but for everyone at home they are..."

Caes tried his best business like tone. His meagre media training had passed him by, he just listened to what Truus had to say about his TV performances!

"What we would like from the public is any information they can give us at all. I think the number is on peoples' handouts, but it is..." Caes carried on.

"No connection between the three young women?" a Radio M reporter asked.

"They all went to *Universiteit* Utrecht, but roughly thirteen thousand women attend there so it may or may not be a connection. We can't rule anything out."

"Classes together?" Radio M followed up.

"Some... but as far as we can see they did not know each other as friends."

"You also have two murders?" The De Telegraaf reporter asked.

"Yes, but at the moment, they are being treated as unconnected."

"But might they be?" De Telegraaf followed up.

"We are looking into them; it is too early to say."

"The name of one of the girls is Sterre Vossen?" the AD reporter asked.

"Correct." Caes said.

"Daughter of former policeman Thijs Orman." Radio M followed up.

"Yes."

"Any connection to his work?" AD asked.

"Again…" Caes said.

"Or his sacking?" Radio M tried.

"We have an open mind on that, but we do not think it is connected to his time in the force."

"Who reported the missing women?" it was the De Telegraaf reporter again.

"Mr Orman and a confidential informant." Caes said.

"For both the other girls?"

"Yes."

"Who was this informant?" De Telegraaf pushed.

"That is not important."

We had to protect Mevrouw Haan, even though it was pointless.

"Are the girl's friends?" AD asked.

"They have some classes together." Principal de Vries said, "but I'm not sure they were friends."

"But they could be?" AD said.

"We are a big *Universiteit*, there are many friendship groups." de Vries said.

"Orman's daughter, what did she study?" The woman from Radio M enquired.

"I'm not sure that's relevant." Caes interjected.

He could see they wanted to personalise this.

"The murder of Spliker. He had just been released from prison. Was his crime linked to the girls?" Radio M asked.

"We are not following that line of enquiry. At the moment, we see the murder as separate." Caes said.

"What do you think though, *Hoofdinspecteur*?" Radio M asked.

"I am considering different avenues."

"Did he know Orman?" Radio M said

A young man from the ridiculously named Bingo FM radio station asked.

"Why should he?" Caes replied.

"*Hoofdcommissaris* Coeman, this has been a bad week for the police?" AD again.

"In what way, we cannot legislate for murder. The kidnapping came to light by chance…"

Madelon interjected, "It is perhaps unnecessary to say this, but the girls who have disappeared had very few if any relatives in Utrecht. They had no real support structure. They may have been targeted because of this. No one would miss them. The police cannot be surrogate parents. We rely on society to

216

assist us. If no one notices these girls are missing it is a sad indictment of society. To criticise the police for this is absurd."

"But the murders..." AD attempted.

"A murderer is to blame, not the police. We will find whoever did this, but we do need help." Madelon was impressive,

"People have to think, did they see anything unusual or out of the ordinary at Vaartsestraat, at the park, was there something or someone strange? Something different? This is not a time to blame people, but a time to work together."

This was going nowhere. The police had put all the information into the public domain, they would now have to try to keep the press and the sicker parts of society away from Vaartsestraat, away from Thijs, away from *Universiteit* Utrecht. They would now interfere in everything, slowing things down, making absurd comments on the case and any progress or lack of it. Generally, they would just be in the bloody way! The police would now get hundreds of phone calls from bogus witnesses, mistaken witnesses, the usual time wasters, the mentally unbalanced, but maybe one or two would have seen something. All they had to do now was to wait for just the one meaningful phone call.

Universiteit Utrecht, 12.00.

Truus still felt she had to go to her Sociology lecture even if she was going to change degree subjects soon. She laced up her Doc Martens and stood up. Looking into the mirror she was pleased with what she saw, her leggings showing off her well-defined legs, and she had on a sloppy sweatshirt just below her bottom negating the need for a skirt. She loved her old denim jacket, well Pappy's old denim jacket, it was comfortably too big and she enjoyed this as it wrapped around her as if she were in her pappy's arms. She scraped a vivid red lipstick onto her lips and pressed them together then pouted, not knowing why, but she was pleased with what she saw. After rubbing a little kohl around her eyes, she was satisfied. Finally, she pulled her beanie on and shoved a few stray hairs under it and blew a kiss to herself in the mirror.

"Look out Utrecht I'm on my way!" she laughed to the glass.

The cold hit her straightaway. Snow was in the air and bit into her cheeks. She regretted at once that she had not added a scarf to her outfit. At least her ears weren't frozen. She shivered and further regrets were added as she realised her bottom was freezing. She dug her hands deeper into her pockets and kicking at the snow, hurried ontowards the bus stop.

She sat and rubbed her gloved hands together. The windows were steamed up and she rubbed a small gap. She looked out at the grey scene as they left the city behind. The incessant gabble from fellow students filled the bus, but it surprised her that she didn't recognise any of them. There again, would they know Elise or Giselle, she wondered. It may be a small world, but people very much led their own insular lives. She eventually jumped off the bus at Uithof and crossed the road into her lecture hall. They were still discussing the bully, this time at work. The docent had asked about the bully, what made them tick and how you should confront it. No one had much to say so Truus thought she ought to try. She put her jacket on the back of her chair and pulled off her beanie. She tousled her hair with her fingers and prepared to listen, but was soon involved.

"The bullying may not be deliberate as the person concerned may not realise how their behaviour has been affecting you. If you can, you should talk to them directly but it's important that you work out what to say beforehand. You should describe what's been happening and why you object to it. You have to be brave to do this, if you can't get a colleague to do it for you or perhaps involve your Union." Truus suggested quietly.

"In addition to the effects on individual workers, bullying at work can also have a major effect on an organisation. Truus, have you anything on that?"

"We know that victims of bullying are likely to suffer from stress-related illnesses leading to significant levels of sickness absence. Given that a third of all sickness absence relates to stress, this can have a staggering effect on organisations." Truus said rather grimly.

"That's right." Heren Medel said.

"Failure to deal with bullying also costs the employer in other ways as it can have an effect on the culture of the whole organisation. If it is not tackled, then it will be seen by others to be acceptable behaviour. If cases result in an individual taking their employer to an industrial tribunal, which comes to the attention of the media, it can have a very bad effect on the organisation's reputation." Truus continued, feeling on quite a run.

"Excellent, Truus." Medel smiled. Truus felt herself going red, not knowing why.

Kroonstraat Police Bureau, 16.02.

The police had so far received two hundred and thirty-five meaningless phone calls in the first six hours. Since then there was an upsurge every time the news conference was mentioned on TV or on Bingo radio, but they were starting to peter out as attentions wondered. Utrecht had actually beaten PSV this week, so people were thinking of happier things. Sods law, having not been to the *Stadion Galgenwaard* for a while Caes had missed this one after falling asleep at his desk at home.

Many of the names of the callers were known to the Utrecht police. Consensus amongst them was that they should just send out a man to give them a kicking when they wasted their time. Caes supposed that knowing who these people were, helped as they were able to eliminate them immediately. It was the unknown freaks that caused the problems. They had to decide what they had to offer, but they had nothing. One or two leads later did seem promising, but after further investigation and many more wasted man hours they were shown to be futile.

There was the caller from Amsterdam who had seen the three girls performing in a Sex club, the woman who had spoken to Elise on the Stena Line ferry to Harwich and had seen her with her friends. Airports from Schipol to Maastricht Aachen reported sightings, but what they were doing in Beek, god alone knew as no one wanted to travel there. At least this was easy to check. Then there were the parents of children who had also gone missing and the heartache that these stories brought back to them. Not that a lost child was ever forgotten, but they just hoped we had found something of their own children so this just meant more time explaining and apologising to unhappy people. We had calls from all over Holland, sightings in Arnhem, Groningen, even Surinam. It was pointless. They all knew they would mostly be found here in Utrecht. It was just where in Utrecht and who had them?

"How's it going, Caes?"
Caes looked up to see Frans Aartsen poking his head around the door. His body followed as he came and sat down.

"Ah, ADs blue eyed boy." Teased Caes.

"Any luck?" Aartsen asked smiling.

"Not really. They've been seen all over Holland."

"They always are; its crap isn't it? I sometimes wonder if those press conferences ever help."

"I know. I hate doing them. Anyway, what brings you here?" said Caes.

"Oh just to say there was never any follow up after Mevrouw Haan visited us. You know I passed it all back to your guys, but she never came back." Aartsen said plainly.

"Thanks, Frans." Caes smiled.

"Don't forget, if we can help in anyway." Aartsen offered.

"Sure Frans…"

Caes waited thinking then,

"Actually what did you really feel about Thijs Orman?"

Aartsens face seemed to freeze for a moment.

"What about him?"

"What did you think about him as a man?" Caes asked.

"Not a lot, not as a police officer either…"

"No redeeming features?"

"None." Aartsen was firm.

"Not even before he took to drugs?" asked Caes.

"I always found him to be untrustworthy, have you questioned him as a suspect?"

"Not as such…"

"Unreliable, too aggressive with our clients…" Aartsen said.

"The broken jaw?" wondered Caes.

"He was on drugs by then, wish I had known. But he was always suspect, it was in his nature." Aartsen said almost bitterly.

Caes was a bit puzzled, this didn't seem like the Thijs he had known, but Frans had had first-hand experience with him.

"Do you know anyone who might bear him a grudge?" Caes asked.

"Too many to mention, Caes. He upset a lot of people over the years. Horst Vos?" Aartsen suggested.

"Don't think so, we have had a chat…" Caes said.

Frans smiled, "Nice man isn't he…"

"If anyone had a grudge it was him, but nothing concrete on him."

"He is a devious bastard though." Aartsen said.

"Vos? But like he says why now, why would he bother." Caes was plain.

"There must be all the dealers he pissed off and ripped off?" Aartsen said.

"Dead, prison or left Utrecht. We are asking, but it seems hopeless…"

"It is so odd, Caes. Still you know where I am if I can help." Aartsen said.

"Thanks, Frans." he smiled.

"Keep me in the loop."

He held out his hand and they shook, then he moved to the door.

"Give my greetings to Truus." Aartsen smiled.

"Will do, *ziens*, Frans." Smiled Caes.

He closed the door quietly, but it was almost immediately opened again by Madelon.

"What did Aartsen want?" she asked with obvious distaste.

"Nothing really."

"Gives me the creeps!" Madelon said vehemently.

"Madelon!" Caes was surprised.

She shrugged and smiled,

"Anyway, more reports. The follow-ups will take forever, but we've had a bit more staffing from our beloved *Commissaris*."

"Getting a bit jaundiced are you, Maddie?"

"No, not really…" Madelon smiled.

"Anything stand out?"

"Nothing really."

"Nothing from here in Utrecht?"

"That's what puzzles me. Nothing at all. Not even those stupid false sightings." She sighed and sank into the chair opposite Caes,

"What do we do now?"

"I have no idea. More house to house, another television appeal later in the week. No one's seen them, it's as if they just vanished off the face of the earth. All around the same time into a puff of smoke." Grunted Caes.

"Truly does not make sense…" Madelon smiled.

"Never does. We need a different angle…"

"Three girls disappear. No ties to anyone. Same education, schools Universiteit. All three know Truus, have we followed up that angle!" she laughed.

"Steady, Maddie, you are in a mood today!" Caes smiled.

"People know of them, but don't really know them." She was quickly back to serious.

"Then with Thijs's daughter it's the same save that there is someone interested."

"Belatedly though." Sighed Madelon.

"But she does have someone. Was this a mistake?"

"Did the kidnapper know who she was?" Madelon wondered.

"Targeted?"

"Or did he think she had no ties either?"

"If he did I think they will be dead."

"So let's be positive and assume all are targeted. Sterre is the only one who can deliver anything to the kidnapper." Madelon said.

"What are you thinking?" asked Caes.

"Were the first two practice for Sterre?"

Caes hadn't thought of that. It made some sense, but again they could be following a dead end. Still they had nothing else.

"You may be right. We'll have to have another closer look at Thijs and more detail into Sterre."

"I'll get Maaike onto it." Said Madelon.

"Okay, that is a different angle."

Caes felt excited, but not particularly optimistic. The dread was that if it was a practice run through he had no real need for them alive, so what was their future. A shiver ran down his spine. Then he thought of his last conversation.

"Commissaris Aartsen didn't think much of Thijs." Caes threw into the mix.

"Really? Everyone else seems to quite like him."

"I know I did." Caes affirmed.

"But if he was a pain in the neck?"

"I always thought he kept it well hidden. Addicts do until it's too late. Still he was, and I still think is, a good man."

"Well I'll leave you, *baas*. I'll speak to Maaike. Doeg!" Madelon smiled.

"*Doeg*, Maddie."

Caes picked up the phone and dialled an old colleague, Bert Maarwijk. He arranged to meet him at O'Connells for lunch.

Binnenstad. 16.50.

Bert already had a beer at his side. Caes ordered a coffee and went and sat opposite him, shaking hands with a firm dry grasp he said.

"How's tricks, Bert?"

"Fine, how can I help?" Bert Maarwijk smiled.

"Thijs Orman?"

"A right mess, isn't it? Good lad Thijs, shame it ended as it did."

"Know anyone who might want to harm him?"

"That bastard Vos for one." Bert said.

Then he pondered.

"We could have sorted that mess out if we'd been allowed. Top brass got involved too soon for my liking."

"Water under the bridge now, Bert. Anyone else?"

"Usual assortment of pimps and dealers, but none who would take his daughter. They didn't have the brains or if they did they'd be rotted away by now." Replied Bert.

"I knew him as a good cop. What did you think?"

"Reliable till the drugs took hold. Always had your back. I think that's why he lasted so long. Despite the drugs he was a popular guy."

"Protected?" Caes asked.

"Only by his mates on the force. We didn't know how bad it was till it was too late. A few of us tried to help, but when he smacked Vos it gave someone the final excuse. He went downhill really fast."

"I know. Frightening really, being at a different station I never realised. Never heard…"

"Well it was never going to be banded about was it, Caes?" Bert almost snapped.

"Don't suppose… it was all rather sad."

"And what could you do? He had to decide…"

"Could have got help?" Caes asked.

"Didn't want it, said he didn't need any help. He didn't think he had a problem, then his wife up and left him, he attacked Spilker then beat up on Vos, stole his stash…"

"All leads to Vos really, but I don't think he is involved."

"But why now, even if it is Vos, why now?" Bert asked.

"That's what is nagging at me. If it was Vos he would have sorted this out all those years ago, not waited. It isn't his style. He would attack first, think later."

"If he ever thought!"

"He is an opportunist. Lost his stash, did nothing… now look at him."

"Powerful man by all accounts." Bert allowed.

"Don't you worry, Bert, I'll get him one day. Look thanks for the chat. Keep in touch."

Bert raised his eyebrows at Caes.

"Sorry, Bert, you know what I mean."

They shook hands.

"I know what it's like. Give my love to Truus."

"Will do. *Ziens*, Bert." Caes said.

Caes needed to speak to Vos again, perhaps on his turf. Try a different angle. Who knows? All seemed to point towards Vos, but he still wasn't convinced.

Det Zweet Fabriek, Herculesplein. 18.35.

Having missed last week, Caes visited his gym again. It should have been a twice a week personal torture chamber visit, but he had too much on to spare so much time. He needed a better work life balance. That would only happen once they had sorted the murders and the missing girls out. This job really was interfering with his life! Did he need a career change?

Caes stayed on the weights, Bogdi was there on his own so they worked together. He thanked him for helping Truus out at the club. He was a bit disapproving of her working in a place like that and said what a bastard this Izzie was, but they moved on. Bogdi forced Caes back to concentrating on his weights programme, but insisted they lift heavier weights, with not so many reps. It was certainly different. He explained how this was more to emphasise strength than power. His physique reflected this. He was very bulked up, Caes was not too sure how this kind of weight lifting would be appropriate for him as he needed to nip about swiftly, as well as sometimes he had to chase and bring people down. He didn't need all that bulk, Caes also didn't like the heavy muscled look of it either. As long as Bogdi could catch the felons he'd be able to swat them down. Heavier weights with less reps meant Caes finished earlier than usual, he showered and sat in the small café attached to the gym. Bogdi sat beside him and sipped at a mineral water. He smiled at Caes.

"So Keeeys, what is happening in big wide world?"

"You've seen the news?"

"Murders in Utrect. We settled here because it was safe..."

"It still is Bogdi." Caes smiled grimly.

"I know that, but outsiders? They see news and think worse..."

"I know, I hate that my city gets dragged down into the dirt."

The conversation depressed Caes. He loved Utrecht. Born and bred there, he felt he belonged. Not to a city of murders and kidnapping. He loved the Utrecht of cobbled stones and hurrying cyclists. Students and colour and noise. At the moment it might just be snow and slush, but it still didn't diminish his love for the city. He bade farewell to Bogdi and wandered across Utrecht towards the gentile delights of home. The Dom towered above him, sparkling in the snow. He shivered and put his head down against the wind. What could he do, the case was filling up his waking hours and he couldn't think where it would go. The clues were conspicuous by their absence and he didn't know where they were heading. Where were the two missing women? Why had Spilker been killed? It was just getting murkier as time went by.

Vagevuur.

He pushed the door open and shouted.

"You, get out."

Sterre seemed to shrink and Elise stared at him.

"What are you going to do?" screamed Elise panicking.

"Just do as I say!"

"Leave her be, what is it?"

He marched over to Elise and slapped her across the face, then grabbed her by the hair and started to drag her to the door. Sterre was in too much pain to move and could only hurl abuse at him. He pushed Elise back into the cell next door and locked the door. Elise banged and kicked it in frustration.

"What do you want?" Sterre asked ashen faced.

"A message for Papa."

"Why?"

"Because I want you to." He sneered.

"You can fuck off, I'm not helping you."

He grabbed her broken finger and squeezed, she howled in agony and then screamed.

"Do what you are told you little slut or there's worse to come."

Sterre could not stop crying. She had never known pain like it and felt as if her whole body was on fire.

"What have I ever done…?"

"Not you, your fucking father! He ruined my life!"

"Who are you? What has he done?"

"Too much, way too much."

"But why me, how does this help?"

"Don't be so stupid, this is for me."

"But please, my hand, please don't…"

"Tell your father this."

He thrust a piece of paper in front of her. She read it quickly to herself.

"But…" she didn't understand. Her father?

"Do you want more?"

He stepped towards her and she tried to push herself into the wall.

"No please, don't!"

He had what he wanted and now to proceed. The police were no nearer finding him. They had no idea who had the women or who had murdered the old woman and Spilker. He just had to tie up the loose ends. Destroy Orman and dispose of the women. Quite simple really. Orman though, did he deserve to face his crime or should he just get rid of his daughter and tell him? He had at one stage decided to get rid of her and to leave Orman in limbo, now though he had other plans. It would be good to confront him, man to man and tell him what he thought. That way he would feel the pain and see the power he had over him. He had his daughter. He was in control. Yes, that was it. He would confront him and before he killed him he would explain how his daughter was to die. Perfect.

Chapter 16

Vrijdag, November 21, 2014.
Kroonstraat Police Bureau, 09.15.

Maaike asked to see Caes as soon as she got in that morning so he spoke with her before morning briefing. She was pale and had black circles round her eyes, she looked tired and had lost a little of her usual sparkle.

"You're not right, are you, Maaike?"

She seemed very mixed up.

"Not really, *baas*."

"Coffee?" Caes asked.

"Please."

"What can we do?"

"I was with Jeltje de Bruun late last night, she tried to kill herself." Maaike blurted out.

"Jesus," Caes's blood ran cold.

"Freddie came with me, without him there…"

"Oké."

She started to cry.

"Without him there, I don't know what I would have done."

"He's a good lad." Caes said softly.

"She is so young and has been so badly treated."

"I know, but that's really not your fault, Maaike."

"I know that, I do, but we should not let it happen at all." Maaike said.

"I know, Maaike."

"People may want to pay for sex, I accept that, but not with such a little thing, she is so damaged…"

Maaike wiped her eyes.

"No, but there are many perverted people out there." Caes wasn't sure how to proceed.

"And then, not to be beaten by some bastard if she doesn't do what he wants."

"I know."

Caes agreed, he was just letting her talk it out.

"But what can we do, this goes on and on."

"Not as much as you think, but yes."

"On and on, *baas*, under our noses and how do we stop it?" Maaike affirmed angrily.

227

"Well as long as prostitution is legal there is not much we can do, but it's the violence that is so wrong."

"And underage girls?"

"Of course, we need to crack down on that."

"When though?" Maaike almost pleaded.

"Well since we have had Jeltje come in, the Bureau Jeugdzorg are going to look closer, so you did good there."

"But…"

"You can't do everything at once. If you would like I could task you and Madelon with looking closer at the problem in our area?"

"Could you?"

"But we cannot have this taking over your work or more importantly your life."

"I know…"

"You will need to liaise with the Bureau Jeugdzorg and get their advice." Caes said.

"Oké."

"Truus and I spoke about this the other night. You have to be sure you can leave most of your work here at Kroonstraat, don't take it home with you."

"It's hard though…" Maaike said.

"It's almost impossible, Maaike, if you are a good officer as you are and you care as you do, it is very difficult."

"Compartmentalise things?" she smiled.

"I say you should try, I have been in the police for over twenty years and I still find it hard." Caes smiled.

"How do you do it?"

"I talk to Truus, she's only young I know, but it helps to talk. I have friends I meet sometimes. I never go into too much detail though; I don't want to scare them off!"

"No," she smiled.

"You have your parents and Freddie."

"Yes we talk a lot, could we talk too much?" Maaike said.

"No, you never can, but again, don't take it all home. Leave it here sometimes."

"I can try."

"You have Truus?" Caes smiled.

She blushed,

"Yes I have Truus. You are fine with that?"

"Of course..."

"It is early though... but what else can I do?"

"I exercise a lot, weight train, I run to get the old endorphins shaken up to make me feel happy." Caes said.

"I could do more then?"

"And take time away, we have been away a few times, just for the day or for a couple of days, just get away and forget everything."

"Right." Maaike said.

"You have your Judo and your dancing! You love dancing, don't you?"

"I do, me and Truus had a good time the other night."

"Then dance more..."

"I'm not sure... seems frivolous."

"Maaike, that's the whole point." Laughed Caes.

"I suppose..." Maaike seemed unsure.

"Well you could give it a go. Just do something different a few times a week."

"Oké."

"And if you want to talk, I am always here or on the phone and you know I'll never mind if you want to chat to me on your visits!"

"*Dank, baas.*" Maaike blushed again.

"And your non-police friends, you have many?"

"We have a few, from school still."

"Well they are important as they will not always want to hear police talk, unless it's really gory!" That made her laugh,

"Come on then, Maaike, let's go to briefing, we'll suggest to Madelon our project and let us move forward."

"*Oké, baas, dank...*"

They left the room together to go to morning briefing. Caes thought he was becoming a sort of therapist to ease his co-workers through the pitfalls that faced them. He had to grimace at the idea. They entered the room. At least everyone still looked positive which was a good thing. They were soon in full flow. Highlighting the successes, they had achieved and trying to work out why they had not been more successful.

"*Dank.* I haven't had time to firm this up yet, but after Maaike's great work with the young girl Jeltje de Bruuin, I want her to look into a project to try to do something about this problem of violent pimps. If anyone has any thoughts speak to Madelon, me or Maaike. This is important, we have a group of men who think they are beyond the law and women who seem to tolerate it. I know it goes much deeper than we can see and I also know we can't do this in isolation so maybe get in contact with the collective or the PIC. You can do this formally or informally. We'll look at a strategy in more detail later this week. Madelon?"

"*Bedankt, baas*, nothing new on the murders, or the missing girls. We continue house to house and photos going out at the Universiteit and locale, but nothing. The murder of two people does not seem to have affected anyone, especially as the two would be what could be called misfits and are indeed missed by no one. A shame in one case I know."

"Ernst?"

"*Dank, baas*, pickpocketing down, I can't believe how taking one person out makes such a difference, but when we searched his rooms, man, you could see he had been busy. But keep a look out, especially you Freddie!"

There were laughs as they remembered he hadn't noticed he was being pickpocketed the other day.

"*Dank*, Ernst!" Freddie snarled good naturedly.

"Izzie and his mob charged and awaiting bail hearing. Hopefully they will be put away, but we can't be sure. Still no cars stolen since they were arrested." Ernst laughed.

"That's three good results in a very short time. Well done everyone involved. Anything else? *Oké*, have a good one everybody." Caes smiled.

Amaliastraat, 10.13.

Truus had decided to write this morning and was at her bedroom desk. She kept looking out of the window. It hadn't stopped snowing, she decided a poem was appropriate and started to think. Rhyme or prose? She preferred prose poems. They gave her more room to work, she did not feel restricted. Story of her life really. She never wanted to be restricted, held down, squeezed into a format that she didn't want to be part of. Looking out of the window she thought of the ice and the snow and decided to be predictable and write about the seasons. She tried to invoke her muse and connect the different seasons with contrasting feelings, trying to work on the imagery that presented itself, looking for words that could convey more than one meaning. She liked words, to be able to manipulate them and get them to play her game. At times, they would pour from her fingers and she could hardly control them, hardly order them. At other times, it was a struggle to find just the right one, the word that meant everything, that would explain away a hundred thoughts in just one space.

When she hit upon that special word it made her feel so good. Words did bring her alive, the right words anyway. When she came across the wrong words it was sometimes as if she had been punched or knocked off balance and she had to take time to regain her balance and get into the flow of things. Words still took her to places she had never been, gave her feelings she had never had. She loved the journey. She loved her destinations as well at times, if it seemed right. She always wondered what was right. Who was to judge her work? She kept most to herself, she didn't want to share everything because a lot of her work came from very deep inside her and was a place only she could enter, but this work on the seasons was different. She thought she should share this and then started to wonder who the audience should be. It was all so confusing. *Why can't I just write for myself and not worry about anyone else*, she thought. Then it was back to the keyboard, checking off ideas in her notebook that she had written the other day.

Kroonstraat Police Bureau, 10.15.

Danny barged in without knocking, Caes was just about to shout at him, but he started first,

"*Baas*, we've found her!"

"Who?"

For an instant, he had no idea what he was talking about.

"Gisele de Groet!"

"Where?"

"Front desk, *baas*, she just walked in!" then he rushed out again.

Maaike opened the interview after the necessary introductions to the tape machine,

"You are Gisele de Groet?"

"Yes, I don't really understand…"

"Mevrouw Haan said you were missing." Caes said.

"I'm not though, where is Elise?"

"Where have you been?" Maaike asked.

"Staying at Texel by the sea. What's happening?"

Her face was pale. She had been crying as her eyes were red against the white skin. She looked desolate. She held her handkerchief to her nose. She seemed to be on the verge of disintegration, just holding herself together.

"Please, I don't understand. I saw the news, my picture, then Elise and Sterre was it?"

"Coffee?" Maaike suggested.

"Please… I'm sorry. Please explain. I saw the news, grabbed a newspaper on the way here, but… Elise where is she?"

"We don't know." Caes said.

"I thought she'd left me."

"Left?"

"I thought we were in love. I was in love. Then she disappeared, I thought she'd gone, left me got fed up… I was so unhappy…"

She started to cry. Great drops of tears left her eyes.

Maaike came back with coffee and sat beside Gisele. She put her arm around her,

"Let's start at the beginning, Gisele…"

"We met at College, Universiteit. We had known each other at school, with Truus, *Hoofdinspecteur,* but we drifted apart. We all drifted. My mother found a new man when Pappy died. She left me here and went to America. I was on my own, we met again at Universiteit. We didn't have much to do with each other until about two months ago when we started chatting. She was on her own as well. Her parents were dead. We both had no one…"

She paused and Maaike squeezed her hand gently.

"Have some coffee Gisele…"

She sipped her drink and smiled thinly.

"We kept bumping into each other. We made friends again, we kept talking, we went out together, got closer and then… I moved in with her." Said Gisele.

"When was this?" asked Maaike.

"I can't remember, but we were so happy. It seemed so perfect. I hadn't realised that I could be so happy."

"But you left?" asked Maaike.

"She, I thought she'd walked out and left me. There was no message, no note…" Gisele said.

"When was this?"

"Three weeks ago. Her clothes were still there. I don't know why but I just thought she'd left me; I don't know why…" Gisele was nonplussed.

"So no police?" asked Maaike.

"No. I did try the hospitals, but nothing… I don't know why I didn't try the police. Her mobile was gone; I must have been mad. She didn't answer her phone, always to voicemail then it went dead. Thought she was ignoring me. I feel so guilty…"

"Why did you leave?" Caes asked.

"I was upset and angry, it's so stupid, I packed all my stuff, didn't leave anything, didn't really know what I was doing."

"Why Texel?" Caes asked.

"We always went there when my Dad was alive, we loved it. Every summer, so beautiful. I suddenly thought that's where I should be." Gisele smiled.

"You wanted to escape?" said Maaike.

"I suppose so. Yes, I did. I thought I'd be safe there. That if she had left me I was in a happy place."

"Were you?" asked Caes.

"Not really. I was sad. Mad really."

"Not at all, Gisele," Maaike reassured her.

"I really thought she had left me and wouldn't be back until I'd gone."

Gisele was again on the verge of tears.

"But still no police?"

"I know it was stupid. But where is she?"

"We think she had been kidnapped." Caes said.

Gisele gasped,

"But why. Who would do such a thing?"

"We have no idea."

Caes was of course at a loss.

"Do you know Sterre Orman or Vossen?" asked Maaike, moving things along.

"Sterre Vossen, yes. She's in some of the same classes as me. But she has gone too?"

"We think they may be together. We have some kind of motive for Sterre, but do you know anyone who would want to harm Elise?" said Maaike.

"No she was perfect…"

A small smile appeared on her lips, but soon faded.

"She didn't have many friends, but no enemies either." Gisele continued.

"Do you have any?" asked Caes.

"Me? Why should I? I didn't hurt her. I love her. She is everything to me."

She snatched her hand away from Maaike.

"Why would I?" she started to sob again.

Caes tried to explain,

"Gisele, we have to ask. We can't not ask…"

"I know, I know, but to think I'd hurt her." Gisele was affronted.

"We don't," Caes said, "It's just the way things go. Some questions need to be asked. We can't second guess answers. We have to pursue every clue."

"I'm not a clue, *Hoofdinspecteur*. I don't know anything." Snapped Gisele.

"So there was nothing unusual before Elise disappeared? Someone outside the flat?" Maaike asked.

"Nothing sorry…"

"Any phone calls that ended abruptly when you answered?"

"Only mobile calls and we always knew who was ringing. Like I said there aren't that many people who would ring… anyway Elise would have said I'm sure."

"What about at Universiteit or in Utrecht. Could someone be jealous of your happiness?" Maaike asked.

"No one knew. We had no one to tell. We were both loners really."

Caes looked at Maaike, she shrugged.

"What about Sterre?" asked Maaike.

"What about her?" replied Gisele.

"Did you talk?"

Gisele thought for a moment.

"Not really, no not ever…"

"Even in class?" Caes wondered.

"I can't remember. I don't think so." Pondered Gisele.

"Did she know Elise?" asked Maaike.

"Everybody knows everybody in a way, but not as friends just as classmates." Gisele said.

"She is a Facebook friend though?" Maaike suggested.

"There are so many. I think we 'liked' everyone at Freshers when we first met, but we don't talk."

"To Elise?"

"I don't think so. Though she would have told me everything. We just did."

"So no secrets?" Caes said.

"None, we were very open. What can I do, *Hoofdinspecteur*?" asked Gisele.

"Keep your phone on. All we can do is wait. She may call. It maybe she wanted a break and is fine, just as you are, but I think we must accept that she has been taken. One last thing. What about Mevrouw Haan?"

"She was a funny old lady." Gisele smiled sadly.

"She thought you and Elise were her daughters. It was she who reported you missing."

"And now she's dead. Am I in danger?" Gisele looked up wide eyed.

"I don't think so, but to be safe we'll put you in a hotel for a while," Caes said.

"But Mevrouw Haan, Gisele?" Maaike asked.

"We went round to her house once. Just to be polite. We could see from the outside what it would be like. It was awful, a pigsty. It was really sad. We offered to help tidy up, but she asked why. She seemed happy in her world, but she smelt awful. So did her house. We only went there once. She didn't want seem to understand why we would want to help."

"Some people are like that, Gisele, as they get older," Caes said.

"But maybe we should have tried harder, I don't..."

"There's no point thinking like that. Social Services knew about her, kept an eye on her, but it is never enough. Some people don't want to be helped. Though with her I think it was perhaps dementia. She was happy in her world. I hope so anyway." Caes said.

"Is there anything we can do for you, Gisele?" Maaike asked.

"Just find Elise and Sterre. Was it the same man who killed Mevrouw Haan do you think?"

"Maybe, but we cannot be sure. It could be coincidence, all living in Vaterstraat, but..." Maaike replied.

"Please find her, Hoofdinspecteur." Pleaded Gisele quietly.

"We are trying, Gisele, believe me we are doing our best. Now Agent Meijer will sort you out with a hotel. Do you need anything?"

"No, I left some things in Texel, but have enough for now..."

Caes gave her his card,

"Ring me at any time. I will answer or you must come in to the station if there is any problem."

"I will, *Hoofdinspecteur.*"

Particulier Onderzoeks Bureau, Blokstraat. 13.35.

Caes, Truus and Thijs sat at Orman's desk. The small recorder a powerful messenger. Sterre could hardly speak the words, her sobs breaking up each sentence.

"*Vader*, I have to read this to you. He… I am alright. My hand hurts and he says he will do worse. He just wants you to know that I am suffering. He will keep me as long as he wants to. There is no escape for me. Think about your past and what you have done. Think about the people you have hurt."
There was a pause as they listened to Sterre triying to stop sobbing, but it was heart wrenching. Thijs was grey and looked twenty years older. Truus was silently crying at the desk.

"He says you know what you have done. There is no escape. I am here for as long as it takes. *Vader*, I love you. He's a bastard…"
There was a slap and a muffled cry as the recorder went off.

"What in God's name does he want?" Thijs said.

"It's no clearer…" Caes answered.

"All we do know is that it's a man," Truus said.

"What have I done, who have I hurt so much?" Thijs asked.

"Sounds like the work of a madman, Thijs." Caes said.

"Then there is no hope?" cried Thijs.

"If he is playing a game, there is hope. He will keep her alive, just to torment you."
Caes replied.

"The bastard, what can I do?"

"We have to wait. We'll go through your records again, re interview, widen the net. We have to find the person you have annoyed." Said Caes.

"I have no idea, Caes. None."

"No prints, no background noise, nothing. Millions of these little recorders sold."
Caes said aimlessly.

Amaliastraat, 17.15.

"You saw Bert Maarwijk?" smiled Truus.

"Yes, he sends his love…"

"I used to really like him. It's funny how we drift apart."

Truus smiled at the memories.

"I know, different places of work, assignments. Nothing stays the same."

"Will your team?" asked Truus.

"What?"

"Stay together?"

"For the moment I hope, though Maddie is looking or rather has been asked to look."

"Really?" Truus was interested.

"Maastricht, by the baas."

"That's too far away. She's really nice."

"I know, a good officer."

"No, Pappy, a really nice woman. Do you want her to go?" Truus smiled.

"Not really, but she'll have to decide. I told her to go down and have a look."

"Pappy, fight to keep her!" Truus was suddenly very serious.

"Why?"

"You'll see she's worth the fight."

"We'll see, Truus. Anyway, back to this problem. I just need to focus. We all remember Thijs as a good guy, all except his last baas Frans Aartsen."

"I remember his name vaguely." Truus said.

"He really doesn't like Thijs; thought he was a waster."

"Each to their own."

"Everyone else really liked him despite his problems."

"I remember telling him you respected him at my interview."

Truus grimaced at the memory.

"I did once, and probably will again."

"It's strange, Pappy how we see someone and think all is well, but underneath they hold a great secret that can affect so many."

"What are you trying to tell me, lieverd?"

"Not me, Pappy! You know all my secrets."

She started to go red.

"Do any of us know what is going on in other people's head's?"

"I sometimes dread to think what's going on in yours, Truus!"

"Pappy, seriously. I try to see everyone as an open book. I don't expect them to be hiding anything from me. What's the point? Most people don't try to hide things, but when they do is it ever for a good reason?"

"I don't know..."

"Everyone is different, Pappy. We can't always be open it seems, but are we hiding things for the wrong reason? To protect ourselves, to protect others? In normal life, we don't have to worry about that, but in your work people always seem to have an agenda, always trying to stay ahead of you..."

"I understand people can be devious, but I don't see all people trying to trick me. Anyone can lie and cheat." Caes said.

"But, Pappy they can also be warm and caring and wonderful." Truus responded.

"Exactly, Truus and that's the angle I always take. I always look for the good in people. Even though you may feel down at times and feel everything is against you, you must see people as honest and true, you cannot think the worst of people."

"Like Frans Aartsen does?" Truus stated.

"He has a jaundiced view it must be said, but I don't really know him since he left the academy and that's a long time ago."

"Is that why you get disappointed?"

"I think so, when people seem to let you down. Crime is letting us down; criminals are working against society not with it and that's painful to me."

"You have me though, Pappy."

She put her head in his lap, her blazing red hair like a beacon and he stroked it gently.

"I'm not a replacement, but I am here."

Caes wasn't sure how she had moved onto this, but smiled.

"I know, *liefje*, I know."

Caes felt a bit wistful, he did try to see the good in people. Femke had always pressed this on him from his early days in the police and hers as a teacher. She always thought that her students were intrinsically good. It was hard to believe when she told him what some of them got up to, but he would smile at her tales and expect to see them personally as they all grew older. When Femke died, it was hard for Caes to see the good in anyone when such a terrible thing had happened. Everything seemed pointless for such a long time. It was only having Truus that dragged Caes through it. Indeed, she almost physically dragged him onto his feet. He couldn't be doing with offers from outsiders of help, it all seemed pointless and meaningless. They could never fill the hole that had been left. He wanted to be on his own with his darling daughter and no one else. It had been Caes and Truus ever since. Now he tried to keep Femke's maxim at the core of all his beliefs. Truus spoke and sent more shivers down his spine.

"If Thijs is a good person, Pappy, then person who has Sterre is quite evil and how do you deal with evil?"

As Caes sat on his settee he thought about what they had so far. It wasn't very much. The girls were still missing; the police hadn't made any real progress. In fact, with the two deaths they had added to the list of concerns. The link between murders and missing girls seemed tenuous, but he felt for some reason they were all linked. Caes rolled over onto his side and looked at the window. He could see ice formed on the outside and wondered how cold it must be. Through the chink in the curtain the moon shone through. He had to find a link. The fate of the two girls depended upon a link. The only pertinent link was Thijs Orman. Someone he had upset in a past life. Someone who knew he had a past with Spilker. That narrowed it down slightly. It hadn't been common knowledge that he had assaulted him. Caes was sure it wasn't Horst Vos. Madelon had been to reinterview him in his own lair to try and put him at ease. He had been too laid back and phlegmatic Madelon had thought, with a clear answer for everything. He had convinced her of his innocence. In this case, anyway and Caes respected her judgement. So, Elise, how did this connect with her? Did she know Spilker? Had she been a victim of his tendencies, was it revenge? She knew Mevrouw Haan, had she been involved in Spilkers circle? The more this went on the more questions were being asked, more leads to investigate... he slowly drifted off to sleep, seeing the picture of Mevrouw Haans body in the snow.

Geen Angst Cross Fit, Daalsedijk, 19.15.

Maaike had rung up Truus to ask if she could join her at Cross Fit. They met up at Geen Angst at about seven. Truus usually enjoyed the later night workouts. It meant she slept soundly unless Maaike returned home with her, but they were both going out tonight.

Maaike was stretching slowly as Truus came into the gym.

"Hi, Truus, you oké?"

Truus leant forward and kissed Maaike on the lips. The familiar surge in her tummy returned. Maaike smiled at her. She was so beautiful.

"Good, good to see you. Freddie oké?"

"He's fine, what do I do then?"

"The coach will tell you what to do. If in doubt, ask. Don't go too hard too soon though."

They went through to the Studio and Truus saw Maaike's nervousness increase. The coach was the Amazon and she had just finished a group session and the participants were all lying on the floor, not moving. Their chests were heaving and sweat was pouring down their faces, but other than that, there was no movement.

"Are they dead?" Maaike asked looking on in bemused panic.

"No, well, not really." Truus said.

Gradually the exhausted group began to drag themselves off to the showers. Then the Amazon began anew. She explained to Maaike as she was new that there were dozens of Cross Fit workouts to ensure they didn't get bored and that their body didn't adapt to the exercises.

"Today, we're going to do a workout known as 'Fight Gone Bad.'"

The Amazon demonstrated the five moves involved, then she had them perform them slowly to ensure that they were familiar with them.

"That's great," Amazon said. "Don't forget to breathe… like this, phhhttt."

"Right," Maaike said, feeling self-conscious, but oddly exhilarated. Then they got started. First they had to squat onto a medicine ball, while hurling a second medicine ball against the wall. This was just for a minute, a really, really long minute. Maaike looked as if she was going to cry, Truus kept encouraging her, but her arms were burning at the same time and starting to feel incredibly heavy.

Then they had to race to a twelve-kilogram kettle bell and perform a so-called Sumo Dead-lift High Pull, a combination of squatting and lifting the kettle bell to their chests. More arm work, luckily the next exercise was sixty seconds of jumping on and off a wooden box, but then it was followed by a minute's worth of what the Amazon called a Push Press which was a barbell lift combined with another squat. Last, it was a minute's recovery on the rowing machine, a minute's rest and then they had to do it all again. And again.

"I can't, Truus." Maaike moaned.

"You can, keep going, just dig in there. It's doing you so much good."

"But it hurts!" Maaike pretended to cry, but Truus was too exhausted to laugh.

The full three sets only took fifteen minutes, but they were both exhausted.

"My thighs are on fire; I can't feel my arms and I'm covered in sweat." Maaike said.

"Don't you worry, Maaike, it's gonna hurt even more tomorrow, but we need to do it again. Soon. Remember it was only fifteen minutes. Let's go through to the weight room and pump some iron!"

Truus had planned a short circuit, but was going to make it intense and repeat it several times. She had devised a session looking at the abs, but this meant they had to make sure that they concentrated on form. Truus put her hands on her tummy and was pleased that it was so hard. There was flesh there, she didn't want to be anorexic, but she had good definition, just like Maaike she noticed.

She hoped Maaike would cope as it had been quite a tough set so far, but she needn't have worried. They went through the routine methodically. It was a real killer. Maaike collapsed first and Truus followed, then it was a drink. They then did a set of one hundred skips before they went through the whole lot again.

Truus's stomach was so sore after the third set, but she had promised herself that she would do it five times and so five times she did it. They faced each other for the final set of skipping with Maaike gurning at Truus as she bounced up and down effortlessly, sometimes flicking the rope through twice for each skip or doing some ridiculous boxing skipping trick that she had learnt somewhere. They finished and Maaike started to stretch out in front of Truus as she slid down onto the floor to complete her cool down. She smiled and blew Truus a kiss.

"Good effort, Maaike." Truus said.

"You too. Making it look so easy, I hate you."

"Not feeling too easy though," Truus smiled, "that was hard work."

"Well I can see the benefits on you, that's good."

"Can't stop though, now can we? I don't want to go to seed."

"Fat chance, Truus, why do you think that?"

The question was answered with a smirk.

Good session? It was horrible; Truus could hardly walk to the bus stop. Her arms felt so heavy and her tummy was just being stabbed by some little bastard every time she breathed in. Truus put her palm across her tummy. She thought she could feel it throb, which made her laugh to herself which of course made her wince even more as it hurt so much. Truus made it onto the bus like some old lady and slumped into a seat. Truus thought she should have sat in the ones reserved for the disabled as she felt truly disabled. Truus couldn't move, she hoped to god she didn't seize up. Then her nightmare continued as Maaike jumped on her. She almost made Truus cry as she elbowed her in her tummy.

"I'm in agony!" Truus almost shouted, but she didn't have the energy to push her away.

"Lucky I'm here to look after you, look what I have. Bath oils." Maaike said proudly.

Amaliastraat, 20.35.

Once home, Truus was able to luxuriate the aches and pains out of her body as she lay submerged in hot water and bubbles. Maaike sat on the loo and smiled at her.

"Nice?"

"Wonderful, this is just what I needed."

"Thought so, I love two for one sales, they are so useful when you want to impress your girlfriend."

"Such a nice thought," Truus laughed.

"That's me, ever the thoughtful one!" Maaike said. "I'd join you if you weren't such a physical wreck!"

Maaike leaned over the side of the bath and started to gently sponge over Truus, dabbing and teasing and caressing her.

"No, Maaike, please don't..."

Truus pleaded as Maaike touched her where she knew she loved her fingers to play.

"Maaike, noo, it's too nice."

"You spoilsport, Truus..." moaned Maaike.

"It's pain and pleasure,"

Truus smiled through gritted teeth.

"I am in so much pain, I think I did five hundred sit-ups and god knows how many press-ups."

Maaike stroked her breasts.

"Maaike please..."

"Don't you love me?" she tried to look upset.

"If I could move I would show you."

"Well, don't move," Maaike smiled and undressed and slipped into the bath beside her.

"Let me show you..."

So she did and this time Truus didn't ask her to stop

Truus and Maaike were off to see Depeche Mode at the Ajax ArenA in Amsterdam. Truus thought she'd go for an ironic look at the concert. Pappy had an old white Fred Perry polo, so she added that to her jeans and a pair of Pappy's red braces and her Doc Martens. She was like an Ajax eighties skinhead throw back, but she managed to get two nice bunches in her chilli red hair into white ribbons. Truus looked at her face in the mirror and drew crimson onto her lips, making them stand out and brushed kohl around her eyes. Maaike looked over her shoulder.

"Beautiful, my love," she whispered and then kissed her ear.

Truus turned round, Maaike was very emo, dressed completely in black, tights, short dress, cardigan and lots of mascara and jet black lips. Her Doc Martens were a shiny black and laced right up. Her only concession to colour was a red kerchief in her auburn hair. Truus pulled her to her and kissed the black lips.

"You taste nice tonight."

"You too," she said. "Come on, we'll miss our train."

Ajax ArenA, 22.10.

From Utrecht Centraal they got the sprinter across to Amsterdam which became packed as they got closer to the destination, then they found themselves being carried along by the crowd as they walked the last few metres to the ArenA. There was too much expensive memorabilia on sale in the auditorium, so they went up to the bar. Truus got them both a couple of cheeky drinks and they stood wedged together in the crowd. Truus of course did not mind being so close to Maaike and could feel her body heat through her polo. She felt as if she was dissolving into Maaike as she sipped her overly expensive drink. Truus looked into Maaike's emerald eyes and wondered if they reflected her love for her. Maaike smiled her smile and Truus knew the truth. She leaned over and kissed her cheek.

"I do love you." Truus smiled.

"Already?" Maaike seemed surprised.

"Yes, I am sure of it."

"I know and I love you as well."

Truus had only ever told her mammie and pappy that she loved them. This was weird, but she felt she had been with Maaike forever and that her feelings were there, open for all to see and her feelings for her were intense. She felt she loved her, she needed her, and she wanted her. This was ridiculous, so fast, but this was love. Truus curled her arm around Maaike's slim waist and felt a tingle of excitement. Wrong place, wrong time in so many ways! Then they moved into the Arena to watch their heroes. Forget the support act, they had listened to them from the bar, and were only there for their boys.

It was magical, though Truus hadn't really liked their latest record, they had played enough of the old tunes to send them out happy. They all blasted out. Synth poprock at its best, from the best. Dave Gahan's voice was like gravelly honey. If I ever fancied a man, thought Truus, they would have to sound like him! And what a stupid thought that seemed now!

The encore included Pappy's' favourite from the good old days, 'Just Can't Get Enough' and finally a barnstorming, as the old folks would say, rendition of 'Never Let Me Down Again'.

Her throat sore from singing so loudly, Truus's legs ached from dancing so much and her clothes were soaked in sweat from the heat of bodies, the movement, the dancing, the everything. Maaike's hair was also wet and matted and Truus dreaded to think what hers looked like. Her ribbons, though still in place, were damp and limp. A bit like she felt in body, but her mind was alive with the electricity of the evening.

"Do you want to come back to mine?" Truus asked.

"To sleep?"

"Eventually..." Truus giggled, "Sorry that sounded so slutty."

She felt herself going red.

"No, it sounded so nice…" Maaike smiled.

It took hours to get back to Utrecht. The sprinter trains were all packed as the crowds left the ArenA, they had to queue for ages, but the thought of what awaited them at home, tired or not, fortified them both and they spent most of the time staring soppily into each other's eyes.

Vagevuur.

Sterre lay on the mattress sobbing, her hand throbbing and pulsing with pain. He had slapped her and twisted it again. She couldn't move, her whole body rocked with agony. She had never ever known anything like it and had been sick.

Elise was shoved in again and hurried over to her. She found a towel and went to the sink and returned to clean her up and to comfort her.

"It hurts so much, Elise, I can't bear it."

"You have to, I'm sorry, you have to. Try to sleep, I'll look after you."

"What's my pappy done to make this happen? He's really a good man, what can he have done?"

"This man's insane, Sterre. I don't think it matters what your pappy did or didn't do. He's mad and that is really scary."

"What can we do?" Sterre asked.

"There's nothing here, no weapons, you can't fight, what can I do?"

"I don't know, he's too strong. If we had something…"

"There's nothing, the room's bare, nothing…" Elise replied.

"He's hurt my hand so much." Cried Sterre.

"Take it easy, try to sleep, try to relax." Elise stroked her head gently.

Elise's soothing words seemed to calm Sterre and she fell into a fitful sleep. Elise looked down on her. Every so often a tremor would make its way through Sterres body. Elise was cold, she was hungry and she was frightened. What she was doing there was the thing that scared her most. It was as if she was an afterthought. He'd made no demands upon her. Well just the early attempt, that had been enough, but otherwise why was she here? There was no one to save her, no ransom to be gained from anyone. She was surplus to requirements. Story of her life it seemed up until she had met Gisele and now this was happening. She just couldn't catch a break. Where was Giselle? What was she doing? She must know she was missing, was she looking for her? This was a disaster. She closed her eyes and wished it was all a bad dream, a nightmare. She opened her eyes to discover it was only too real.

Chapter 17

> Zaterdag, November 22, 2014.
> Amaliastraat 10.12.

Maaike turned and smiled at Truus.

"Dungarees again?" Maaike pointed disapprovingly.

"Yes, what's wrong with them?"

Maaike suddenly made Truus feel all defensive.

"You are showing off your tummy again."

"Well, my darling, if you have it you flaunt it!"

"But dungarees!"

"I like them; I think I look cute."

"And a sports bra, have you no shame?"

"What?"

"It's inappropriate! So non rigeur."

"Dungarees and sports bra on the fashionista Maaike Meijer's no no list? I wonder why?"

"What do you mean? I was thinking of the weather!" Maaike said.

"Tummy." Truus replied.

"What?"

"You love my tummy." Truus boasted.

"So?"

"You love my boobs." Truus smiled.

"Your point being, Miss Heda?" Maaike was smiling.

"You don't want anyone else to see what's yours and lust after it!"

"God you are so full of it!" Maaike snorted.

"But?"

Truus raised her eyebrows, waiting.

"Alright! I wish you would wear a sack so no one could see you!"

"How very old fashioned you are!" Truus smiled.

"Roll up the legs, that'll look better."

So Truus obeyed and it did.

Kroonstraat Police Bureau, 11.00.

There had been no more breakthroughs, *Hoofdcommissaris* Coeman had been onto Media Affairs and they suggested appearing on Saturday nights crime programme, *Opsporing Verzocht*. Caes hated the thought of being on television so asked Madelon to appear. She had a face for television!

Madelon was cool and composed as she sat at the high table looking into a battery of lights, reporters and the inevitable microphones. She opened the session with an account of what they had done so far and what help they now needed. Everyone then started speaking at once, but she only had to raise a hand for silence to take over the proceedings.

"One at a time..." she said.

"Brad Veerten. AD News... What is the progress to date?"

It was if her previous statement had already been forgotten.

"As I said in my preliminary, we still need help from the public. One of the young women has been traced and eliminated from our enquiries. Gisele de Groet is not a suspect, but an innocent victim of a misunderstanding. The other two young women have simply disappeared and no one as yet has seen anything that can help us."

"What precisely do you need?" Bingo Radio asked.

Madelon again repeated what she had said earlier. Caes admired her patience.

Flash bulbs went off and cameras whirred. It was quite distracting, but Madelon stayed on point.

"Where you in *Vaartestraat* on the dates in question. Did you see anything unusual? At the Universiteit did you know the young women. Were they having any problems? I know it seems a cliché, but was there a problem with partners, was anything out of the ordinary. We have to think outside the box. Did something unusual happen in the days or even hours before they disappeared. Arguments? Fights?"

"Miriam van Peert, Radio M. Could this be a love triangle gone wrong? Do you think there is a sexual connotation to this?"

"We are hoping that the women will not be harmed. We do not know if there is a connection between them at the moment. Evidence has not come forward to support this, but if any of their friends does know they should come to us at Kroonstraat and help us. Everything will be kept in the strictest confidence. We really do value anything that could help us no matter how insignificant you may think it is..."

Madelon was firm and reassuring.

And so it went on. At least the reporters seemed interested, if only the general public would get involved. In a positive way that is. Caes left Madelon to it and went out into the crisp fresh air and the snow.

Vismarkt. 12.15.

Maaike sat in Coffee Company slowly stirring a cappuccino and fiddling with her beanie. Her eyes lit up as she saw Truus enter. Truus kissed her cheek and went to order a drink. Maaike picked hers up and went to sit in the more comfortable chairs away from the students who bashed away at their laptops and tablets. Still snow outside, but it didn't seem to slow down their output. Maaike nearly disappeared into the deep leather chair and had to steady her drink as she balanced herself. She saw Truus laughing at her predicament as she waited for her drink to be served. Maaike managed to show her the finger before she had to readjust herself again. The seat was too low and sucked her in, making her feel foolish. Truus laughed as she sat opposite her.

"You are a sight, Maaike, get a grip of yourself."

Maaike snorted and reached for her drink.

"I have a surprise for you," she announced.

"Will I like it?"

"Not sure..."

She whisked off her beanie hat and Truus was faced by a girl with newly dyed ash blond hair. It stunned Truus at first as it was so different and so unexpected. She reached to touch it for some reason as if she didn't believe it was real and Maaike leant into her caress.

"Beautiful, Maaike, makes you look like an ice princess..."

"You really like it?"

"I love it."

"I thought of red like yours, but didn't want to copy..."

"So you went for the ice princess look instead. We'll lose you in the snow if you go bare headed!"

Tamada Kick boksene, Johan Buziaulaan, 15.00.

She had earned an extra kick-boxing session. Truus got loosened up and went through her stretches. She felt good today. Writing had been a lot of fun and her mood was high. Truus set the clock for five minutes, and then began her heavy bag workout by throwing some easy punches and kicks. She started to pick up the pace as she became looser, and started to feel the sweat pour down her back. Truus wondered if she was odd, as she loved that feeling and then blinked more sweat from her eyes as she started to stick and move as if she was fighting a real person. Truus had got into her sequence, she was going kick, punch, left side, right side then mixing it up, no defence but all offense as if this was a real bout. Once the five-minute round was over, Truus rested for one minute.

She drank some water and stayed loose during the brief rest period bouncing on her toes. Then it was back to the heavy bag and she started the next round. This time she added an imaginary leg sweep, so hit the floor and then got back up again as quickly as possible and into the kick and punch routine. Truus felt as if she was floating on air, everything was moving so naturally. This was always a great point in any exercise, when it just came so effortlessly. She kept hearing her explosion of breath as she punched the bag, it made a great sound combining with the glove on leather echo. As she got warmer, Truus increased the ferocity of the kicks and punches, with the leg sweep she moved around it while keeping her guard up. She had another rest and wiped her face and drank some more water. Then was back to bouncing on her toes again. After another five minutes, she started to hit the ground, and roll under the bag and then popped up and delivered another barrage of blows from the opposite side. She carried on for a good thirty more minutes, alternating, punching, kicking and sweeping with the roll under the bag. It felt great.

Tamada called her over, he had been watching.

"Great work, Truus, now some defence,"

and he made to strike at her, but she instinctively blocked him.

"Good!"

And so this went on with feints and blows and kicks and sweeps and Truus just kept blocking and moving, moving and blocking. Her calves were aching and her legs were feeling like lead, but she made herself move. Truus could almost feel the bruises coming out on her arms as she parried blow after blow and every so often a foot would whistle past her head as the incredibly flexible Tamada swung or round kicked. Finally, it was over, but not before the obligatory hundred sit-ups and hundred press-ups.

"Great job, Truus." Tamada said as she hobbled off for a shower.

Praise indeed from the master!

Truus stood under the shower letting the water teem over her body and slowly slid onto her haunches. She felt exhausted, but exhilarated. She really loved this. Pushing her body to the limit, trying to extend the limit every time she worked out, trying to be as fit as she could be. Truus sat there and rubbed her tummy, all the workouts were making her so toned and hard, but still she felt girly, not a butch sportsperson.

Truus rubbed her hands through her hair and reached for the shampoo and started to rub it through, just daydreaming and tired. She wanted to get home to bed. It was a lovely feeling to be fit, but it made her so tired! She needed a bit of pasta for supper and a kiss from Maaike and it would be a perfect day.

Amaliastraat, 17.30.

That early evening Truus was listening to Depeche Mode at home, reliving the concert, through her headphones trying to concentrate on some writing at her desk. How could anybody like a boy band, she thought? She suddenly thought as the electronica crashed through her head. She closed her eyes and turned it up louder, destroying her eardrums but deep into the music. She could listen to 'Precious' over and over again and often did. None of todays so called music appealed to her with so many silly little boys and their floppy hair and tattoos, how could you call that music. Truus opened her eyes and looked down at Maaike. She lay on the floor, reading. Her legs up in the air, she kept bouncing her heels one after the other on her bottom for some reason. She looked up and gestured at Truus to turn the music off.

"Truus, did you know that in French, you don't really say 'I miss you.' You say 'tu me manques,' which is like 'you are missing from me.' I love that so much. I think that it means you are a part of me, you are essential to my being. They say you are like a limb, or an organ, or blood and that I cannot function without you. That is just so true of how I feel about you when you are not with me."

Truus scrunched her nose up and shook her head wondering where Maaike was going with this gambit.

"And only the French could express it like that," Maaike said,

"Dutch doesn't have much romance about it, does it?"

"Not really, everything is black and white I think, but emotions like love are reds and pinks and vivid scarlets, all flashing brightly, blazing in front of us, burning up inside of us, too difficult to describe sometimes, too difficult to feel at others. My love explodes for you in a crimson ball of flame!" Truus said and smiled.

"I love you in blood red..."

"That goes a bit dark, Maaike..."

"My heart pumps red blood, my heart is your heart, my blood is your blood. My love for you is blood red. That makes you my Blood Red Love."

Maaike said as she pushed herself up from the floor and came over to Truus's desk.

"Whatya doing?" Maaike asked.

"Just some writing."

"About?"

"Nothing really, I can't seem to focus."

"Switch your music off then."

"Usually I don't need to; I find it helps me..." Truus smiled.

"Want to come out for a run?" Maaike asked.

This was a good idea, escaping to run was always a good idea. They got to the newly built, but unopened Vaartsche Rijn railway station, without too much effort. There was a lot of fresh snow on the ground and Truus loved to run in the snow. The paths under the bridge were untouched by snow at the moment, then they turned back on themselves through a few footprints on otherwise virgin snow under the moonlight and made their way across in a long circuit, nice and steady. Maaike was chatting away about nothing in particular which was a good sign as far as their fitness was concerned.

"Push a little harder, sweetheart,"

Truus said, thinking they ought to stretch out and suddenly Maaike was gone, shooting ahead into the far distance, street lights flickering on her as she seemed to glide over the snow.

"Where on earth does that come from?"

Truus gasped when she finally caught up with her at Albatrosstraat.

"I have no idea. I just seem to have it, I always have. Even though I hate it!" she laughed. "Come on, let's get going I'm freezing..."

So, they carried on along Briljantlaan then Socrateslaan back to where they had come from at a steady pace. They nearly fell through the front door then fought to get up the stairs, pushing each other like ten year olds in an absurd race to the top. It ended up with Maaike climbing over Truus to the top of the stairs and then holding the door closed to her bedroom as she tried to get in. Luckily her pappy was out so the noise meant nothing and Truus eventually shoved the door open and then Maaike jumped on her. Truus started to give her a nuggie on the head, which as ever was a big mistake. Maaike forced her onto her back, sat astride and started tickling her, she was a monster, Truus tried to fight back as it was really hurting to laugh so much, but Maaike was so strong! Of course, it ended in tears as she caught Truus on her nose and it started to bleed, but Maaike did remorse so well! Truus did adore her, blood red love and all.

    Truus woke with a start, forgetting where she was at first. She found herself all entangled in Maaike, her arms around her neck, legs folded around hers, like a lover's knot. Bodies sweaty, but chilly as the eiderdown had fallen to the floor. Her body was soft but sticky and Truus had to ease her way out from her limbs. Each brush of flesh against flesh was electric and Maaike moaned at the most inopportune moments. Finally, free of her, Maaike moved and snuggled into her pillow as Truus retrieved the duvet and pulled it over her shoulders. Truus lay down and she automatically moved into her, moulding her body with hers so they became one. She whispered something in her sleep and did what she often did, sleepily kissing Truus's shoulder which only meant more surges through her body. All Truus could see was her perfect face framed by her now ash blond hair, like a sleeping angel. Truus closed her eyes and thought wicked thoughts.

Vagevuur.

Elise sat with Sterre holding her close and stroking her hair. Sterre was a bit feverish and Elsie was worried about her hand. It was very swollen and Sterre was in a great deal of pain. She didn't want to touch it again and had manufactured a sling with Sterres jumper to keep it raised. This was slightly more comfortable for her and had allowed her fitful sleep, =but there were dark rings under her eyes, as she imagined there must be under hers.

"How long have you been at Vaaterstraat?" asked Sterre.

"Nearly a year now…"

"It's madness. I've been there nearly two and I've never seen you…"

"We live like that though don't we. We have our own worlds, our own friends…"

"But at Uni, we must keep passing like ships in the night…"

"Crazy…" Elise smiled thinly, "But when we get out of this we can be friends."

"You are very positive Elise."

"We have to be. He may be a nutter, but we have to be positive."

"Not sure what we can do, only three hands between us…" Sterre said.

"Kick him in the balls next chance we have." Giggled a rather hysterical Elise.

"Probably hasn't got any, that's his problem!"

"Yea, no dick!"

They laughed for the first time in a long while.

"We will have to go for it though. Can't let him have a free run." Said Elise.

"I know, it's scary, but we have to."

"I think you'll have to kick him. I'll jump on him after and you make a run for it."

"Seems rather simple…"

"Well, when he shoved me out last time he was kind of distracted so we'll have to hope for the same."

"Are we strong enough Elise?"

"We'll have to be. So, next time he's close enough we go for it, promise?"

"Promise…"

Chapter 18

Zondag, November 23, 2014.
Vredenburgkade 22.00.

Truus and Maaike went down the road and across the canal to Tivoli to listen to some Industrial Punk from Savages. Short aggressive songs from their hard-looking lead singer. The band were all dressed in black. Truus and Maaike were in black, as little clothing as possible because they knew it was going to be hot and sweaty, but enough covering them to be decent. Black shorts and DM's for Truus with long black socks and a black crop top. She looked real hard as well. Maaike mirrored Truus, but wearing bright yellow tights. Despite the lack of clothes, they were sodden with sweat. Truus's hair looked like it did at the end of a cross fit session. Maaike had her face streaked with streams of sweat and mascara. What a mess they were! Truus pulled her close and her hand rested on her back. That too was wet with sweat, but only made her want to get closer to her and move towards her so they danced joined at the hip to 'She Will' one of Truus's favourite songs. They pumped out all the favourites including 'City's Full' which Truus also loved. The beat just reverberated in her head then through her body. They moved into the mosh pit at the front and were bouncing around off people, onto other people, just devoid of any cares, taken along by the music.

There was none of the floating precious Maaike in these dances, it was all stomping and jumping and careening around, hardly bothering to put any method into their madness. The sweat was dripping off them both as they listened to 'Strife', then Maaike grabbed Truus's hand and dragged her through the throng to the side and they collapsed against the wall. Compared to the snow bound city it was like a desert in the club.

"So hot, my love, so wet..." Truus gasped.

"I know, I'm so sticky, it's stifling..."

"I'll get some water."

Truus found her way out and into the queue at the bar and got four bottles of water, Savages were well into 'No Face' when she got back. Maaike was still slumped against the wall. Truus gave her a bottle and opened another and poured it over her head. She raised her face to her so it splashed over her cheeks.

"Soooo nice, Truus, so nice..."

Truus poured the remainder on her own head, she was too hot to worry about what people may think and drank another almost in one go. They shared the final bottle and attacked the dance floor again for their last two songs. They bounced around again, getting bruised and battered, but they didn't care. Nobody did. Everyone was in such high spirits and having a great time. Savages left the stage to huge applause.

Their encore was loud, 'Flying to Berlin', Truus and Maaike were flying nowhere, they were knackered. They sloped out of the Hall and made their way home like two beaten up, damp old ladies.

Amaliastraat 23.55.

Caes had made them all a coffee and looked at the two bedraggled women who sat stunned at the kitchen table almost unable to move.

Truus, still not used to normality, shouted,

"My ears are still ringing and I feel a bit woozy."

"Too loud Truus tone it down!" Caes laughed.

"Oops sorry Pappy!" Truus still shouted.

"What on earth happened to you two, you look washed out?" Caes asked.

"We just danced, Pappy, we just danced…"

"It was so hot; we are so sweaty…"

"I can see that, girls, delightful I must say," Caes smiled, "But you enjoyed it?"

"Oh yes!" they said together.

"They are fantastic, Caes, progressive post punk I think they call it. Very punk I reckon!" Maaike said.

"Takes me back to my day…" Caes started.

"No, Pappy, you didn't wear safety pins in your cheeks and grease your Mohican up did you?"

"How old do you think I am? I was in nappies during the punk revolution. No. I was listening to Manics, REM…"

"Not Vengaboys?"

"Not really a Vengaboys kind of guy though I do like 2 Unlimited. No, it was Depeche Mode."

"Of course you have such good taste…"

"No darling, that's why you have such good taste!" Caes laughed.

"Touché." Truus replied.

"Blur…" Caes offered.

"Love them too," said Maaike.

"Massive Attack, Radiohead…"

"So eclectic, Pappy." Truus said.

"That's me, Truus."

"Excellent." Maaike agreed.

"Then of course the God that was Bruce…" Caes tried.

"Who?" Truus laughed, teasing him.

"Shame on you girl," Caes said, "Springsteen, The Baas. Your mammie and I went to see him in Barcelona and Edinburgh in the nineties, when we were sooo young."

"You abandoned me for a rock concert by Bruce who?" Truus said in mock indignation.

"Springsteen!" Caes shouted as Maaike sniggered.

"We had an amazing time in Spain, Nearly four hours of solid rock. I loved Barcelona, I must go again."

"Come on, Maaike, I think we need to go..." Truus suggested.

In tribute to her *vader* Truus found some Springsteen on You Tube as she ran the bath. He was soon filling her bedroom with guitars and a beautiful saxophone.

Truus slid into the water and Maaike slipped in forward facing her at the other end. Their legs rested on each other as they sank as low as they could. It felt so nice. The warmth of the water, the fairy light bubbles, the warm and silky skin of Maaike beneath Truus's legs. Truus found one of her feet and adjusted her body so she could massage it, then found the other. Truus ran her hand up her leg, slowly caressing it. Maaike shivered violently, then stood up like a bubble covered mermaid and turned and sat between Truus's legs. There was just enough room, but she didn't really mind being so close to her. Truus put her arms around her neck and she hugged her body into her breasts, they were complete.

Maaike sat at the top of the bed. Truus lay with her head in her lap as Maaike slowly stroked her hair. Truus had her eyes closed. She felt her body tremor at every touch of Maaike's fingers. It scared her that she should feel so much, so soon. That Maaike was having this profound effect on her. Scared her and comforted her as well as this was just what she knew she needed. She put up her hand and took Maaike's, moving it to her lips and kissed it.

"This is so nice, Maaike, I've never felt like this before."

"Me neither. Who'd have thought?"

"For a few weeks I had been thinking..."

"Of me?"

"Yes, you started to give me feelings in my body every time I saw you. I didn't really understand what they meant."

"Couldn't you tell?" Maaike asked.

"I've never felt like this about anyone. It was all new to me." Truus replied.

"Really?"

"I've never been with a boy, so couldn't relate."

"Me neither, never wanted to either." Maaike whispered.

"It's so strange, all this time…"

"I know. Have you never…"

"No, no kissing, no touching. Maybe that should have told me something…"

"Told you what though, it's all so complicated"

"This seems really natural."

"Freddie always fancied you." Maaike giggled.

"No…" Truus shrieked blushing, "I had no idea…"

"But then he found Magda…"

"Pappy suggested Freddie, but only once, quite recently really. He never interfered."

"Your pappy is fine with us being together?" Maaike asked.

"Yea, of course…"

Maaike bent down and tenderly kissed Truus on the lips. Truus still held her hand and moved it towards her breast.

Vagevuur.

Sterre had no idea what time it was let alone what day it was. Her hand hurt so much. It was discoloured and bent and made her retch when she looked at it. Elise slept at her feet. It was reassuring to have somebody with her, but she doubted this was going to help in the long run.

She wondered what her father had done. She knew he had had some scrapes and that he had been sacked, but she couldn't imagine her father doing anything that wrong, not now anyway. She hadn't seen him for a while, but she thought she knew him well enough... but what did she know? He could have done anything and she'd have had no inkling at all.

She rested her throbbing hand on her shoulder and leant against the wall. It was cold. She was cold. Elise stirred and looked up at her,

"How'd you feel?"

"Lousy..." *Sterre said.*

"Still hurting?"

"Not so much," *Sterre lied.*

Elise shuffled up and sat beside her.

"What does he want?"

"My pappy I suppose..." *Sterre whispered.*

"But why me, I hope to god..."

"I think he needs us for now, but I am scared. He doesn't care that we see him, so..." *Sterre faltered.*

"I know; I know that's what scares me so much." *Elise started to cry.*

It was as if their world was on a loop, a never-ending loop. They had no idea as to how long they'd been there. They didn't know where they were. The awful thing was that both recognised their captor from somewhere but could not place him. Had he been on TV, in the newspapers? Lecturer or neighbour? He had that ordinary kind of face that would fit in anywhere, but his eyes stood out for their coldness and utter contempt he had for them especially Sterre. It was obvious he hated her, but what could have caused that hatred? What on earth had her father done to him? Whatever it was it couldn't have been recently. Sterre knew he had become a Private Investigator. She couldn't imagine a case he was following would engender this antagonism, but anything he had done as a police man was so long ago. She had no idea. She found herself back on the loop going around in circles trying to imagine what could have happened, what he could have done. Elsie just felt trapped and caught up in something she didn't really understand.

Chapter 19

Maandag, November 24, 2014.
Amaliastraat 07.20

Next morning, Maaike stood naked by the mirror. Truus looked at her. Pale skin, with her newly dyed hair. Her slim figure firm and enticing.

"You look like an icicle, Maaike!" Truus laughed.

"Nice, good boost to self-esteem, Truus." Maaike pouted.

"No, your hair's so... so white! Really, stand to attention and you are an icicle!"

"Am I too thin?"

"Not at all, perfect. Sorry it was just a thought." Truus smiled.

"Well icicle or not I have to go to work. Good luck with your interview."

Maaike kissed both cheeks, but Truus pulled her closer and kissed her lips passionately.

"I do love you Maaike..."

"I know; I love you too..."

Maaike was breathless and looked into her loves sparkling blue eyes.

"Of course..."

Caes hadn't seen Truus so nervous for a while. It was weird, but an English and Creative Writing interview at Universiteit Utrecht was obviously very important to her.

"How do I look, Pappy?
"A bit pale to be honest, my love, just try to relax."
"No, my clothes, not too casual?"

She looked so pretty, a bow in her hair, wearing his once favourite denim jacket, skirt and pixie boots, not her usual Doc Martens, leggings and sweatshirt.

"You look lovely, Truus, perfect." Smiled Caes.
"Will I impress them?"
"Of course. Do you have your portfolio?"
"Yes, all here. Wish me luck!" Truus grimaced.

"You don't need luck, but I wish you it anyway."

He kissed her cheek. She moved towards the door, paused and came back. She hugged him.

"I love you, Pappy." Said Truus.

"Get going, you'll be late!"

Departement Engels, Universiteit Utrecht. 12.15.

"Truus, why do you want to switch courses?" Ruud Neeskens asked.

"I just feel I'm going nowhere with Sociology."

"But your lecturers are so impressed with your work..." interjected Neeskens.

"At times it really does command my attention, but at other times, it just doesn't move me."

"And writing?"

"I love to write; I should have chosen this originally."

"Why didn't you?" asked Docent Stam.

"I thought I should do something relating to one of my interests, but it was silly really as it wasn't my real interest which has always been writing."

"What can you bring to the course?"

"Imagination. Enthusiasm. I really want to write; I want to become a better writer. I'm not sure if I'll be any good, but..."

"Your portfolio is very exciting, some of your poetry shows great promise." Neeskens said.

Praise indeed from such a famous author in his own right, Truus thought feeling pleased with herself.

"I just feel that this is for me, so much more than something so dry as Sociology. I want to use my imagination. I want to develop my skills."

"Well I cannot see any problem with a transfer, but you will have to start the year over, it's too late to pick it up now." Stam said.

"That's fine, I didn't expect to just start now, *dank*."

"In the meantime keep writing. Try as many different ways as you can. A novel perhaps or start a blog on line. Try as many different avenues as you can. You are welcome to come in to any lectures we are running now, but perhaps look at next years' programme to make sure you don't double up. Is that oké?"

Neeskens said with great enthusiasm. He was a charismatic bugger, she thought.

"That's fantastic, dank."

Truus was so happy, she felt a load off her shoulders and had something to look forward to. Did she have the novel in her? She would have to see.

Kroonstraat Police Bureau 13.15.

Madelon and Maaike met to discuss how they would move forward.

"We have to ask how many street girls want to stop."

"I don't think we can ever stop prostitution, Maaike, some actually want to do this."

"Then we have to prevent violence happening in the first place by changing the attitudes and beliefs of those who use them and run them."

"It's the pimps who are the problem, we have less reports of clients assaulting girls."

"But they don't need pimps. I can't understand it."

"I think it's because of the pimps. They want the money, they want to control their profits and push the girls to get as much as possible."

"So we need to intervene at an early stage when violence does occur to stop it continuing?"

"But that assumes it will happen anyway, how can we stop it before it happens?"

"We have to find a way of dealing effectively with the perpetrators to stop the violence."

"But we saw how effective that was the other day. They don't want our help."

"The collectives need to get more involved with the Eastern girls and the non-European girls. The girls need to know what choices they have. We need to support victims and their children to rebuild their lives and reduce their risk of experiencing further violence."

Maaike said, "But if they come here illegally where are they going to turn to?"

"I think the biggest problem is that women and girls are forced, coerced or deceived into entering prostitution and their pimps are keeping them there." Madelon said. "We need more work in their home countries, but it is not simple, it's not just a police thing, the government needs to act."

"I spoke to Truus and we thought that trafficking and then all of the recruitment, transportation and exploitation of women is the problem. We need to get to these countries and stop it there."

"The perpetrators range from total strangers to relatives and intimate partners, but most are known to the girls in some way. It can happen anywhere and we need to show the girls that it is not acceptable under any circumstances. That is the most difficult problem facing us," Madelon said.

"Violence, coercion and intimidation are all too common, the victims have a limited availability of choice resulting from their own vulnerability."

"What can we do?" Maaike said.

"It's all about choice, Maaike. Personal choice. We need to show the girls they have choices and that they don't have to take the path they are on. We can show them that violence is not an option."

"But how?"

"If they understand that it is wrong, and for many in an abusive relationship that is the first problem, we can then show them the choices they have. No pimp, work in a collective, health care, childcare. This is a huge issue, Maaike."

"I understand."

"I hope you do, it will mean a lot of work and a lot of liaison with other groups and you cannot do it all on your own."

"I know."

"You cannot, Maaike, that's most important. I know Caes has spoken to you. Try not to take this home. Try to put work to one side when you are at home or socialising. Work and the rest must be separate."

"I'll try."

"But you seem so much happier today."

"Yes, I had a lovely weekend, I am in love, I think."

"Well that will surely take your mind off work."

"It may, but I still need to care. I have to feel something about the work I do."

"That's true, but …"

"Compartmentalise! Yes, Caes told me that as well. I do understand." Maaike smiled.

"And be happy in love."

"I will be, I am happy. Dank, Madelon, for giving me this opportunity."

"You deserve it, keep working hard, I am sure you will go far."

"Dank." Maaike did feel better.

"Compartmentalise!" she smiled as Maaike left the room.

Totale Judo dojo, Balearen, 15.00.

Maaike went to her dojo and literally hit the mat. Maaike had just finished her session with *Ukemi* where she faced at least fifteen consecutive opponents, some saw this as old fashioned, but Maaike loved the challenge of fighting different weights and attacks. She hit the mat a few times, but more than held her own against the majority. Her opponent would rush at her and would either hit the mat or thrust at her depending on instruction and the bout would commence. It was exhausting stuff and Maaike would feel drained at the end of it.

She was only fitting one session a week in at the moment and knew this wasn't enough to gain the next step on her belt. She hoped things would calm down a bit at work or did she just need to commit and work those extra sessions. She then saw the image of Truus and wondered if she could give up her precious time with her for the tatami. Once it would have been a no brainer, but now she was in love and all sorts of conflicts had arisen about time and where she wanted to be. Despite her love of judo, she knew that she was now distracted by a different kind of love. Oh well, she thought and left the dojo.

Maaike made for the weights room to finish off her session with her usual back breaking routine. She hated it, but also loved it. She pulled off her *judogi* and put her hands on her stomach. Hard as iron she smiled to herself and adjusted the weight on a dumbbell.

Maaike finished off her circuit concentrating on her grip. She didn't want to be swiped away as she had been when she was younger. She wanted an iron grip. When doing pushups or squatthrusts or burpees, she would try to push the ends of her fingers into the floor, as if trying to get a grip on a basketball. Every time she finished a session and took off her *gi*, she would wring it out a few times as if she were trying to get the sweat out. After a hard session, this was even harder as her hands and fingers seemed to be like jelly, but she knew it had to be done. Needs must.

Particulier Onderzoeks Bureau, Blokstraat. 15.10.

Truus had just got into the office when the phone rang, her stomach was sore from this morning's session and she winced as she sat at the desk.

"Orman?"

"It's his secretary." Truus answered.

"Get me Orman."

"He's not here, can I help?"

"I want Orman."

"Who's speaking please? Can I take a message?" Truus asked feeling uneasy.

"Get hold of him, it's about his daughter."

Truus went cold.

"Sterre? Where is she?"

"I'll ring again in thirty minutes. No police. Get Orman!"

"No don't ring off…"

"Get Orman, I'll ring back at ten."

Truus thought quickly. She had to tell her father so rang the police Bureau.

"That's all he said?"

"Yes, Pappy."

"Oké, don't you worry. Freddie and I'll be outside; we'll follow him if he gets another message."

"Oké."

"Just ring my mobile when he leaves, though we should see him."

"Right, Pappy."

"And you stay in the office. Ring Thijs now."

"I will, Pappy, don't worry."

Thijs was flustered and panicky. The phone rang. He breathed deeply and picked it up. All he said was,

"Orman…"

Thijs just listened, Truus watched his face going grey and then he put the phone down.

"I've got to go, Truus. Say nothing to anyone."

"*Oké*. Good luck, Thijs."

She picked up the phone,

"Just left, Pappy."

Vaaterstraat 18.00.

Despite what she had said to her father, Truus thought she should try just one more time to find Elise, now that Thijs was out meeting this man who had Sterre, she couldn't do anything else and felt helpless. The other evening at the night clubs had made her more determined than ever to find Elise and to try and make things right however absurd that seemed.

She knew that Mevrouw Haan's house had been searched and sealed off by the police after her murder; she glanced at the tape criss-crossing the dirty front door as she passed by and shrugged to herself. It left just the pretty house on the other side of hers, number two as the only one she had not visited. She kicked her way through the snow, just as she had as a little girl. She smiled to herself. She thought of what her father had said about back up, but she was in the wide open here, with people walking up and down the street all the time, these were nice houses and nice people must live here. She knocked on the door, shivering in the snow. The door opened and a man holding a mobile phone smiled a greeting at her, a man who she vaguely remembered from a long time ago. Where had she seen him before? He ushered her in from the cold, covering the speaker as he moved.

"What can I do for you, young lady?"

"Hi, I wondered if you could help. I'm Truus Heda, I work for a Private Investigator called Thijs Orman."

"Oh yes, I've heard of Thijs, what's the problem?"

"We tried your door a couple of days ago…" Truus started.

"I've been away, come into my lounge…"

She was ushered into the front room. It was cold and seemed neglected. The cold hung in the air and sent chills down her spine, or was that a feeling of foreboding. He offered her a chair.

"I'll just finish this phone call..." he said and left the room.

Truus stood up and looked at the room. It was sparse, unlived in. There were some books in the bookcase, an atlas, tourist guides to Surinam, encyclopaedias. She could hear the man talking on the phone, he sounded quite sharp. Where did she know him from, he really was familiar? How had he heard of Thijs, he wasn't a household name? The voice stopped speaking and he returned smiling to the room, then she heard the faint sound of a girl crying…

Dom Plein, 19.25.

Freddie and Caes had spent most of the afternoon trailing after Thijs. He kept driving to various locations in the city, stopping, waiting and answering his mobile. Then off he would go again.

"This is bloody ridiculous..." said Freddie.

"We'll just have to keep at it, but this is frustrating..." Caes replied.

They drove past the Dom for the third time. They weren't even going in circles, just a zig zag across the city. They passed the Museeum and turned towards one of Caes' favourite restaurants. His stomach grumbled in sympathy.

Caes was fed up; they didn't need a sightseeing tour of the city. Whoever was on the phone had Thijs on a leash and was pulling him in all directions, tormenting him, making him suffer. It was torture. Every so often his car would stop and he would talk again on his mobile. They should have organised a phone tap thought Caes, but it was too late now. Pointless also to get more police involved as they would certainly be seen in this weather, as so few cars were about. Caes was amazed they hadn't been spotted by Thijs already. There again he had more important things on his mind. Caes looked at Freddie who shrugged.

"Shall we step in?" Freddie asked.

Every time they thought they might have reached the end, Thijs would be off again. It must have been driving the poor bloke insane. It wasn't doing much for their mental health either and Freddie was getting agitated. He banged the steering wheel of the car.

"It's not likely to be anywhere near here…" Caes said

"The middle of the city is not the place…"

They were both hungry and thirsty, they hadn't planned this too well, but didn't dare stop to get anything. They just had to concentrate on Thijs. His car moved through the city centre at Neude. They found themselves cut up by a Number six bus and had to take evasive action to re connect with Thijs. He stopped again. An alert policeman would have booked him for parking in a bus lane. Where were the police when you needed them thought Caes? Onwards past the Centraal station and Caes knew where they were going as Bleekstraat appeared on their left. The car rounded the corner and pulled into Vaaterstraat and stopped. Where else? Caes thought to himself as he glanced at Freddie. Caes pulled up in the forecourt of an old medical school along Catherijnesingel and waited. This time, Thijs got out of the car and started walking across the road towards the canal. They waited and watched before they finally got out of the car and followed.

Pulling up his jacket collar Caes tried to ignore the snow drifting from the sky, he was quickly frozen. Freddie shoved his hands in his pockets and looked up into the steel grey sky. He breathed out a great sigh, his breath instantly clouding the air in front of him.

It was very secluded and getting darker as the trees were casting long shadows on the canal side and on to both their faces. Thijs was talking to a man at the edge of the canal.

"Who's that?" asked Freddie.

Caes recognised the man. Why was he talking to Commissaris Frans Aartsen?

Catherijnesingel 20.25.

Aartsen looked out over the canal, and then turned back to face Orman.

"We had some good times, Thijs, we were a good team..."

"I was never on your team." Thijs said.

Aartsen ignored him.

"Then you blew it, you got greedy..."

"Just a bit of dope. Greedy? I was just stupid!"

"You fucked it all up for me, I got demoted because of you, and it's taken me seven years to get back to where I was..."

"Still, you make no sense. Greedy...? That's not why I am here. Have you got Sterre?"

"Don't try to deny it, you took my customers, you wrecked my business..."

"Your business? What the fuck do you mean...?"

"Don't try and con me, Thijs. I had everything in place; I had the runners, the dealers, the suppliers. I get the boot, sent to fucking Surinam to get myself sorted out, to be retrained, because they said I wasn't any good at leadership after you fucked me up. I didn't have the skills they told me. You need to re-evaluate whether you should stay in the force, they told me. This is my life, Thijs, I should have known you were no good. Me, I got punished because you were a smackhead."

"But I still don't...Where is Sterre?" Thijs pleaded.

"They sent me thousands of kilometres from Utrecht, thousands of kilometres from fucking civilisation. I come back six months later on leave and you'd taken…"

"What? No Frans, I didn't take anything. What the fuck did I take? What's Sterre done?"

"My business! My fucking drug business! My fucking police career, you fucked me up completely!"

"Hell man, you must be insane!"

"Thijs…" his voice darkened.

"And what business? Why didn't you just pick up a phone?" Thijs asked.

"We never did business like that, it was always personal."

"What the fuck has this to do with Sterre? I had no idea what you did, Frans, what you had, we weren't friends, you were just my baas and a fucking twat at that!"

Aartsen hit him, just once and Orman was out cold, crashing down into the snow that covered the ground.

Caes held Freddie back as Aartsen felled Thijs.

"Wait…" Caes hissed.

But they had to move fast when they saw him start tying his feet to the stone. It was obvious what he was going to do next, the canal awaited him. Meijer flattened Aartsen with one punch as Caes rang for an ambulance.

"How dare you?" Aartsen sat in the snow astonished, holding his face.

"Forget it, Aartsen…" Caes said.

"I am a police officer, Com…"

"Forget it, you bastard, you are nothing…"

Freddie grunted, as he heaved him back to his feet and punched him again.

Kroonstraat Police Bureau 20.50.

Aartsen just didn't seem to have a care in the world. Despite the swelling on his cheek and eye, his face was wreathed in a smile that kept turning into an ugly smirk. He was really annoying Caes.

"I just collect, money, power, the girls, why not?"

"But why?" Caes asked.

Aartsen paused, relishing the fact that he had an audience. He was in no hurry, but finally admitted,

"I collect, they are pretty."

His bruised face almost lit up with a smile. He was so pleased with himself. Caes felt sick.

"You hurt them?"

"No I don't want to get dirty…" Aartsen said smugly.

"You hurt Sterre." Caes said.

"Hurt her? Oh, that, it was nothing."

Again, the sick self-satisfied smile. Caes was finding it hard to control himself. He had heard the screams from Sterre. He knew she had suffered horribly, yet here was her abuser sitting smugly and calmly in the interview, seemingly secure in the knowledge that he felt he was in control.

"Elise Cuijper, why?"

Caes tried to change the balance of the questioning.

"I collect, I needed the company." Shrugged Aartsen.

"You what?" Caes was sickened.

"To tell you the truth, Caes, you don't mind me still using your first name do you, Caes?"

"Get on with it!" snapped Caes.

Caes was beginning to hate this man, a man he had once considered quite a close colleague if not a friend. His mind flashed back to his chat with Truus about hitting criminals, how he had tried never to do that, but his patience was getting thin. The smug face needed a slap.

"She was a distraction, a bit of fun."

"You?" Caes said.

"No, I needed them to confuse, how much time have you spent?"

Aartsen was so please with himself.

"You bastard…"

He was starting to make some sense. This had been thoroughly thought through, but what was his end game wondered Caes.

"Well, by the number of your reports that came to us at Taap Koorndreef it worked." Aartsen said.

"So Elise meant nothing?" Caes asked.

"Not to anyone else it seems; she was all alone in the world."

"But if the old woman hadn't…"

"Well that helped, when she came into the Police Bureau at Kroonstraat, then Taap Koorndreef it was great, another distraction. It kept you all off balance. I couldn't have planned it better."

"But you killed her?" Caes shouted.

"Well what was her point?"

He was contemptible and for some reason seemed so full of himself, showing off his achievements as if he was beyond the law.

"For fuck's sake, Frans, she was just a sad lonely old woman…"

Caes was on the edge of losing it. He turned to Ernst who had been stood silently seething in the corner. Caes knew that he wanted to batter Aartsen, but knew he couldn't.

"Again, distraction."

"So you just killed that poor old woman." Ernst asked.

"She knew too much." Aartsen just smiled a thin smile.

"You saw her at the station, she knew absolutely nothing." Caes said in response.

"I could not be sure. She had seen something, god knows how, but I had to make sure."

"And Spliker?" said Ernst.

"He was a worthless shit; you know that, he didn't deserve to live. That one, I was doing us all a favour."

There was the smirk again.

"He was still a human being!"

"Was he though? What did he offer us, anyway it put Orman in the frame, gave him something else to worry about?"

"The two girls?" Ernst asked.

"Two?" he smiled, "Well they'll be oké as long as I get back to them."

"You know there is no chance in hell of that happening." Caes said bluntly.

"Well then…"

Aartsen seemed to gloat.

"Don't be a fool, Frans, this is only going to end badly, don't make it any worse."

"Any worse? What could possibly make it any worse," he smiled again, then looked up straight into the face of Caes.

"Oh yes, have you heard from Truus today?"

Caes felt his blood run to ice.

"You fucking bastard…"

Ernst had to be quick to stop Caes getting to Aartsen. He held him tightly, Caes soon relaxed and stopped.

"Where is she?" Caes snarled through gritted teeth.

"Caes my good friend. You let me go, I let her go…"

"Don't be ridiculous…"

"On your head…" Aartsen started.

Caes shrugged Ernst away and lunged at Aartsen grabbing him by his collar. As he yanked him up he could see no fear in his eyes. The man was a psychopath thought Caes.

"Harm my daughter you bastard and I will kill you…"

Caes hissed, then shoved Aartsen back into his chair. Ernst put a hand on his shoulder and they walked from the room.

As he closed the door behind him Caes shivered. He had not known fear like this for a long time. It hit him between the eyes and then his body seemed to fill with ice. He remembered when he had last felt like this, when they had told him that Femke was going to die. How afraid he had been then. How his world had threatened to come to an end. He couldn't bear it, not his Truus. She was all he had, she was what he lived for. He felt desolate, had no idea what to do. He shrugged off Ernsts hand and slammed the door to his office shut. He slumped into his chair, elbows on his desk and head in his hands.

"What the fuck do I do now?" he said to nobody and everybody.

Caes gave a quick briefing to those who were still in the office. He felt frozen, didn't know what to do at first. Nothing could have prepared him for this. He had tried her phone just in case it was a bluff, but all he got was her answer machine. Would that be the last time he heard her voice?

Marie Hartmann put her hand on his arm.

"Do you need anything?"

"Just my daughter..." was all Caes could think to say.

He sat in his office, head back in his hands, despairing. He couldn't think what to do. His daughter missing. A psychopath in custody, but at the moment one not prepared to say anything about the whereabouts of the three women. His mind started to wander. Were they already dead? Had he harmed the others as much as he had harmed Sterre. Was Elise still alive? His head started to spin around and round, he tried to stop the momentum inside his head and felt he was going to be sick. Thoughts just tumbled about, trying to get out. Different scenarios came to the fore and he had to dismiss them as fanciful or too extreme. He wanted to scream, he needed to regain control. He rubbed his forehead and ran his fingers through his hair almost as if he was trying to clear his mind. Decisively he stood up. Thijs needed to be spoken to, he may have something. It was better than doing nothing.

Vagevuur.

Truus lay on her side, whimpering silently in pain. She could taste her own blood in her mouth, and she was finding it hard to breathe as the tape around her mouth was so tight. She hoped her nose wasn't broken because it was getting increasingly difficult to breathe through it. It really hurt. Both her arms hurt, pinned as they were behind her back. Her whole body really, really hurt. She tried not to cry, but everything hurt her so much. He had given her a real kicking and her stomach pulsed through with pain. She thought she must have a broken rib or even more as there was a nasty stabbing pain like needles in her side every time she took a breath. She tried to take shallower ones, but it was so difficult with the tape around her mouth to get enough air in through her nose.

Every so often she had to take a deeper breath and it made her whole-body spasm and rock with such pain, as if she was on fire. Every time she inhaled it hurt her so much. She just thought I really want my Pappy here to look after me. She tried to get onto her bottom to sit up, but each tiny movement was a stabbing agony, she cried in pain, but only a dull muffled moan came out of her taped mouth. The real cry was inside her head, a primeval scream taking over from the pain. She just wanted to scream out loud. Tears now mixed with her blood as she shuffled moaning onto her backside. She couldn't breathe, she was all blocked up with blood and snot, she had to stop, she had to relax, to calm down. Where's my pappy, he should be here looking after me, I really want my pappy.

She tried to look around, but it was too dark. Christ! She couldn't see anything out of her right eye, God was she blind? She tried to open it, but it too really hurt, slowly she started to see her surroundings. A room, empty, a door with a thin shaft of light coming from the bottom, newspapers, boxes, nothing else, just a room. She felt her wrists sting as something cut into them, she could feel blood or sweat there as well. Truus could just see that her feet were wrapped tightly together by some tape so she assumed that was what was cutting into her wrists as well. What in God's name had she done? How had she gotten into this fucking mess? How was she going to get out of it? She moaned again loudly as her ribs suddenly stabbed into her insides, making her almost choke in her agony. What had she done?

Truus vaguely remembered walking in the snow, knocking on a door, but where? Waiting, shivering in the snow, then the door opening and a man had smiled a greeting at her, a man who she remembered from a long time ago, Frans... Aartsen. It was him. Commissaris Aartsen, he said he was on a job, he asked her to step inside the house. The lounge, the unlived in look, the phone call. Then she remembered she had heard the faint sound of a girl crying, he had looked shocked, then he had hit her, she had kicked him in the balls and had started to run, but he had caught her, tripping her up and she went flailing towards the exit, just trapped inside the doorway. So much for not needing any backup, she almost sobbed again in self-pity. Dragging her back inside, he had punched her again in the face and then kicked her and kicked her and kicked her and then it had all gone black and here she was. Perfect.

Fucking Frans Aartsen. Commissaris Fucking Aartsen. Well at least she had solved the case, she thought, she was better than her pappy, but where was he? When would he come to save her, to look after her? Where was her good old reliable pappy, he should be taking me home now and putting me to bed, safe and sound at home. Where the fuck was he and then she started to cry again. Where was he? Commissaris Frans Fucking Aartsen. The bastard. But why?

Kroonstraat Police Bureau, 21.30.

"I couldn't stop him punching you, Thijs." Caes tried to explain.

"But why follow me?"

"I didn't trust you, Thijs. I'm Sorry."

"Why didn't you leave me with him?"

"What?"

"He would have taken me to Sterre." Thijs said.

"No, Thijs, he was just about to drop you in the canal when Freddie Meijer hit him."

"You don't know…"

"He had tied a block to your feet, you were going into the canal, I suppose he had played you long enough." Caes said coldly.

"He said I'd ruined his life, destroyed his business. The man's insane, what had I done to him?"

"We'll find out, Thijs."

"Sterre?"

"Still alive, we hope, somewhere…"

"Elise?"

"We hope so…"

"Where's Truus?"

"Yes, well, he's got her locked up somewhere as well…"

"Christ!"

If it were possible Orman's face had gone even whiter.

"You do know he's insane, don't you?"

"That's my worry, he thinks we'll let him go and he will be able to return to the girls…"

"Maybe…"

"You know we could never do that, Thijs…"

"Even with Truus, Caes?"

"Even with Truus! I just can't."

"Caes, always by the book, even now…"

"The book? Fucking hell, Thijs, if I thought he would lead us to them, to Truus, do you think I wouldn't just re write the fucking book, just kick him out? He's fucking insane, he's not going to help us. I've got to go."

Thijs reached out, "Sorry, Caes, I'm sorry."

Where would he have them thought Caes? He had a house in De Baarsjes and a small flat in Zeeburg. Where had he got the money for those? If he owned those was there somewhere else? They had both been searched. Empty. Where were they?

Elise lived on Vaartsestraat, but no sign of anything suspicious. It all looked like Vaartsestraat, but they had searched the flats and the houses. Caes knew he had to stay in control, but he was angry, he felt panic invading his head. What had he missed? Someone must know something.

"Freddie! See who owns what on Vaartsestraat again. See if we can get a link with anything. Ernst get plans of all the houses, let's start over again, we may need to rip some apart! Danny! Get over to Binnenstad again, rip that fucking house apart! Adrie, get onto his bank, see about recent, no, see about payments anywhere for the last five years."

"Five years, baas, that'll take…" Adrie started.

"Just fucking do it, Adrie! Madelon, Madelon Verloet! Get pictures of Aartsen, circulate the whole fucking street, and see if anyone knows him. They must take some notice of something down that fucking street!"

Hoofdcommissaris Coeman came to the door,

"You oké, Caes? This is a fucking mess."

"Yes, I think so."

"Are you too close to this? I have to ask."

"No, it's oké, we think they are still alive."

"If you are sure?" Coeman wondered.

"Baas, if you took me off it, I'd still carry on, so best leave me to it."

"Well it's still your call, Caes, at least for the moment. Take care though. Where's Aartsen?"

"Interview room three."

"Do you want me to talk to him?" Coeman asked.

"Can do, it can't hurt. He's not going to say anything though; the bastard is off his head."

He didn't say anything about the girls; he had decided not to speak to anyone about that, but his 'work' as he called it was another matter. He was so proud of what he had done; he was with Coeman for a long time. It seemed that several years ago, he had been one of the biggest drug importers in Utrecht; everything was done by word of mouth, almost like a terrorist cell, no telephones, all through couriers. He didn't use the phone, he had all these contacts and because he trusted no one, he couldn't control anything when he was not there, he certainly hadn't thought that through, but he had been worth millions of euros; that was how he had all the properties. When Thijs got the boot, Aartsen had been blamed for a lack of leadership skills and was offered a training post and sent to Surinam. This involved teaching the Surinam Police how to police their state. What a great irony that was! Incredibly, and this was hard to understand, his drug empire just collapsed and others stepped in and filled the vacuum as they were bound to do. He was stuck thousands of kilometres away in Surinam and couldn't do anything, it was ridiculous, but I suppose it said a lot about Aartsen. Part of me wondered whether this was where Horst Vos had stepped up his accumulation of wealth. We knew he was a big player now, but evidence?

Well we could whistle for it; how ironic this would be though. Aartsen of course had blamed Thijs. He served his time overseas, regaining his reputation and ticking all the right boxes. Keeping his head down, Aartsen made his way back up the greasy leadership pole to where he had once been as a Commissaris, he was lucky and left Surinam when a vacancy occurred at Taap Koorndreef and started his 'work' all over again, trying to muscle back in on the drugs scene, but having more opposition so he was now mainly small fry and not making the euros he once had. Caes supposed he could have gone for Vos, but would he have opened himself up to further scrutiny if Vos knew something. Well they could go for Vos another time. There were more important matters to concern them. But he had always festered over Thijs and this was his revenge.

This whole business though was so extreme. He had planned this for a while, the distractions with Elise, how she had just fallen into his lap. How he had seen that Spliker was to be released so had enticed him into friendship with his visit to Wolvenplein and his introduction to the Twilight Club as a pretext to meet again so he could finish him off and thus implicate Thijs a little more. That Thijs had a solid alibi with Truus had messed that up and so that was another pointless murder, but after all his plots and well laid plans, we had him, but he had the girls and where were they?

Vagevuur.

It had seemed to take Truus forever to crawl towards the crack of light that she assumed was coming from under the door. Every single movement she took sent a wracking stab of pain through her ribs. Drenched in sweat, she wanted to vomit, but was so scared of being sick, of choking, just as she was scared that she would not be able to breathe through her nose. In truth, she was just terrified, stark staring terrified, she didn't want to die, not like this, not ever, but especially not like this, the thought petrified her, making her more determined in her move to the door in her own shuffling, body wrecking way. She had to stop to try to regain some control over her body. She was shaking, with a mixture of frustration and fear. How the hell had she managed this? Pappy would be so angry with her. He had told her to always remember back up. Once again she had known better. She kept wiggling her fingers to make sure blood was still circulating, irrational fears swept through her head, what if the circulation stopped, would she lose her hands, would she suffocate if she was sick, would she just die when no one came. Where the hell was her pappy?

So much for her kick boxing Truus thought, she had not been very successful this time. She knew she had caught him with a good kick, but he had over balanced her too easily and then got his retribution. Being on your feet and swinging was all well and good, she hadn't spent too much time on the floor trying to fight an animal off. She shivered and then felt the hot tears trickling down her cheeks and began to get all snotty which again panicked her so she tried to regulate her breathing through her nose. She closed her eyes and just tried to calm down. What would Maaike be doing now, did she know where she was, did she know she was missing? She imagined Maaike's soft skin against hers and started to cry again. At last, after what seemed hours of agony, she made it to the door and then all she could do was to bang her head on it. Hoping against hope, that she would be heard by someone, anyone as long as it was not Commissaris Frans Fucking Aartsen.

Kroonstraat Police Bureau, 23.00.

Caes couldn't control his thoughts. His head was spinning. Where had Aartsen known the old woman from? What might she have seen and where had she seen it? Was this coming back to Vaartsestraat? Was that the real link, that strange little cul de sac? My mind went back to the houses we had searched, to the emptiness of Mevrouw Haan's home, I closed my eyes and pictured again the mess, smelt the smell, heard the loud tapping from the heating, where was that. What was it? Why would the heating tap? Christ! It suddenly dawned on me just as Adrie came running into my office. "Baas, payments to Pararius, agents for a property on Vaartsestraat, he's got a fucking house on the street!"

"I know, it's next door,"

It suddenly all became clear,

"I heard them knocking, fucking hell how stupid!"

"But we went through them!" Freddie Meijer said.

Ernst Hoewegen came in with a set of plans.

"Baas, a cellar!"

"For fucks sake!"

Caes couldn't believe how stupid he'd been. The door slammed behind him as he rushed towards the car outside.

Vaartsestraat, 23.23.

They raced around to Vaartsestraat where some officers had already kicked in the door next to Mevrouw Haan's home. There was a lot of movement upstairs, but Caes bellowed for silence. He again heard a dull tapping, no it was a muffled thudding on a door, coming from under his feet. Eventually finding the trap door under the kitchen carpet he clambered down the steps and saw the dark corridor ahead. Caes found Truus wedged against the door as he pushed it slowly open. She looked just like a crumpled sack of rubbish.

"Pappy?"

Caes could barely hear the words that she mumbled through the tape that was wrapped horribly around her mouth. Blood seeped onto it from her nose, it was a shocking sight.

Her face was so battered and bruised, his lovely girl, what had Aartsen done to her? Her right eye was almost closed, swollen red and black; there was caked dry blood on her clothes. Caes left the gag and unwrapped the tape from her wrists; she cried behind the gag as the blood started to circulate again, a horrible guttural sound. She stiffly tried to put her hands up to move the tape from her mouth, her fingers numbed and not working.

"No, leave it, lieverd, you'll tear your face."

Caes kissed her cheek, then took her arms and tried to rub the circulation back into them, he held her hands then massaged her wrists. She pulled away and tried to get the tape off again, fingers scrabbling impotently at her face.

"No, lieverd, wait, we'll have to soak it off, it'll hurt too much. There's an ambulance outside, please, just wait a little bit longer."

In fact, the medics had to pull Caes from her as they tried to get her onto a stretcher. He could not let her go, he could not stop crying.

Sterre and Elise were hugging each other in a corner when Freddie Meijer burst in, gun in hand, followed by Adrie.

"Just fuck off out!" Sterre screamed at him.

"No, no, it's oké, Police. I'm Freddie Meijer, Agent Frederik Meijer, you're safe now, both safe."

Kroonstraat Police Bureau, 23.55.

Aartsen was still smirking when Caes hit him, he flew across the room. Caes dragged him back onto his feet and raised his fist again. He looked at him and then shoved him back into his chair. Aartsen wiped blood from his face and looked stunned. So, he should the bastard.

"I could beat the fucking shit out of you and no one; no one would give a fuck. Everyone here? They despise you, you are nothing to anyone anymore, you bastard!"

Suddenly Caes felt deflated, what was the point of hitting him again. It wouldn't make it any better. Truus was still hurt. He couldn't take that away or make her better. He felt empty. When she had needed him the most he had not been there for her.

"That's all you're going to get from me and from Truus. I'm not wasting any more of my time on you."

Caes shoved him back into his chair.

"Prison will be a joy for you, murderer of an old woman, policeman, you will have fun. I don't envy you."

At least Aartsen had stopped smirking.

According to Elise, Mevrouw Haan had met her and Gisele the very first day when they had moved in together. She thought they were her daughters in her own befuddled way. She had called them over from across the road and they had reluctantly joined her. She thought they visited her and cleaned for her when it appears they were around at her house just the once. They could not bear to return to its squalor and stench. She had still remembered their names and thought they were both her own. This was the saddest part, Caes could deal with the death of Spliker, it too was wrong, but he was a worthless piece of shit who had already damaged so many children and would probably have done so again if he had lived. You can't cure his disease. But poor Mevrouw Haan, she was in a world of her own. There was no connection between her and Aartsen, just the coincidence of her living next door to his house and imagining the girls were hers and he had killed her, what a bastard. Caes hoped he hadn't decided that time they had met at his station in Taap Koorndreef, no, he would have seen her anyway, seen the notes the clerk made. He hoped he would get his dues at Demersluis or Het Veer. The trouble was that they took too much care of their fucking prisoners these days.

Time was crawling towards midnight. It had been a long day, but Caes had one more thing to do.

"Hoofdcommissaris Coeman, I hit him, I'm not sorry, but I just had to hit him." Caes admitted.

"I heard he tripped and fell against the table, Caes. So, don't worry about that, all will be well, all is finished. Get back to Truus."

Chapter 20

Dinsdag, November 25, 2014.
UMC, 01.25.

Maaike smiled shyly and got to her feet. She pecked his cheek as she passed Caes.

"I'll leave you to it, baas."

Truus smiled thinly, wincing as she did so, she had a crop top on, the white bandages showing vivid against the mottled bruised flesh that was exposed on her tummy, her right eye was closed and surrounded by strange colours, none of them natural. There were little scabs around her mouth from the sticky painful removal of the tape. Caes sat down at her side and stroked her cheek. She mumbled though bruised lips.

"My tongues too big for my mouth, can that be swollen as well?" she almost laughed, but winced in agony.

"How do you really feel?" He asked.

It was all too self-evident, her face was swollen, her nose was puffy, she looked a complete car crash victim, a wreck.

"Like I've been sat on by an elephant!"

"Oh, well that's *oké* then." Caes smiled.

"What did the *dokter* tell you?"

"Just the two bust ribs, bit of bruising, nothing much really."

"Easy for you to say." Truus grimaced.

"Well I've seen worse after one of your kick-boxing sessions." Caes smiled.

"You are such a bad liar; no one catches me as badly as this when I go there!"

She was indignant and made Caes smile.

"We both know that's not true as well, *lieverd.*"

"Well just Tamada and he's a bloody freak."

"Well it's been good practice, just think how bad you'd look if you didn't do self-defence!"

She laughed then cried out in pain.

"Don't, Pappy, don't make me laugh, that really hurts. Did you hit him for me, Pappy?"

"Yes, but only once. He went down, but I really hurt my hand."

Caes showed his bruised fist to her.

"Poor you, that's a shame for him. How's Thijs? The girl's?"

"Fine, you'd best be careful, Sterre will have your job."

"She can have it, don't know if I want it still," she muttered.

"Truus… you know that's not true."

"No, I know, that's a worry for everyone, isn't it? Do you mind?"

"Yes and no."

Of course, he minded, Caes more than minded, but as before, he would never again be in a position to tell her what she could or could not do with her life. This traumatic episode may make her think twice about things, though who was he fooling?

Falling for Maaike was a very positive thing; though the intensity of Maaike's character might overwhelm Truus at times. Then Caes laughed out loud, they would be like a pair of raging meteorites those two.

"What's so funny?" Truus asked.

"Nothing, just thinking… We'll see how you feel when your ribs are fixed. Did you talk danger money when you signed your contract with Thijs'?"

"Contract? No. In fact, nothing was ever signed; he's not even paid me yet. Sort him out, Pappy; I didn't do all this for free. I don't even know what I earn. I'm such a flop!"

"I'll speak to him. Oh yes, my love, one more thing."

Caes handed her the magazine he had brought in,

"Now I really am a proper Detective."

"Autopress? A car magazine? I hate cars what about a music magazine?" Truus asked.

"Read the by line?"

"Jakob de Welt."

"The piece?"

"This Weeks New Car… Oh…he writes reviews…" Truus was almost lost for words, then,

"How did you find this out?"

"I went around and asked him. I am after all a detective. Every week he test drives a new car and writes about it for the magazine."

"But… what about the Blekkiks?"

Truus would not be beaten.

"Bloody hell, Truus, just leave it."

Hemel.

Caes made his way slowly out of the hospital leaving Maaike with Truus. At least there was no snow falling, in fact the white stuff they had spent weeks getting used to was now turning to slush, slowly dissolving under the heavy rainfall. The streets were almost clear of any snow as rain hammered down. It didn't feel warmer as the wind was howling along the straat. Rain was bouncing up from the cobblestones. Caes looked up at the buildings edging the main road. The snow had almost finished thawing. There was now much less white, more dark shiny tiles reflecting the streetlights and the moon which was full in the sky. Winter could well be over, but would this mean continual dismal wet weather? They just couldn't catch a break. It was almost midnight, the witching hour. Caes shivered, not sure why; as all was seeming to come together. Just his daughter to worry about now.

Made in United States
North Haven, CT
14 July 2024